VIRGO'S VIGILANTES

BOOK 6 OF THE ZODIAC

PAUL SATING

PAUL SATING

Editor: Cindy Niespodzianski

Cover Design: Jake at jcalebdesign.com

ISBN-13: 978-1-7322617-9-2

GRAB THREE FREE NOVELLAS

THE ZODIAC SERIES

To Steve Milroy. You saved me as a kid!

1

UNDERWORLD, UNDISCLOSED

Seconds After Leo

NOTHING SAYS "WELCOME HOME" like having two spear points pressed at your neck the second you walk out of a rift. The self-contained flames of crackling Hellfire dancing over steel tips will get your attention. It definitely got mine.

I'm not saying Azazel had this planned all along—he didn't and wouldn't—I believe that, because I was in no position to distrust him after what he had done in Olympia just moments ago when he handed me the supposed coordinates to the missing Horn. Well, coordinates to an ancient, powerful artifact and a message of warning and empowerment. Enemies and friends awaited my return to Hell. With the spear points, I'd already met some of the enemies and was really looking forward to seeing the friends.

The problem was, I was in no position to request or demand much of anything. He knew that. Distrust of the elderly Founder wasn't something I needed to waste energy on. Now standing in the Council chamber, I had enough to go around with the other demons I was about to confront.

The rulers of Hell, Lucifer's Third Council, had called me home to answer for something I did to upset them. It would be outlandish. Trumped up. Laughable. Gross. Spurious. In other words, everything you'd expect of politicians.

This farce wasn't about crimes or not-crimes. This was about getting me back into the Underworld so they could force me in the direction they wanted me to march. A death march. Beyond any other evident truth there was this; Lucifer's Council wanted me dead.

One way or another, I was here to fill that destiny.

Dropping my bag at my feet, I raised my arms, showing the pair of unintelligent chamber guards I was no threat. They took synchronous steps back, spears raised back to vertical positions without a word. A statement of power, as if I needed to be reminded the Council ruled here.

The guards were not the only demons awaiting my return from Olympia. I wasn't surprised because Azazel had prepared me before leaving the apartment, but there was still an ounce of turmoil rocketing around inside my brain at seeing who the Council had gathered for this latest farce. My parents stood across the room, about as far away from me as possible. The other pair of demons were two I'd include on the invite list if the Council had asked.

"Wow, it's so good to see you," Bilba said as he approached, his arms outstretched long before he was close enough to embrace me. We hugged, only long enough to not lose any cool points, before separating. I turned to the tall, handsome demon with perfect jet black hair who stood next to him.

"Zeke, great to see you," Ralrek said with a sad smile.

"Ezekial," I corrected, pausing to ensure he flinched. I only allow my friends to call me by my nickname. For six thousand years, Ralrek hadn't been counted among those few.

That changed only in the past few years, but toying with him was still a favorite pastime.

We clasped hands, bounced chests off each other, and separated as quickly as we joined.

"What are you guys doing here?" I asked.

Ralrek tipped his head toward the front of the chamber where a long jade table so dark it might as well have been black sat upon a riser, dominating it and the room. The table had to weigh more than ten chimera. "They told us we had to be here."

A group of ancient demons sat behind the extravagant table, leaning toward each other and speaking in low, conspiratorial voices throughout the seconds of my return to Hell.

Lucifer's Third Council. The five most powerful demons except for the big guy himself. Azazel was one of them, but not one of them. Not anymore. I was still trying to wrap my head around the fact that he was actively, if not subversively, working against them. What that meant for me was unclear. Too much to ponder at the moment. Upon leaving my Olympia apartment, Azazel had warned me not to forget I had friends here, that over-reacting might be to my detriment. As we returned through the rift between the Overworld and Hell, I was not a lamb being led to slaughter. What I was, though, was unclear. I guess I might define that in the next few moments.

The presence of the five most powerful individuals in the demonic realm, only one on my side, was enough to temporarily unsettled my nerves. My angst remained untouched. Heavens, I was still sore from a fight to the death the night before, and missing the friends I left behind, including an angel who saved my ass.

Basically, I was trying to keep my shit together.

I faced Hell's rulers. Yahweh could torture them for eternity as far as I was concerned. Michael, Beelzebub, Seraph, and Apopis, dressed in their formal attire. The fact they had donned those robes meant this little get-together was not going to be fun for someone, and that someone was me.

"Before we begin," Azazel shambled over to stand between me and the table, "I must prepare."

Michael nodded. Beelzebub grunted.

"Hurry up," Apopis hissed, his tongue flicking at the corner of his mouth.

Seraph leaned forward over bent elbows planted to her side. "We would like to move these proceedings, Azazel. Be quick about it, please."

Azazel ambled toward his personal chambers. Never one of the quickest demons at his advanced age, his stride was shorter and wobblier than seconds ago in the Overworld. I couldn't help but smile. So nice of him to provide more time to commune with my friends to calm my nerves.

"Are you okay?" I whispered to the pair. Inside the Council chambers, the Founders could read thoughts of demons. Well, except for me. Not that I could claim any credit for it. My ability to block their mind reading came down to the fact that I possessed the most kick-ass halberd in creation. Creed blocked them from dabbing their claws inside my head. But Bilba and Ralrek didn't enjoy the same luxury.

"I've been better, to be honest," Bilba said, the tips of his protruding ears turning a darker pink. "They didn't tell us what this was about. We didn't even know you were coming back."

"Not until that rift opened. Once it did, it was pretty much a no-brainer. Especially since they are here," Ralrek said, casually tossing his hand in the direction of the older demons who stood nearby.

Next to one of the large pillars supporting the expansive ceiling painted with an image of the Hellfire stood my parents. Underneath the flame of annihilation the cruelty of the Council was proven once more. Bringing my parents in to witness my final demise was no surprise. I expected nothing less juvenile from Hell's rules. But still, a part of me twitched with anger and humiliation. Only a twitch this time, I swear. Old Zeke was still somewhere back in that Olympia apartment. The me who stood in the Council chamber now was a different demon altogether. My parents' presence felt more like a pathetic power play. Too bad the Council hadn't yet realized their extra player advantage wasn't going to sway me.

Mother clamped her hands at her waist, squeezing them tightly enough to meld into a single lump of flesh. Lilith Sunstone usually had deceptively hard eyes, but now they quivered when she looked at me. Her square chin, easily the most intimidating one in Hell, trembled. The incubus at her side was much taller, his gray hair slicked back. His cold eyes stared ahead, toward Hell's leaders.

Oh, joy.

Some things in life repel one another. Oil and water. Magnets. Succubi and incubi who aren't tall, dark, and handsome. Add to those examples this farce with the combination of the Council, my presence, and that of my parents and two best friends, and you've got yourself a party.

My parents' presence only reinforced my belief that Azazel was going to have to call on a miracle of Lucifer to get me out of what was going to be a bad day.

"Did they say why they were called?" I asked my friends.

Bilba shook his head.

Ralrek harrumphed. "Your father wouldn't even look at us."

"Your mom was friendly. She gave us hugs. But your father ignored us. I'm sorry, Zeke," Bilba said.

"There's nothing for you to be sorry for. You didn't do anything."

A door clunked closed from the back of the room, as loud as a hardback textbook dropped on cold tile in the middle of a library. With Azazel in his chambers, I was alone with my best friends, my parents, and the four powerful demons who were going to ruin my day.

My mother shifted on her feet, her hands still gripping each other. My father was stoic, lifting his chin as if aware I was examining him. I couldn't say I was surprised. During my entire Abandonment, I hadn't heard from him once. I wasn't bitter. It was what it was.

"I guess I should go say hi," I said begrudgingly.

"Good luck with that." Ralrek sniffed.

"She loves you, Zeke." Bilba shot Ralrek a sneer. "This is just a lot to deal with. Most demons never go through this once in their life. Your parents have been dragged through it over and over. Be patient. She misses you, and this is how she is reunited with you? So cruel. So unjust."

"Be careful," I said with a nod toward the four demons behind the jade table before tapping the side of my temple.

"I don't care what they think about me," Bilba said, his tone firm.

My friend's determination was encouraging, but his timing still sucked. Any other day, any other time, any other situation, I would have praised him for his display of fortitude. But not with the Council on a mission. They didn't need to be handed anymore victims.

"Do it for me then." He shot me a confused look, so I clarified. "They're on the warpath. They have something planned; I don't doubt that. Let's just keep their attention on me and away from the two of you. Whatever they're planning, I'm pretty sure I'm going to need you to get me out of trouble."

"Again?" Ralrek said, a faint smile playing on his lips.

"Just think how boring life would be if it wasn't for me constantly getting in trouble," I said before going to my parents. Four heads from behind the jade table moved to watch each of my steps. Their conversation continued while I crossed the room, but they made no secret they were more interested in watching me than they were in each other's words.

My father stiffened as soon as I stepped their way. My mother looked like she could have crumbled. But neither moved toward me.

I hugged my mother first. "Hi."

She pulled me against her, cupping the back of my head as if I was still an impling. "Oh, Ezekial. I never thought I would see you again. My boy. My precious boy." She pulled back, keeping contact but making enough room to look me up and down. "You've lost too much weight. I need to put food in you. No worries. The first chance I get, I'll cook something special. I promise."

I didn't want to bring up that I might not have the freedom for her to cook for me. Also, the last way I wanted to be welcomed home was with my mother's cooking. Culinary arts aren't much of an art for Lilith Sunstone. But I love my mother far more than my desire to be honest with her. If I made it out of this, I'd eat a thousand of her dinners.

I turned to Kanthor Sunstone. "Father." A single word. Nothing more. Yet so difficult to form.

His gaze remained forward. "Ezekial."

I waited, but he offered nothing else.

My mother wrapped her arm underneath mine. "I'm so glad you're home. After this is over, we need to catch up. I'll make tea. I've got a few boxes at the house from a new product line I'm testing. We can have that. I plan on hearing your stories long into the night. No early bed for me."

The click of a door handle brought my attention back to the corner where Azazel had disappeared, pulling me away from teasing my mother about her ever-deepening involvement in pyramid schemes. The ancient Founder stepped out, now wearing the official black robe. He ambled toward the jade table at a pace that would make a sloth look like a sprinter. Never once did he cast a glance my way.

Time crawled as he climbed onto the riser, shuffling to his position at the end of the jade table. Behind his chair, he paused, putting a finger to his lip and tapping it as if he'd forgotten something.

"Will you hurry up?" Beelzebub growled from the second chair. The demon, as big as a chimera and hard as brimstone, crossed his arms, flexing his biceps underneath his robe. His dark eyes fell on me, a satisfied grin on his face framed by the pork chop sideburns he bleached blond to contrast his dark skin. The jig was up.

The bad news train was barreling down, and I was tied to the railroad tracks.

Azazel patted his chest as if he had left his note-taking material inside his robe. "I seem to have forgotten where I set my quill and paper. Allow me a moment to return to my chambers."

"Just send the guard. We don't have an eternity," Apopis snarled, his eyes scanning the chamber guards. He pointed at the nearest one. "You, there. Go retrieve his quill and paper."

The guard snapped to attention and almost ran to Azazel's chamber.

"Quickly," Apopis shouted after the guard, who sped into an actual run.

Azazel frowned.

"Mr. Sunstone, step forward," Michael, the leader of Lucifer's Third Council, said from the left side of the table. The first chair. He still wore the neatly trimmed beard and mustache he always did. His light brown eyes fell on me unflinchingly.

I moved in front of the table. Creed hung in collapsed form from the loop at my side, warming at Michael's attention. I ignored it for now.

"Unfair, but necessary," a voice whispered. From where, I couldn't tell. I snapped my head to the side, not expecting someone to sneak up on me in such a serious situation.

No one was there. Bilba and Ralrek were a few feet away. After a moment, Bilba squinted as if confused. I scrunched my eyes. The smartest demon I knew, he could be thick-headed, especially when it came to defending me. The confused glance he and Ralrek shared at my examination hinted it might not have either of them who'd made the comment.

Deciding to ignore the voice and move on to the Council's latest screw job, I faced the jade table.

"We won't spend long on this hearing, Mr. Sunstone. Understand, it is of utmost importance that we dispense with this as soon as possible," Michael said.

"Which shouldn't be difficult considering the gnat's actions in the Overworld," Beelzebub said. A deep chuckle rumbled somewhere in his chest.

Creed thumped against my hip. "What actions are you talking about?" I asked, my eyes sliding across the members behind the table.

"Your actions that upset the Balance," Apopis spat, his close-set eyes narrowed to slits.

Unlike the past, his half–tattooed faced no longer bothered me, though I was still curious to discover what the stupid inscriptions said. I imagined it was a dare from his college days.

Creed warmed a few more degrees. He didn't like Apopis either.

I answered the thin Founder, but my eyes were firmly on the only succubus on Lucifer's Third Council. "And what actions were those?"

"Would you like us to read the entire list of infractions, Mr. Sunstone?" Seraph asked, her voice raised in a haughtiness undeserved for someone so despicable. Until recently, I found the slim Founder stunning. Now her cheekbones were too bony. Her long, blond locks, too stringy. The slivers of wrinkles that hinted of the possibility of mature seduction looked more like cracked porcelain.

My mouth moved before my brain engaged. "I would be honored. In fact, I would be happy if, for once, just once, this blessed Council was forthcoming about something."

So much for playing it cool.

Behind me, my mother gasped. Ralrek groaned, and Bilba made a noise like a trilling ember cat. And those were the funny reactions. Not so funny were the Council member's reactions.

Azazel, whether fabricated or not, blubbered something to his chest. His long goatee, gray but tipped with orange, poked his stomach. Beelzebub actually had the audacity to make a fist and pound it into the open palm of his other hand. Apopis pulled his lips back and hissed. Seraph's icy blue eyes flashed. Only Michael remained composed, which I would expect.

He leaned forward, tapping the jade table with his finger. "Mr. Sunstone, you have worked for the Council for years. You understand the duties and responsibilities we hold, and, despite your recent actions, I had hoped you would be civil enough in these proceedings that we could address the challenges before us without antagonizing one another. This is not pleasurable for any of us. But it is something we must do."

"It is necessary," Apopis said.

"Again, I'm at a loss over what I've done that is so bad to be called back from Abandonment. I didn't even think that was a thing."

"It has happened before, though not for many ages. Not common, definitely a unique situation," Azazel said.

"A situation that, nonetheless, must be addressed," Michael said, sitting straighter. He held the air of authority with his posture and his position, and he knew it. "Azazel is correct. Calling someone back is rare, indeed. But there are times when it must be done to preserve the Balance."

"Still not sure how I affected the Balance," I said, eyeing each of them before tapping the halberd on my hip. I swear they flinched. Even Beelzebub. "Unless you're talking about me using this, which of course, I wouldn't have had to use if you hadn't sent your assassins and your nephew, Seraph, to kill me."

Lucifer, it felt good to name her. Petty? Maybe, but I was past caring about pettiness, especially toward the pettiest demons in creation.

"You think too highly of yourself, boy," Beelzebub laughed, crossing his arms. "You were Abandoned. We would have no reason to bother with you, never mind sending someone to kill you."

"Yet, you did," I pressed.

"We did no such thing," Michael interrupted as Beelzebub's arms flexed.

"True enough. We didn't. Yet we cannot explain why Chax Vicu, Seraph's nephew, was in the Overworld," Azazel said, bringing his goblet to his lips, looking straight ahead as he sipped and waited for a response.

"I have my reasons." Seraph's head snapped in his direction. "None of which is any of your business."

"They may not be, but it provides cause for young Ezekial's actions," Azazel replied.

"You dare justify the murder of a demon by an Abandoned?" Seraph shot to her feet, her knuckled hands clenched. "That demon was my nephew. My family. And he was killed in cold blood by that criminal."

Azazel slowly set his goblet on the table. Even from thirty feet away, his hand shook noticeably.

Heat rose up my neck. My pulse galloped. "Chax Vicu has been after me since I wanted him to halt a curse on an innocent demon. The demon you knew about and did nothing to help. Because you supported your family's vendetta."

"This is highly unconventional," Azazel blurted in a wobbly voice.

"Insolence," Apopis spat.

"Michael, do something about the boy, or I will," Beelzebub boomed, tipping forward.

Behind me, my mother whimpered, infuriating me. How dare they put her through this?

Creed pulsed.

"What will you do?" I challenged.

Bilba gasped.

We were in Hell; the Founder could do nothing to me here any worse than what the Council already had done. Without permission from Lucifer, they were powerless to kill me. Besides the big guy Himself, no demon could kill another in Hell. Well, except one.

Me.

If Beelzebub wanted to dance, I was ready to tango. I had Creed and two left feet. My day might not be enjoyable, but I would walk, or crawl, off the dance floor. Beelzebub lacked that same guarantee.

"Enough!" The command from Michael boomed across the chamber. "Enough," he repeated, softer this time. "I will not allow this to be reduced to a juvenile squabble. Seraph, sit down."

All attention in the chamber moved to the succubus standing at the fourth spot. She was still half-facing Azazel, about to protest.

"Sit," Michael repeated.

Her eyes flashed once again before she whirled to her chair, yanking it back. The chair legs cracked against the riser. Sitting in a huff and scooting forward, she waved her hand in a few rolls. "Well, then, let's get on with this business before we completely capitulate to this imp."

"I don't believe that's what we're—" Azazel started.

"There will be no capitulation," Apopis said. "Regardless

of his desires, thoughts, or opinions on the matter, we should be done with this discussion and move on to the punishment."

"So I'm to be punished for defending myself."

"You murdered a demon in the Overworld," Michael said as if it settled the argument. "And that is not the worst of the matter."

"The heaven it isn't," Seraph said.

"Seraph," Michael tilted to see around Beelzebub, rotating his head in her direction and basically cutting off everyone in the room who wasn't in his line of sight. "You will get your say in the matter. I'm going to ask you... again... to stay true to our purpose."

"What purpose is that?" I asked.

"To determine the punishment for your crimes," Beelzebub snarled from behind his crossed arms.

"It's not a crime to defend yourself against someone trying to kill you," I argued. "You'll need to do better than that."

"And consorting with an angel?" Apopis retorted. "What would you say to that, Sunstone?"

Well. Shit.

Beelzebub barked a laugh. "The boy thought we didn't know."

Honestly, I didn't care if they knew as long as that knowledge didn't put Cassie in danger. She proved she could handle herself against someone like Chax and his crew. She could deliver pain and death in a sneak attack when the rest of the Underworld didn't suspect her presence. The same way she did as part of the angel crew that attacked the First Circle at Gemini's attempted execution. But I doubted she had the same chances when it came to facing down a Founder or two. Even if she could stand up against them, that didn't mean I wanted to poke that blazebull. Cassie would have enough troubles back in the Overworld. Best to keep her out of the matter.

"I'd say your spies need to get better at their jobs," I said, hoping to plant doubt. "Either that or you are imagining things. Angels? That's ridiculous."

"Our reports say that Angelfire was used in your attack on Chax," Seraph said.

"Again. Defending myself, not attacking him. Though, I guess you're not going to listen. He didn't listen to me either, and look where that got him."

She shot to her feet.

Creed burned against my side.

I concentrated and projected my senses outward. If someone was tapping into their Ability, I'd know it the instance they touched it. In the past, I only felt when a spell was being prepared. As my Creed-gifted senses improved, I was even more sensitive to magic, and honestly, I'd take any advantage I had. Pricking at the fabric of the room, I reached, my Sensing coming back empty.

But one wrong movement from her, or any of the Founders not named Azazel, and I'd have Creed in my hands, ready to do to the Founder what I did to Taurus. And the assassin. And Chax. This list was getting long.

Before returning to Hell, Azazel asked me to not rush into any situation, to trust I was not alone in what was to follow. Maybe he should have begged.

The last thing I felt was the comfort of company. Even if Azazel suddenly reversed the aging process and became a more youthful, powerful version of himself, even if Bilba and Ralrek made the bad decision to fight on my side, I doubted it would end well for the good guys. Someone I cared about, someone who was on my side, would pay a heavy price. No one needed that.

"Trust," someone whispered, the voice wispy and ambiguous.

I risked a glance away from Seraph, half-worried I had just made a mistake. The succubus was conniving enough to use the diversion, but she didn't. Whoever spoke gave away no sign. Disguised in ambiguity, the voice gave no hints to the speaker.

Trust what? Trust who? Was I just hearing things? Had something happened inside the rift on my way back through to the Underworld? Rifts could be dangerous, even to experienced travelers. Though I had crossed between realms numerous times since working for the Council and never experienced any severe reactions, there was always the chance I would. A matter of when rather than if, I guessed. Maybe I was hearing remnants of traveling through the magical device.

Great. A convenient bout of delusion to go along with whatever the Council was readying to serve up.

"Murder. Consorting with angels. The death of Cancer Nijal," Michael said, his voice steady. "That is why you are here, Ezekial. To face the charges and, if found guilty, be sentenced. Stop with this other folly if you want to preserve what few rights you have left."

"Wait. What? Cancer?" I said, shocked and stumbling through broken thoughts.

"She's dead, boy," Beelzebub taunted.

"Abolished, Sunstone," Apopis said.

Cancer? Abolished?

"How?" The word creaked out of my throat.

Apopis's laugh sounded like a rattle. "As if you don't already know."

Cancer.

I hadn't heard from her since she flew to the other side of the Overworld to return to the war zone to serve humankind. Abandoned along with me, she was decaying—dying, as mortals said. Everything dies. Humans. Demons. Planets, suns, and their solar systems. Nothing is free of death's touch. A natural process for immortals and mortals, it happened much more quickly for us when we were cast to the Overworld. Her desire was to leave a positive mark on the world with the time she had left. I had figured I would hear from her when the time was right. Now...

"I... I..." Forming a response was impossible. Somewhere behind me I heard Bilba say he was sorry. A disembodied comfort.

I felt detached. Cancer, gone.

"There's nothing to hide, boy." Beelzebub's deep voice shook me out of my thought-tornado.

Seraph said nothing, just bore holes into me with her gaze.

"But... I haven't seen Cancer since—" I cut myself off out of instinct to protect her. Whatever this was, I knew I was innocent. If something had happened to her, it wasn't at my hand. The guilty party was likely sitting in front of me.

"So unfortunate," Apopis said, shaking his head.

I swore he was smiling, but my eyes were blurring with tears.

Something ruffled to the side of the room, but I was too busy mourning the loss of my friend. I drew a breath and lifted my head, readying myself to ask the Council's favor for a moment. I needed to collect my swirling thoughts tucked behind the image of Cancer's face. But Michael wasn't paying attention to me. Instead, he gave a slow blink and head nod to a guard at the side of the room. It was only then I realized that the ruffling was from a guard going through my personal items.

Dizzy, I couldn't think straight. Any momentum I had gained by coming out swinging at the Council was lost.

A thick incubus with brown skin that never met a razor, he straddled my bag, which gaped open. In one hand, he held my copy of *The Histories of the Balance*, the most important book in Hell, gifted to me by my ex-boss, Dialphio Tywald. The Council feared the book so greatly they had my original copy burned, by Apopis's own admission. Now, they had their filthy hands on the last copy. The guard also pulled out the only demonic notebook I brought home, leaving a bundle in my apartment in hopes Cassie would find them.

"A demonic notebook?" Seraph asked. "How does an Abandoned book stocker afford one of those?"

I shrugged, hoping I looked more nonchalant than I felt. "You paid me well to do your dirty work."

"Hmmmm," was all she said in response.

"Doesn't matter. Bring the book here. Leave the notebook," Michael ordered the guard, who complied.

Numb, I watched as the incubus delivered my book to the leader of the Third Council. His black armor rattled as he stretched to set the tome in front of Michael, who didn't touch it until the guard departed. Beelzebub looked at it as if it were a coiled snake. One corner of Apopis's lips pulled back, spreading his smile half across his face.

"Is that what I think it is? The heretical writing?" Azazel asked.

Michael nodded. "It is." He tipped the book so that it stood on its end.

"Where did you come by this, Sunstone?" Apopis said, his head rolling to the side, jutting in my direction.

I wanted to smile. They thought they had the upper hand, but the book was something I didn't need any more. I understood enough about the nature of Hell's history, the magical halberd I held, and how astray Lucifer's Third Council had gone from its original intent. Let them keep the blessed thing. Plus, knowing Dialphio, she'd probably made another hundred copies by now.

"I found it in a bookstore in the Overworld. It's the most popular book up there. All the mortals are reading it," I teased.

Apopis's brows drew together. "You treacherous, little bastard."

Bringing my height into the discussion was a low blow.

"Possession of heretical items, murder of my nephew and

of another Abandoned, and consorting with an angel." Seraph tipped her fingers down to the table, pressing them so hard against the dark jade that the tips turned white. "Is there anything more to discuss, Michael? Or can we finally dispense justice? It's obvious Mr. Sunstone has committed a number of egregious crimes. We have too many things to accomplish to spend any more time debating his future."

Michael watched me, stoic. Not a hair in his well-groomed beard twitched.

Beelzebub slapped the table. My mother yelped. "I agree with Seraph. Let's be done with this."

"It would be appropriate to take a vote," Azazel said.

Michael slowly set *The Histories* down, his hand lingering on it. When he spoke, it was as if he were addressing the book. "Agreed. It is time for us to deal with this permanently." He looked me in the eye. "Mr. Sunstone, you've been given many opportunities to change your course, yet you continue to take the wrong path. It is unfortunate, but our attempts to help you see the light have failed. We have done all we could. Now, we determine your fate."

"I say we Abandon him. This time we choose where he spends the last of his days, rotting away. Some particularly grim locations come to mind," Beelzebub said, sitting back, extending his arms. The balls of his biceps twitched.

Was he seriously flexing?

Seraph snorted. "How many times do we send him to the Overworld where he can cause problems? Plus, if we Abandon him again, he will just reach out to the angel. Do we want to give him that chance?"

Apopis's tongue flicked to the corner of his mouth. "We can't take chances with this one. I vote that we keep him closer, here in the Underworld."

"But if he remains in the Underworld, he remains immortal," Michael countered.

"We have to do something. Something permanent, and

something now, Michael," Seraph said, swatting one hand at him. "His consequences must be as grim as his actions. We need to make a statement."

There was silence behind me, both from my parents and my friends. I was grateful for that. I didn't want any of them to make a comment. This chimera wagon was rolling, gathering speed, and anyone who cared about me would get run over.

"Then are we ready for a vote? Because it doesn't sound as if we are," Michael pointed out. "We can discuss the terms and conditions later. First, we need to determine if he will be Abandoned or imprisoned. Once we set that, then we can decide how he will spend his remaining days."

"There's always another option," Apopis sneered.

"Would we be willing to discuss that?" Michael asked.

Seraph turned to take in the slender, half-tattooed Council member. "Get approval for an execution? Do you really want to go through the process? Public trials, where he'd have witnesses and could appeal. The time it takes. Time I would rather spend on other things than seeing Mr. Sunstone for one more day."

"Seraph is right," Beelzebub chimed in. "I'd rather not spend another day on this issue. Heavens, I don't want to spend another hour dealing with this gnat. Let's choose. Abandonment or imprisonment? Let's be done with it. If we go with Abandonment, I will take care of the logistics."

Azazel slowly raised his hand, a finger extended.

Michael acknowledged him. "What do you have?"

The oldest Council member chimed in, his voice weak and wavering. "There is yet another option besides imprisonment, Abandonment, or wading through an execution trial."

"Such as?" Apopis sneered.

Azazel spread his hands. "We know nothing we've tried has worked. We have already imprisoned Mr. Sunstone. We have already Abandoned him. Yet he continues. We want swift action, which is why we are here. Past Abandoned were always adjudicated at lower levels. So there is a way that we can swiftly address this."

"What way is that?" Beelzebub grumbled. "Out with it."

"A trial by combat," Azazel said.

My mother gasped. My eyes shot open. Ralrek scoffed. But the wheels were turning in the minds of the Founders. They were entertaining Azazel's proposal.

"Interesting. Definitely interesting," Michael said, tapping his finger absentmindedly on *The Histories of the Balance*.

Beelzebub rolled his bottom lip out of his mouth, sitting back and crossing his arms. "I would be okay with that. We could take him to the fighting pit in the Seventh. I haven't been back in ages and would love to visit my old stomping grounds to watch Sunstone being torn apart, limb by limb."

Seraph watched me as if I had already found the unlocked door and was waiting to dash to freedom.

"Interesting proposition," Apopis said. "Do you have an opponent in mind? Someone carrying the criminal guilt equal to Sunstone?"

"I have a few candidates. There's a demon in San Jose who offered to spy for the Upperworld," Beelzebub offered.

Michael tilted his head, his eyebrows raising. "We do have the Jordanian politician. It would be difficult, of course. But he needs to be brought to justice as well."

"Hardly an opponent worthy of young Ezekial," Azazel said.

With that, Apopis agreed. "That is true. Sunstone would walk free a minute after combat started. No, he needs a more dangerous opponent."

"There is the former Third Circle Administrator—" Seraph said.

"I don't want him back in the Underworld," Beelzebub barked.

"We have to choose someone, or go with another option," Michael said before another verbal battle kicked off.

"Do I get a say in the matter?" I risked asking.

Beelzebub lunged forward, his finger shooting out in my direction. "No! And say another word and we will cast a Silencing spell on you. I promise, it will be a permanent one. You won't even be able to say goodbye to your loved ones. Keep your mouth shut."

Michael pushed his hand to the floor as if he were trying to subdue a faerie. "Let's keep this moving." The leader of the Council looked down the table at the opposite end where the oldest among them sat. "Azazel, this was your idea. Do you have anyone in mind?"

Just above his long, pointed goatee, Azazel's lips rolled in and out. "Actually, I do. Another demon who has gone... wayward. Someone I believe can be more than a match for young Ezekial."

"Good then," Michael said. "Who is this demon?"

"I'd... rather discuss that in private. Young Ezekial should not be privy to this information out of... security concerns." Azazel wagged a finger at me.

Heads turned to Michael. Including mine. Had I not been completely thrown off my game learning about Cancer's death, I might have confronted Azazel's apparent setup with a dose of Creed for the Founders. Right now, I could barely remember to allow my automatic biological processes to do their thing.

The leader of the Council nodded. "We'll talk about the specifics later. I think—"

"We're going to take the word of this senile bastard?" The shout cut Michael off. Seraph was on her feet again. "Enough of this. I'm not just going to roll with whatever is thrown out, without thought. We need to be deliberate and we need to do this right. I'm not willing to take a chance on Sunstone escaping justice again. Beelzebub?"

"I am of no mind to give Sunstone any breaks. Whoever we choose, it needs to be done quickly, and with the right opponent. Like Seraph, I am no longer willing to take chances."

"Are we all comfortable with a trial by combat? Can we take a vote on that, at least?" Michael asked his peers.

The Founders voted in favor of a trial by combat in less time than it took my mother to burn dinner. Apparently, my fighting days were no longer behind me. Though I had done nothing wrong, I was now going to have to fight for my life. And by the speed at which everything was moving, it was going to happen soon.

"Now, the matter of Sunstone's opponent," Seraph said, finally re-taking her seat.

"If you will just give me time, in private, I'll explain my—" Azazel tried to speak but Michael cut him off.

"This is a matter we will continually circle around," Apopis said.

Beelzebub grunted. "I'll fight the gnat myself if I have to."

I welcomed that proposition.

Seraph closed her eyes, breathing in slowly through her nose. Her agitation was palpable. "Let's call on Him. A quick conversation and all will be settled. Let's not waste any more time."

Beelzebub leaned forward without unlocking his arms. "Are you sure? You know how He can be. The vote needs to be unanimous."

"Highly unconventional. Highly unconventional," Azazel complained.

Her top lip peeling back, baring her teeth, Seraph said, "Again. We need to move forward. Invoking Him will be faster than making the allowance for an execution trial. We agree a trial by combat is the way. Let's make this next decision even simpler. I invoke Lucifer."

What in the heaven did that mean?

"I second the motion," Beelzebub said, slapping the table.

Michael's hand slid to his side to where he kept the gavel. He picked it up, raising it at a slight angle. "All in favor?"

"Aye," Apopis said.

"Well, I have already stated that I believe this is highly unconventional. I believe that we can make the decision ourselves without invoking Him," Azazel argued, his cheeks wobbling in frustration. "If you but listen to my justification for—"

Beelzebub leaned back in his chair, tipped on its hind legs. His massive hand gripped the jade table so he didn't tip over. I imagined those thick fingers around my neck. "Yes or no? It's that simple."

Azazel blinked a few times before answering, looking at the others for help. None came. "Then… yes."

"Aye," Michael said. "We will invoke Lucifer and return to this matter. We're done here." He tapped the jade table with the gavel.

Accused of murder and consorting with demonkind's eternal enemies, facing a trial by combat against an unknown opponent selected by the Lord of the Underworld Himself. Talk about an epic homecoming.

2

UNDERWORLD, UNDISCLOSED

CAN a homecoming be considered a homecoming if you never actually see home? These are the things you think about when you have too much time on your hands.

Straight from the Council chamber, I was escorted by a squad of guards. I'm not being hyperbolic. When I say a squad, I mean a squad. It wasn't two or three. They didn't even add the pair at the chamber door. No, after Michael concluded the meeting, a guard opened the side door as the Founders prepared to leave. No less than fifteen guards lowered long spears, tips burning with Hellfire, as they surrounded me.

That didn't do much for my mother, who crumbled against my father and cried quietly. She only pulled her head away from his chest long enough to let me see her tear-stained face as she watched me be marched out.

"We've got you, Zeke," Bilba said as I passed.

Ralrek gave me an affirmative nod.

Out of the chamber, I was taken down five flights of stairs. Lower and lower. Only the guards' armor clinking accompanied my spiraling thoughts.

The Council was doing whatever they could to make sure I couldn't share the truth—with a capital 'T'.

Shoving me into a prison until my trial by combat prevented me from letting the rest of Hell know one of its Founders thought it was okay to curse other families and to attempt to kill an Abandoned. Each step lower, I found myself regretting the times I trusted Seraph enough to share anything with her. Those freely–spoken words were back, chomping bites like a hellhound coming off a diet. Seraph had gotten close after earning my trust, and I thought she had done so because she saw something in me and was giving me a chance the others on the Council didn't seem interested in. But it had been a ploy to get a better understanding of who I was and what I was capable of. With each step deeper into the prison, I realized the Council had been playing the long game because they understood my nature better than they ever communicated. Their concern was not for me, but for what Hell's Segregate could do to hinder their ambitions.

We reached a new landing, and a guard stepped forward, unlocking and pulling open a thick door through which only a small barred slat was cut. Heavy security. He stepped aside, allowing half the contingent to step through while the others remained behind me.

"Move," one barked.

I stepped into a long hallway that stretched into the darkness below, illuminated by sporadically placed torches that burned with the azure of Hellfire.

"Nice place you've got here," I said to the guard behind me.

He had the good humor to snicker.

This wasn't his fault. It wasn't the fault of any of them. They were just like any other demon, doing the Council's bidding any time the Council bid. No thinking, no questioning. Such was their grip on the residents of this realm.

Being Hell's only resident without magic had always been

a blessing, one that created incalculable headaches and even more lonely nights. Most weren't interested in associating with a demon like me. When Aries gifted Creed during my first mission, I thought he had given me a further blessing, for all the trouble the halberd was. Over time, though, I discovered Creed caused more problems for the Council than for me. In their chambers, my mind was untouchable. For the bonus, no matter how powerful they were, the Founders couldn't take it from me either. No one could without special equipment, and even then, that was tricky. My mind and body, alive because of Aries's gift.

"Trust."

I glanced over my shoulder, squinting, to find which guard spoke the one–word comment. Maybe a friend? An ally, even?

But they looked straight ahead, their gazes only flicking at me after I turned.

"Keep moving," one said. He had a huge bend in the middle of his nose. He must have seen his share of fists up too close.

"What did you say?" I asked the ugly guard.

"No one said nothing," a less ugly guard said. He lifted the butt of his spear and used the flat end to press against my lower back. "Move."

Ahead, a guard stopped by a cell door. It was the first cell I'd seen in the hallway. I was getting more privacy than anyone ever wanted.

His keys jingled as he searched out the lock, before cranking. It sounded like large stones smacked together in a cavern. Under my feet, the stone vibrated slightly, as if an enormous mechanism underneath the floor had been freed. My skin prickled.

The forward contingent stepped into the cell. I followed, turning to see the second contingent spreading in an inverted V-shape at the door, one guard inside, two standing behind him, three behind him. The squad was making sure I stayed put.

"Put your halberd in the rack," the one in front of the inverted-V said, lifting the spear and pointing toward the wall.

I turned to see two blue-burning torches bordering tarnished silver clamps bolted to the wall. The cell wasn't atrociously damp, but it wasn't the most arid either. How long before I found myself in the same condition down here?

"What if I don't want to?" I asked.

He stared dumbly, mouth hanging open. "I—well, you need to."

I raised an eyebrow. "Need to?"

"Well… yes, of course," he said.

"Why?"

"Well—because—you're—you're a prisoner," he said.

"I don't really feel like making a prisoner of my halberd," I said, tapping Creed with my palm. "He hasn't done anything to anyone. But then again." I waved at my new surroundings. "Neither have I and look where it landed me. Almost as if the Council is trying to oppress me and what I might have to say." I patted Creed, which was noticeably inactive. "I think I'd like to keep him by my side. For company, you understand? Don't want to get too lonely."

"Just do what he asked," a guard from the back rank said.

I stared at the demon. He stared at me. Neither of us flinched. Someone's armor jingled.

"Trust," a voice said, intimately close.

The guards, those in the second contingent by the cell door, and the first along the wall near the brackets, watched. None had spoken.

I was clearly losing my mind, and I just stepped into this cell. Whatever rift Azazel created, its taint had dug deep into my gray matter. For a flash of a second, I hoped that hadn't been his intent all along, that he hadn't tricked me, just as

Seraph had before him. It wasn't unconscionable to think that I had fallen for Azazel's "harmless," ancient personality. Like chicken wings and beer, I might be damned for all eternity to be partnered with a lack of trust. The way things were working out, I'd have plenty of time to reflect on my reasons for flickering doubt in the goateed Founder.

Had I even been played by him? Him giving me the coordinates to the Horn, an item I was supposed to find now, appeared farcical. Of course he would compel me to trust him by asking for help in stopping the growing force that was Seraph. It opened me to the possibility that I did have a friend on the Council, someone I could lean on, but it would also convince me to step through the rift. Though I could detect magic before spells were cast, that didn't mean I understood the nature of the spells. Detecting the magic of a rift was one thing. Understanding what I was subjecting myself to was another entirely. Azazel could have easily tainted me while keeping me clueless. Not until I started hearing things.

Oh joy, when are the hallucinations coming?

"Look, we're just doing our jobs," the guard from the back rank said, returning my attention to the here and now. "We don't want trouble, but I was told to remind you that you're in prison while your family and friends are up there." He jerked his head toward the ceiling. "We are the messengers, but you know what that means. Right?"

It was a tried-and-true tactic of the Council, to always threaten the life, limb, and safety of loved ones to get me to comply. And it always worked. Like now.

"Fine." I yanked Creed free.

The guards near the wall jumped. One of the younger incubi shifted his spear as if ready to attack.

"Careful there." I wagged the collapsed halberd in his direction. "This thing has a mind of its own and, for the life of me, I can't get it to listen. It's got quite an attitude, and I can't be responsible if it decides it doesn't like your face and wants to free you of it."

The young incubus looked at his peers. One with a permanent shadow of a mustache titled his head up. The younger guard raised his spear tip and stood at attention.

I smiled as I stepped past him, lifting Creed. "Sorry, old buddy."

The halberd jiggled, barely perceptible as I set it in the bracket.

"Clamp it shut. We know we can't touch that blessed thing," the guard outside the cell—really brave of him—said.

When I closed the clamps, the tension melted from the guards. The one in the back rank giving orders smiled. "Thank you for complying."

"Sure thing."

The guards parted at the cell door, allowing the contingent stationed inside to march out. They waited as the last one locked me inside.

The order-giver hung back as the squad formed into two columns, aimed back down the hall. "Chow will be brought in a few hours. Let's go, boys."

By the time I found the most comfortable place to sit—which was an accomplishment considering the entire cell was nothing but black brimstone with one small, goat-hair rug—the clinking of armor had faded behind the thick outer door.

The world got very quiet, very hastily.

Meals came, if you could consider the slop I was served food. Funny, how instantaneously culinary snobbishness fades when the only meals you eat are prison meals. I lost track of how many I'd eaten at around twenty-five. After that, everything tasted the same, and the days of dark solitude took a mounting toll. I passed the time thinking about Cancer and even talking to her memory from time to time. It never spoke back. I did laps around the cell, counting the steps each time. Eighteen-by-twelve Zeke-sized steps, in case you were wondering. I did more pushups than sit-ups, since the stone floor raked my spine any time I did a short burst of core work. I even entertained thoughts of working on some of the fighting techniques Leo taught me, but I looked ridiculous—yes, even though I was alone—fighting the air. I even used my senses against the brackets holding my halberd and practiced sending them through the stone walls. I never got much in the way of feedback.

No matter what I did to occupy myself, the long days of solitary imprisonment were tough.

The Council was trying to break me, that much I understood. But I'd also fooled myself into thinking I would only be in prison for a matter of hours. Maybe a day or two at the most. Turns out, I was wrong.

Without a line of sight to the outside world, I had no idea how many days passed, but consuming more than two dozen terrible prison meals implied I had been in the cell for well over a week. Once, I asked a guard and he, almost apologetically, told me he was not allowed to tell me. Either way, expediency of death seemed less important with each passing meal. So much for Seraph being in a hurry to have my head chopped off.

The lack of other prisoners didn't help. The last time I was locked behind bars, I had Ralrek, who was still only just separating himself from being Hell's asshole at that time. Still, being forced to share space with an asshole is better than sharing with only yourself and the voices in your head, of which had begun to hang around more often. After a few days, I had figured the taint from Azazel's rift would have faded and the voices would have stopped. But the days proved me wrong. The ridiculous company I kept commented at all hours of the day and night.

"Trust."

"Believe."

"Balance."

I never knew when I would hear them. Tainted magical rifts or simply losing my mind, I didn't know, but sanity was on its way out the cell door. At least one of us would be free. If only I had hallucinations to accompany the voices. The party inside my head would be a lot more fun.

Talking to Creed didn't keep me sane. The stupid halberd had entered sleep mode or something. Not a rattle or even a single vibration in all my time since I put it in the brackets. I think it was pouting. Or the brackets were imbued with a nastiness similar to the clamps Marijon had used against me in the Eighth Circle when she became the only demon capable of stealing the halberd.

That thought kept me occupied for a while, let me tell you.

The halberd's attitude might have been attributable to whatever my senses were picking up on in the prison since the moment I was shuffled down the corridor. Unlike the voices, my prickling skin was a constant. Magic was at work here. Which type, I didn't know, but at this point, I didn't care either. I was more agitated by its unwelcome company.

None of the guards who brought my meals seemed inclined or informed enough to educate me on it. Whatever the feeling, it was constant. A spell to tame my halberd. Thankfully, whenever I called to it, Creed would vibrate against the clasps. I was confident it would break them, but I didn't want to push my luck unless I needed to.

At some point in this ambiguous existence, the prison door unlocked and multiple feet slapped against smooth brimstone floor. This was the first time I'd had multiple visitors. I moved to the cell door, pressing my face against the cool iron to look down the hall as far as possible. After a few seconds, a goofy grin split my face.

I had company, and it was company I wanted.

"Zeke!" Bilba shouted, his voice echoing.

"Quiet," the guard said.

"Screw you," Ralrek snapped, striding along with Bilba to reach the cell door first.

"Hey guys. I never thought I'd be so happy to see your ugly asses," I said.

Bilba reached through the iron bars and patted my shoulder. "Good to see you too, Zeke. You're getting fat."

I slapped my flat stomach. "Can you believe they don't have a gym on the premises?"

"Unconscionable," a feminine voice rang out. A familiar voice. A succubus I longed to see.

"You better not have brought me any work," I called.

"Not that you would get any of it done. And if you did, I'd just have to go behind you and correct it," Dialphio said as she stepped into view.

Her emerald eyes, bordered by faint green eyeshadow, sparkled, even here. Even in the murky cell, her auburn hair looked lighter, as if it had lost its vibrancy. Still cut short, she had it styled now in spikes, as if a constant wind blew it back. Shortest of the bunch, Dialphio moved between Bilba and Ralrek, facing the cell door. I was relieved to see how healthy she looked. I had not seen her since my trial after Baghdad. With her presence alone, Dialphio made the world feel a little more sane. Cancer would have liked Dialphio.

"You're a sight for sore eyes," I said.

Dialphio's eyes softened. "As are you, Ezekial." She snapped her head toward the approaching guard. "Hurry. Unlock this door. You've kept him alone long enough."

The guard rushed forward, as if Dialphio was the one who paid his coin. He opened the cell and stepped out of the way. My friends entered. He closed and locked it once more with an apologetic shrug. "Sorry, just procedure."

The four of us spent the next minutes hugging.

Glancing over her shoulder at the guard, Dialphio said, "Are you going to stand there all day?"

He gave her an unblinking look.

"Go!" she said, shooing him with her hands before pointing at the iron bars. "He won't go anywhere, I promise. Give us privacy. You stripped him of enough dignity as it is."

The guard hefted his spear and walked away. The clinking of his armor faded.

Dialphio turned back only after he was out of earshot, a devilish grin on her face. Reaching into her blouse, she paused when her arm was elbow–deep. "You boys might want to look away."

We did.

After a moment, she cleared her throat. "It's fine now."

I twisted to see her holding a book in her hands. "So they," I said with a jerk of my head toward Bilba and Ralrek, "told you about my copy of *The Histories*?"

"No. What did you do with it now?" Dialphio asked.

"Nothing. The Council searched my bags when they brought me home and confiscated it… again."

"So you lost another copy of the most important book in Underworld history?" Dialphio said, but I noted a playful hint to her tone. She shook her head, waving her hand. "No matter, copies are being made. I might let you borrow another one, though I'm sure you'll lose that too." She held out her hands. "This is not a copy of *The Histories*. Just a notebook."

"Magical?" I asked, knowing Dialphio wouldn't have snuck in a regular notebook. This one was demonic, a magical device that allowed users to communicate vast distances across not only Hell, but even from here to the Overworld.

"It is," she said.

"You shouldn't have done that. You could get in trouble," I said.

But Bilba was shaking his head. "The cell has a suppression system for magic. I'm surprised you haven't noticed that, Zeke." So that was what I'd been feeling. He continued before I could revel in the fact that I was now detecting a new type of spell. "Anyway, it's designed to cut off magic at larger levels. No spellcasting in here. But things like demonic note-books are too low–level to register."

I squinted. "They didn't frisk you for contraband?"

Dialphio planted her hands on her hips. "They would not think about touching me where I had that stashed. Not if they knew what was good for them."

I took the notebook, pinched between my finger and thumb.

"Don't be cute. I'm sure you've been exposed to grimier situations then a notebook carried in my blouse, based on what I know of young incubi. You probably have dirtier things in your bag they searched through." Dialphio chirped.

I smiled and gave her a hug. "Thank you. This will help with the loneliness."

She squeezed, not letting me go. "I heard about your friend, Ezekial. I'm so sorry." Another warm squeeze. She could have held me forever if she wanted.

"Thank you," I somehow managed to choke.

Dialphio held me for a moment longer, until my breathing slowed, and stepped back. Her cheeks were flushed and the rims of her eyes were red. Her hand shot to the cover of the notebook just as I was about to open it to distract me from thoughts of Cancer. "There's also something in there. Wait until you're alone. Make sure no one is around."

"Okay."

"And as for *The Histories*, don't worry," Dialphio said. "I have plenty of copies, so that's not a worry. Plus, you hardly need it anymore. You're well-versed on the origins of the Council. And you know enough about that thing," she said, half–turning to point at Creed hanging on the wall. "Further reading won't do much for you."

"Because you're not smart, is what she's saying." Ralrek poked my arm.

"That," Dialphio piled on before I could respond, "and what you know just needs to be applied. Knowledge in itself is hardly useful. One must apply themselves before it can become beneficial."

"Well, I should have plenty of time to work on it down here. How long has it been?" I asked.

Bilba's head hung. "Almost two weeks."

"Two weeks? Wow." I was getting very good at estimating the passage of time in prison cells. A benefit of spending too much time in them.

"We're trying to find more information, but it's difficult. The Council is tight-lipped, as always." Dialphio frowned. "From what I hear, it's a matter of dragging this out as long as possible to weaken you. So, it's important that you spend this time sharpening your skills with the halberd and keeping your mind equally sharp. You don't want to be dulled, regardless of who or what they choose as your opponent."

"I would if I could get to my halberd without anyone finding out."

Dialphio's face scrunched. "It's right there."

I hung my head. "I haven't tried because... because I figured I was being monitored, and if I misstepped, the Council would punish one of you, or my parents. Heavens, everyone."

Bilba's shoulders rose and fell in a quick shrug. "They already are. You might as well make sure you're ready for the fight, when it comes."

"What do you mean they already are?"

Bilba's head dropped.

Ralrek's arm slid to his back. "Dumbass here has been getting pressure."

"Pressure? From who? About what?"

"The Passage," Bilba said to the floor.

"Hey," I said as I approached, putting my hand on his shoulder until he looked up at me. "What about it?"

The Passage was a test very few demons had the privilege of taking. A test of their Abilities, if passed, the demon gained the title of Major demon and all the societal benefits and power that came along with it. Normally, it is a great honor to be selected, one most demons spent their lives only dreaming of—especially those who had a fair shot. Hell did have its fair share of dreamers though, too. My friend wasn't the latter; he'd studied the arcane arts for thousands of years already. Now, that study was paying off. Bilba was taking it early in life, far earlier than maybe he should have. But he'd been preparing for the test throughout my time in Abandonment. I would have thought he'd be bursting with excitement by now.

"I keep hearing they might move it up. My test date, that is," he finally said.

"Isn't that a good thing?"

His lips pinched together, unsure.

"It's a very aggressive schedule," Dialphio answered for my best friend, her eyes on him.

"Are you not ready?" I asked.

"I'm… I'm not sure." Bilba shuffled from foot to foot.

"Then tell them that." It made sense to me.

"It's not that simple, dumbass," Ralrek said.

"Sure, it is. If you're not ready, tell them you need a later date," I said, hoping against everything I knew about the Council that they would be reasonable about this.

"I have, and it was rejected. Twice," Bilba said.

Oh, that was a problem. The Passage was not risk–free. Not by a long shot. Taking place outside of Hell, if Bilba wasn't ready, he could be put in a situation that could kill him. Call that a Light Bulb Moment.

"Is this their doing?" I asked, looking at Dialphio.

From the bracket in the wall, Creed vibrated. Sure, stupid halberd, now decide to keep me company.

Creed vibrated louder, rattling the brackets.

Everyone turned to look, Bilba included.

"Has Akimon petitioned for another date? As your father,

maybe his request will carry a different weight?" I asked, trying to think of any way to delay the pressure on Bilba.

Bilba's head dropped again. "He tried. Denied him too. Now he tries to support me as long as I'm confident."

"And you told him you were?" I asked, even though I knew the answer.

"Yeah. He's my father, Zeke. If I tell him the truth..."

"And Melchiot?" I finished, trying to rescue him from dwelling on a son's guilt.

Melchiot Zeistane was the mentor Bilba hired while I was Abandoned. It was her job to prepare him. She was also a Hex user, capable of casting a rare magic supposedly used to initiate the curse that afflicted Cancer and her family. During my time in the Overworld, she had been helping Bilba look for a cure. So far, they had come up empty.

"She's bothered by it, to say the least," Bilba said. "It's not normal, she says. But, honestly, she is acting guarded. She said I am strong, even if I don't feel like I'm prepared. She doesn't think so either, but said this might be the only chance I ever get."

"Tell him the rest." Ralrek looked down at Bilba without adjusting.

"I don't want to get into it," Bilba said.

"Tell me what?"

Ralrek straightened. "Everyone thinks he's being monitored."

"Monitored? Like, being watched?" I asked.

"That's what it means, dumbass." Ralrek smirked. "It basically started when you were Abandoned. Subtle things here and there, even when he's at work or home. Especially when he's training with Melchiot. Nothing threatening, at least not right now. More like they're just keeping tabs."

"Why? Bilba?" I said his name slowly and with emphasis when he ignored me. "You've been playing around with spells, haven't you?"

"Maybe," he peeped. "But either way, that doesn't have anything to do with the Passage."

"You can't know that for sure," I said. "Plus, you should know how the Council is." I didn't want to shame him, but it was so blessedly difficult to deny how harsh the Council was. "They're looking for justification."

"I... I'm just testing things in case we find ourselves in a situation where we need it, that's all." Bilba sounded as guilty as an impling caught with his hand in the cracker jar.

"Like what?"

"Like anything required to support the Great Prince," Ralrek snorted.

I shook my head. "Don't you start. Not now. Keep it up, and I'll trick the guard into locking you in here and setting me free."

"You've got to admit, it's still funny." Bilba smirked.

I looked to Dialphio. "Want to help me here?"

She waved a pudgy hand at me. "Oh, you seem to be doing fine on your own... Great Prince."

The three laughed, and it wasn't long before I joined them. "Well, at some point, I might go looking for the Horn again, if you're so ready to help. Not much I can do in here."

Bilba's head snapped up. "Really?"

I looked toward the dark ceiling and spread my arms out to my sides. "Not like I'm going to talk about it as long as I'm in here, but you might hear something soon." I tapped the demonic notebook in my hands. "I received a... note while I was Abandoned that might come in handy."

"Well maybe it was a good thing they brought you back?" Bilba offered.

"Yeah, nothing like always being the exception to the rule," I said with a harsh chuckle.

"You're hardly the exception," Dialphio said. "Plenty of demons have been brought back from Abandonment before."

"Yeah, there's nothing special about you," Bilba said right

on the back of her statement. "The Council has done this dozens of times from what I've been reading. They might want us to think something different, that Abandonment is permanent, but that's not the case. Even if you were the exception, which you are not, in case I wasn't already clear."

"You guys are trying to make that very clear, thank you," I said with a wry smile.

"In fact, it's a new punishment, relatively speaking," Dialphio said. "This wasn't necessarily used in a punitive way for much of our early history. At least, it hasn't always been the default punishment."

"Seems to be more of a recent tactic.," Bilba said.

"Shocker." Ralrek wasn't much help.

"I don't think anyone, at least those of us in the cell, are surprised that the Council is being less than honest," I said, my eyes slipping to Creed. Even the halberd was a prisoner of sorts to the Council.

"Demons have crossed over all the time. It's just a lie," Bilba said, his voice rising. "Just another lie. One of many we've been told."

Dialphio made a small noise, like a muffled bird chirp. "Imagine what else they're lying to us about."

We fell into silent agreement, interrupted by the clanking of approaching armor. I tucked the notebook in the back of my pants and pulled my shirt over it.

I sighed. "It looks like our visit is over. I hope I get to see you soon?"

"Hope so," Ralrek said.

Bilba moved in for a hug. I gave it to him.

Dialphio shuffled forward when he vacated the spot. The guard was already unlocking the cell door. Too soon. My ex-boss's mouth was near my ear. "Remember what I said. Use that halberd. Don't cast, just focus on staying physically and mentally sharp. The time is coming soon."

She pulled back and gave me a motherly smile.

"I will," I promised.

With her hand in front of her body so the guard couldn't see, Dialphio made a square shape in the air and pointed at the notebook I hid behind my back. She mouthed, "Read it."

"Let's go," the guard said.

My three friends lingered for a second longer before departing. He shooed them down the hall, away from the cell, as the lock clicked back into place, separating me from the living.

"Get moving. Visiting time is over," key boy said, lowering his spear toward the mouth of the hall.

My three friends waved and departed. I waited until the clanking armor faded to ensure no one was hanging around in the hall, long enough to be sure no other guard was hanging back for nefarious reasons. Now that I knew they had a suppression spell in place, I wasn't worried about being watched by magic, so I pulled the notebook out. A folded piece of paper was tucked inside the front cover envelope sleeve. With excitement, I fought the note open.

I recognized the handwriting immediately. Cassie. The angel who saved my life only weeks before.

Saved my life in the very ambush during which I supposedly murdered a demon.

CASSIE: *Hi Zeke. I am sorry I haven't written more often. A lot of things have been happening. I understand they are with you as well. I'm sorry about all of this. I wish I had a better reason to be writing, and I feel horrible saying this, but I need your help. I can't believe this is happening. Demons are causing problems in Olympia. Leo is going through something, but he's not involved. Please, Zeke, the Balance is being affected, worse than before. Can you help? I don't trust this notebook enough to say anything else. I need to see you. I know you're involved in stuff, but the second you break away. I need you. If that's not possible, is there someone else, like Ralrek, you can convince to help. Someone trustworthy and powerful. We need you.*

WALKING TO A TORCH FRAMING THE BRACKETS HOLDING CREED, I burned the note.

Well, wasn't this great? Imprisoned for something I didn't do, begged to return to the Overworld to help in a situation I couldn't alter by an angel who was supposed to be a mortal enemy. My "mortal enemy" was more trustworthy than the ancients who put me on trial.

Things were never simple, were they?

3

UNDERWORLD, UNDISCLOSED

"WELL, IT LOOKS LIKE A PARTY NOW," I said, eyeing my best friend's rigid expression

Ralrek snorted at my reaction to Bilba. "Aren't you at least a little nervous, Zeke?"

"Yeah, they're not playing around. They fully intend on following through," Bilba said, scratching his slimmer-than-pre-mother's-heartbreak cheek with his black–nailed fingers.

My best friend wasn't looking as healthy as before I was Abandoned. With context, knowing what my friend was facing, the demands of the Passage were weighing on him. Bilba was stronger than he knew, but maybe he was carrying too much weight. Between trying to support his father by taking the Passage and being best friends with the hurricane of doom that was me, the stress was showing. He could, I swear, handle stress as well as he handled himself around succubus.

The Council chamber wasn't abuzz with activity—we demons do enjoy our buzzing—but it was busier than the last time Hell's rulers dragged me into their showroom. Even though the long jade table at the front of the room was unoc-cupied, that didn't mean this space was devoid of life. Small pockets of demons dotted the wide expanse, no one group hanging too close to the other. Chamber guards stood by each of the doors in pairs. Conspicuous by their absence, the Council still hadn't shown up. I took in those around, dressed in fashionable robes, or high-class slacks and blouses. A few wore suits. The staffs a few carried were gnarled and knotted, appearing millennia old. One succubus hung a wand from her brown leather belt that was polluted with mounted stones cast to resemble unicorns. The way it hung heavy, the wand had to be made of solid gold.

"Do you guys have any idea who they are?" I whispered, waggling my finger at the different pockets.

Ralrek pinched his lips together and shrugged.

"Influencers from around the Circles," Bilba said with his own conspiratorial whisper.

"Why are they here?"

"To witness the event." Bilba shuffled forward a couple of inches. "From what I hear, your stance caused serious headaches for the Council. According to Dialphio, they've been fighting and arguing amongst themselves about you since you came back. But the in-fighting goes back to before that. Throughout your Abandonment, actually. Having to bring you back and deal with you exacerbated the internal fighting. Supposedly, they're not agreeing on anything."

"How did I do that?"

"For some reason they think you're more badass than you are," Ralrek said, his dark eyes scanning the room.

Ralrek's snarkiness was always good for my ears. He had changed throughout my time in the Overworld into something I didn't like. Far from being the jerk I'd known him as for six thousand years, he also wasn't the same incubus I came to enjoy being around during the Gemini mission or our service in Baghdad in the Army. During and since my time above, he was losing hope. When I had needed him to be engaged and active in the Underworld, to help me manage the mess that my situation was becoming, he had been the least passionate of our small group. Back then, I had told Bilba how I wished to be home, so I could kick Ralrek's ass back onto the right path. Bilba even agreed I would have helped the taller incubus. Though I was back, I wasn't free to bring light into his life, but seeing him full of snark gave me hope that at least a sliver of his old personality was returning. And not a moment too soon.

"So they're still planning on going through with this?" I faced the front of the room, trying to ignore the obnoxious stares of the older, affluent demons. I'd been escorted from my cell without a word. After the short first minutes standing around, I was still unclear how I felt that my friends were in attendance. No Dialphio. No parents. That meant something. A curve. A twist.

Funny aside. The Council did attempt to put Creed in silver brackets on a side wall similar to those in my cell, but the halberd copped an attitude and broke them within seconds. Apparently, neither the Council nor their guards thought to install backups. None of that would have made a difference and only served to slow proceedings, but it was as funny as smoking hot angels attempting to say demon's names.

When all was said and done, the weapon was on my hip again. Oh, and giving not a single nudge in either direction.

"Are any of us surprised? I'm not. If for no other reason, they have to go through with this to save face," Bilba said, waving his hand around as if casting a spell. "They want to make that statement now. That's why these influencers are here. For better or worse, I think we're going to find out what their plans are for us."

I shot him a look. "For us? You mean, for me."

Bilba shook his head. "Something tells me this isn't all about you. It may look like it at first, but they've got something up their sleeves that will impact Ralrek and I as well. Maybe even Dialphio."

"Dialphio?"

Ralrek grunted. "She's not doing herself any favors by showing allegiance to you. Even just coming to the prison sends a signal."

"And the Council is always watching," Bilba said. "And she's involved, somehow, someway."

"What do you mean?" I asked.

Bilba scooted even closer. We were now almost shoulder to shoulder, not that it mattered. If they wanted, the Council, stashed away in their personal chambers, could eavesdrop on our conversation or whatever dorky thoughts were pinging around in my best friend's skull. Apparently, they didn't want to bother. "I don't know how, but she has word about the Council's plans. She couldn't, wouldn't, give me specifics because she didn't want me involved on a deeper level. Too much risk, I guess. But she told me enough. It seems like they have agreed, with conditions, on the volunteer to fight you in the trial by combat."

I raised my arm, swinging it and a half–arc. "Then what is this for?"

"Like I said, to make a statement," Bilba said.

As if on cue, five doors opened at the side of the massive room. The guards protecting those doors snapped to attention as Hell's rulers entered the chamber from their individual rooms.

The five fell into a silent single file, Michael in the lead. The Founders were dressed in their formal black robes with red bands embroidered on the sleeves, cuffs, and seams. Michael paused when they passed a clump of older demons, draped in finery of the higher-class. He shook hands and smiled like a typical slimy politician. Heads were brought together in whispers of promise, conspiring, and favors traded by the looks of it.

Someone growled.

It was me.

Bilba whispered, "Keep your head, Zeke. You can't let them rile you. We have witnesses, and don't think for a second what happens here isn't going to spread around the Circles as soon as everyone leaves. If you give them reasons to talk, they'll talk. Float the higher road."

Honestly, his use of one of Hell's time-test maxims that not only taught demons to value being the better demon, but also simultaneously ascribed that honor to our wealthiest as if it were an intrinsic value of theirs annoyed me. The problem? Bilba was right, of course, but that didn't mean I had to like it.

After another round of handshaking, smiling, and obnoxious head nods, the Council moved along, pausing again at a third group, repeating the grotesque political display. Soaking in the adulation like celebrities.

One aspect differed as they approached the table. Unlike every time before, the Council wasn't moving as a single unit. At least two body lengths divided them, never interacting with each other, only with the affluent demons who demanded attention. Fractures? Or was it fissures? I couldn't remember. It didn't matter.

A Council divided and trying to keep up their public image.

Finally, at the jade table on the riser, they stood behind their chairs, facing the gathering. Each of the five Founders lowered their heads, almost synchronized. I felt the weight of attention and glanced around me. Everyone's eyes were on me.

"Mr. Sunstone, present yourself," Michael ordered.

Because one of the few bragging points I have is the fact that I'm quite experienced with Council presentations in the chamber, I knew precisely what he meant. I moved forward, centering myself on the table, twenty feet separating me from them. Creed warmed against my hip at my approach.

"Shush," I whispered.

The heat from the halberd flashed against my pants, scorching my skin so bad that it felt like it seared through my jeans.

"I'm going to turn you to kindling."

"We're here to set in motion a necessary, yet unfortunate event," Michael continued as the Council members took their seats.

The crowd shuffled forward, their footsteps barely audible, as if they, too, feared drawing the Council's attention. The influencers practically vibrated with excitement.

I was so happy for them. Nothing I appreciated more than a crowd so bored with their own lives that they were forced to fill their days with entertainment through someone else's crumbling. Good demons, let me tell you, are hard to find.

"You have been brought here as witnesses to this day," Michael announced. "You are privileged to witness this event because you are trustworthy members of our society who can carry word to those who need to hear it. Egregious crimes have been committed by Ezekial Sunstone, and it is necessary he faces consequences for his decisions." Michael scanned the room but avoided me. "You may remember he, along with Mr. Ralrek Burning, was responsible for bringing angels into the Underworld. Angels who attacked us, killing over three hundred."

"Never forget," Azazel said from the opposite end of the table.

"Never forget," the other Council members muttered in unity.

The cultural trope spread around the room as the clusters of demons repeated the saying.

Way to build a case against me, false as it was, by leveraging a tragedy I wasn't responsible for committing or even knew would happen. Since when were facts relevant, though?

"Mr. Sunstone was also part of the human Army when he

blasphemed Lucifer," Michael soaked in the revulsion from the crowd, muttered in whispers behind hands, as decorum demanded. When they died down, he piled dirt on top of my coffin. "For which he was Abandoned. But he did not stop there. While in the Overworld, serving what was supposed to be a deserved life sentence among the mortals, Ezekial Sunstone murdered one of our community."

"A demon?" someone in the back of the room shouted.

Michael nodded. "That is, unfortunately, correct. Ezekial Sunstone murdered, in cold blood, Chax Vicu, a member of a prestigious family. Though he had brought no harm to Mr. Sunstone, nor did he affect the Balance, Mr. Sunstone took it upon himself to seek vengeance against those who serve Lucifer."

"Heretic!" an older incubus shouted, shaking a fist adorned with obnoxious curled rings at me as if she was ready to throw down if the Council allowed.

"We've set a trial by combat which will determine the fate of Mr. Sunstone. He will face another who has wronged Lucifer, and the victor shall earn his freedom once more, as is our custom. We have only yet to receive the approval to set the combat. And that is what we will do now."

Excited whispers buzzed around the room.

In the corner, a door clicked, and the whispering stopped. Every head turned as if connected. A figure appeared between the largest, most dangerous guards I'd ever seen, standing at attention. Soft rattling at the side of the room caught my attention. One guard I had seen on previous visits shook, literally, in his armored boots.

The volume of the excited whispers arose again, circulating faster. One incubus fell to his knees. A succubus on the other side of the circle fainted. Five Council members shot to their feet, even Azazel, who I'd never seen move with anything that could be misunderstood as speedy.

The figure in the corner room stepped out and moved

along the back wall, past the wall sconces burning with Hell-fire. The flames grew broader, taller, and brighter as the incubus passed under them.

Lucifer.

No, I wasn't using the Lord's name in vain. The Council had called on Lucifer.

Not tall or short, the ruler of the Underworld walked parallel to the back wall, His eyes cast at the floor. His hair was gray, holding enough hints of a distant past's blond. Lucifer wore it greased back. Hooked strings still fell forward. He had a full beard and mustache, which was curled at the tips, rising toward His bent eyebrows, making it appear as if the two were somehow connected. Lucifer's black robe was embroidered to match His Council members, but with more flourish—the designs grander, the loops bigger and broader.

Thunk. Thunk. Thunk. Each step, like the tolls of a death march. The plain staff clunking filled the chamber.

Throats were cleared. Succubi found jewelry to fiddle with. Incubi suddenly realized their neckties needed straight-ening. Elderly incubi and succubi stood straighter as Lucifer reached the steps of the riser. A guard on each side raised their arms just underneath his elbows as if they were preparing to catch Him should he fall. Lucifer didn't look either way. Instead, His head still cast down, it appeared He had to concentrate on each step.

Thunk. Thunk. Thunk.

Atop the riser, He turned toward Michael, who bowed at a ninety degree angle. The other Founders and all attendees followed suit. Bilba's bow was as awkward as mine.

"Lord," Michael said demurely, slowly backing away.

Beelzebub, directly behind Michael, looked over his shoulder even as he backed. I didn't think I would ever see the day the massive Founder acted subserviently. Each Founder moved further down the table to new seats. Had the table not been so long, their new seat assignments would have pushed Azazel off the riser.

Lucifer leaned His staff against the jade, the wood knocking against the hard stone. His skin was the color of sand, lacking any of the age spots that clung to Azazel. A guard moved to pull his chair out, the chair Michael had sat in from the time I knew of Lucifer's Council, but Lucifer swatted the black gauntleted hand away. When He sat, He did so with a grunt. He faced those gathered, His bottom lip jutting out slightly further than His top. Lucifer's eyes were small ovals dominated by those thick, angled eyebrows. His irises were pure gray.

"Let's proceed," the ruler of the Underworld realm, the immovable force opposed to Yahweh, spoke for the first time in front of me, not looking bothered in the least. Maybe that was because of the way His thick eyebrows dropped precipitously at the ends, and deep creases ran the length of His forehead.

The five Council members scrambled to take their seats like they'd just discovered they had them. Demons shifted as if they needed to move to meet the expectations of the grandest of demonkind.

Michael picked up the gavel and slammed it once against the jade. Lucifer flinched.

"We are here to receive your approval for the opponent to face Ezekial Sunstone in a trial by combat," Michael announced, only turning to recognize Lucifer after making his full statement.

"Make your case." Lucifer's voice sounded like rust.

"Our case is as it's always been," Apopis said, thrusting his shoulders back.

"Do you presume to speak for all of us?" Seraph shot back. All heads, except Lucifer's, turned in her direction.

"Remember, in turn," Michael chided.

"Michael, it is far beyond time to decide," Beelzebub said.

"We've been around and around this topic. We have our fighter, let's just get the approval."

Azazel raised a liver–spotted hand. "I contest the matter that we have our fighter. We have a majority, but nothing more."

"I prefer it be unanimous." Michael sounded tired.

"It would be, if these two conceded." She thrust her finger toward Beelzebub and Apopis.

Throughout the spat, Lucifer sat, his tiny gray eyes peering out to a distant point.

Michael cleared his throat. I swore a few minuscule blotches of red appeared on his cheeks just above his beard line. "We needed to be unanimous to receive approval."

"Was this matter not settled before you called on me?" Lucifer said, never turning to even glance at the five demons who administered the Underworld for Him.

Apopis shifted in his seat. Michael arced his chin, as if stretching his neck free of the black robe cinching closed around it.

"We had," Michael said carefully. "But this is a most diffi-cult decision, my Lord. A special case by every measure, we are ensuring we select wisely to not dishonor you."

"We've already provided you with the two names, Lord," Seraph said, adding the official title as if it were an afterthought. "They are on the scroll in front of you."

Lucifer looked down. His eyes lingered. If there were just two names listed on the scroll, they had to be the longest names in history of our kind. Probably full of consonants too.

When He lifted His head, He peered at that distant point again and remained silent. The Founders waited. Michael turned, seeking silent guidance from his peers. Beelzebub blew out a breath with puffed cheeks then tipped his head to his shoulder in a shrug. Seraph's eyes flashed with that familiar danger. Azazel mumbled something unintelligible.

Apopis rolled his hand to Michael before flicking it in Lucifer's inattentive direction.

"Um, Lord," Michael said, shifting his chair to cock it in the direction of the Lord of the Underworld. "We seem to be unable to unanimously decide. So maybe, if You would be so gracious, You could choose the one most appropriate?"

Lucifer's tiny eyes never so much as blinked. "I know nothing about these two."

Michael's head swiveled to his peers again. Finding no answers, he turned back to Lucifer, frustration clear on his face. "Lord, if You approve the trial by combat, we will utilize a majority vote for the fighter for your approval... if that is okay with You?"

Michael's tone hinted that he didn't care if it was okay with Lucifer or not, as long as he got a decision from Hell's king.

A thick silence hung in the air. I was so fascinated by the apparent disinterest from Lucifer, I didn't think about the fact the eternal ruler of Hell was here in my presence—or that I was in His. A demon, the demon who could smite me where I stood if He chose. Here I was, a perpetual threat to Hell, in the face of the one who negated threats for breakfast, and yet nothing was happening. Seeing Him as fragile and disconnected as He appeared, I understood a lot about the reality of our realm and kind.

"Yes. Yes, fine," Lucifer said in his rusty voice. "You have my approval to set a trial by combat and opponent. Just make it equitable."

With that said, He grunted as He pushed himself to his feet. The two guards hovered behind him, but ever–present, ready to support the ancient in case His body betrayed Him. Acknowledging no one in the room, Lucifer cranked around, picked up His staff and used it to thunk His way out of the chamber.

The room of demons watched Him go in stunned fascination. I imagined the thoughts going through everyone's mind at Lucifer's arrival and departure, so underwhelming as it was.

And now my future was set for a trial by combat against… someone. At least my destiny was partially solidified.

Michael swallowed noticeably and cleared his throat. "We will proceed then," he said. "With a simple majority, we will determine your opponent, Ezekial Sunstone. Agreed?"

He wasn't asking me, which was a good thing, because I wouldn't agree on any of this. Instead, the question was asked in my direction but aimed at the Council members. The four agreed.

Michael waved at the guards toward the rear of the chamber. "Bring them in."

As I turned, so did everyone else. A pair of guards pulled the tall doors open in unison, revealing two demons. My jaw dropped.

Both were large, far larger than me—but that's not saying much since I'm nearly a half foot under six feet. Height aside, both were heavier than me too. But I knew plenty of imps who hadn't finished puberty who outweighed me, so that wasn't what shocked me either. Of course, the Council would select oversized opponents. Anyone who knew how they operated could have guessed that.

The incubus on the left was broad and carved into a V-shape of rock–hard muscle. His cannonball shoulders rivaled even Beelzebub's. His lats were so well-developed that his arms couldn't hang loosely at his side. This demon would make a meal of me without breaking a sweat. I imagined him swinging me around by my feet, slamming my head into the ground while eating a bucket of fried chicken with the other hand.

That intimidating force had distracted me from the marginally smaller, shaven-headed incubus, sporting a mustache and beard. An incubus who could brag about good looks. Also bigger than me. Every bit a formidable fighter. I knew that because I had fought him. I had trained with him. He taught me as many mixed martial arts tactics as possible in our short time together. I had even fought by his side in a life-and-death struggle only weeks earlier.

"Leo," I groaned.

Man, fuck the Council.

The two incubi were marched into the chamber, but my eyes never left Leo Neto.

Why him? How? He had been Abandoned just as I was and had only been a target of Chax Vicu and his gang because of me. Was this punishment, likely constructed by Seraph, for turning his back on Chax and siding with me?

The larger demon kept his gaze on the Council as he approached, but Leo watched me as I watched him. A confident, charming demon, he looked like a fragment of himself. His eyes drooped, and his mouth formed a grim line. He gave me a quick head nod as the pair saddled up next to me.

"We will now take a vote on which of these individuals will fight for their freedom against Mr. Sunstone," Michael announced. "Members, cast your vote. We'll start with you, Beelzebub."

"Goliath will not hesitate crushing the little gnat. I vote, Goliath," Beelzebub said. The larger incubus dipped his head.

What a stupid name. I would be sure to tell him that right before he rang my neck.

"Apopis?" Michael asked.

"Goliath receives my vote," Apopis said.

The last thing I wanted to do was fight Leo, especially in a trial by combat, but the mountain of a demon to his side wasn't exactly an enticing prospect either.

"Seraph?" Michael said.

She locked eyes, flaring with hatred, on me. "Leo."

"Azazel?"

Azazel waved his liver-spotted hand in the air. "Well, as it is apparent we will not have a unanimous vote, you know where I stand on this matter. I—"

"Just vote, you knob," Beelzebub boomed, drawing a few snickers from the room.

Azazel's furry eyebrows, white as parchment, scrunched together. "There is no need to be unprofessional. Mine remains the same. I vote, Leo."

Wow, Azazel. Really? He had told me I had friends in this fight, but now it looked like he meant me to fight one of them. What was Azazel's game here?

Two to two. Great. Michael was going to be the deciding vote again. Who knew, maybe he would throw a wrench in the plans and vote for neither of them, forcing the Council to decide whether or not I could be ganged up on. Thank Lucifer —really, thank One, but I had enough on my mind—for Creed blocking that thought from the counsel's attention.

"Then let's settle this matter once and for all," Michael said.

My fate was about to be determined. Regardless of which way he went, this proclamation did not bode well for me. But at least with the giant, I wouldn't be riddled with guilt if I was lucky enough to survive the combat.

Right until the moment Michael cast his vote.

"Leo," Michael announced, his hand sliding to the side and reaching for the gavel, which he lifted above the table by only a few inches. "Therefore, it is set. Tomorrow, in a trial by combat, a battle to the death for your freedom, Ezekial Sunstone, you will face Leo Neto. May you both spend this night reflecting on your past and what you have done that led you to this unfortunate place. Spend your hours wisely, as for one of you, they will be your last."

With the official proclamation made, Michael rapped the gavel onto the jade, filling the chamber with a sharp slap.

For whom the Bell tolls, and all that.

4

UNDERWORLD, SEVENTH CIRCLE

PRE-GAME JITTERS ARE A THING. I played enough blazeball in school to know that. What I didn't know was that they were even more real in life and death struggles. Right now, I had a bad case.

The shouts of the crowd in the stands above my head didn't help. In a perfect world, I would block out the noise and focus on my combat preparations. Sadly, at least for me, Hell was not, never was, and would never be a perfect place.

"Trust," a voice whispered from somewhere deeper in the room, maybe outside the closed door, just loud enough to rise above the din created by the spectators in the stands over my head.

I whipped around, dropping my boot as I looked for the source. Just as before, I was alone, without a clue what was happening inside my skull. Maybe if Leo cracked it open, he could deliver a diagnosis.

I was dying or Leo was, unless one of us figured a way out of this. Right now, I was all out of ideas. Heaven, I could barely maintain my sanity, hearing things when there was no one else around. Knowing my luck, distracting visual hallucinations would start showing up as soon as Leo was swinging a mallet at my head in the fighting pit.

Resuming my boot-tying, I laced the black steel-toes I selected. This room, separate from Leo's—though I was assured his was identical—was filled with armor and weapons from which to choose. The incubus who was supposed to attend to me, who I'd sent to find me something to eat, said the room wasn't this well stocked for the other fighters he'd attended to over the years. I guessed the regular fights weren't nearly as well-funded by the Council as the rare trials by combat. Apparently, the Council went all out providing devices of destruction.

The attendant, Pedent, returned after a short while, giving the up and down on my apparel. "Are you sure you don't want these?" he asked, holding up another pair of boots that looked the same as the pair I was wearing. I told him that. He smiled, "Watch this," he said, and then dropped the boot, slamming the heel on the floor. A thin blade shot from the toe, three inches long.

I gulped. "I couldn't do that to him."

Pedent shrugged, picking up the boots and returning them to the shelf. "Fine to have morals in here, but don't think for a second that applies out there. I've been working here for a few thousand years and have seen tens of thousands of fights. Trust me or not, that's up to you. You don't want to use them? Don't. He probably will."

"Go warm up my food. Please."

According to the rules briefing, this trial by combat wasn't going to be technical. Technically, there were no rules. That's as far as it went, as far as anyone was concerned. The expectation in the stands was for blood. Lots of it. How else did you have a trial by combat, where only one combatant walked out of the arena, right?

Not that I expected the attendees to be passive. Word from the guards who escorted me through the gateway to the

Seventh Circle was that locals were particularly riled up for the spectacle. A guard, whose complexion was as repulsive as his breath, told me the stadium sold out in a matter of minutes. When I asked him how many people the stadium could hold, he estimated several hundred, though he'd heard they were adding extra seating for this fight.

Several hundred—or more—demons, so hungry to see violence, that they bought up every seat in the time it takes to visit the bathroom?

The guard, excited by my apparent interest in not losing my guts all over a plot of matted sand, told me wagering was heavy not only in the stadium, but the Circles as well. Seems the Council had brought their marketing game.

A full stadium. The ruler of the Underworld purportedly planning on attending. The Council watching along with residents from every Circle—including the bloodthirsty demons of the Seventh. Weapons, a ringed pit from which there was no escape, and two incubi fighting for their lives. Hell sure knows how to throw parties.

I tried to settle my mind, feeling better about my decision to forgo the bladed boots for the steel-toed ones. I wouldn't stab Leo with my feet, but at least my precious toes would remain intact if he decided my toenails needed a little trim. I needed to be as clear-headed as possible. Getting wrapped up in the moment's drama helped no one except those who wanted me dead. Thinking about Leo, the pressure Bilba was under to take the Passage, Cassie's call for help, all of it pulled my mind away from where it needed to be. All of them combined played second priority to Cancer, though. I couldn't shake her memory. I didn't want to. Wherever she met her demise, I hoped she got to change a few lives first. Somehow, I knew she had. I couldn't very well help anyone if I was dead. With clear thought, I might just be able to partner with Leo and devise a way out of this before one of us was looking toward the roof of the Underworld with glazed-over eyes.

It was worth a shot.

Leo had worked with Seraph' nephew, Chax Vicu, as an unknowing-yet-desperate Abandoned demon. He and his whole family had the misfortune of being related to Aries the First and had been Abandoned because of it. Chax promised Leo and his family a return to Hell if he would help hunt me down. Once Leo learned the truth, though, he changed his position. That put his life in direct conflict with Chax's—and by extension, Seraph's—ambitions, and Leo had almost paid with his life.

Leo wasn't in this position because he wanted to harm me; he was here because he fulfilled his promise to protect his family.

Just how the Council put him in that position was something I didn't know. But I planned on finding out as soon as we stepped into the pit.

I found shin guards and strapped them on, and was struggling with my breastplate when Pedent returned with my meal, a pile of coleslaw, three potato wedges, and a thin slice of meatloaf. The potatoes were cold, the coleslaw warm, and the meatloaf as hard as my father's heart.

"Great last meal," I mumbled, not to Pedent specifically, but he was the only one around to hear my complaints. Well, him and my invisible friend who was driving me mad.

"Sorry, that's all they had," he apologized. "I tried to keep everything warm, but with everyone clamoring for their food before the fights, the kitchen is overwhelmed."

I waved. "Was hoping for chicken wings."

Pedent looked at me as if I had just plucked wings off a faerie. "You would eat the wings off a chicken?"

In his wide eyes, I had just become the monster the Council made me out to be, at least to this one incubus in this secluded room, under the Seventh Circle fighting pit stadium.

"Let's just say—" I started, about to explain the glorious delicacy that is mortal chicken wings, but by the horrified expression on Pedent's face, it wasn't worth the effort. A monster, I truly was.

"Let me help you with that," he offered, flicking a finger at the breastplate I still hadn't been able to buckle. As he helped, he said, "The stands are full. Quite a festive atmosphere."

"Good for them," I said. "Anyone important out there?"

Pedent's hands stopped moving as if he recognized I had caught him, and then resumed. "Oh, yes, everyone who is anyone in the Seventh, by the way I understand it. Plenty of others from different Circles. Looking at the way they're dressed... and the fact that they could travel, they must be important people."

"What about the Council?" I asked, shoving the last potato wedge in my mouth and trying to ignore the way it chilled my teeth.

"I've heard they're here as well," Pendent said, leaning closer. "Even heard our Lord will attend."

So it was true. This was going to be a big deal, a performance for the ages. "How much time do I have?"

As if on cue, heavy-booted feet stomped down the hall. Three guards entered the room without knocking, one smirking as Pedent struggled to clasp the breastplate closed. "Are you girls ready? The Underworld is waiting."

"Give me a minute?" I said by suggestion.

"Ain't got a minute," a second guard with an explosion of freckles said. "Was told to come get you. Everyone is ready."

I wanted to inform him that was good for everyone, but that I wasn't ready. Since I was one of the two fighters in the main event, it was pretty important I be included in that club. But I didn't think any of them wanted to hear what I had to say any more than the hundreds in the stands above me waiting to witness the bloodletting.

I stood. "Fine. Lead the way."

Freckle-face looked at me quizzically. "Ain't you get no

weapon? Bring whatever you can carry into the pit. Best take everything you're able to hold."

"I've got all I need," I said, patting Creed, which hung from the loop just below my now-clasped breastplate.

The first guard, the oldest of the trio, chuckled. "A stick? That'll do you a lot of good in the pits, even if it's half as dangerous as rumors say. You must have serious coin riding on the other guy."

The three guards laughed before turning and walking back into the hall. One of them chuckling and commenting about how disappointing my stick was. I let the criticism be. Creed needed a little grounding from time to time.

Pedent stood to the side of the room now. "Good luck," he said, not sounding like he meant it at all. How much had he bet on Leo?

I stepped into the hall behind the three guards. They led the way, taking a right at the next intersection. The crowd noise cleared when I rounded the corner. At the far end of the hall, bright blue light shone, a sign of the waiting day. The ray of the Hellfire wasn't the only thing waiting by the sounds raging down the hall from the opening to the pit.

"What are they excited about?" I asked.

Without turning around, freckle face answered, "Had preliminary fights before yours to get everyone warmed up. Get 'em in the spirit, you know?"

"You're the main event," the older guard said.

I looked behind me. "Where's my opponent?"

I had hoped to have a chance run-in with Leo while we were preparing out of sight of Lucifer and his minions. Spoiled again by the Council making sure we didn't have time together. Anything I had to say to Leo would be said in the company of several hundred of our closest demonic friends.

A roar went up, accompanied by the thundering of hundreds, no, thousands of feet.

"We missed the end of the fight," the oldest guard said. "Damn shame too, I had money riding on that, can't wait to find out if I won."

"Looks like you're up," Freckle-face said, shooting a glance over his shoulder at me.

"Great," I responded.

At the mouth of the tunnel, the guards stepped aside, allowing me a clear view of what lay before me. A broad expanse of brown stretched away in an oval. The fighting pit. Above it, row after row of stands stretched into the Seven Circle afternoon Hellfire, and each space was filled. Pleasure and anticipation were the name of the game if what I was seeing on those faces was a hint. A day of festivities. Banners flew, food vendors made their way through the throng, grown men traded high-fives and hugs. The smell of cooked meat was thick in the air. Somewhere in that mass of demons, a band played a traditional pub song.

A regular happy–happy, joy–joy day.

The fighters from the previous match were leaving the pit, one coming in my direction, and his defeated foe being dragged, unconscious, toward another tunnel.

"Good luck out there," the incubus said, one eye swollen shut, and half his face covered in blood.

"Thanks," I said absentmindedly as he passed, my eyes following the incubus he defeated, unsettled at seeing him being dragged out of the pit to harassing catcalls and taunt-ing. The mouth of the opposite tunnel swallowed him.

Leo appeared in the space vacated by the vanquished incubus and those dragging him. He squared on the fighting pit. He was too far away to make out his expression, but by the way he stood, he was ready.

I felt as sorry for him as I did for myself.

A short succubus, middle-aged and thin as a reed, walked to the middle of the pit, carrying a trumpet almost as tall as she was. Once at the center, she raised it to her lips and blew out a short round of melodic bursts before lowering it. Off to my right, a pair of feet shuffled. A warm wind cut across the top of the stadium, ruffling banners. The rest of the stadium, though, was so quiet I heard the banners flapping in the breeze.

"And now, our main event," the succubus shouted with a surprisingly powerful voice. "The next match has been sanctioned by our Lord, Lucifer, and will be a trial by combat, a fight to the death!"

The stadium erupted in a cacophony of chaos.

Creed warmed.

The announcer waited for the din to die before raising a hand. The last noisemakers trickled into silence. "And we are cursed to have in our attendance, Lucifer Himself." She made a grand wave of her arm toward the main stand where the Council sat. Halfway up the stands, velvet ropes and a line of honor guards, adorned in their black armor, separated a box of seats from the rank and file. They bracketed a 'U' around the back and sides of the select seats, one noticeably empty. A call went out from the mouth of a tunnel halfway up the stands. Another contingent of honor guards marched from the depths underneath the stands out into the Hellfire light. Their metallic marching echoed into the day before they did. When they came, they arrived with spears tipped in Hellfire in one hand and shields in the other. The guards made two lines, forming a security cordon for the ruler of the Underworld.

Lucifer was in his ceremonial robes. He walked out of the mouth of the tunnel and stopped on the landing.

Creed buzzed. "Don't you start," I whispered at the magical halberd.

Surrounded by His guards, His hair swept back in a thick wave that fell to His shoulders, He raised a hand and the day's attendees responded. As they cheered His name, He made His way to the empty chair in the box to join the other

Council members, who were standing to receive Him. The chair looked more like a small throne. The adulation went on, the fervor growing, until Lucifer took His seat. Once He did, so did the Founders, signaling to the announcer to continue.

"From the Fifth Circle, sentenced to a trial by combat, sanctioned by Lucifer, for the crimes of murder and consorting with angels, Ezekial Sunstone," the announcer finished. A wave of hisses, insults—too many of a particularly nasty flavor—and boos rang down. Somewhere underneath that noise was the distinct sound of a few dozen hand claps and cheers. At least I wasn't totally despised in the Seventh.

The announcer raised her hand again, and the response faded as I crossed the sand, feeling the warmth of the Hellfire on my face for the first time in far too long.

"And his opponent, from the First Circle, sentenced to a trial by combat, sanctioned by Lucifer, for the crimes of murder and consorting with angels, Leo Neto."

Far be it for me to say hatred is a good thing, but it was nice, in a strange way, of course, to hear Leo receive a similar reception. Neither of us was going to be a big smash, regardless of the outcome of this fight. They just wanted us to get smashed.

I arrived at the side of the announcer as Leo crossed the pit. He stepped with purpose, slow and measured. If I had been that smart, I would have taken my time and analyzed the layout of the fighting pit and stadium for advantages, as he was probably doing now. Instead, I'd hurried to get on with this matter as my mind still scrambled to figure a way out. Advantage, Leo.

He was dressed in light leather armor, unlike my steel breastplate and shin guards. He wore a leather skullcap. The weight he saved with his armor was more than made up for in the arms he carried. Two swords crossed his back. One hand held a large, pointed shield ringed with heavy rivets. In his right, a bulb-shaped mace, its spiked head as large as a cantaloupe. From his hip, a chained whip flopped as he strode toward me. Quadruple-advantage.

Apparently, Leo was looking for a fight.

He marched to the side of the announcer opposite of me. She looked at both of us before whirling toward the main stand, raising both her arms in our direction, and announcing, "My Lord, I present to You, Your fighters."

Lucifer, seated, slunk back, his elbow resting on the arm and his chin resting atop his curled hand. With his free hand, he rolled it in a lazy circle.

The signal to proceed given, the announcer shouted, "We fight!" She raised the trumpet to her lips once more and blew out another succession of quick bursts before spinning on her heels and marching off the sand, leaving Leo and I alone in the middle of the fighting pit.

We turned to face each other, the roar of the crowd dissolving into the background as adrenaline focused my attention on my friend–turned–opponent.

"Good to see you," I said, giving him a flicker of a smile.

"You're just as ugly as I remembered," he said in a friendly tone. "How have you been?"

"Better. You?"

Leo paused, looking around, a shadow passed over his face as the crowd called for us to fight. "Same." He hefted the mace and raised the shield, his eyes finding me once more. "We're going to have to give them what they want or both of us pay."

I sighed and gave him a wide berth as he circled. "I've been trying to figure out a way out of this. Any ideas? I'm happy to walk away."

"Oh, yeah?" Circling. Circling. "How has that been going for you?"

"I wish I could say I had an epiphany when I was taking my pre-game shit, but between my constant imprisonment and lousy prison food, I can't say I've been thinking clearly ever since leaving Olympia. You?"

He hefted the mace in Creed's direction. "Is that the only weapon you brought?"

I lifted my arms and flexed my biceps. Someone in the crowd catcalled me. I think they were being sarcastic. "I also brought the guns."

Leo's mustache and beard twitched in a quick smile. "They're not playing around, Zeke. We're going to have to do this."

I stepped back as he stepped up. "I know. Just give me time to think. You're more than welcome to help, you know?"

The mace raised. "There's nothing we can do. Blessed Lucifer is here. Fight me, Zeke! Don't let it end like this. Draw your weapon. Let's give them a show, at least. Some of them spent serious coin to be here."

"Perverts," I quipped. He didn't smile this time.

I backed away as he circled closer and closer. My hand slipped to my hip, and I pulled Creed free, keeping it collapsed in its truncheon form. "Is everything okay in Olympia? Any questions get raised about what happened?"

Chax and a gang of his hired thugs had tried to kill me in Leo's gym. The result was a bay full of corpses, and a nice display of blood on the gym's rooftop. Leo, another Abandoned named Virgo, and the angel Cassie were the only survivors of the skirmish, and I had left Leo with a mess to clean up, literally and metaphorically. I meant to go back and help him with the former, but Azazel had caught me in my apartment while I was still recovering from my injuries. I never saw the Overworld again.

Leo circled. "Things are good. The gym had to close for a few days, but Cassie helped with her connections and Virgo brought in a bunch of his people. Cool guy, by the way. Be sure to tell him I said hi when you see him again. You and he are going to need to talk. No one noticed anything about the gym. Had a few members who were upset about it closing, but that's how gym rats are. You can take their freedom, but don't ever close their shrines."

He swung. I dodged. The mace bit deep into the sand, spraying grains all around it.

"That's good to hear. So Virgo and that group are good?"

Leo feinted a charge before drawing back. "Yeah. As a matter of fact, a lot of them are members in the gym now. That helped the bottom line. Plus, it's always good to have someone like him on your side. Seems like the other Abandoned have taken to him now that Chax isn't around. Virgo's got them in shape. They were even willing to agree to a temporary peace."

"They're not bothering any of the Abandoned, demon or angel?" I asked. That was interesting.

"Right on, man," Leo acknowledged. "It's made things a lot easier now that we don't have to worry about them."

"I imagine."

"Fight!" a pre-pubescent voice shouted from the stands.

I flicked my eyes in the direction of the voice to find its source, but I lost the owner in a blur of faces, which wasn't helped when Leo charged, swinging the mace again.

He was a better fighter than this, much more strategic in how he approached fights. He was doing this for show, giving me the time I needed to find a way out. Still, I didn't need to stumble my way onto the end of one of the mace's spikes.

"Cassie, though, she's still a pain in my ass," he said as he charged me, ramming me with his shield. The move was a surprise, distracted as I was by the swirling exit strategies in my head, waiting for one to stand out from the others.

Pulling myself off the desert sand, I ignored Creed buzzing in my hand. "Are you going to keep things amicable?"

In the middle of his trimmed beard, Leo broke into a smile. "Don't worry, man, I'm not messing with your girl."

"She's not my girl," I said.

"Hit him!" a succubus shouted from above. I wasn't sure which 'him' she was talking about, but I don't think it mattered, if the growing agitation in the stands was any sign. These demons had come to see the first trial by combat in some time, and they had paid for a spectacle. We weren't giving them their money's worth. Such a pity.

When I glanced up to check the reactions of the Council members, they had an interesting mix. Lucifer, leaning back in his chair-throne, traced the embroidering on his sleeve with a finger. His five leaders contradicted His disinterest. Azazel was the only one who didn't appear outwardly agitated, but four sat toward the edge of their chair. Beelzebub paced between the chairs set out for the Council members and the cordon of guards protecting them from the commoners.

While I was distracted, Leo charged, plowing into me with his shield and knocking me to the sand again. The crowd hollered their blood lust. Some cheered, some booed, and a few hissed, thrown in for diversity's sake, I guessed.

I rolled over to stand, but not before Leo made his next move. He jumped on my back, wrenching my neck in a chokehold. I was caught between his thick biceps and powerful forearm. He squeezed, pulling my head tight against his chest. I widen my eyes to clear my vision at the sudden impact of the shield and the subsequent lack of oxygen flowing to my brain.

"That thing you were told about Cancer's death," Leo said, his mouth close to my ear as he wrenched, "isn't necessarily true."

I slapped at his arm, trying to shove my hand between my neck and his bicep. The move would create space for my throat to open and deliver enough oxygen for my brain to function. Maybe then I could determine if I'd heard him correctly. "What... what are you talking about?"

"They told you Cancer was dead, but that might not be

true," Leo whispered. He rotated, keeping my neck locked in his grip, flipping me over his body and landing on his other side. The move put the Council and Lucifer to our backs. This had been a deliberately benign attack. "Azazel wanted you to know, but he couldn't risk telling you himself. She might still be alive, man. That whole stuff about you being charged with her murder was just a set up. You know that. He doesn't want you giving up hope. Break my hold."

"Wha—what?" I gasped.

"Break my hold," he repeated.

I jammed my hand between his thick arm and my neck. It sliced through too easily. I was free.

For good measure, we scrambled to our feet. As I adjusted my breastplate, he punched me square in the nose.

My head rocked back as sharp pain burst from my sniffer, spreading up my forehead and even around to the back of my head. Within seconds of the punch, my entire face throbbed. Blood warmed my lip.

"First blood!" an incubus shouted from the stands. Cheers went up in the opposite direction in his voice, but the demons around him didn't react.

One succubus stood, stabbing her finger in his direction. "Sit down!"

I blinked behind the stabbing pain, sure Leo had just broken my nose. "Are you sure? Why would Azazel tell you that?"

Leo bent to pick up his mace and was swinging it with circular motions of his wrist, keeping his arm steady. His shield lay behind him, and he was trying to back up to it. "Like I said, he wanted you to know."

"Why?"

It might have sounded like a dumb question to Leo, but it was one I needed an answer to.

"Because you have allies who see how important you are,"

Leo said, his green eyes flicking toward Creed, which lay at my feet. "Pick it up, man. We have to finish this."

Leo gave a wide berth. I decided to show off. Raising my arm away from my body, I opened my hand and called to Creed. The halberd popped up like a rebounding yo-yo, slapping into my palm. There were a few 'ooohs' and 'ahhs' from the masses. Not enough. Let's see them do something that cool.

Leo continued swinging the mace with a wrist flex as he backed to the shield, snagging it. We were both fully armed once more. Leo moved with ease. I, encumbered by my decision to wear steel armor in the middle of the desert Circle under the powerful rays of the Hellfire, wasn't so mobile.

Cancer. Cancer could still be alive.

"Did he tell you where she is?" I asked, countering Leo's movements and pushing him back.

The frustration in the stands drowned out our conversation.

"Someone do something!"

"This is boring."

"I'd rather talk to my mother-in-law."

A round of cackling from the crowd followed that last one.

Leo shook his head, but before he could answer, the sand between us erupted, showering the pit in dust. A rumble rolled through the spectators. Leo turned toward the main stand, his back exposed to me, to look at the Council members. Beelzebub's hand extended in our direction.

I hadn't even noticed someone conjuring. I was off my game. Another slip-up might be my last.

Creed buzzed.

"Danger," a voice whispered. Leo was too far away and no one else was in the pit. An opportune time for a tag team handicap match against Leo and Insanity.

"You're insulting your Lord with this farce. Fight now, or the next time I won't miss him," the muscular Founder threatened, his voice carrying across the quiet stands. The Prince of Demons raised a finger to his lips in mock pondering. "I wonder, who will be the lucky one I select for my next fireball? I had a substantial breakfast this morning. It should be an especially powerful one."

His chest jiggled with a sharp laugh. Apopis sneered. Then an awkward mimicking of his laughter spread around the stadium as if compelled, slowly at first from the section surrounding him, spreading outward in both directions.

Leo stepped back. This time I felt a rough scratching across my exposed skin coming from his direction. "We've got to do this, man."

I growled, fearing the escalation of the fight, and agonizing over the fact that I still hadn't figured out how to stop it. Giving Creed a shake, the halberd reacted quicker than ever before. I had barely stopped my hand movement by the time it sprang to its full length of six feet. Gasps filled the stadium when the wavy dagger jutted from the butt and the half–moon ax atop the haft was partnered by an asymmetrical blade. Creed had already captured the spectator's attention, and they hadn't even seen its full glory yet. Yet. But if Beelzebub threatened me again, they just might.

"I don't want to," I said, knowing how petulant it sounded.

"It was always going to come to this after Chax," Leo said.

"There has to be a different way," I argued.

Leo released his spell. The rim of his shield flickered with its first flame. That flicker turned into a steady crackle, the flame growing three inches in height and spreading around the border. The center of the shield glowed with Leo's spreading spell.

"Don't do this, Leo," I said, backing away.

The section the crowd closest to us was attentively quiet. To the left, a large section of demons stood as if feeling the rising tension. Excitement painted the air.

"Someone was always going to have to pay for that, man,"

Leo said, circling, his shield growing brighter as he flicked the mace, it's spiked head catching fire. Flames danced off the weapon and shield, shooting tiny embers into the air. "And neither one of us could have stopped that. But one of us can do something now."

The scratching on my skin intensified with the oncoming spell. Before Leo thrust the mace forward, shooting a fist size ball of flame, I was on the move, sprinting to the side, tucking and rolling. The flame hit the sand with a loud thump, spraying grains.

"Stop."

"It feels good to have my Abilities back, I've got to admit," Leo grinned, stretching his shoulders back as if sucking in the afternoon air intensified his Fire Abilities. The head of his mace glowed orange. "I guess you can't understand what that's like since you didn't lose yours when you were Abandoned. But, let me tell you, it feels good." He said that last word with a roar, flinging the mace head forward again, shooting another fireball, this one larger than the last. I dove forward underneath the roaring ball that sizzled as it passed over my head, exploding behind me.

Close to Leo, I swung Creed around as I spun on my knee, sweeping his feet out from under him. Leo collapsed on his back as a small cheer went up from a section of demons near us.

I spun away on my knees before jumping to both feet in a fluid movement. Leo was still getting to his, the shield still aflame, and his mace reigniting.

"But the thing about having the Abilities is what you can do with them, man," Leo reasoned, plodding forward and raising his shield. "The only thing I was doing in the Overworld was helping people. But I couldn't help my family. You met them. You know what they were going through."

I did. "How is Nana?"

The mace roared forward, this time shooting a circle of fire that expanded as it neared. No diving would help me avoid this spell. As it was, I barely had time to raise Creed and begin spinning it to create a barrier.

I was too slow. Creed's shield was too small. The circle of flame screamed over and under Creed's spin. The flames licked at my hair, and I smelled too many follicles smoldering. The flame did more than that to my steel-toed boots.

Large sections of the stadium stopped cheering and started laughing as a small column of flame burned at the end of my boots, melting them. I screamed, dropping to the ground and trying to pull them off, forgetting I'd laced them. Leo charged and I had the wherewithal to stab Creed in his direction with one hand while hurriedly untying the steel-toed heat blankets around my feet.

"Stay back or I will light you up."

He didn't.

I groaned, swiping at him while kicking off one boot.

My feet were stabbed in a million different points as the fake leather took on a sheen as it melted. The pain was excruciating. My fingers fumbled to pull the laces loose. I tore at them. Finally, I got the second undone while arcing Creed wildly to keep Leo away. I yanked the last boot off. My sock came with them. My skin was red and as agitated as I now was.

"What the fuck, Leo? This isn't what I want." I stood, trying to ignore the pain in both feet. I lowered Creed to mid–guard.

"Neither do I, but they do," he said, tilting his head at the Council.

I risked a glance, seeing Beelzebub, his arms crossed and a broad smile on his face. Apopis's fingers were templed. Michael was stoic. Azazel's brow furrowed. The bloodlust that emanated from Seraph disgusted me enough to almost forget everyone else. Even the Lord of the Underworld, who still didn't look like He cared one way or another.

"We don't have to give them what they want," I said, hoping some miracle idea would strike me.

"And we're not. That's what this is all about," Leo said, raising his mace, glowing orange, ready to throw another spell.

I brought Creed in front of me and began pinwheeling it, expanding the shield. This time, his circle of flame wouldn't touch me, no matter how large a spell he cast. I was invulnerable, at least from the side of my halberd's barrier. I couldn't say the same about any other direction of the stadium.

"What are you talking about?" I asked. "I know they set us up."

Leo snickered, throwing another fireball, which exploded against Creed's shield. A growing section of the crowd cheered, encouraging him. "You were, man. And you will continue to be because they want your ass dead."

"I'm well aware of that."

"And yet you'll throw away this chance at freedom?" Leo said, moving to the right.

The commotion in the stadium grew in frustration and excitement as Leo attacked and I defended.

"Neither one of us is free," I said.

Leo jumped in the air, light on his feet for someone his size. I felt the rough scratching of a new spell even before he spun, face-on. I extended Creed's shield. As he rotated around and loosed a large fireball, half his size, it met the invisible barrier halfway, exploding in a shower of orange. The demons in attendance cheered as if they were watching a blessed firework show.

"But one of us will be after this is over. It needs to be you," Leo said, now panting.

"Wait, wha—what are you talking about?" I asked, feeling his building spell.

"If I walk away from this, what happens?" Leo asked.

What a ridiculous question in the middle of a fight. I kept

Creed spinning, my countermeasure ready for anything Leo cooked up.

When I didn't answer, he said, "Exactly. Nothing. I can't change a blessed thing. You can. You need to be the one to get out of this arena. You have to be free."

"Leo—" I started, but felt his spell build. Creed gained momentum. He released a short wall of flame, forty feet wide.

I backed away.

The flames approached, spreading out and growing taller.

Leo sprinted forward as the flames bent around and behind me. He dove over the wall and rolled up to my feet as the flames reached shoulder–height all around us. They crackled, licking at the air. We were now standing together, trapped inside a circle of fire with a diameter of less than twenty feet. Black tendrils of smoke escaped into the air.

Then it dawned on me. Leo gave me a goofy grin.

I lowered Creed. "Pretty smart."

He cast a glance to the side. "Only the demons at the top level of the stands can see us. Soon, the smoke will block them out too. Don't imagine we'll have much time, man."

I shook my head. "I doubt the Council will be okay with us hiding in here for long. They've got trust issues."

Leo's face was wiped of humor. "Listen. Azazel cut a deal with me, somehow got the Council to buy off on it. My family is back. Here, in the Underworld. All of them. And they get to stay. They're back. Safe and healthy. Even Nana."

"What? That's great!" I stopped, noting his lack of joviality at the news. "But they only got that if you volunteered to fight me, right?"

Leo swallowed hard, nodding.

I was about to speak but a gust blew through the stadium, pushing the flames aside into the sand, extinguishing them. Small embers floated off, carried by the dying remnants of the wind. I spun, my eyes finding the box. The five Founders watched Lucifer.

The Lord of the Underworld adjusted in his seat after casting a spell that blew out Leo's fire. A spell I hadn't detected, even after being more attentive after missing Beelzebub's earlier fireball. "Resume," he said in his bored voice.

Leo backed away. I backed away from Leo. His shield caught fire at its edges, as did his mace. I spun Creed. We circled. Portions of the crowd, now able to see us once again, reanimated their hostile encouragement for blood.

"You… you can't," I said, stunned by Leo's revelation.

He raised the mace, its head burning. "It was the only way to get them home."

"No. There has to be another way."

"There isn't," Leo growled, flinging the mace forward, a stream of fire jumping from its spiked head.

The blazing trail raced across the sand. I hopped to the side, but Leo swept his weapon back in my direction. I hopped again. And he traced my avoidant steps.

Whoops and shrieks from the stands filled my ears, even over the raging fire, as those rooting for Leo encouraged their champion while those few on my side took up my call. Good thing there was coin riding on this match or the Council might inquire into anyone who supported me.

I sprinted away, tucked and rolled, and the flame followed me. It pushed me toward the wall of the pit, spreading out into two branches that must have looked like a giant 'Y' to those observing above. Closing in on the wall, I sprinted toward it, leaping and pushing off in a fluid movement. My momentum carried me over the growing flames nearly pinning me in.

The crowd was in a frenzy now. Leo was saying something, but I couldn't hear him over their din.

"Aren't you getting tired?" I shouted at my opponent as I stalked forward.

Leo shook his head. "If I don't make a good show of this, they will send my family right back, and you know what will happen then. I have to make Lucifer believe this was an honest effort, man. Otherwise, it was for nothing."

"We have to change this," I argued, rotating Creed again.

Leo raised the mace, dropping the shield, and reaching behind his back to pull one of the swords free. He set its blade on fire, the orange flames dancing above its tip. "We can't control them. But we can control how we react to the positions they put us in."

The large fighter stomped toward me, swinging mace and sword. I stopped Creed, lowering it to mid–guard.

Leo swung his mace. I brought Creed up in a cross block. The blow sent vibrations down into my shoulders. He raised the sword for a slashing strike. As the sword arced down, I rotated my halberd, catching the back of Leo's blade with my half–moon ax. The combined momentum propelled Leo's sword into the sand.

He arced another strike with the mace over his head and I barely blocked it. My hands were numbing.

"Promise me you will look after my family, man," Leo grunted as he swung, sweat flying off his arms with the momentum.

I blocked each blow, backing away.

Mace. Pound. Mace. Pound. Thump. Pound. Blow after blow came as Leo pressed his attack.

Around the stadium, demons stood. Stomped. Clapped. Regardless of who they cheered for at the outset, they were now fully engaged, getting their money's worth. My extra sensitivities to my surroundings let me to pick up on the fact Apopis and Seraph were on their feet along with the crowd. Michael rose from his chair, as did Azazel, who was taking longer.

Swing after swing, block after block, I stopped Leo's blows.

"My brother is going to need you." He heaved. "Harvest is

an absolute mess. Kick his ass if he needs it, but get him straight, if you can."

"How about you do that yourself?" I blocked another blow and swung the haft of Creed at Leo's midsection to avoid catching him with any of the blades.

Leo tilted his mace down, blocking my strike. "Don't be lazy. They'll know. And stop" –he grunted, bringing the mace up and over his head in a straight-down strike which slammed into the sand— "thinking another way exists. You are the one who can change the mess the Underworld has become under them. Please make sure no demon is ever treated like me and my family again. My uncle would ask the same of you."

Leo's horizontal blow from the mace almost took me in the ribs.

Leo was right. If Aries was here today, he would remind me I was the one, that I was the liberator bestowed the gift of Creed, proven by my ability to hold the blessed stick. The Great Prince. This was about honor and duty, not about want and choice. If I didn't carry out this day to the satisfaction, no, the requirements of the Council, neither one of us would walk away in the end. Those we cared about would be made to suffer. This would have been for nothing. Everything, stretching back to Aries and his sacrifice. All progress erased. All hope extinguished. If I didn't do what needed to be done.

"How can I ask you to fall, Leo?" I asked, my throat clenching.

"This is for my family, man." Leo took a wide swing, which I pushed away.

He was tiring. I wasn't. I had been on the defense throughout the fight, reserving energy because I wanted to avoid that which could not be avoided.

Mace, pounding. Relentless.

Creed vibrated in my hands now, even when Leo wasn't sending strikes. The ends of my fingers were numb. I was sweating and breathing heavily. Leo was relentless. One slip, one mistake, and I would be the one skewered, and he would take up the mantle of righting the wrongs of the Council.

I had the crazy thought that maybe the demon who separated the supposed Great Prince from Creed would wear the crown. Wishful thinking. Just like everyone in Hell, even its rulers, Leo could only dream of holding my halberd. Except that wasn't Leo's dream.

Vitriol fell from the stands. Spectators called me names for avoiding going on the attack.

Leo had a distant look as he swung blow after blow, once almost knocking Creed from my grip. For the first time in the battle, I feared this was the end. I didn't know how much longer he could go, but driven to protect his family, and knowing his character, Leo didn't quit. He couldn't.

I threw blows back at him. Low attack, swinging high, and always making sure I caught his weapon with my blades. To make this look genuine, I even cracked out most basic form. Rising Dawn, a slow, looping form, I sped it for the battle, knowing Leo could anticipate and deflect the arcing blows. The only time I purposely landed strikes were the few I aimed at his ribs and legs, and only with Creed's haft. The strikes would leave bruises, but that was better than severing limbs. As I went on the attack, I shot glances into the main stand. The Council gawked, except for Lucifer, whose aged cheek skin wrinkled over the ends of His fingers.

I pushed back against Leo, forcing him toward the center of the pit. Blow after blow, delivered with contained ferocity, as I scrambled to find any way out of this. Even if I made him pass out, it wasn't enough. One of us had to die here today. If that was me, everything ended. If Leo did, his family would be safe if—that was a big if—the Council kept their word. Nothing would change for the rest of Hell. If both of us did, no one won.

I pushed and pressed. Leo must have sensed my

newfound energy. His attacks were reinvigorated. His blocks staunch.

I dropped to my knees, swinging Creed in a backward strike which Leo leapt over. I had anticipated that and was on my feet, the halberd now in both hands, delivering a cross-check that sent the big fighter stumbling backward.

I closed on him, but just as I did, my skin tore with rough scratching.

I hitched my stride, shocked Leo could draw so much power, more power than I'd felt from him in this entire fight. At this stage, with him looking worn out, it shouldn't be possible. But the sensation of the fire spell wasn't coming from Leo, but from directly behind him. From the main stand.

Behind the Lord of the Underworld and the four Council members standing in front of their chairs, Beelzebub conjured.

Before I planned my attack, the ground underneath me erupted. It shot me into the sky, tumbling over and over as the world burst open in flame. I was unable to distinguish sky from ground or ground from sky until I fell back to the surface. Contrary to popular belief, sand is not soft. Not when you slam into it from fifteen feet in the air. Lucifer, I hate heights.

The Founder was interfering. My head was too cloudy to register any of the reactions of his peers or of Lucifer. As for the crowd, they didn't have a problem with it.

Enraged, I shook my head, trying to catch my breath. If Beelzebub wanted blood, blood he would have.

I pushed myself up, roaring, ready to destroy. At my feet, Creed lay half-buried in the sand.

The crowd thundered.

Leo stomped toward me, his mace and sword blazing with his Fire Ability.

I snatched Creed and...

... the world recalibrated as the three-bladed halberd burst to life with Hellfire. My blue flames more than matched Leo's, even at his strongest.

I threw my hands up to my side, crushing Creed in my grip and howling. Then I slammed the wavy dagger blade into the sand. A circle of blue flame erupted, racing away in an expanding orb. When it struck Leo, it flung him backward, halfway across the pit, well over sixty yards. Banners tore from their poles. The spectators toppled over benches. Even the awning in the main stand protecting the Council from the warmth of the day was not impervious to my—Creed's—wrath. It ripped from the ringlets attaching it to the poles and floated over the edge of the stadium.

I'd never heard silence like in the moments that followed. I moved toward Leo, not seeing him, but the faces of the Founders in his place. All of them, even Azazel, flashed over Leo's own well-groomed-but-battered face.

As I neared, Leo struggled to his knees. His right arm, his dominant arm, bent at an awkward angle in a place where arms aren't supposed to bend. He held it against his body. Blood dripped from his nose, the corner of his mouth, his ears, and even from the corners of his green eyes.

"I'm sorry," I choked out, then sobbed.

Arm pinned against his chest, his eyes filling with tears, Leo offered a bloody smile. "I'm doing this for my family. You do this for the entire Underworld. Undeniable love demands meaningful sacrifice. But it's a sacrifice gladly given, man."

I swallowed, unable to respond.

"I'm ready," Leo said, raising his head to the sky.

The buzzing rolled toward me from the stands much like a wind whipping through a storm. My mind swirled in its tumult, replacing the peaceful face of Leo with the masks of the Founders, flickering from one to the next. Seraph being first, Beelzebub next, Michael and Apopis, interchangeable. Azazel was there too, but blinked away.

I lifted Creed, rotating the wavy dagger blade forward and plunging it into Leo's chest.

Just as I had with Taurus, a golden light radiated around the wound where blade met flesh and blood. It expanded gradually, but only for an instant. Mournful, scornful, and celebratory shouts mixed with indistinguishable voices. With a thunderclap, the light pulsing in Leo's chest exploded outward, washing Hell in golden light.

When it faded, Leo was gone, and I was free.

5

UNDERWORLD, SEVENTH/SIXTH CIRCLES

Honestly, I don't know how long I kneeled in the sand next to the small pile of white ash that had once been Leo Neto. My mind disassociated the ash from the incubus who had breathed hope into my fortunes during the short time we had known each other. Though he probably never knew because I never told him, Leo taught me about sacrifice, and helped me see that my self-pity was holding Cancer back from serving those she felt called to help.

Leo enlightened me to what Aries's sacrifice meant on a deeper level, along with the payment it required. Leo made me see the sacrifice he was willing to make for his family.

The stunned mumbling of the hundreds of spectators was nothing more than faint background noise. My chest heaved with exhaustion. Creed pulsed in my hand. The Hellfire evaporated from its blades.

At some point, a squad of guards had walked out into the pit and circled me, giving me a wide berth. I barely registered them. They didn't matter. Very little did right now. All I wanted was to reflect on Leo and what he had done, believing I could make a difference against the Council.

What kind of incubus was I if I didn't do everything in my

power to put his wish into action? I swore I would tear down the entire stadium, brick by brick, if a single one of those guards even tried to prod me out of my kneeling reverie for the fallen fighter.

None of them did.

I'm not sure how much time passed before I heard soft, scuffing footsteps moving across the sand.

"Well fought, Sunstone," came the raspy voice of Apopis.

"Fuck you."

Apopis hissed. "You're a free incubus now. Best not spend the first minutes of your newfound status insulting one of my station. That could land you in trouble and..." I don't know what he was pausing for, "haven't you had enough of that? Aren't you ready to live your life as a free member of society, away from this trouble and strife?"

Sucking air through my nose, I picked up Creed and stood. The ranks of guards shuffled backward, and a few of them lowered their weapons to mid-guard. Good.

"And I assume that's why you're here to bother me?" I said, meeting the Founder's eyes evenly. "You and your stupid half–tattooed face want to taunt me one last time before you kick me out to some heaven-hole in an austere corner of Hell. Am I right?"

I don't know what felt better; me getting my opinion about Apopis's facial tattoos off my chest, or watching the narrow slits of his eyes widen. Either way, it was the first ray of positivity I'd felt for a long time.

"So, so smart, Sunstone," Apopis hissed, cocking his body to look at the guards behind him, and wagging a finger. "So smart that you're absolutely correct. I'm here to escort you to your new home. Make this easier on everyone."

I rotated just enough that my back wasn't turned to the devious Founder. Most guards carried a spear that burned with Hellfire. Two, on opposite sides of the circle, held short swords instead of spears, accompanied by large, silver clamps in their opposite hands. The two wore thick gauntlets on the arms that held the clamps. I knew what those were for, I had seen something similar held by a succubus named Marijon in the Eighth Circle.

"I won't let you take it," I said as I turned my gaze back to Apopis. "You can try, but I promise, it will be your last mistake."

Apopis's eyes narrowed again, his imperceptible cheek-bones pushing up as he smiled. "Were it up to me, you wouldn't have a choice. But," he paused, blinking rapidly as he glanced up at the main stand, now nearly emptied, "we have to honor the conditions of the trial by combat. You have earned your freedom. These incubi are here to protect me from you should you make another poor decision. They are not here to steal."

"Good." And it was. Who knew if I could follow through on my promise to make Apopis pay. I wasn't confident, to be honest, but sure would give it the good old army try. I stood, brushing my knees off. "Then take me home. I'm assuming you have an apartment for me already, one that will be watched constantly?"

Apopis stepped closer. "Unfortunately, as part of the condition of your freedom, we won't be able to watch you as closely as we would prefer. Such a shame. But, it is what our Lord demands, as he wants to honor the agreement. Count yourself fortunate." The Founder slid closer, his light feet gliding over the sand. "But know, you'll never truly be free, Sunstone. We will always be watching you. Watching and waiting."

"Yay. Lucky me."

"Don't pout. It's unbecoming," Apopis said, his tongue flicking to the corner of his mouth. "I would advise you to stop raising Heaven now that you have this freedom. It would be such a shame to waste it, to waste Leo's death, and find yourself under the Council's administration once again.

Plus, were we to have to get involved again, I fear Lucifer wouldn't be so forgiving. Imagine what that means for those you care about. Such a shame, should an accident befall them, and you could not be there in their time of need."

His newest threat delivered, I stepped toward Apopis. The Founder flinched. The wall of guards behind him shuffled closer, aiming their spears. The wall stopped when I flashed them a look. "I'm leaving, and I'm leaving peacefully. What I do with the rest of my life is my business. If you want to get involved, you better understand I will protect my rights, my autonomy, however I need to. Now, if you're done throwing your trite threats, I need a shower. The Seventh Circle is hot as blazes."

I turned from the Founder, aimed at the open tunnel and the ring of guards standing between me and it. Adrenaline surged through me at confronting the thin ancient who could still break me in two with his Ability if he chose.

Could he? I had to wonder. Well, maybe once I cared again. Right now, I was so far from caring that it would have to send me a holiday card at Samhain to update me on its life.

But it felt good to snub the Founder. Lucifer, so good.

The three guards who were in a direct line of the tunnel backed away, forming a short cordon. The others remained in the shrinking formation, falling in behind me. I walked to the mouth of the tunnel. My chest loosed a shaking breath at the sight before me.

My family and friends stood between me and that opening.

Kanthor Sunstone wore slacks and a button up with a tie. The last time he dressed like that was at my grandmother's funeral. His gray hair announced a fresh cut, but still lusciously full and white as a blinding light. My mother was in a conservative sundress, one she'd never worn before. The straps of her sandals sported a few too many diamonds for my taste or comfort. A red leather purse hung over her shoulder had an obnoxious gold latch that filled half its face. Of course, tears welled in her eyes. My father's were as dry as the Seventh Circle and aimed at Apopis, one of his heroes.

Further along the reception line was Ralrek. The tall, handsome incubus's jaw was locked. His fierce gaze gave him an unapproachable look. I never expected Ralrek to be happy that I survived—I'm joking, we've come a long way—but I didn't expect him to appear aggressive around a Founder. This was an incubus who looked like he was ready to chew the head off a dragon.

Bilba stood between my parents and Ralrek, and he was the only one in the group offering a genuinely joyous smile, as if he didn't recognize the significant danger I had just been under. The tips of his ears were pink. His cheeks were flushed. Dressed in a polo shirt and dark jeans, I hadn't seen him look this dashing since the last time we went out to scour bars for any succubus desperate enough to let us buy them drinks—we never succeeded, if you're keeping score. As I approached, his mouth dropped open, but he clamped it closed with a snap.

I wanted to say something. I wanted to tell my mother she would never have to live another day thinking about me slowly decaying in the Overworld. I wanted to ask my father if he could find it within himself to be proud of something I had accomplished. I wanted to ask Ralrek if he was ready to fight. I wanted to ask Bilba to check into what Leo said about Cancer, and the lesser concern that her supposed death might just be the Council's way of trying to break me down before my life and death confrontation.

I didn't get to do any of these things.

"Keep moving, Sunstone," Apopis said behind me. "You've earned your freedom, but that doesn't mean you have the freedom to waste my time."

I clenched my teeth, half turning to shoot the Founder a nasty look but let it go as I approached my family and friends. The last thing my parents needed to see was me confronting one of Lucifer's Council. My father looked more than ready to defend Apopis. My mother had just been guaranteed of getting her little incubus back.

As we walked past, I gave them a wink. "I'll see you soon."

Behind me, Apopis rattled. Maybe a laugh?

We entered the tunnel, my heart thudding at the exciting times ahead. Lucifer Himself had guaranteed me freedom. I now stood moments away from that. I couldn't wait to see home again, with its familiar sights, sounds, and faces. I couldn't wait to head to The Book Abyss and squeeze the life out of Dialphio at the first chirp of laughter from that wonderful bookstore owner. I couldn't wait to get to Chilly Willy's and buy an iced coffee from Gigi, if she still worked there. Part of me—a lot of me—hoped she did, and not for the reasons I had in the past. I couldn't wait to hit Old Towne and spend coin sampling the bland food and lukewarm beer its restaurants had on offer. I couldn't wait to be home.

In the room where I dressed and prepared for the fight, I stripped out of my shin guards without the help of Pedent. Apparently, winning won me no favors or privileges. One guard was kind enough to help with the breastplate while the other thirty plus the Founder watched. My shirt stuck to me, and there was a grotesque warmth radiating in my nether region that made me want to take a shower very, very soon.

"I'm ready," I told Apopis.

He nodded, and the air in the middle of the room buzzed. At first, a black spot hung just a few feet from the floor. As the gateway grew, the spot turned into an elongated oval that stretched toward the ceiling and to the floor. Through the blackness, orange light flickered. The gateway provided no clear detail. Murky to represent my future? Enlarging until it touched the ceiling, the gateway crept wider. Apopis stood to the side and gestured with both hands. "Let's go, Sunstone. Give him his bag."

A guard brought the bag that was taken from me the second I walked back into the Underworld with Azazel. He dropped it at my feet and spun away.

"I don't imagine you returned my copy of *The Histories of the Balance*?" I asked. Apopis didn't need to know that I didn't need the tome anymore. The copy I had stashed in my bag was a note-free version, so even if they had flipped through its contents, they wouldn't learn anything.

His thin lips spread. "Hardly. I told you that the last time you held that heretical writing. You won't see the book again, and Lucifer willing, you'll never see another. We're already seeking the source. But that's not for you to worry about. You're going to spend the rest of the immortal life you don't deserve in peace and serenity. No more trouble, Sunstone. I mean it. You won't like the consequences."

"I never liked consequences, Apopis," I said, feeling good at using his name so casually. "In fact, I've disliked them as much as I dislike you."

Armor rattled, but my focus was on the scrawny ancient at the side of the gateway.

I nodded toward the gateway a few feet away. "Where does that open to? It doesn't look familiar, and it's dark. Not like anyplace I know."

Now Apopis's smile widened, and I knew I'd been had. "That is the Sixth. An appropriate location for you to spend the rest of your life. In your bag, you'll find the address and keys to the apartment we procured for you. The first three months' rent has already been paid, praise be to Lucifer and His generosity. After that, you're on your own, just like any other demon. Exactly what you wanted."

"I didn't want to live in the Sixth. I wanted to return home. To the Fifth. With my family and friends," I snarled.

Apopis shrugged, nonplussed. "Not my concern, Sunstone. Have a good life." He glided away. The guards parted. Once he stood on the other side, they moved forward, lowering their spear tips. As the circle closed, Apopis stretched his head as high as he could to address me, "Oh, and stay out of trouble, Sunstone. I heard the Sixth can be a... difficult place to live. You could find yourself in trouble sooner rather than later, and it would be such a shame if you never lived long enough to reach your full potential."

The guards were so close now any one of them could have skewered me in a flash. Caught in the small room underneath the stadium with no one around except for Apopis and his guards, anything could happen. How much could Lucifer see? How much could he know about the actions of his senior demons? With my family and friends a few yards away in the stadium, if I caused trouble, Apopis could march the contingent of armed incubi out into the fighting pit and take out his frustrations on them.

With a growl, snatching my bag. I stepped into the gateway before Apopis agitated me into doing something stupid.

The world spun as the floor dropped out from underneath my feet. Gateways and rifts can disorient, no matter how many times you've gone through them, but none had been this distressing in a long time. I figured it was Apopis's way of screwing with me one last time while he still had the chance. Dipping. Falling. Spinning and rotating in nothingness. Not knowing up from down or left from right. In another flash, I was back on firm ground and looking at my future.

6

UNDERWORLD, SIXTH CIRCLE

WHAT A FUTURE this was going to be. Demons say first impressions are forever impressions, and the Sixth really needed a new PR person based on what greeted me in my new home.

I faced a wide street. Crackling blue flames jutting from the sidewalks and storm drains drowned out the buzzing of the gateway. It wasn't until I turned to ensure one of Apopis's guards wasn't going to shove a spear through my back and leave my body sprawled in the street that I discovered the Founder had closed the gateway.

I set my bag on the rough brimstone sidewalk.

So, this was the Sixth Circle of Hell.

The street was four carriages wide. For as far as I could see in both directions, white buildings appeared connected. One long stretch of identical structures hugging the street. The facade looked like white stucco. Every thirty feet, a small archway hovered over a door. Only two stories tall, the edges of rooftops were easy to spot with tendrils of smoke curled into the air from the roofs as if they were on fire.

Bluish smoke wafted off the sidewalks around the open-ings that spit flames, and from the demon–hole cover. From the storm drains, short bursts of flames popped every few seconds. Even between the seams of the sidewalk, Hellfire licked between the cut blocks of brimstone. Talk about a need for a public safety voting initiative.

The Sixth Circle smelled like meat that had gone bad when I was still wearing diapers.

I pulled up the collar of my sweaty T-shirt and covered my nose as I bent to unzip my bag. Pulling it open, I saw an envelope sitting on top of my rumpled clothes. The Council had taken measures to search through everything, and oh, how I hoped to Lucifer, they had rummaged through my dirty underwear. Funny—not in a funny, ha, ha-type of way—though. As much time as they took looking through my belongings, they didn't take half the care to put things back. At least the envelope was easy to find.

I pulled it out, zipping the bag closed. As the envelope dangled, a weight inside shifted to the end. Keys. I clamped my hands around the heavy end. Knowing my luck, the keys would break through the paper and tumble into one of these burning storm drains.

I peeled the envelope open and emptied the keys into my palm, shoving them into my pocket before taking out the slip of paper with the address to my new home. I read it and looked around for a street sign, finding none. Living in Hell has many disadvantages. The mortal realm taught me that much. The obvious one is that we have terrible food compared to what mortals cook up. Another disadvantage is living under gazillions of tons of bedrock that block satellite signals. A GPS navigation system would have come in handy right about now, but we all know the Founders opposed anything that made movement around the Circles easier. They're draconian like that. As it was, I had to wander until I found someone who could point me in the right direction.

Time in the Underworld is set on a consistent schedule, regulated by the Grand Chamber which contains the Hellfire, and thus the light that provides our sense of night and day. Strategically located clock towers kept the time, but being new to this Circle, I had no idea where the local ones were. For those regions not close to the towers, small animated magic spells known as Callers helped keep time. As magical creatures, they don't interact with us, and often make great efforts to not interact with us. After walking for an hour or so, it would have been nice to come across one. I was that desperately lost.

I assumed the gateway would have been opened relatively close to the location of my new apartment, but with Apopis being the one who dispatched me, that was foolish. For all I knew, he could have put me down on the complete opposite side of the Circle.

When I finally saw another demon, it was a succubus on the other side of the broad street. I waved, meaning to cross and ask for assistance. She returned my wave hastily enough, but then dashed up the few steps to her door like she was late for dinner or a hot date.. I sighed and continued taking in the Sixth Circle, one interchangeable block after another.

The few stores I passed, none opened, provided clues to the neighborhood I was in. Noise came from around the corner. Quiet conversation. Clinking of what sounded like porcelain-on-porcelain. The signs of life.

A building's awning stretched out over the sidewalk, underneath which small, white iron tables and chairs were set out. The awning smoldered, loosing thin tendrils of smoke into the already-polluted air. Demons sipped tiny cups of coffee at a few tables.

An incubus sat at a table by himself, reading a paper and drinking from a child-sized cup. I approached, setting my bag down a few feet away. He glanced up once before his gaze returned to his paper, and then once more at me when he saw me approach, keeping his cup to his lips but not drinking.

I held up the piece of paper. "Excuse me. Could you help me find this address?"

The incubus set down his tiny cup and folded his paper closed with a snap. "Sure thing. Let's see it."

I breathed a sigh of relief. The Circles of Hell can be tricky. Demons don't enjoy inter–Circle travel, which is prohibited and controlled by the Council, so few of us get to experience the different ways of life in its different locales. I was one of the lucky ones—or not so lucky, depending on how you look at it—to have experienced our different Circles. My experience in the Second taught me Hell can be as wet and rainy as Seattle. The Eighth taught me that ugly demons can proliferate an entire Circle, creating an equally ugly culture. The Fifth was my home for six thousand years, and I knew I was biased, but it was by far the best of the bunch. Somewhere toward the bottom was the First, where my only experience had been a walk of shame past thousands of demons, to the square where Gemini was to be executed. In my short time there, the residents of the First failed to impress me. So far, the Sixth was off to a much-needed strong start.

"Hey, Sirus," the incubus said over his shoulder to another sitting a few tables away. This one, looking like a relative except for a nose so broad it encroached on his cheekbones, sat with an attractive succubus, hunched over the table, slurping her coffee. "Do you know where Lacus Hill is?"

"Ain't it up over by Yuli's old place?" The incubus named Sirus said with another jerk of his head. "Swear it is. The place we used to have those poker nights. Wasn't that the name of the park up there?"

"You're right," my helper said, slapping the table in sudden clarity and turning back, handing back the paper. "Keep going up this way," he said, pointing down the street, "and take your first left. Three blocks more, you'll be walking up a hill. At the top you'll find a park. Probably full of impling's at this time of day. Ask someone there. Bet they'll know where to find that place."

I thanked him for his time and offered to buy him a new tiny coffee—I have no idea how something so small could be satisfying—which he refused.

"Not a problem, my friend. Not a problem," he said, picking up his small cup and taking a loud sip before snapping open his paper again.

I followed his directions, hoping the gain in elevation took me above the grotesque meat smell, but my hope was dashed. Block after block of identical buildings, all connected, with the same archways hovering over the same, indistinguishable doors, each crackling with unseen rooftop fires, I concluded that the Sixth's smell was woven into its terrain. How long before I got used to this? A deeper part of me wondered if I ever would.

The tiny cup incubus was correct. A large park sat at the top of the hill, full with implings and watchful parents. Twice as many trees as demons populated the park. The tops of each red pine burned with a cone of blue flame. More and more smoke drifted into the upper region of the Sixth. In my cursory glance, two medium-sized mounds of dirt, barely taller than me, emitted smoke. Between them was a flaming geyser, two hundred feet in circumference. It was dormant right now. No security barrier protected the little ones from a very bad playtime. But there was a sign with the name of the geyser, so that should count for something, right? The impling's played around it as if it wasn't a potential death trap.

"You're in luck. That address is just over there," a succubus way too hot to be a mom, said. She pointed down the street to my right.

I thanked her and headed off, wondering how these demons didn't get lost. I must have looked like an absolute outsider. Wandering the rough brimstone, I looked between the paper and house numbers, some stenciled, others hand-written. A couple doorways were decorated with numbers that looked to have been seared into the white facade.

Finally, I found my place and headed up the three steps to unlock the door. The lock resisted as I turned the key, but popped open with enough determination. I stepped inside, my skin prickling. Not magic, but the temperature of the entryway. Laughing at myself, I closed the door. I was being paranoid, letting the Council get to me.

I dumped my bag next to the wall and loosed a sigh. During my expedition across my new home Circle, I had to hold my shit together. Now that I was alone, I could let it all out. My chest shook. I leaned against the wall, holding myself up as I felt the first burning tears come.

Tears for Leo.

Tears for Leo's family.

Tears of hope that Cancer might still be alive.

Tears for losing my friends and mother before I had a chance to reconnect with them after Abandonment.

The tears came, coursing down my cheeks and dripping to the floor. I bent, hands on knees, and didn't stop them. When the sobs came, I didn't stop them either.

"Are you going to keep crying like a big baby all day or do I have to get my own drink?" a rough voice said from the other room.

I shot up. Ralrek? "Hello?" I said.

"Hi," another familiar voice, this one higher–pitched and jovial, said. Bilba.

I shot around the corner. "What the heaven are you doing here?"

As sure as Apopis's half–tattooed face was ugly, my two friends were sitting in my new living room. That in itself would have shocked me, but the fact they weren't alone distracted me from being shocked about my shock.

Bilba and Ralrek sat on separate chairs in the far corner of the sparse living room. Plain walls showed their pale green paint. A calm, if not ugly, environment. The chairs, mismatched, were polyester blends of reds and yellows. The couch looked to be green leather from the way it creaked as the succubus who sat on it adjusted.

She was older, in her early thirty-thousands, with light brown skin. Her jaw jutted out, as did a large, arched nose. Dark irises nearly filled her eyes that danced around the room as if she were watching an invisible sylph flit about the place.

"Uh, hi," I said to the stranger before turning to my friends. "What in heaven are you doing here? How did you get here? Who is this? Not to be rude, sorry," I added to not... well, be rude.

Bilba got to his feet, bouncing. "Oh man, you are a sight!" he squealed as he closed in, embracing me in a hug I didn't ask for but gladly accepted. He pulled back. "You're free, Zeke. Free. Do you get that? Oh, we brought you a house warming gift."

Ralrek leaned forward at that and tapped a stack of demonic notebooks on the table. "Actually, they're from Dialphio. She didn't want you to have any excuses to not check in, she said."

"Yes, Dialphio," Bilba said. "Sorry. I wasn't trying to steal her thunder."

Ralrek was on his feet. I wiped the tears off my cheeks. He moved in, giving me a warm smile. "Stop being such a baby. Bring it in." He wrapped his arms around my neck, my head in the middle of his chest. After the quick hug, he pushed me away gently and went to the kitchen. "You need a blessed shower, Zeke. I'm going to check the refrigerator and see if you have anything. Anybody want something to drink?"

Still stunned, I mumbled, "I'll take whatever is in there."

"Me too," Bilba said. "Same for Melchiot, please."

"Melchiot?" I said, registering the name and turning to face her.

Melchiot Zeistane was the mentor Bilba and his father had hired to prepare Bilba for the passage. I extended my hand to her.

"Nice to meet you," I said. "He's told me all about you. Such an honor. I can't thank you enough for your help looking into the issue with the curse."

I felt like I was rambling, so I shut up.

She extended her hand, her slim fingers wrapping around my palm. "You're very welcome. And I've heard a lot about you from Bilba. He speaks highly of you."

I punched Bilba in the arm. "As he should. Now, can someone tell me how in the heaven you're standing in my brand-new apartment?"

"The fridge is empty!" Ralrek called out from the other room. Coming back in, he said, "Let's do this now. I'm thirsty and I'll be hungry before too long."

I threw up my hands. "Wait a second. Someone needs to make me a lot smarter than I feel right now."

"That's going to be a challenge," Ralrek quipped, collapsing back into the chair.

I looked from one to the other and back again. "No, seriously. How did you guys find me? How did you get here? Wait," I said, a sudden thought coming to me. "Is there a certain," I shot a quick glance at Melchiot and edited my question, "powerful... friend who helped you find me?"

Bilba confirmed my suspicions. "Yes. The, um, incubus helping find the, um, thing with the," Bilba stumbled and paused, raising his hands to both sides of his head and hooking his black-nailed pointer fingers, making chubby horns, "thing, gave us this address when everyone else was distracted at the fighting pit. Nice fight, by the way."

"Yeah, I was impressed with that whole Circle of Hellfire thing you did. And at the end—"

I held up my hand, stopping Ralrek. "Please guys, this isn't something I want to get into right now. I'm not in the right head space. Leo was a wonderful guy. You didn't know him, but Ralrek, you would have gotten along with him."

"I bet. If I was in the market anymore," he said.

"Not like that." I wasn't interested in delving into Ralrek's existent or nonexistent love life. "If it wasn't for Leo, I would have never made it out of Olympia. He saved my ass."

"Sorry, Zeke," Bilba rubbed his hands together. "I didn't mean to make it sound like it wasn't a big deal. I guess I just got carried away being happy that you're free, safe."

"I don't know how safe I am, or how safe I'll be," I said, taking a glance at his quiet mentor again. "But I guess I'll find out soon enough, won't I?"

"Do you think they're going to keep messing with you after that? I don't think so," Bilba said, moving to sit beside Melchiot on the couch, leaving the chair free for me.

I groaned as I sat. It had been a long day. "Why not?"

"Let them. We're by your side all the way," Ralrek said, his fingers gripping the arms of the chair.

"Simple," Bilba said, pulling my attention back. "That trial was sanctioned by Lucifer. There is nothing they can do to override His decision. And His decision was formalized when you won. You are free. If they try to do something sneaky, they'd risk drawing His attention. The way I understand it, none of them are in a position to do that. Not right now. Maybe not for a long time. You have plenty of time to get your life squared away and figure out what comes next."

"Honestly, the only thing I want to do right now is sleep for the next week. I'm so exhausted." I groaned. "If you guys weren't here, I'd be scrubbing my balls in a hot bath." I swiveled to look at Melchiot. "Sorry, I'm not usually this rude," I said as I adjusted in the chair, my back stiffening. The thought came hard and sudden, my gut seizing, "Did the Council banish you from the Fifth as well?"

The tips of Bilba's ears turned pink. "Nope. We got here by a gateway. I was going to explain."

I scratched my face, impressed with Melchiot's brazen actions. "Thank you for bringing them," I said to her.

She sat up straighter, shaking her head. Her gaze fluttered around my living room like a fairy. Tear-drop earrings dangled from her ears, exposed by the long black curls she had pulled back into a broad ponytail. "Oh, I didn't open it. I can't."

"Oh, then our... powerful friend did?" I asked Bilba, confused.

Ralrek chuckled, leaning his head back in the chair, scrunching into a more comfortable position, his finger lazily hanging in the air, pointed at Bilba. "Nope. Dumbass did it."

My mouth dropped open. "You? You can open gateways?"

Pink extended from the rims of his ears to his earlobes. "Yes. I've been able to for a while. I've been focusing on them throughout your Abandonment." He looked at Melchiot before he continued. "I'm doing this to prepare for my Passage, Zeke. But I did a lot of reading—"

"Of course you did," Ralrek and I said.

"Ha, ha." Bilba's smile spread. "Anyway, I tripped across an old book of spells thanks to... another friend... and that was the end of it. I started practicing what I read, and before I knew it, I understood how gateways are constructed."

"Not just gateways," Melchiot said, her eyes cast to the floor as if she were thinking the deepest thoughts.

"What—what does that mean? What else can you do?" I asked, stunned and excited by what I was hearing. If Bilba could open gateways—"Wait. Can't you get caught? They're all over us, bud. We can't ever let our guard down. If the Council finds out you opened a gateway here, they'll have your head. I mean, I love you guys, but we can't take that chance. Did you not watch what I had to go through? Are you ready for something like that?"

"Oh boy, here it comes," Ralrek said, his eyes closed and a

half smile playing on his face as if Bilba and I were arguing about which was the best professional blazeball team.

"Here what comes?" I asked.

"He's just giving me a hard time because he's jealous," Bilba said that last part teasingly. "I can..." Another glance at Melchiot. Another pause.

How much control did his mentor have over him that he had to seek her permission to talk about his Abilities? To me, of all demons?

"What, Bilba?" I said firmly, knowing a hot bath was waiting. No matter how much I missed these guys, at some point soon I was going to have to wash the funk away and decompress from a day I wanted to forget but knew I'd remember forever.

"I can also open rifts," he said as if he were apologizing for the most heinous of crimes. He waved both hands, his palms outward in my direction, as if begging off a fight. "But only recently. They're a lot harder to construct than gateways. But... yeah, I can do those too."

Gateways and rifts. Bilba could travel everywhere. Whether or not he wanted to think about it, that was a threat to the Council. He'd become a target if they ever discovered his Ability.

"You can't, bud," I said, leaning forward. "If the Council finds out, they'll have your head."

Then Bilba laughed. "That's the thing, Zeke. There is no stain from my spells. The Council can't detect them."

Next to him, Melchiot shook her head. "It's like he's not even casting. I don't understand it, to be honest."

"Are you saying your spells are... invisible?" I asked.

"Not the right word, but more like oxygen. We know it's there but we can't see it," Bilba said, the pink at the tip of his ears darkening.

"They can't be seen?"

"That's what invisible means, dumbass," Ralrek snorted in the chair opposite me.

I corrected myself, "No one can detect them? No one who didn't directly see you open one will know it was you who cast it?"

"Bingo," Bilba said with a wink. "It's quite a useful skill."

"It's unapproved and unregulated. It's also illegal," Melchiot said.

"Are you sure?" I said.

"Very," Bilba's eyes were alight with excitement and pride. "After you have time to settle in, there's someone I need to take you to see."

Melchiot sniffed.

I only half heard her response. "I need to get back to Olympia. Can you take me?"

"Why there?" Ralrek asked.

"When you came to see me, there was a message in the notebook D—," I stopped myself from exposing Dialphio's name in front of Melchiot, "that was brought to me. That note was from Cassie. Bad shit is going down in Olympia involving demons. She begged for our help."

"She's an angel, Zeke," Ralrek protested.

"She's a friend," I said. "And she needs my help. I need to see what's going on. You don't have to help if you don't want to change things. For me, there is no choice."

"I shouldn't be hearing any of this," Melchiot said, her dark eyes sucking me in. Prying. Maybe, or maybe I was being paranoid.

"When I was in the pit with Leo, he told me others are trying to set up something that could be beneficial. I need to get back. If your rifts are undetectable, maybe we can get away with trying. Right?"

"Well, technically," Melchiot answered.

"I've got the time," Bilba said, spreading his hands. "Plus, then Ralrek can get back up there and see these mortals he's constantly talking about. He's ruined too many movie nights talking through every scene with some hot guy in it."

"Not looking to date, my friend," Ralrek said, nonchalantly tapping the arm of the chair. "Plus, sorry, but Hollywood must be flooded with hotties. It's not my fault mortal movies are full of them. But, if you're going to force me to go, I guess I could make the sacrifice. For Zeke, of course."

"Gee, that is so kind of you," I teased. "Only if you promise to be on your best behavior. Cassie is a friend. She isn't who you remember from our Gemini mission. She treated us far better than our own kind did, if you'll remember."

Ralrek pursed his lips, closed his eyes and nodded his head. "You got me there. I'm up for it if you guys are. This place... stinks, and you're not much better."

"I don't know how I'm going to get used to that smell." I turned to Bilba. "If we're ready, we should do this, while the Council thinks I'm recovering and too exhausted to get myself in trouble. But first, I need a shower. I hope they at least stocked the house with shampoo and soap."

"Heavens, at this point I would be glad for you to just run water over your nasty body." Ralrek chuckled. "Go clean your ass up for your girlfriend."

"She's not my, my—she's not my girlfriend!" I said, then teased with a smile, excited by this unexpected turn. Before I jumped into the shower, I'd write a quick note to Cassie and let her know where we're on our way. Never a dull moment.

7

OLYMPIA

FOR REASONS I don't understand, any demon talented enough to open gateways can open them in any Circle of Hell. But rifts require something extra, something special. According to Bilba, a demon needed to have been in a location before they could open a rift to it.

Since Bilba never had the distinct pleasure of making it to Olympia during my Abandonment, the closest he could get us was Joint Base Lewis-McCord, our duty station before the deployment to Baghdad. Let me tell you, few things are as uncomfortable as four demons plopping into the Overworld, seemingly out of thin air, in the middle of a vast military installation, surrounded by thirty thousand armed mortals. Fortunately for us, I had plenty of boring evenings to familiarize myself with the post. We found the front gate, which we walked through while waving shyly at the military police, who watched us with suspecting eyes, and off the installation. By sheer, brilliant luck, a taxi was dropping off a young soldier who should have spent the day doing something besides drinking by the way he stumbled out and dropped his wallet, plastic cards tumbling to the road.

We waited for the embarrassing debacle to end before

approaching the driver. When he found out we were headed to Olympia, he smiled. He'd eat well on our fare, for sure.

I gave him the name of Leo's gym. He looked it up and punched the address into his phone—Lucifer, I love GPS magic—and got us to Olympia before Bilba's fascination at being back in the Overworld wore off. Thankfully, he didn't accidentally blabber in front of the driver. Another thing Bilba did well? He kept his plastic card and remembered his security code-thing to withdraw mortal currency from his mortal bank account he'd kept open after serving in the Army. That dude, smart, I swear.

While Bilba paid, I faced the Lion's Den, the structure Leo built. A dark cloud of responsibility hung over me. Adding to the feeling was the fact that the parking lot was empty of angels. Cassie hadn't made it.

Ralrek stepped beside me, putting a hand on my back. "You okay?"

I nodded. "I'm just angry. Everything the Council's doing." I cut my comment off, not sure how much to share in front of Melchiot. She was listening without making it obvious. The way she avoided any direct eye contact for more than a few seconds helped the illusion.

"There. There's that, all done," Bilba beamed, joining us.

I grinned, taking joy in the clear pride in his face. "You sure that rift won't be detected?"

"Almost as if we were never here," he said.

I nodded. "Good. Let's head inside and see what we can find."

It was strange, being back here so soon, back where Leo's spirit was prominent. I half expected to see the husky fighter in the gym's bay, working out a member or twenty. Pain tugged in my chest. Leo was nothing more than a pile of white ash, swept away with the grains of sand of the Seventh Circle or trampled under the feet of the next round of fights.

I stepped into the small lobby, hoping Cassie might be in

the gym. The entry was decorated just as it had been when Cancer worked here. Accolades in frames on the wall. Cheap chairs underneath. The television playing sports programming. Refreshingly, something else was the same. The middle-aged woman with yellowed teeth sat behind the reception counter.

"Hey, Debbie. How are you?" I said, moving toward the counter with an awkward wave.

She did a double-take, before recognition spread on her face and her expression warmed. "Hey... you." It was obvious Debbie had forgotten my name. Maybe she never knew it. "I haven't seen you around the gym in a while."

"Yeah, I've been a little busy. You understand."

Her smile fell from her face. "Oh, if you're looking for Leo, he's not here. But if you're trying to restart your membership, I can help you with that."

Good old Debbie, always the business-focused person at the Lion's Den. "I figured he's been busy, so I didn't want to bother him. I was wondering if you'd seen someone else."

She gave me a firm look, the same she gave me the first time I visited the gym, when she thought I was there to creep on female patrons. Debbie didn't play around, not when it came to Lion Den business. Probably not ever. "You know how busy the gym gets. I see lots of people. Do you want to narrow it down for me?"

"I'm actually looking for one of the guys he used to train. I fought him once, raised quite the ruckus when he almost broke my neck," I said without embarrassment. "Goes by his fighting name. Virgo. Lanky. Light brown sk—"

Debbie was already nodding. "Oh yes. Virgo. I remember him. He was in earlier today. I don't expect him back until tomorrow, most likely." My disappointment must have shown because she said quickly, "I can take a note for you. Pass along your message."

That wasn't going to work. We couldn't be away from Hell

for an entire day. Yes, we could make multiple trips to and from, as long as Bilba's spells remained undetectable, but I didn't want to risk asking that until I felt safer. I'm a skeptic, not a cynic, okay? "Is there any way you can let him know I'm looking for him? Just tell him Zeke needs to see him, and it's pretty urgent. I'm not going to be in town long, so if that message could find its way to him today, I would really appreciate it."

I hoped Debbie picked up on my hint. She seemed to. "I'll see what I can do."

"Thanks." I pulled back from the reception desk to peek into the bay toward the octagon where I had a lesson in ass-kicking taught to me in one of the most frightening ways possible. "Any chance I can step into the gym and see if I know anyone hanging around? I'd like to catch up with anyone I can."

She rolled away on the chair she rarely left to the side desk where forms were stacked. "Be my guest."

"Thanks." In the bay, several patrons worked out on the bags or the mat. Three older men were being walked through the basics of fighting stances. I didn't recognize anyone. No Cassie either.

"Let's get out of here," I said. "I have another idea how I can find him."

"You're the boss," Ralrek said.

I didn't know what the chances were I would find Virgo and his group of Abandoned, but we didn't have options. We could hang out in the gym until Debbie threw us out and never see him. Four demons walking around the streets of Olympia would draw attention from the Abandoned soon enough, I hoped. Basically, I'd be happy to come across any group holding a modicum of trouble in their appearance and behaviors. It was the best chance with the limited time we had.

As we stepped out under the overcast gray sky, my day

was brightened.

"Is that Creed in your pocket or are you just happy to see me?" a sweet, sweet voice, like water trickling over rocks, said.

I stared into the perfectly symmetrical face framing crystal eyes. Her horizontal eyebrows highlighted her dark, thick eyelashes. Cassie threw her arms open and hugged me. The Overworld never smelled better.

"How in the heaven are you?" I squeezed too hard and for too long.

She laughed. It was ugly, like a snort mixed with a cough, which only made me laugh along with her. "Two seconds into seeing each other and you're already cursing, Z-Zeke." She wore a backpack which she slung off her shoulders and tapped. "I got your note."

"I hoped so. That was the whole point of making sure you had a notebook. When I didn't see you in the gym, I got worried."

"I couldn't pass this up. Too many important things are going on," she said, checking out the rest of the group. "Hi, R —Ralrek."

"Cassie," he said in curt response.

"And I assume you're Bi—Bilba?" she said, Ralrek's abruptness apparently not bothering her.

The tips of Bilba's ears gained a faint shade of pink. "That's me. Can I get a hug too?"

Cassie brightened. "Of course."

When she stepped back, she turned to Melchiot. She extended her hand. "Hi. I'm Cassie."

Melchiot's black eyes danced around the angel, as if seeing something no one else could. "Nice to meet you. Name is Melchiot."

Introductions made, we got down to business. Cassie said, "Let's walk and talk. I want to take you somewhere."

"Sounds good," I said as we left the parking lot and

walked east across the small city. "What's been going on?"

Every single one of us, maybe even Melchiot—since I wasn't sure if she'd ever been to the Overworld—knew we had to be careful how we talked about immortal issues. We didn't want to draw attention to ourselves or our purpose, though I figured we had more allowance than we had been brain-trained to believe. Heavens, we could use magic in the Overworld and it might go undetected if it was a reserved spell. Unwittingly, the Council had made me smart enough to be more than a major headache. Cassie was careful as well.

"You might think I'm crazy," Cassie reached behind her and tapped the backpack, "but I've been taking notes for a while."

"Notes about what?" Bilba asked, huffing up beside her.

"Demonic activity affecting the Balance," Cassie said.

Melchiot made a sound that resembled a low growl. I ignored her, for now.

"Could it be the Abandoned?" I asked.

"Doubtful." Cassie shook her head. "You know that's not their game. They're more about making sure our type doesn't affect the Balance either way. They want to remain neutral. The actions we've received reports on are anything but."

"We?" Melchiot inquired from the back of the group.

Oh boy. How were we going to tackle this issue? The less said, the better. I jumped in, taking the lead. "Cassie has access to high-level reports. She gets to hear tons of stuff most of us don't."

Silence told me Melchiot bought the line, at least for now.

Cassie seemed to pick up on the uneasiness. "Yes, yes. Of course, I can't say too much about it here, but prominent figures have been shifting the Balance by influencing small pockets of mortals."

"How bad is it?" I asked, my mind flashing back to my previous time in Olympia and discussions of the eternal struggle between Hell and Heaven.

"They've got these groups that walk around the city targeting those who don't align with them. It started out as harassment," Cassie said.

"Sounds like it has progressed?" Ralrek asked.

"Unfortunately," Cassie said, her face twisting and something with looked like confusion. "To the point where they started these takeovers. They harass organizations that try to do good works. When protesting didn't work, they started harassing employees. That worked slightly better, but not enough, I guess."

"What makes you say that?" Bilba asked.

"Because they started forcing their way into these establishments."

"Why would they do that?" Ralrek asked.

"To shut them down," Cassie said. "If a shelter or a food bank couldn't open its doors out of fear for their safety, then they wouldn't be able to serve the very people they needed to serve."

"That's a cruel thing to do," Bilba said, measured heat in his voice. "To deprive mortals in need to shift the Balance? I wouldn't even expect that out of the Council."

Cassie's mouth popped open and closed in the blink of an eye. She'd given the answer away.

"They are involved, aren't they?" I asked.

Cassie's crystal eyes slid over to me. "From what we understand, yes. At least one of them."

Behind me, Bilba whistled, accompanied by a Ralrek growl. Melchiot was quiet.

The Council getting involved in matters of the Balance in Olympia. Who and to what degree? I needed to figure that out. At the moment, I wasn't worried about their reasons. That Cassie believed Founders were putting their filthy hands in the mortal realm was enough.

"This is bad, Cassie. I don't doubt that it's a colossal headache for your side," I said, forming my apology, "but I'm not sure how we can help, even if only half that information is correct."

Her tiny chin dropped. "Whatever you can do will help. We... can get involved. To a degree. I have approval. But we must be very careful or it might tip the scale in a way neither side wants. But with your help, I think I can set a few things in motion. "

"What do you need us to do?" I asked, knowing this wasn't a matter of discussion or contemplation. I'd help in any way imaginable with whatever Cassie needed. She just had to ask. Okay, maybe not 'any way.' That was most likely her pheromones, or something, doing the talking. But still, if she asked, I'd probably do what I could.

"I need you to convince Vi—Virgo to get involved," she said.

Virgo. There he was again. I had looked for him because Leo had urged me to find Virgo during our life-and-death fight. Virgo could help in the matter of Lucifer's Third Council, Leo had said. Now, Cassie was pulling out his name.

Virgo, it seemed, was a central figure in this eternal struggle.

"Is he giving you trouble?" I asked.

Cassie rolled her thin lips. "No. That's the problem. He's not doing anything. Says he doesn't want to get involved in these... matters. Said this is an example of why they've done what they've done. The Abandoned see their place as a sort of peacekeepers."

"If I may," Melchiot said. "You keep saying Abandoned. What are these Abandoned?"

I took a moment to educate Bilba's mentor about the group. After I explained about the demons and angels who had been kicked out of their respective eternal realms to die a slow death in the Overworld, only to form a pseudo-formal organization, I could have driven a chimera carriage into Melchiot's open mouth.

"They would do that to our kind?" she asked.

"They do it," Bilba said, his eyes on me. "None of what I told you about Zeke's Abandonment was fabricated."

Melchiot's head dropped again as she shook it.

"Well, it sounds like the Abandoned won't have peace for long," I said. "Especially if influential demons are screwing with the Balance. What is Virgo thinking?"

"That's why I need your help," Cassie said. "He will listen to you much better than he listens to me because… well, you know."

"Is that where we're headed now? To see him?" Bilba asked.

Cassie's head rocked as if on a fulcrum.

"Okay," I said, and prepared myself to convince Virgo to play nice.

We caught up on each other's lives while we made our way toward the downtown harbor. It hadn't been that long since we had our last face-to-face in my Olympia apartment, but a heaven of a lot of "c-rap" had happened in between I felt she needed to know. Through my short stint back in Hell, Cassie had been busy. She was upset when she heard about Leo but used the opportunity to highlight why she needed our intervention with Virgo. None of us—well, maybe Melchiot—needed convincing.

At the harbor, we stood in front of a tall hangar, painted drab green, with a row of rippled, eight-foot tall windows running along the top. The building and the slabs of surrounding concrete were fenced in—closed, of course. A small armada of vehicles was parked diagonally up both sides of the fence line.

"The Abandoned's hideout," Cassie said with a grand gesture.

Even before I knew this was our destination, I noticed bodies moving behind the windows near the roof of the building. To the left, in the middle of the line of trucks and vans, stacks of rotting pallets leaned precariously, forming a barrier. Behind it, subtle movements revealed hidden Abandoned. Enough to cause a problem for anyone they wanted to cause problems for. To the right, a small boat had been lifted onto a dry storage rack. Inside its cabin, a shadow ducked when my head swiveled that way.

"We're being watched," I said, extending my senses for immortal signatures of magic, picking up on nothing. None of the watch-people were Abandoned demons. "Have you been getting chummy with Virgo?"

That wonderful, thin–lipped smile made another appearance. "I wouldn't say it's been chummy. I've been causing him headaches. I think he'll be glad to see someone's face besides mine."

I wanted to argue how wrong she was, but thought better of it, knowing it would be used against me by one or both of my friends.

Cassie inched the gate opened, and we approached with slow steps. I constantly swiveled to keep watch on the hiding spots on both sides. I wanted the Abandoned to know I knew they were there. We reached the door at the side of the building and Cassie knocked. Inside, dragging feet neared.

"What do you want?" a voice asked.

Cassie pressed her mouth close to the door. Lucky door. "Tell V–Virgo Cassie is here to see him, and that I have brought a friend he'll want to see."

This time, the dragging steps were even slower than their arrival.

"Now what?" Ralrek asked.

"We wait," Cassie said.

Turns out, we didn't have to wait long. Minutes after the footsteps inside shuffled away, they returned. Not reluctant, but hurried. The door was thrown open, and a stocky mortal greeted us. I knew that because I was Sensing constantly and he wasn't emitting any signature of Abilities, leaving him as mortal or angel. Based on Cassie's reaction, the latter was not true.

"Come in. Virgo will see you," the man said.

We were escorted into the hangar. The long, gray cement floor was empty of over-sized machinery, vehicles, or airplanes, making it little more than a really open hangout with inefficient environmental controls. Only sporadically placed furniture broke it up. Five tables lined both walls. Most had chairs around them. Two solitary tables must have been for other purposes. Along the rear of the building, a basketball hoop hung on the hangar door. It didn't look at regulation height. A basketball sat on the concrete underneath it. Near the wall to my left, three couches were spread out in a 'U'. A handful of Abandoned watched a movie on a large screen television from the days of hair band heavy metal. An action movie I'd never seen halted me at an awesome explosion—hey, I'm an incubus, I can't help myself.

"Keep moving," Ralrek said behind me, giving me a playful shove.

On the far wall, three doors stood in line side-by-side. The mortal escorting us walked us to the middle one. "He's waiting for you in there."

Eight Abandoned sat around a long oak table, at the head of which sat Virgo. He stood as we entered. Just as a few weeks ago, he was the embodiment of fitness. The black short-sleeve shirt he wore exposed enough of his biceps and cut forearms to announce to the world he was not someone to antagonize. His hazel eyes were just as fierce, but I swore a corner of his mouth twitched in what could have been a Virgo–specific smile.

"Hey guys," he said, coming around the corner of the table. As we approached, he extended his arm, hand formed into a fist. We all fist bumped, even Melchiot.

"Nice place you've got here," I said in a light tone.

Virgo was an interesting case. Throughout my Abandon-ment, I had taken exception to him because I thought he was targeting me—he was. He was part of Chax's group who had nearly killed Cancer by running us off the road. He was part of the plan to get me inside the octagon in Leo's gym and beat me to within an inch of my life. He was Chax's personal bodyguard on the night three dozen of the demon's crew tried to finish the job, only turning when Chax's motives were proven to not be altruistic. As enigmas do, he made the picture murkier by being the first one to volunteer himself and the Abandoned to clean up the mess left behind from the resulting battle. Basically, I'm saying, I was still feeling Virgo out. But, if Leo vouched for him, I was going to give him the benefit of the doubt.

"Did you come into some money?" I asked, only half-serious.

Virgo's intense gaze fell on Cassie. "No. It was a gift. It seems someone appreciated my efforts with that situation you had a few weeks back."

I turned to Cassie, shocked. "You did this?"

"Well, I had assistance. But, yes, we wanted to make sure the Abandoned had someplace to call home. A place where they could meet and relax," she said.

"And organize," Virgo said.

Cassie conceded. "And organize."

Virgo pointed his chin at me. "Is that why he's here with his crew?"

"I'm hoping he can talk sense into you," Cassie said with a smirk.

"I'm not looking to get into the middle of a lover's spat," I said, trying to lighten the mood even more.

Cassie wagged a finger between herself and the tall-dark-and-fierce ex-demon. "We have more of a love-hate thing going on."

That seemed to tickle Virgo. His mouth twitched for the

second time. A few of the people sitting around the table chuckled.

"Makes things more entertaining for the rest of us, Cassie," a human at the table said.

Only after he spoke did my thick skull register that the voice was familiar. My eyes must have been the size of blaze-balls—slightly too large to be gripped by your average adult incubus. Yes, my hands are too small and I have to use both to hold a blazeball. No short jokes, please. "Steve?"

"I was wondering when you were going to stop being rude and say hi," the man said, getting to his feet and coming to the table. We embraced. "I hope things have been going better for you?"

I met Steve through a gang of bigots targeting him in a park in the middle of Olympia. I hadn't been in the city for more than a few weeks before that day. We even had beers once, and Steve shared his personal story. It was an inspirational conversation, one I enjoyed and wished to repeat, but never had a chance to.

"Well, to be honest, interesting things have happened since the last time we chatted," I laughed. "How in the heaven did Virgo talk you into getting involved in this mess?"

"Funny story, that," Steve chuckled. "You have a way of drawing attention. Not long after our chat, I heard about you around the city. Seems some funny stuff happened at the Lion's Den shortly after that. Heard you were involved. And, well, since I knew you were a good guy, it didn't take much to put a few things together and do some asking around. That's when I met this crew. Been like a family ever since. Man," he said, slapping his hands, "it's so good to see you."

"I don't want to be rude," Melchiot said, "but we don't have a lot of time. Our absence is going to be noticed. We're already taking a chance by doing this... unapproved activity."

Virgo's face scrunched.

"She's the party pooper," I whispered.

He gestured at the table. "Make room for them. Let's talk so you can get on your way."

"That's fine, you don't need to—" Bilba started to say, but the Abandoned were moving with the speed of adherence. Virgo ran a tight ship.

We took our seats. As I did, I pushed my senses out and swallowed a cloud of emissions. Virgo's signature combined with Bilba, Ralrek, and Melchiot. Someone else was giving off a strong signal. The room was too small, too crowded to separate one from the other.

"V—Virgo, we have to figure out how to make this work," Cassie said. "If we don't work together, nothing gets solved. This problem isn't going away."

"Is it safe to talk about this in front of everyone?" Ralrek said, with the tact of a chimera in a China shop.

"I'm as pissed as anyone about what they're doing, but you know our stance on this," Virgo said, raising his arms in a wide V to include everyone in the room. "We are a mix. We don't prefer one side to another, because both sides have failed us. Even the mortals among us" —the reaction from Bilba, Ralrek, and Melchiot was hilarious, as unsuspecting as they were that such matters would be talked about openly— "are failed by the Upper and Underworlds. Our entire purpose for existing is to ensure the influence of immortals doesn't touch us. That's not entirely possible; we understand that. But we are going to do everything we can do to minimize it. We're tired of the immortal games."

"But that's what's happening, and by not getting involved, you're enabling that influence to grow," Cassie said, scooting forward in her chair. "I'm not asking you to take a side. I've said so before. That's why I asked Z—Zeke to help. I want you to see it, I want you to hear it from my own lips in front of him, that I don't want any preferential treatment. I've never asked for it, and I won't start now. But I can't do it alone."

"How is that?" Virgo said, leaning to the side.

"Someone with much more say than me or anyone in this room, is going to decide. They'll involve even more powerful players. Before you know it, this spins out of control," Cassie said. "It's happening. You know the reports we've received. Are you happy with what's been happening around the city?"

"Of course not," Virgo answered.

"That won't stop," Cassie said as if she anticipated the response. "In fact, it's only getting worse. You've seen how these groups are growing. The more they unsettle the people they oppose, the more vitriolic their message becomes. The more brazen their actions. Give it another few weeks and imagine what it's going to be like, V—Virgo. And if my side has to counter, we will. We all know where that leads."

The air was thick with tension as everyone waited on Virgo. I leaned forward. "I haven't been around, I know," I said, "but I can assure you, if Cassie says it, it's true. Shit has been rolling downhill, in bigger balls, all the time." I briefed Virgo on what happened to me since being plucked from the Overworld. To his credit, he listened, his fierce gaze locked on me the entire time. No one in the room even as much as coughed, not even when I mentioned Leo's fate. "Now, I don't know who's behind riling up all these idiots and causing problems for mortals and you, but I don't trust anyone in Hell as far as I could throw their gooseneck sow's tongue asses. They will stop at nothing to gain influence, and none of them are willing to intercede on behalf of what is right. Well, with one exception I'm still feeling out. If you don't get involved, the choice will be made for you." I let the sentence hang as I looked around the room, taking in each of the Abandoned standing counsel to the fighter. "For all of you."

That got a reaction. Fear will do that to a demon, angel, or mortal. None of us are immune.

Noise filled the room as everyone began talking over each other. The hostility was aimed at the immortal forces screwing with the Overworld. I felt guilty, but only partially.

If Virgo insisted on maintaining neutrality, he was going to answer for it to the very people who would suffer because of the decision. That was the thing with tough guys, they only saw the world from their tough guy perspective, thinking they could conquer anything they set their minds to. Virgo wasn't a bad guy. He put himself in harm's way to help me. Bad guys didn't do things like that. But his autonomy blinded him, and that might hurt others. He needed to know that cost.

"I've lost track of how many times they've attempted to kill me. All my missions, everything that's happened, the war, my Abandonment, a trial to the death that took Leo's life," I said, letting that last one land hard. "That's just the beginning of this mess for the rest of you. It doesn't stop here. And let me tell you. If they suspect Upperworld involvement, they're just going to crank up the intensity. None of you want that. What's stopping you?"

Arms crossed, standing to the side of the room, Steve answered. "Leadership. We have none. Not formally, I mean."

I nodded, appreciating his honesty. A new member of the Abandoned, he may be, but at least he had the courage to say what was needed. "Then nominate a blessed leader and do what's right. No one needs to suffer over something that could be solved." Then I focus on the sole individual who needed it, now more than ever. "What's stopping you from stepping up?"

"I'm not a leader," Virgo said, his arms placed on the table, his hands contracted into fists.

"That's why we need you to lead us," Steve said from the wall. "You won't be reckless. You'll make sure we're safe. That's why you must lead."

"Yeah," another man said, this one well into the second half-century of his life.

A woman stocky enough to remind me of the bulbous nosed Chain Queen I had taken out inside the Lion's Den, slapped the wall. "Right on!"

Cassie leaned forward, reaching out and touching Virgo's fisted hands. "They need you. Olympia needs you. And, it's quite possible the whole Overworld needs you."

Virgo didn't pull his hands away. He didn't scowl. His fierce eyes bored holes into the table. Everyone let him consider what was said.

After a time, he spoke. "If I do this," he said, raising a hand at the excitement that followed, stressing, "if I do this, it has to be done our way. You two." He wagged that same dangerous finger at me and Cassie. "Bring whatever you want to me, share all the information you have, provide guidance and advice, but you do not form decisions for us. Understood?"

Neither Cassie nor I could agree swiftly enough.

"Absolutely," I said.

"Deal." Cassie's crystal eyes sparkled.

Now, the wall was free of the bodies propped against it throughout this meeting. Like those attendees, I found myself leaning closer. Melchiot's monochrome eyes never blinked.

"Fine," Virgo said.

Hand clapping and backslapping accompanied his response. The celebrations stopped when he held up his hands. "But if I am going to lead this rabble, I'm going to want to know what it will be called."

Confusion passed over most faces. No one stepped up to ask, so I did. "Called?"

"Any serious organization needs a name, doesn't it?" he said, spreading his hands once more. "So, if you all want this so badly, let's have it. What should we be known as?"

Steve stepped forward, a big chimera–dung eating grin on his face. "Let's call ourselves," he paused, a wicked smile on his face, "Virgo's Vigilantes."

The new moniker hung in the balance for approximately two-one-hundredths of a fraction of a second. I'm sure Abandoned across the hangar heard the cheering agreement.

And so, Virgo's Vigilantes was born.

8

OLYMPIA

"Virgo's Vigilantes," I teased as I rolled the name over in my head.

"Not convinced myself," Virgo said, walking us to the front of the hangar, past a jubilant throng of movie watchers and socializers.

As soon as the meeting broke, word spread. The newly named Vigilantes were ecstatic. Many watched as we crossed the vast cement floor. Beaming smiles and broad grins told me how much this formalized step meant to them. With the name given, they believed. In themselves. In a greater role, a grander purpose.

As someone who knows something about belief, this could go a long way. Hell's rulers made a huge mistake by putting me in a trial to the death. Now free, motivated by the weight of responsibility and empowered by a stunning angel and an Overworld gang looking for justice, I was ready to become the nightmare they feared.

If this is what the wheels of momentum felt like, I would ride this as long as I could hold on. Something was building here. It electrified the air.

"I don't know, it's sort of catchy," Bilba said.

"We should leave," Melchiot said, tilting toward Bilba and casting a nervous glance around the hangar. "Very soon."

Melchiot was going from party pooper to annoying. Leaving now would deprive me of the chance to talk with Cassie and Virgo. Mostly Cassie. Sure, we'd gotten our business done, but hadn't really talked as friends, except for the walk to the hangar. Too many ears had been hanging around then. Plus, after such a big decision, racing off wasn't the wisest decision we could make. I'd been on enough teams to know that. We needed to bond before we split into the winds.

"Give us a little time, will you?" I asked my friend.

Bilba's head swayed between me and his mentor. "I can open a rift back to the Fifth for you, Melchiot. We'll follow later. How does that sound?"

"We shouldn't," she said, moving closer still. "This could jeopardize several things."

Bilba pulled back. "Like what?"

Melchiot watched us as we watched her. "Well... your Passage, for one."

"And? You've already told me the way this is set up is abnormal. And this," Bilba paused, gesturing at our small group, "is important. Maybe the most important thing any of us will ever do. I will not pass it up. I'll open a rift, and you can head back. But I'm not. I'm staying here."

To drive home the point, Bilba mumbled, his hands moving. The rift sizzled before the air split open. It was narrow, smaller than the one he'd opened to get us to Olympia. Around the hangar, decaying immortals and mortals alike watched.

Melchiot hung by the rift. "Please do not put your hard work at risk."

"I'll let you know when I'm home," Bilba said.

Dismissed, his mentor turned and scurried through the rift. A white dot outlined her body as she was absorbed, then sucked in on itself. Bilba let the rift go and the rip in the air faded.

"Still so cool you can do that," Ralrek said.

"I could teach you," Bilba said, his ears pink, from humility or dismissing his mentor, I couldn't tell.

"Fat chance I could ever pull that off, but thanks," Ralrek said.

Bilba nodded and then smacked his hands together. "So, now what?"

"I have tasks to get to," Virgo said, nodding to the door. "I'm sure you guys know your way out. Remember what I said about this agreement. It's only as good as both of you and your kind honoring it."

"I get that," I said.

Cassie reached over and grabbed Virgo's hand. If decaying demons could be lucky, Virgo was that. "Thank you for taking this chance to trust me."

Virgo nodded, gave a squeeze of Cassie's hand, and let go. "I'll see you later," he said, returning to his business to leave us to ours.

"Now what do we do?" Bilba prodded. "Well, unless you two need alone time? Me and Ralrek could go grab a coffee or play some of that roundball." He pointed at the basketball on the concrete. "When you're ready for me to bring you home, give me a shout, or wait for us to come back if we go for coffees? I don't know." He gave Ralrek a shrug, not committing to either action.

My neck heated even as I stumbled to think of a response. Cassie's eyes were wide, with humor... I think.

"Let's get something to drink. If I remember correctly, there's a pub down the street," I said before turning away and walking out of the hangar, knowing the other three were close behind. I needed to stay in front of them long enough for the color in my cheeks to fade.

The chilled air and gray sky didn't sour my mood. I was

with my two best friends and my favorite angel in the entire universe. I was free. The Council wasn't after me, at least not yet. Covertly, I was part of a small gang who enjoyed true freedom of movement. Things couldn't get better. Well, unless the pub was open, serving beer, and dishing out free all-you-can-eat chicken wings. Too bad there was no such thing as miracles.

"I know it's only been a few weeks, but it feels so good to see you again. I'm so glad you could make it. Bi—Bilba, thank you so much for doing this," Cassie said, locking her arm around his elbow.

This time it wasn't only the tips of his ears that flashed pink. "You're—you're welcome. It—it really wasn't a big deal."

"No one likes a braggart," Ralrek said, a sly smirk.

"It's the least we can do. Especially after what you did for me," I said, swallowing something stupidly thick in my throat.

"I only did what was right. What any angel would have done," she said.

Ralrek snorted. "Any? Doubt it."

"Be nice," I warned. "Cassie, be honest. Are you putting yourself at risk with your Council? I imagine you are, if yours is anything like ours."

"Worse entities exist than our Council, that's for sure," Cassie said. "But don't worry about it. I did what was needed. What the situation called for. And I'd do it again, a thousand times over."

"Why? Because you like Zeke?" Bilba giggled.

Ralrek stopped, turning on our shorter friend. "What are you, nine hundred years old? Grow up. Plus," he added, waving at me and the angel, "look at them. It's obvious they're infatuated with each other."

Leaving us embarrassed, Ralrek walked away. The way his shoulders bobbed, he was laughing.

"Ignore him," I said to Cassie.

"Uh, sure. I just hope he doesn't hate me."

I shook my head. "He doesn't. He's been Hell's asshole for six thousand years and pretty much embraces the title."

Cassie snort–laughed, the cutest combination of joy and bodily functions I'd ever heard in my life. The laugh I couldn't hear enough of, ever. "Seriously though. Please don't worry about me. I didn't get in any kind of trouble."

"Well, that's good to hear. That was a powerful spell you used to save my ass. If a demon tried that, it would get registered around all Nine Circles of Hell."

"Chax got what he deserved," the angel responded. "I feel terrible that what I did caused you so many headaches. I hope that's the end of it. Otherwise... well, you don't deserve any further struggles."

A mortal couple rounded the corner, their arms interlocked, looking every bit of mutual happiness and satisfaction. How long would mortals be happy if they knew what was happening in the underworld of Olympia. Virgo's stubborn resistance, having to be cornered into agreeing to get involved, lingered. Did he consider couples like them when he questioned his involvement in this eternal struggle?

After they were out of earshot, I said, "I doubt it'll be long before one of the Founders bothers me again. That seems to be their style."

Cassie shook her head. Her cocoa hair with its blond highlights falling over her smooth neck.

"What is that all about? Did I say something wrong?" I asked.

"No. No." She drew a breath. Her shoulders stretched back as her chest expanded. I kept my eyes focused on her beautiful eyes. "I worry about what I did and how that might antagonize Seraph. I don't imagine this is sitting well with her."

"Oh, I expect Seraph to be a problem for," I paused, swinging my head like a pendulum in mock thought, "about the rest of my existence. At least as long as she allows me to live."

"That's not funny," Cassie mumbled.

"I didn't mean it to be."

We walked for another block, sharing only our parallel steps.

"Excuse me, but I need to talk to Ralrek about... something," Bilba said, scurrying ahead to catch up with the taller demon who didn't even know where the pub was but was leading the way.

What a good friend, that Bilba Ravenous.

"Can I ask you something?" I broke the silence.

"Of course, you can ask me anything," Cassie said almost as soon as I finished.

"You once told me part of the problem with Seraph was she owed someone a favor. The way I remember it, you were trying to tell me she's dangerous in a different way. Maybe I'm remembering it wrong, but I know she's dangerous. What favor does she owe, though? To who?"

Cassie flinched like I'd hit a tender spot. "I... I don't know if I should talk about that."

I was confused. "Come on, you know what's at stake. What I could walk into when we get home. What I might deal with for the rest of my life. Throw me a bone here, please."

Cassie stopped. Right there, in the middle of the sidewalk, she stood, an immortal creature with immense power, drawing the attention of my universe. A blue sedan passed. The mortal driving craned his neck, checking her out. Only Cassie's expression stopped me from laughing. Thankfully, she didn't notice.

She came toward me, each step measured. "My father, Z— Zeke. That's who S—Seraph owes a favor. It's difficult because it's a sensitive situation, not in terms of my feelings, but politically."

I pulled back. "What? Is your father important or something?"

She nodded more than she needed to. "Yes. And he did a political favor for Seraph eons ago that she never repaid. Not that he expects her to repay it, considering her position in the Underworld."

"Yeah, I don't think Seraph is under any impression she needs to pay on things owed," I laughed though it was definitely not funny.

We had caught Bilba and Ralrek, who were walking slower, obviously noting our deep discussion.

"I promise, she will never repay a thing owed. She's dangerous," Cassie continued. "I don't know if you guys understand just how dangerous. Se—Seraph's political connections go back a long way. Almost back to the beginning, just like any Founder, yours or ours. She's connected and has been only gaining power ever since. According to my father's stories, she set herself apart early on. She was smart. Her moves and ploys were subtle. He always warned me she never stood out to most angels, so they did nothing until it was too late and that forced our Council's hand. By the time everyone recognized her ambitions, she was practically untouchable."

"She was untouchable? Even in Heaven?" Bilba asked with obvious fascination.

Cassie nodded. "She was. That was, in large part, what led to her Fall."

"We find that term offensive," Ralrek sniffed.

"I thought it was a trade. A swap," I said, covering for Ralrek's brusqueness.

"Sorry, I didn't mean to offend you. I can see how that is an insensitive term," Cassie said to my dark-haired friend. "But yes, Asmodeus and Legion were... swapped for her and M-Michael. The way I understand it, the negotiations took months, but it was because of her. Poor Mi-Michael wasn't a threat, but there had to be a balance to the exchange before Yahweh and L—Lucifer agreed. M—Michael was the innocent bystander in the mess. I am worried for you guys, because there's nothing I can do to help you stand up against her. I wouldn't put it past her to be exploring ways she can make you pay for what you've done, Z—Zeke. She's not a good immortal."

"You can say that again," I agreed. "Tell me something?"

"Sure."

"I feel like you have more to say but aren't sure how to say it," I started, shooting Ralrek a firm look. "I know you have history with us," I said, thumbing at the taller demon. Then I pointed at Bilba. "And you don't know him, yet. But I swear, I trust these two more than anyone in Hell. Anything you have to say can be said in front of them. In fact, it would help if it was, so everything doesn't rest on my shoulders. I have a way of getting myself in a lot of trouble, and if anything were to happen to me, then these guys and everyone helping them will be back to square one. Best we all hear it."

Cassie's eyes drifted across the three of us. "Okay, then. Ser —Seraph is devious—"

"We know that already," Ralrek interrupted.

"Let her finish," I said with enough force to remind Ralrek that he might not be Hell's asshole anymore, but he could regain his title.

Cassie cleared her throat. "S—Seraph is devious. She's manipulative, and she has a history of fooling even the most perceptive immortals. She'll use whatever tactics she can to reach her goal. And if that goal includes revenge for Ch— Chax, she will do it. Make no mistake, guys, it isn't just the Underworld you need to worry about. She still has many connections in the Upperworld. And she will use them against you. Count on that."

9

UNDERWORLD, FIFTH CIRCLE

"ENEMIES IN HELL AND HEAVEN? When Zeke does something, he goes all in," Ralrek chortled.

"Hey, I'd appreciate only partial laughter at my misfortune," I said.

"Sorry, bud, but that deserved a hearty laugh."

Sometimes, I swear, Ralrek is even more twisted than I knew.

Minutes ago, we said farewell to Cassie, who headed back to the Upperworld to do whatever angels do there—which I'm sure are the same things as demons in Hell, but it's fun to craft controversy and conspiracies sometimes. I'm sure it was something important since Cassie herself was more important than the three of us incubi combined. Whatever Cassie's assignment, she was deep in this Balance issue in Olympia. With her returning to her tasks, it was time for us to get to work.

"Ready to take us home?" I asked my best friend, burping up a healthy dose of chicken wings.

Bilba held up a finger. "First, can you give me a chance to get away from the pub before I make a scene that scars these mortals for the rest of their lives? And second, we're not going home."

I squinted. "What do you mean we're not going home? We have to. We've been gone long enough, and I still need to hit the store before you guys drop in on me again and Ralrek complains that my fridge is empty."

"Zeke, remember when we were in your new place and I told you I had someone who wanted to see you?"

The way Bilba's mouth disappeared under an avalanche of cheeks as he smiled told me this wasn't someone I needed to worry about. "I remember."

Away from the pub on an empty side street, Bilba mumbled, resuming his invisible dough ball manipulation gesture with his hands. The rift soon sizzled to life, filled with a murky vision of a stairwell.

"Where is this?" I asked, jabbing a thumb at the watery image of someone's stairs.

"To someone who told me to bring you to her before she rang my ears," Bilba said.

I grinned. "Dialphio," I said excitedly and stepped into the rift.

The world fell away, as it always does in these things. I soon found my feet again, this time in a place I missed as much as any in Hell. The Book Abyss, Dialphio's bookstore. The first place in the Fifth Circle brave enough to employ me. I stepped out of the tear between worlds and onto the main floor of the bookstore, the rift splitting the air right between two book displays.

When Bilba stepped through, I pointed at the displays and his rift. "Luck?"

He wore a reserved grin. "Nope. I can't tell you how many hours I've spent in this bookstore, making sure I knew the exact layout. I don't know about you, but I'm not crazy about the thought of Dialphio's reaction if I shredded a display."

"Is that who think it is?" a birdlike voice called down the stairs.

"The prodigal son has returned after seeing the error of his ways. To right his past wrongs and all that," I announced.

Ralrek snorted. "And you call me cocky."

"Because you are," Bilba and I said together.

Dialphio hung halfway down the stairs, one chubby hand gripping the railing. She set her feet on different steps, watching us with sparkling emerald eyes. I felt like an impling getting caught tugging his little sister's hair.

"Are we in trouble?" I asked.

A strange smile appeared on the bookstore owner's face. It wasn't of happiness and joy, nor was it sad or remorseful. This one landed somewhere in between. "No. Not at all, Ezekial."

"Good," I chuckled, "because the look you just gave us made me feel like we were, and I was trying to decide whether to blame it on Ralrek or Bilba, or both."

Dialphio chirped. "Seeing you home again fills my heart. Thank you for bringing him, Bilba."

"Of course," my friend said. "We would have been here at the planned time, but Zeke wanted to see his girlfriend."

"She's not my girlfriend," I said.

Dialphio descended the stairs to the main floor. "And how is Cassie?" Her question was still dangling on her lips by the time she had me wrapped in her arms. Her squeeze was like a warm blanket on a cold Overworld night.

I hugged my ex-boss. "She's doing well, but she's very busy handling things in the Overworld."

"Things?" Dialphio asked, cocking her head.

We took turns filling Dialphio in. Dialphio took in every word, her expression neutral. No emotion, not at the activities of the mysterious Council member in Olympia, the Balance, or even at an angel asking for help. She didn't get excited until we mentioned the formation of Virgo's Vigilantes.

"This is an interesting dynamic. One that could be advantageous, but one that could also cause some problems if the Council finds out, which I'm sure they will. How they react will tell us everything we need to know." She paused, clicking her fingernails on a nearby book display, looking toward the front door of the store. "Of course, these Abandoned bear the brunt of the risk if they get too involved. This could be tricky."

"Why is that?" Bilba asked.

"The mortal war continues without an end in sight," Dialphio said, still clicking nails on wood. "The war will keep everyone distracted. The world war can have many unanticipated effects on the Balance. With so many countries fighting, and such great strife for mortals, the attention it receives from the two Councils is justified."

Bilba snapped his fingers. "Giving anyone who wanted to shift the Balance an opportunity to move subtly?"

Dialphio nodded. "Exactly. With a distraction like that, anyone with ulterior motives who wanted to go unnoticed could take advantage. There are a million ways they could do it. If Cassie's reports about these… I don't even know what they would be called. Hate groups, maybe? But, if accurate, this could be early signs of powerful demons working their agendas."

Her voice trailed off as if her thoughts were taking her somewhere else, somewhere that wasn't in the middle of the main floor of a bookstore in the Fifth Circle of Hell. I waited. There was a reason she had Bilba bring me to The Book Abyss, more than giving me the opportunity to catch her up on my chaotic life. Not that I didn't appreciate it if a short social call was the only reason we were here. Being back in the store, even if for only a few minutes, was doing me a world of good. The displays and stacks of books weren't half as chaotic as I imagined it would have been, a tendency Dialphio had any time I wasn't working for her.

The small store, filled with thousands of books, held the smell only bookstores have. An aromatic decay of paper of all ages hung in the air. The store was quiet. Looking out the front door, on which hung her CLOSED sign, nightlife in the Fifth was waking. Soon, the street would fill with demons seeking entertainment. Sights, sounds, and smells combined to remind me that this Circle was my home, and I missed it.

Dialphio blinked and refocused. "All of this makes me more grateful to you, Bilba, for bringing him here. We can't dally. Too much is happening. Now that we know they're maliciously manipulating events in the Overworld, we have to assume Olympia is not the only place this is happening." Her voice drifted away again. "Likely many locations, I'll bet." She looked at me. "Ezekial, have you given thought to your role in all of this? Have you considered how you will help? You will help, of course?"

"Absolutely," I said.

"And not simply because you have a crush on this angel, I assume?" Dialphio said. That was definitely not a question.

"I don't have a crush on her. Cassie is a friend. A friend, I can't believe I have to remind you, who recently saved my life. I sort of owe her."

"Many are involved already, and many more will join your cause," Dialphio said. "It is time for you to recognize that. Some do it because they care about you, but others, take for example Virgo's Vigilantes; they're doing what they're doing to help the cause as well, because of your power. You lift others. It is your role. Your responsibility. You know this. We've had this conversation."

"Doesn't mean I'm comfortable with it," I said.

"With what?" Ralrek asked, moving to the foot of the steps and taking a seat.

Dialphio's eyes never left me as she said. "Based on the research I've done, I believe Ezekial is the one spoken of in

The Histories of the Balance as the Great Prince. Did he not share that with you?"

Ralrek snorted. "Yeah, we know about that. Some great prince," he said, looking me up and down. "I expected him to be taller, fitter, and not so ugly."

I blew him a kiss.

But Dialphio was all business. "The Great Prince isn't something you're elected into. It is deigned, if you will. Destiny. Mandatory. Required. Fated. Your responsibility. However you want to categorize it. As such, you alter things."

"Huh? Like how?" This was the first time Dialphio had mentioned anything along these lines. Not that we had time to discuss it. That was probably by design. The Council's design.

Her cheeks bulged as she blew out a breath. "A tall mountain alters weather patterns. You, your presence, your proximity changes the way people, angels, and demons act around you. You don't do it consciously, so it's not like you're using anyone. A result of who you are, something you haven't tapped into and may never."

"I wasn't there when this started in Olympia, I don't think. I was sitting in the Council's prison," I said.

"But you were in Olympia before," Dialphio said. "You dealt with Chax, Leo, Virgo, and Cassie. Each of those interactions, you were influencing them."

I rubbed my face in frustration. "Are you saying I pushed the Council toward rallying groups of idiots to harass and threaten mortals to shift the Balance while the war distracts everyone?"

Tap. Tap. Tap. Dialphio rolled her fingers, tapping her nails on the book display. "Honestly? I'm still working this out. But, in a way, yes. Think of that example with the mountain. Weather moves as weather does, but when it comes upon a mountain, it's changed. Not wholly. It remains what it was. But the mountain forces it to take a different course. That would explain many of these challenges with the Council. It would explain why they never saw what you were, though credit still has to be given to Aries for his insight." Dialphio's face brightened. "Of course, this is under the influence of One. For all we know, this could be part of Their design, a role you were always supposed to play."

"I told you, thinking about that gives me a headache," I admitted. Dialphio had guided me toward thinking about One and the nature of Its existence in the All, a concept too large for a simple demon like me to wrap my head around.

"Let me give specific examples. Remember the Angelfire attack in the First Circle?" Dialphio asked. Silence fell over The Book Abyss when she stopped tapping her fingers.

"Of course. That's not something I'll ever forget," I said.

"None of us should," Dialphio said. "Do you remember what happened after the attack, after those who fled tucked tails and ran home to hide while the brave and caring tended to the injured? While the mournful searched the devastation for loved ones? While you looked for your parents?"

My mind raced back to the details of the attack. The square was a pile of wreckage of roof tops and storefronts, the hangman's platform upon which Gemini was to be executed, and of the bodies that littered it. I could recall a lot about that day, along with some finer details I'd rather forget. Details made obscure by the immensity of the tragedy.

"Someone gave you a note about Creed," Dialphio said, nudging the conversation.

A cloaked figure handed me a note after I had spent hours searching the bodies for my parents. That note served as another clue to what Creed was. I never learned who the stranger was or how they found me in the chaos of that day. Until now. My eyes widened. "That was you?"

Bilba sucked in his breath.

Dialphio's unwavering eyes locked on me.

"But the Council was still around. Their muscle-head

guards were around. You could have been caught. They would have imprisoned you, Dialphio." The sudden role change felt odd, me becoming the parent of the bookstore owner who had been as much a mother to me as my biological one.

"Yet I did it because it was needed," Dialphio said coolly. "It was my role. Someone had to do it. Fate or circumstances, it doesn't matter how you look at it. I was in a position to alter your course. That is the effect I'm talking about, Ezekial. You do that. No doubt you've been doing it to these two for thousands of years." Dialphio waved her hand at Bilba and Ralrek. "Look at the chances they're taking to support you, even though in the back of their minds, they understand the risk, and everything they could lose because of that support. Life would be simpler if they never had supported you. Still, they do it because they love you."

No smart ass snort from Ralrek this time?

"But they also do it because they're compelled," Dialphio said. "Just as I did in the First Circle by slipping you that note. I made sure you received the messages about Creed in ways that were safe and didn't put you in danger. Your impact continues, not just with me, but with so many others. Some powerful others."

Again, Dialphio was saying something without saying it. I needed clarity. "Who, specifically, are you talking about?"

Dialphio's nostrils flattened as she drew a breath. It came out with a shiver. "Azazel."

"What about him?" I said cautiously, still confused by the ancient Founder's recent actions, but hopeful his intent aligned with keeping me healthy, happy, and alive.

Dialphio raised her eyebrow. "Do you think all the information I've had, as timely as it was, was coincidental? Do you think I'm uber-perceptive or that luck plays such a role? Don't you think it's strange that I haven't suffered consequences even though the Council knew you worked for me and could have guessed you acquired *The Histories of the Balance* from my bookstore? Honestly, sometimes I'm convinced you play oblivious too well."

"He is a proven dumbass," Ralrek said from the stairs as he started walking up. Dialphio ignored him.

"These things didn't happen by chance. I was fed information, and in turn, I tried to feed it to you," Dialphio said.

"From Azazel? He's been helping me all along?" I asked, stunned.

She nodded slowly. "When it is safe, sit and talk with him. I'm sure he has interesting things to tell you about his personal story. One that links with Aries. Those two go way back.

"Wow," Bilba said in a raspy breath.

Wow, exactly. "Why you? No offense."

"He's my cousin," she said, the motherly tone refocusing the conversation. "For all I know, this may be part of the effect you've had all along."

"Because I'm fated?" I asked.

For too long, I had pondered and pouted, resisted and complained about the concept of fate. But that time was past. The facts were clear. From Aries to Leo, and everyone in between. Receiving Creed. Being a commodity in a trade between Taurus and someone—Seraph?—on the Council. Assigned to chase down an angel operative in Gemini and connecting with Cassie. Meeting Cancer and helping in her battle against a Founder. Not a chance meeting. It opened my eyes. Being deployed to the same installation as Chax was a script written by a… well, god, forcing me to cross swords with Seraph. Picking Seattle for my Abandonment, only to not be able to afford it and move to Olympia, where I met Leo and learned his family's story, how they suffered because they were family to Aries. How Leo tried to save his family, working through Chax, of all demons. Killing him in self-defense, placing me directly in Lucifer's path. The absolute apathy the leader of the Underworld showed, remaining uninvolved while His Council members ran rampant. The way the Council tried to force me into the grave, and the way they racked up the body count by forcing me to kill Leo to serve a greater purpose.

If fate wasn't real, then it went by a different name.

Whatever I was becoming, someone, or something, was behind it.

Dialphio grabbed my hands in her warm ones. "I'm not here to explain the nature of One. That's impossible. But I can try to explain to you what is happening. That's why I pushed you so hard during your Abandonment. You'll accept that you are the Great Prince, or I'll spend the rest of my life twisting your ear until you capitulate. Many depend on you accepting this role, just as many others have accepted what has been thrust upon them."

I tried to ignore my skipping heartbeat. "I'm trying. I really am." I hated hearing the way my voice shook.

Dialphio squeezed my hands. "I have something I think might help. Let me show you. It's the reason I had Bilba bring you here. Now is the perfect time to show you, to help you understand. Follow me."

Ralrek slid out of the way, allowing us to pass. "After you, my liege."

I gave him a light punch in the stomach, which he returned with a good-hearted slap on my back that almost made me trip. I turned to Bilba who wore a knowing gaze. Even he was aware of what was on the second floor, a level of the store where Dialphio prohibited entry. In fact, I remembered my first day on the job when she warned me from ever thinking of snooping around there. The secret was about to be revealed, at least to me. My friends already knew, those sneaky jerks.

At the landing, a single lantern that hung from the wall

illuminated a small door next to it. Behind the door was low mumbling.

"What's going on? What are we walking into?" I asked.

With her hand resting on the door handle, Dialphio said, "That's what you get to decide."

With that, she pushed the door handle down and stepped into the room.

The mumbling ceased. I took one more look behind me at my two friends.

"Keep moving, dumbass. Everyone's been dying to meet you, and you can't expect them to wait much longer. They'll tear the blessed place down if they don't see you soon," Ralrek smiled.

Blowing out a big breath to calm my nerves, I stepped onto the landing and into the room. The space was small, just large enough for us to crowd into. A single chair next to a two-foot tall table capped off with a modest lamp giving off a bright blue light sat along the wall to my left. An incubus sat in a chair, reading. Toward the back corner, only a few feet away, was a second door. Closed. Dialphio waited by it.

The incubus looked up from his book and shot to his feet. The book thumped on the floor and Dialphio groaned. "Mr. Sunstone, so great to meet you," the incubus said, stepping forward, his hand extended.

I took it, and he shook furiously. I looked at Dialphio, who was smiling. "Nice—nice to meet you," I said.

"Nostris," the incubus said, as if sharing his own name was an honor.

"Nostris, yes, nice to meet you," I repeated, not knowing what else to say while he still gripped my hand. At least the shaking had stopped.

"We need to meet the others," Dialphio interrupted this awkward introduction. "Let him go, Nostris. You can drool over him later."

"Ugh," Ralrek said behind me.

"Yes. Yes. Sorry. Again, great to meet you," he said in a rush before bending to pick up the book. He sat back down in the chair and flipped the book open. His eyes didn't return to the page as I made my way to the door.

Dialphio stood at the door, her hand resting on the handle. "You get to choose where this leads but know this; these demons have been working feverishly for years for you. Don't take that for granted."

I was stunned. "For me? For years?"

Bilba moved close behind me. "I told you when you were Abandoned, things have been moving."

"You knew about this?" I asked my best friend before looking at Ralrek. "And you?"

He shrugged nonchalantly. "Maybe a little. It's not like you didn't know I've been going to meetings while you were chilling in the Overworld with all those sexy mortals."

So this was what this was about. A movement was afoot ever since my return from my first mission. The Council publicly humiliated me because I didn't follow their orders to murder Aries. That humiliation had the desired effect mostly, further ostracizing me from a population who had already rejected me because I was the only demon in the history of Hell without magic. But it also galvanized small pockets of demons around the Circles as rumors spread. The Council kept me busy and so had life. Too busy to give much attention to any rumors of supposed rebel groups growing roots around the Underworld. During my Abandonment, all three demons had told me about how those bands of rebels were growing as I was an example of the injustices of a ruling body. Now, I was going to meet them. Face-to-face. Who said I was ready for this?

"What am I supposed to say?" I asked Dialphio, feeling like an impling on his first day at school.

"Start with hello, and go from there," she said with a chirping laugh and pressed the door handle down.

The voices inside the room stopped, though a sporadic wave of whispers rippled around.

Dialphio stepped into the room. "Sorry. That took longer than expected. But I have a pleasant surprise for you."

"Is he here?" a hidden figure said as I lingered outside the door.

"Really?" another asked.

"Oh my Lucifer, Dialphio. Did you?" a third asked, drawing out the last word.

A beefy finger tapped my shoulder. "Are you gonna hang in the doorway all day or are you finally going to meet the demons who have been itching to meet you?" Bilba asked.

Feeling like a complete idiot who was too full of himself to know how idiotic he actually looked, I stepped into the room.

I would love to say I looked cool, calm, and collected, but my shoulder bumped the door frame, and I stubbed my toe on the floor raised a quarter of an inch higher than the hall-way. My waving arms probably looked as graceless as the rest of me.

Behind me, Ralrek snickered. "Dumbass."

Bilba strode past me, giving a fist bump to a younger incubus half his age and twice his height. "Hey, Ret. How have you been?"

"Busy as heaven," the younger incubus said. "How about you?"

Ralrek received a warm greeting too. He returned it less personally than Bilba, but still wore a not-so-cocky smile as he craned his neck upward, doing those chin-jerks that incubi used to ask "what's up?" without requiring the words. He moved to the back of the room, past the six tables that reminded me of my middle-school chemistry class, and four towers of roughly bound books, and grabbed a can of Satan's Suds soda.

Anchoring my gaze on my two friends was easier than having to take in the rest of the room. Every stranger's eye was on me, and the enormity of what I was to these demons was a lot to handle.

Dialphio refused to allow me to hide. "Close the door behind you, Ezekial. You may be the Great Prince, but I still demand good manners in my store." She chirped a laugh which was accompanied by the others in the room.

I took my time closing the door and turning around. I was unsure what to say or how to proceed. Look, I'm not ungrateful. Anybody who cares enough to help others is a good demon in my book. But for the longest time, for years, I had been told there were demons who were not only sympathetic to my situation, but ready to act against the Council. Now, I was standing in what was a secret room in an obscure bookstore owned by the sweetest succubus in the world, looking into strange faces. Ten demons plus the three closest to me. This was a reading group, not a movement.

Discouraged, I managed a smile, though it felt more like invisible fingers pulling at the corners of my mouth. Remembering Dialphio's demand for good manners, I said, "Hi."

Then the tsunami hit. Ten strangers pushed forward. They introduced themselves and told me how excited they were that Dialphio planned to bring me home. They told me how grateful they were that I had survived the trial by combat. They claimed to know I would win.

As Dialphio encouraged everyone to take their seats and let me get comfortable, a young succubus with large ears and hazel eyes darted around the chairs to the back of the room and put together a plate of fruit for me. Rebels eat healthy, I guess.

The generous welcome overwhelmed me, but I was more than embarrassed when we spent the next half hour recalling my greatest accomplishments. When I say 'we', I mean them. They did the talking while I absorbed facts about my own life I had forgotten, while my ex–boss and two friends sat toward the back of the circle, smiling without rescuing me. These demons knew more about me than I knew about myself. A weird twist to my day, almost like I'd been Abolished and was floating in the ethereal background in another dimension, watching friends and family recall my life.

Dialphio interrupted. "I'm sorry everyone, but Ezekial cannot stay much longer."

Groans of disappointment filled the back room.

"Yeah, sorry, but I've got to get back to..." I started, almost referring to my new apartment as "home" before stopping myself. "Well, I've got to get back to the new place the Council set up for me. I imagine they have someone watching it and will snoop around before long." Intense gazes greeted that statement, so I laughed nervously and tried to lighten the mood. "Hope they think I'm out shopping, which is also something I need to get done tonight. But it was great meeting everyone."

"Not so fast, Mr. Hero," Dialphio said, stepping to take a central spot in the room. "I know this has been overwhelming for everyone, not just Ezekial. But this is an important point in our history. How we proceed from here is crucial, not only in terms of which direction we take, but if we achieve what we want to. Ezekial has a lot on his mind. He's not even settled in his new place. But we also don't know how many of these opportunities we are going to get. For all we know, they may put their grip on him as soon as he returns home."

Well, that wasn't a comforting thought.

"Ezekial, you have heard what they know about you," Dialphio said, talking to me as well as the group. "But what I want you to hear are their thoughts on the future of the Underworld, and what they want to see. Each one of us is privy to your history, I think you know that now." She chirped a laugh that said the depth of the group's knowledge did not embarrass her, but that maybe they had turned it on heavier than she anticipated. "What I want you to take away from this meeting is more than the words they've shared and are going to share. I want you to take away their presence, the fact they are here. Until you arrived, they were busy copying *The Histories of the Balance*." She waved at the stacks of books along the different tables in the room.

So that's what those towers were. Copies upon copies of the most truthful book I'd ever read.

"Why are you hand-copying *The Histories*?" I asked.

"We very well can't go to a publisher, now can we?" Dialphio asked. "Any publisher would report us to the Council before we walked out of the building. So we have spent months making as many copies as possible. We will spend many more making as many as possible. That's not the important point. They're not here to socialize. They were working before you arrived to help others around the Circles to understand their own place in the Underworld a little better."

"And maybe ask questions," an older succubus, dressed in a garish purple blouse said with a biting tone, receiving skeptical scoffs from a younger pair of incubi to the side of the room.

"You've copied all those?" I imagined the hand-cramping that had happened in this room.

"Those and more. We don't keep all our copies here, of course." Dialphio nodded to the older succubus after answering. "Yes, Illis. Hopefully, those who get copies will think. That's a discussion for another day." Dialphio turned to me. "But they are here. They are acting. They are doing something that, if the Council were to find out, would put them in a prison. These demons could lose their way of life. Lose their safety. Their autonomy. And they don't have what you have. None have the access to influential demons you enjoy. And they don't have that," Dialphio finished, pointing at Creed.

"Can we see it?" the young incubus who Bilba befriended, named Ret, asked.

"Yeah, can we?" one of the scoffing incubi said.

"That would be so cool," a younger succubus, definitely the cutest, fluttered her eyelashes as she contributed.

"Dialphio doesn't like weapons," I said lightly.

"Oh, show them. You enjoy showing off your stick," Ralrek said from the back of the room, shoving an apple in his mouth and tearing off a chunk.

"Please, do. Let's get this over with," Dialphio said.

Most of the group clapped excitedly.

I pulled Creed out, making sure I had enough room, and gave it a shake. The halberd sprang to its full six feet, its blades flashing. Most of the gathered group jumped back. "Creed, meet everyone. Everyone, this is Creed, the biggest pain in my ass not named Ralrek."

That drew nervous laughter.

"Okay, okay. You've seen it. Ezekial, please put that thing away," Dialphio said, trying to sound lighthearted. As I collapsed the halberd and slid it back into the loop, Dialphio resumed, "Let's share our vision for the future."

And the group did. I went through the plate of fruit, grateful for the light meal since it might be the only one I would eat tonight, while they shared their opinions on matters pertaining to the governance of our realm. Bilba brought me another fresh plate, this one with meats, cheeses, and two rolls of bread so I didn't have to get up as the group shared their opinions. I nodded my thanks.

The rebels talked about the freedom they craved, the fact they wanted to see a day when they didn't have to worry about what they said and where they went. They wanted to live without fear, of perceived notions that Lucifer and His Council might take offense to any slight. They wanted to live without the nagging paranoia of a Council listening in on the activities of the Underworld to catch anyone who lacked absolute allegiance. They wanted freedom of travel, not only around their own Circle but also between Circles.

Illis, in the garish purple blouse, shared her desire to see the Overworld before she was too old to enjoy travel. She hypothesized Hell's leaders could devise a well–managed, low–risk mechanism and process so Hell's responsible residents could see the mortal realm. She mentioned it could even be a motivational tool for demons of all status.

They had ideas, small and grand. Most of what they communicated made sense.

"This is fine, but you realize the Council will never go for any of it, right?" I asked.

"That's the point," an incubus so gaunt his face could have been chiseled out of stone and then a loose layer of skin draped over it, said. "They won't go for anything that doesn't gain them more power, more influence. Each day the status quo is allowed to exist is another day we lose our ability to change it."

"Hear, hear," Dialphio said. Everyone mimicked her call.

"So how does that happen? How do you change it? Because the Council doesn't care what you think or what you want," I said, pointing at Bilba and Ralrek who hung at the back of the room. "Ask them if you don't believe me. Those two have been through as much crap at the hands of the Council as me."

"Simple," Illis of the garish purple blouse said. "Someone else, you, need to be installed as Lucifer." There were "'uh-huhs" and "mmmhmmms" at the old succubus's comment.

I tried not to laugh, but failed. "I can't be Lucifer."

"Why not?" the wide-eyed succubus who had built my first plate of food asked.

"It's a title, nothing more," the loose–skinned incubus added. "Anyone can be elevated to the title. Why not someone deserving? Why not someone the Council can't touch?"

I couldn't believe what I was hearing. This was heresy on the highest level, far more severe than the blasphemy charge I faced after my argument with Seraph in Baghdad. Dialphio was putting herself, these demons, my friends, and myself at risk. I searched her face for a sign she understood how grievous this conversation was but found nothing.

"That's not even possible, and if it was, how do you see it happening?" I said, stuffing goat cheese in my mouth before I said something I regretted. I had to remember these demons were here for me, had been working to spread the same message I wanted other demons to know. They weren't the enemy. They were dreamers who didn't understand how reality worked.

Dialphio stepped forward. "Well, see, that's the problem. We can't agree on that."

"That's what I've been trying to tell you since you were Abandoned," Ralrek piped in, waving a stick of salami at the group. "All they do is argue over who gets to sit in the seat of Lucifer, and how that happens. How many months now, Dialphio? Still no resolution."

"But you're here now," the young succubus with large ears and hazel eyes said. "That changes everything."

"Not yet, Zenas," Dialphio said. "We have to figure out a way to position someone to challenge the title. Unless we're now agreeing to go with the assassination plan?"

The way Dialphio made the comment told me she thought that was the dumbest of dumb ideas. However they planned on pulling that off, I had to agree. An assassination was the Council's modus operandi. Not ours—was it 'ours' already? I wouldn't be part of anything of the sort.

The group broke into bickering clusters, each championing their preferred plan. It was all noise to my ears. I'd had a long past few days, and the shower I took before leaving to see Cassie and Virgo only helped me refresh. I was tapped out, physically, mentally, and emotionally. It didn't prepare me for a long night of politics and scheming.

"What would you have us do? We can't take them on, but he can," an incubus, six feet tall, with a round face and long forehead sporting a backward blazeball cap said, referring to me.

"We are not risking him. He is the icon," a succubus who would be comfortable in a library said, nudging her horn–rimmed glasses with a knuckle.

A good idea. I liked not being risked. Maybe when I wasn't so tired I'd have better insight for them, but I had nothing at the moment. I was impressed my brain still had the functionality to make my lungs expand.

Dialphio spoke so firmly-yet-softly all the attention turned to her. "Ezekial, your trial threw a wrench into things and we're still adjusting. Zenas is correct. Everything changes now that you're home. With Bilba able to help you move around, we can continue this when you've rested. It was important for the group to see. This will push us on in ways you can only imagine. Take time to adjust and get settled. We should be encouraged," she said, now turning more to the group than me. "I know we have waited for this moment for a long time. But we need to give Ezekial time. We need to understand what he has been through. The compassion we ask of a future government is the same we must show to him now."

The meeting adjourned, and the group approached one-by-one to deliver personal messages of encouragement and gratitude. I accepted them, even though I had done nothing. The fear I would let a bunch of demons down was very real. I kept that to myself.

We remained long enough for me to stuff my face with as much food as possible—since it was now obvious I wasn't getting to a store tonight—before saying our farewells.

Nostris, the informal door guard, stood when I walked out, shaking my hand rapidly and thanking me for the appearance as if I were some sort of celebrity.

My head spun as I tromped back to the first floor.

"Bilba, hold off on a gateway for just a second. There's

something I want to give Ezekial before he leaves," Dialphio said, disappearing behind the half–wall of books at the back of the store where, at least in the past, she hid her desk. When she returned, she carried a small bag.

"No, I can't," I said, recognizing it for what it was.

"You can, and you will, or I'll go right back upstairs and tell those selfless demons you refuse to accept their gift," Dialphio said.

"This... this is from them?"

"Yes," Dialphio said, extending the bag. "Take it. Otherwise, you'd insult them."

I did. It was heavy with coin. Tears were coming. I would not cry in front of Ralrek again.

Thankfully, Dialphio saved me. "Take him home. We all still have notebooks, right, boys?"

We nodded. It was easier than forming words.

"Good. We'll set something up soon," Dialphio said, closing in and hugging me. "Go get some rest. You deserve it."

I turned to Bilba. "Take me home, buddy. The Great Prince needs a nap."

10

UNDERWORLD, FIFTH CIRCLE

"It's a good thing you're a free demon." Bilba laughed, scratching his face with one of his black fingernails.

"Why is that?"

"Then you wouldn't have been able to help me."

That was true. If I hadn't earned my freedom through killing an innocent incubus, I would have been in prison or slowly dying in the Overworld until Bilba and I could figure out how to sneak me through a rift to an eternal realm hideaway. Instead, I was in Melchiot's School for Passage Training. The name, admittedly, was a mouthful and pretty bland. The name was also far less impressive than her facility.

We were in the middle of a huge bay stretching countless yards in every direction. The largest building I'd ever seen in the Fifth, which was so crowded with demons and buildings and homes I didn't think anyone could afford the real estate of something this vast. The walls were padded with white foam, which Melchiot said soundproofed the building. When I asked why it needed soundproofing, she stared at me blankly for an uncomfortable time before explaining, in slight detail, that the tests required it. Depending on the student, their test and the spells it required could be extremely disturbing for the surrounding neighborhood.

"Are you sure I'm going to be helpful?" I asked Melchiot.

Her dark eyes flitted around as if she was nervous. "Most definitely. Of anyone who can test Bilba, it will be you. You too," she added.

Ralrek picked at his fingernails.

The tall demon with immaculate, greased back black hair was two dozen steps away. In between staring at his long fingers, he scanned the open bay. At Melchiot's question, he grunted.

"But you are... unique," Melchiot continued, focusing on me again, "and at this stage, Bilba needs that. Especially now that his test date was moved up."

"What? When did that happen?" I asked, turning to my best friend who looked away.

"Oh... I don't remember," he said.

"The day after we were at Dialphio's," Ralrek said, eaves-dropping from his inspection location.

"They moved your date up after you took me to the Over-world and to The Book Abyss?" I asked, trying ever so hard to keep the edge out of my voice.

"Yes," he drew the word out, drenched in guilt.

"This isn't something to blow off," I waved my hands around. "We have to stop this nonsense. You can't be opening gateways and rifts anymore. Not for me. Not for anyone."

Bilba curled his hands into fists, planting them on his hips. "Oh? And how are you going to get around and attend to important tasks?"

"I won't."

He drove his fists firmer into his hips. "So the rest of the Underworld and the parts of the Overworld you can influ-ence suffer because I have to take a test sooner? No, this isn't a decision you get to make for me, Zeke. Sorry. Just the fact.

I'm fine with this. That's why you and Ralrek are here. I'm ready. These are just the final preparations."

I turned to Ralrek, seeking help. He looked at me with a flash of a raised eyebrow and a half–shrug. No help there.

I tried his mentor. "Melchiot, talk sense into him. If he's not ready, he can't take the Passage. It's too dangerous. We don't need to rush."

Her fluttering dark eyes never found mine. Instead, they always found something more interesting on the floor or in the air around us. "I have said that many times. Bilba has great skill, though untamed. Not one I'd typically approve of testing at this level, but he's taking the Passage anyway."

"He's being made to take it," I corrected.

"I'm going to. I have to do it," Bilba interjected. "We can continue standing around here, wasting time, or you can help me prepare. Which is it going to be? Regardless of what we do here today or until I am standing in the Passage, the Council is going to do what they want, when they want. Either I prepare the best I can, or I lie down for them. Which one?"

Everyone waited for my answer in the silence of the giant bay.

"Fine," I said.

Bilba's ears pinkened, and he offered a soft smile. "That's what I wanted to hear. Thank you." He turned to his mentor. "Melchiot, let's get this thing going. Where do you need me?"

Melchiot started off toward the front of the space without answering. A few solitary footsteps later, she turned, her eyes flicking from Bilba to the floor, to the ceiling, to the walls. "Follow me. I'll show you where I want you for the start."

"Okay," Bilba said, trotting after her.

"What about us?" I called out.

"Just stay there for the moment," Melchiot said without turning around.

I went over to Ralrek, who was standing with his arms crossed, still scanning the bay. "What are you looking for?"

"Nothing," he said with a quick shake of his head. "Just trying to analyze this space since I have a feeling it won't look like this once the test starts."

"Oh, I hadn't thought about that," I said.

"I'm sure there's a lot you haven't thought about, Zeke." Ralrek smiled.

"Instead of being an ass, how about you tell me why haven't you applied to take the Passage? We have a few minutes. Not that I want you at risk either," I said, softening what could have been a hard statement. "You ready to listen to him talk crap about being a Major demon when he passes? You are more the bragging type than he is. I would have thought you'd try to beat him to the punch."

Something flickered across Ralrek's face, but then it was gone. "Do you think I'm so insecure that Bilba becoming a Major demon would bother me?"

"Yes."

Ralrek surprised me by winking. "Okay, that's fair. It's probably true. The fact is, I applied. Just got shot down."

"Sorry to hear that. Did they at least give you a reason?"

Ralrek waved his hand in the air as if he was pushing away an annoying faerie. "They gave me some garbage about my unproven heritage."

"What in the Underworld does that mean?"

He said, "No idea. They talked about my father's undocumented birth. Absolute bullshit. But I'm not bothered by it, to be honest. Yes, I would love to be a Major demon one day. You know how many guys I'd have to fend off if I was? Sure, it's a sucker punch to the ego to know Bilba will be one long before me. But I love him, and I'm happy for him. I'm so disillusioned by all the garbage going on, I can't bother wondering why."

I got that and told him so. I'm not sure at what level

Passage applications were approved, but I'm sure someone on the Council had their hands in it. My mind was put at ease by the way Ralrek looked at peace with the decision. I ignored the nagging part of my brain that reminded me little moved Ralrek's emotional needle lately anytime he wasn't face-to-face with the Council.

Melchiot came back to us. Bilba was stationed in one corner of the bay, at the furthest point from us he could be without being outside. Her eyes danced to various spots on and around us as she briefed us on expectations. "So we will begin soon. This will be an intense test, the most intense he has ever had. You two are critical to his preparations. You need to push his limits. He must be pushed."

"Pushed, got it," I said, trying to move this conversation along. "But what do we actually do?"

"When I begin the test, this," she said, rotating her head in a circle, her eyes dancing from the ceiling lights to the floor mats, "will change. Of course it will be a complex illusion, but still just an illusion. It will feel very real, as will the pain, should you suffer any injuries."

I flinched at that. "We could be injured?"

Melchiot's head bobbed. "Absolutely. All three of you could be. Will be, most likely, if this goes as I hope. It's normal for these types of tests. In fact, I would be surprised if he didn't injure you. Disappointed, because it will mean that he wasn't pushed to his limits, as I hope he will be. As he needs to be. Remember, this is an illusion. We will still be in the Underworld, so there's no fear of suffering something permanent, or becoming a casualty. Please keep in mind, however, the Passage is not in the Underworld, so Bilba will very much be at risk inside the real thing. Which is why you have to push him as hard as you can in this test." She shook her head. "Also very irregular. Too soon. Much too soon. Challenge him, please. Otherwise, he won't be ready."

"Okay," Ralrek and I agreed.

"Then let's begin," Melchiot said, gesturing to the corner opposite Bilba. "If the two of you would stand there, please. As soon as I cast the illusionary spell, you can begin. Your aim is to make him quit, to break, to capitulate, or be injured."

She spun and walked away, her head jittering side to side as though talking to herself.

"Are you ready to hurt him?" Ralrek said, looking down at me sideways.

I shook my head. "No. What about you?"

Ralrek looked to Bilba. "He's a pain in my ass, but no, I'm not ready to hurt him." He drew a breath so deep I could hear it filling his lungs. "We've got to."

"Yeah, we've got to," I repeated, thoughts turning to the Council's rising body count. What Ralrek and I did here today might go a long way toward keeping Bilba from being added to that tally.

"Don't forget, he's such a pain in the ass he'll probably hurt us long before we hurt him," Ralrek said, flattening his hand and running it along the sides of his hair.

"Okay, gentleman," Melchiot called from the front of the bay. She might have spoken loudly, but her voice barely reached us due to the dampening effect of the soundproofing pads stuck to the wall like mosquitoes flattened on the front of a runaway chimera carriage. "We begin, be ready.

She clapped her hands and darkness descended.

"Shit," I said, my hand going to my hip to pull Creed free. My skin itched with Ralrek's budding spell. Giving Creed a shake, I heard but couldn't see the ax heads and dagger open. I wasn't going to hurt Bilba, but Creed would come in handy to keep my favorite pain in the ass at bay.

"I can't see a thing," Ralrek whispered to my side.

I reached over with my free hand to feel him out. I waved the empty air. "Where are you?"

Before he could answer, the shadow of a blackened wall shot up in front of my face as gray light filled the new world.

I had almost stepped into the wall, so close I smelled the wet mildew emanating from the stone. Ralrek, by my side, pushed away from it and turned around. He looked as confused as I felt. We were at the closed end of an alley. Walls on either side crowded us. The alley was only eight feet across.

"What the heaven was that? Where are we?" my friend asked.

"No idea. But I don't like where we are right now. How about finding someplace with less of a... trap feel?" I suggested.

Ralrek tipped his head a couple times.

We crept to the end of the narrow alley, me holding Creed in both hands, not willing to attempt spinning it to create my defensive shield with such a small margin for error. Ralrek walked beside me. His hands began to glow as we made our way toward the mouth of the alley. They were now turning orange with the heat of the spell he held.

Reaching the end, we peeked around opposite corners. I took the left. A street stretched away, empty. No carriages, no demons. No impling's playing. Not even a sylph flitting above our heads.

"Anything?" I called over my shoulder.

"Nothing. Quiet," Ralrek said.

Too quiet. "Let me go first. I can create a shield to throw off whatever he has planned."

"Volunteering to take the brunt of his attack? Sounds good to me."

We stepped out of the alley and I rotated Creed, creating a small shield the size of my chest. Doing more at this point would only kick-start the process of wearing me out before we found Bilba. In the back of my mind, I knew we were only inside Melchiot's school and those walls contained everything I was seeing. But this illusion was so massive, so authentic, it felt like Melchiot dropped us in the middle of the Eighth

Circle. I half-expected to see Marijon stroll around the corner, her staff complete with the C-Clamp she used to steal Creed. Even the sky above burned with the azure of the Hellfire, so bright it almost washed out the rough texture of the stalactites hanging from bedrock above. Best to save as much of my energy as I could for whatever Bilba had planned.

We reached the end of the block with no signs of threat. The intersection gave us three choices. "Any preference?"

"I swear we were facing the front of the building when she turned on this illusion," Ralrek reasoned. "But then we were facing that wall and turned around a hundred and eighty degrees, so we should be walking to the back of the building."

"True, but as far as we've walked, we should have run into the wall by now," I said, feeling slightly helpful.

He shrugged. "Your guess is as good as mine. Let's just walk straight for now and see where that takes us. If we find the edge of the building, we'll know where not to flee if Bilba tries to corner us."

The logic was sound. We crossed the intersection.

Halfway across the street, exposed in the open, I sensed my best friend begin his attack. Magic.

"Get ready!" I shouted, spinning Creed faster to create a larger barrier. As soon as we were exposed, I felt the sticki-ness of a Deception spell. Bilba was near, and he had seen us first. As I scanned the buildings to my left and straight ahead, the crackle of flames of Ralrek's spell burst to life. "Check your surroundings. He's here. I just don't know where. I'm seeing nothing on my side."

After a moment, Ralrek answered, "Nothing here either."

I was about to recommend we get to cover when a zipping sound, faint, but growing, approached at a rapid speed.

A projectile, roughly a foot long and as thin as a finger, pierced the road. Then another. Then another. A fourth. The projectiles came from the same direction and they were miss-ing. Bilba's aim sucked.

"Move behind me," I said, sliding as close to Ralrek as I could without slicing one of his arms off with the spinning halberd blades. Ralrek moved without question as more and more of Bilba's... things pierced the air and punctured the street which was now taking on the semblance of a flattened porcupine.

Behind the shield, we didn't have to worry about those nasty long darts, but we had to find him before he changed tactics. I was tired of operating in reaction mode. "I'll hold this and keep both of our asses safe. See if you can find him."

I did my best to see if I could spot my annoying pink-eared friend while holding Creed's shield. After searching under the storm of pale darts, I was frustrated, and a little sweaty. And I don't like to sweat.

Ralrek growled behind me. "There he is. To your left, third story. Four windows past that sign."

I found the sign. A rectangle of white plastic hung off the building over the street. The plastic had a large hole punctured in the top corner. The sign read "Grand Hotel." By the looks of it, nothing was or ever had been grand about that place. Just beyond it, white curtains billowed from an open window. Each time they swayed to the side, I spotted Bilba's round cheeks.

So I said what all best friends say. "Light his ass up."

I stepped forward, maintaining Creed's shield as Ralrek hurled fireball after fireball toward Bilba's location. I don't know much about aiming spells, since I'm a magicless demon, but either Ralrek sucked, or it was harder to hit something from this distance than I imagined. His fireballs smashed against the sidewalk and front door of the building. Ralrek adjusted his aim and his fireballs burst against the stone walls. One wayward one even caught that white plastic hotel sign and blew it off the bar holding it above the street. The sign was melting as it flew out of sight over the roof of the building.

Though his aim was poor, at least Ralrek's counter attack cut off Bilba's dart throwing. Then the scratching sensation of the Fire caster diminished. It was still there, like Bilba's stickiness, just subtle. Both magic users were holding their power. Holding and waiting.

"We've got him on the run, but he's preparing another spell," I said.

Staying behind me, Ralrek replied, "Got it. I'm ready the second he steps out. By the way, has anyone ever told you how creepy it is when you sense us casting?"

"I get told I'm a creep quite often," I said.

"Shocker."

Good to know he found humor in the feedback I'd received from succubi for the past few thousand years.

"As long as the building doesn't have a back door, we've got him trapped," I started. "We just need to—"

"Turn around!" Ralrek said, panicked.

I spun, shocked at how disturbed he sounded and wondering how in the heaven Bilba had not only gotten out of the building without detection but also outflanked us to launch a sneak attack. My jaw dropped at what I saw.

Bilba wasn't behind us, ready to launch an attack. His darts were. Sounds crazy, I know. What's crazier is that they were no longer darts.

"That little bastard," Ralrek snarled.

I could think of a few more creative names to call my best friend.

The darts he fired with poor aim, the ones sharp enough to pierce the brimstone road, weren't darts at all, but petrified snakes. Now, they were wiggling free and slithering in our direction. Dozens of them, an army of animated reptiles. The last remaining one popped its head out of the road and raced to join the reptilian army.

"I hope you have something up your sleeve, because I

can't fight all of them," I said, not taking a chance to peel my eyes away from these creepy, crawling agents of Bilba.

The scratching sensation of my partner's magic evaporated. I shot him a panicked look.

"I have to change my spell. The one I had wouldn't work against... those," Ralrek offered unhelpfully. "Take care of them until I start a new one."

Well, wasn't this just great?

I stepped forward, part of my mind calling out to Creed to see if I could activate the stubborn halberd. But the dumb stick wasn't looking for a fight. The ax and dagger blades were cold, gray steel. They would do damage to the snakes, but a bit of Hellfire magic would come in handy while Ralrek was doing whatever casters do in their heads to form their spells.

The snakes, though animated through Deception magic, were far too intelligent to attack en masse. They spread out, coming at me from all angles. I attacked the first one attempting to dart past me to get at Ralrek. The wiggling beast was too slow for Creed's dagger. I pierced it, skewering the poor thing before turning and seeing three more.

"Hurry up, Ralrek," I said, feeling my panic rising as I slashed at the three, splitting each in half.

No scratchy sensation. What was taking so long? What kind of spell was he working on? Was he trying to draw on the Hellfire itself? No sensation of Fire magic, but the stickiness of a Deception spell crawled across my skin.

Two more snakes met Creed, much to their misfortune, and I still didn't get help from my friendly Fire dude. The snakes had slowed, spreading out, now encircling me. I flicked my glance behind me in a desperate plea for intervention and saw why Ralrek was letting me do all the work.

Ralrek was in the middle of the street where I had left him, and he was shouting at me. I couldn't hear a single word, even though only a short distance separated us. He thrust both arms forward and slammed his hands in unison. His hands stopped at the same point in the air, as if striking an object. He spun in a circle, thrusting his hands out in my direction and shouting, repeating his movement, this time to the right. Same action. Same reaction. Hands that stopped in mid-air. Then I understood. He was inside some sort of barrier. A box. Bilba had imprisoned Ralrek in an invisible box, and Ralrek never saw coming. I never felt it. Bilba had kept his dart-snake spell active while constructing a second spell, disguising the second behind the first because he knew I could feel his Ability before he finished conjuring. The sneaky bastard. Since when could he do that?

I was fighting a chubby magic user and two dozen snakes all by myself. Thanks a lot, Ralrek.

"You're a real dick, Bilba," I shouted to the empty street, hoping my best friend could hear me. If he could and didn't call off the small boas, he would soon become my second-best friend.

The stickiness didn't dispel.

The snakes came from every direction at once, and I did the only thing I could at that moment, I struck out before being struck at.

I cut down as many of the wriggling bastards as I could while on the move, hoping to slow their attacks. One here. Another there. Creed's blades cut through Bilba's reptilian forces. During one turn, I glanced in Ralrek's direction and noticed he was slamming his hands against the invisible barrier, but I also noticed something else, something more troubling. Ralrek was not alone inside the barrier. He was about to become the victim of his own magic.

A wall of flame grew taller behind him. Gray smoke rose into the air, trapped within the box that contained the tall incubus. As busy with the snakes as I was, I couldn't make out the exact dimensions of the prison, but they were becoming clearer with each second as Ralrek's flames cast off smoke.

I tried to move in his direction, but three snakes cut me off, each pulling back and hissing, ready to strike. One dove at my feet while another launched itself in the air. I took out the one in the air with a slashing move, but the one going for my feet wrapped itself around my ankle before I got a clear swipe at it.

I don't know what you consider gross, but having a foot–long magical snake coil around your foot has to rank toward the top of my list.

I tried to shake the snake off while moving sideways toward Ralrek's prison. Another snake darted at my foot as two others launched themselves. Like last time, I took out the greater threat, cutting the heads off the airborne pair, sacrificing my other leg in the process. Now, I had a small boa wrapped around both ankles, adding a surprising amount of weight to my frame.

I picked up on another inconvenience as I ambled toward Ralrek. My toes tingled. These little conjured bastards were cutting off the blood to my feet. Snarling, I entertained ways to make Bilba pay when this was over.

Ten feet away from Ralrek's invisible prison, his screams still didn't reach me. One hand on the invisible barrier, Ralrek's other grabbed his shirt collar and pulled it over his mouth. More and more smoke filled the box. My friend and fight partner disappeared in a gray cloak.

"Okay, let him out and make this a fair fight," I called into the open air.

Silence.

Four boas darted at my feet. No longer could I move as swiftly as I had before because of the two clinging to my ankles. This was going to be trouble.

I backed toward the invisible prison, the only direction I

didn't have to worry about being attacked by the snakes because Bilba's box blocked the path now.

I stabbed one of the approaching snakes, and cut the tails from two with Creed's dagger, before bringing it up and over. One strike, three dead snakes. A three-for-one deal. A fourth refused to be added to the total.

This snake caught me just above the elbow. Like one of those metal wrists snaps, it coiled around me in a flash and squeezed. Three out of four appendages now carried the additional weight of snakes spending their afternoon constricting my blood flow. Slowed by them, I still had double-digits to take on.

Looking over my shoulder, I could see only Ralrek's hand on the invisible barrier. The hand was at ground level. As revolting as snakes were, Ralrek was having a worse day than I.

Even as the rest of Bilba's snake army charged, I lifted Creed and spun in a half–circle, stealing a portion of the move from *Shadows Fall*, and sliced the air open with the double-ax head. Creed's asymmetrical ax bit through two snakes on its way toward Bilba's conjured prison. When blade met spell, spell lost.

Creed struck the barrier. The collision sent a vibration up my arms and into my shoulders. There was a disappointing fizzle as the halberd broke the barrier—I expected so much more, something cooler, from my powerful friend. Smoke billowed out and into the open sky. Just not fast enough. Ralrek was still in trouble.

At that point, I remembered what Melchiot had told us. Fighting Bilba like this wasn't to our advantage. That's not what the Passage was about. For Bilba to be tested, he had to be pushed to face his greatest fears. What we had been doing was nothing more than an intense sparring session. For thousands of years, Bilba had kicked my ass in Eve's Sanctuary whenever we'd sparred. That changed once I received Creed and became adept with the halberd. But I had been decaying in the Overworld while Bilba had been receiving training from a renowned Passage trainer. He wasn't the same magic user he'd been. This wasn't a normal sparring session. Yet I was treating this as if the situation and my friend were the same I was torturing for fun in Eve's garden.

Melchiot said the key was to push him to his limit. We hadn't done that to him yet.

The way my feet tingled and my left arm dangled because of his stupid snakes, coupled with the way Ralrek lay unconscious in the street, I had no problem using Bilba's fears against him.

And I had to do so now.

Fear. I knew exactly what Bilba feared.

If my friend wanted to fight dirty, I could strap on the cleats and play with the best of them. The Council taught me how to do that for years now.

"You want to know why you're so worried about no one loving you?" I shouted into the open air, hating every bit of what I was going to do, but desperate to throw Bilba off his game so Ralrek and I had a fighting chance at... well, this fight. "This is why, right here. This is why you don't have a girlfriend and never have. This is why no one loves you, except for your father. This is why your mom is gone. This is why she rejected you when you found her at the flower shop!"

Yes, it was cruel. But, in a twisted way, I was doing this for my best friend. Bilba's greatest fear—losing the love of the demons who were supposed to love him.

Bilba's snake army hissed simultaneously. So, he could hear me, huh?

The slithering reptiles attacked. One of the larger snakes raced past me while I was busy with two of its partners, going straight for Ralrek. Reaching him, it wrapped itself around the fallen demon's throat. Ralrek's head flopped as the snake coiled, twisting itself around the tall demon with such force it pulled his entire six-and-a-half-foot tall body over. I gagged.

The snakes on my ankles and arm squeezed. I think I heard something crack. Maybe I was imagining it. Seven more were on me before I could take them out with Creed. Wrapping around my waist, my free arm, my neck. I fell to my knees, dropping my halberd and trying to pull them off in a panic.

White spots blotted my vision as the snakes, together, crushed.

I was going to kick Bilba's ass.

Somewhere in the distance, I heard a loud mumbling like underwater voices.

The world faded, then there was a sudden flash of light, then complete darkness.

I fell forward.

Some point later, I was lying on a cold floor instead of a brimstone street. I snapped my eyes open. We were in Melchiot's training bay, the empty streets and ghostly buildings erased.

I scrambled up, feeling at my neck. No snake. Looking at my arms and ankles and waist. No snakes. A few feet away, Ralrek groaned and rolled onto his back. I went to him. He peered up at me through squinted eyes and gave me a weak smile. "I never thought I'd be so happy to see your ugly face," he said.

I extended my hand in an offer to help him up. "Me either. You okay?"

It was an effort to pull the taller incubus to his feet considering there was over a half a foot of height difference between us, but together, we pulled it off. He nodded. "Yes, yes. But Bilba won't be when I'm done with him."

My gaze had already gone to the other end of the bay, where Melchiot and Bilba were talking in hushed tones. By the way Bilba hung his head, I didn't think Ralrek could do any worse than our friend's mentor was at the moment.

I tilted my head in their direction. "Let's go see what that's about."

Bilba looked at us through his eyelashes as we approached. "Hey guys," he said in a somber voice.

"Nice work back there, asshole," I said, only half-joking.

"Yeah… I guess," he said in response.

Melchiot's eyes darted at us and away. "Good work or not, he failed."

"He failed?" Ralrek asked.

"How?" I asked.

Her eyes never stopped moving. "He didn't control his emotions. When you made the comment about no one loving him, he lost control of his power. Unacceptable. Absolutely unacceptable."

"So he fails for that?" I asked before throwing a sideways look at Bilba. "Sorry, buddy. I just did what I guessed was called for to throw you off. Plus, we were getting our asses handed to us."

The tips of his ears burned pink. "I know. I'm glad you did. I mean, it hurt, but I know you would have never said something like that outside this context." He sighed. His breath quaked. "I've got a lot of work to do."

Turning back to Melchiot, I said, "I guess I don't understand why he would fail for that. He kicked our asses. I'm not all that, but I've given a number of demons a headache. Ralrek is no slouch himself. Bilba can open gateways and rifts that go undetected. Yet, he failed?"

Melchiot cupped her hands. "If a demon loses control of his emotions, he loses control of his reason. Without reason, he cannot control his Abilities. In the Underworld and daily life that's not a problem. But in the Passage it will be. To be a Major demon is a great honor few achieve. The Underworld cannot have demons of that status who are incapable of controlling their emotions, even in their rawest form. It's the most difficult part of the Passage beyond ensuring one's own survival. Therefore, it is a great measure. Bilba showed frailties when you taunted him. He's not ready."

Melchiot spun, walking away as she rocked her head, her long curls shaking.

Bilba hung his head and then looked up. He chewed on the corner of his lip. This was a tough loss. A major setback.

I went to him, wrapping my arm around his shoulders. "Come on. Let's go get a beer. We've earned it."

11

UNDERWORLD/OLYMPIA

ONE OF THE best things about having a strange ability to heal speedily is that, in fact, you heal... uh, swiftly. It's pretty cool.

The day after Bilba abused us during his failed Passage preparation test, I was in the kitchen in my quiet apartment in the smelly Sixth Circle. No offense to anyone with an affinity for the Sixth, but I haven't lived here long enough to gain an appreciation for its unique aroma.

While I cooked, I focused on how good I felt after the ass-kicking. Things could have been much worse. If that had happened in any other context than Bilba's Passage practice test. If another Deception user had been the one casting spells for nefarious reasons. My mind raced with thoughts of what I could have done better, should have done better. Still, I felt well enough to conduct another round of self-criticism. I hoped Ralrek did as well. I reached out to him via the demonic notebook, but hadn't heard back. I hoped he was resting.

Bilba's test had been a test for me as well. Like him, I had failed. I couldn't allow myself to be put in that position again. Overrun by a small army of snakes and a single caster was not okay in my book.

Basically, I was pissed at myself.

Setting my pan to the side of the flame, I turned to the refrigerator to grab hellion eggs, already missing the Overworld version that are far tastier. My eyes caught the notebook on my kitchen table. The seal of Lucifer burned bright with an incoming message. Ralrek checking in?

Eggs forgotten, I went and flipped it open. The message was from Cassie. I wasn't disappointed. Cassie giving me attention could never be a disappointment, even though I needed to know if the tall buffoon was okay or not.

CASSIE: *Hey, Zeke. I hope everything is well and that you are getting settled. I know I'm a terrible friend who only writes when she needs something, but I need to talk. Actually, I need your help. Incidents have inflamed tensions. Let me know as soon as you see this if you can come?*

I pulled the quill out and scribbled a quick note.

ZEKE: *Of course. Let me message you-know-who and see if he can hook me up with transportation. I'll let you know as soon as I hear something. I hope all is well.*

I added the last bit as an afterthought, feeling tacky, then I drew a line under the message, and addressed the next one to Bilba.

ZEKE: *Hey, any chance you have time for a friendly chat?*

"Friendly chat" was our code for a personal visit. You have to be sneaky about these things.

I made my breakfast, periodically checking the notebook for a new message. I wasn't only finished cooking and eating but also on my way to the shower, when I finally heard back from my best friend.

BILBA: *Yeah, give me an hour.*

I relayed the message to Cassie and then got ready for my day. By the sounds of it, it might be a long one.

Bilba showed up. Finally. Ralrek did too. As well-groomed as ever, Ralrek's neck still bore the bruises of Bilba's snake attack.

I was glad to see him looking nearly as handsome as ever. The devil. "Can the two of you do nothing without the other?" I quipped.

Bilba and Ralrek looked at each other and shrugged in unison.

"Dorks." I shook my head. "Ready to go?"

Ralrek was past me, his head bent inside my refrigerator. Obviously, he was feeling fine. "You're living like a bachelor."

"I am a bachelor." A win for Mr. Obvious.

"That's why he wants to go back to the Overworld and see Cassie," Bilba contributed unhelpfully.

"No," I said.

Ralrek poked his head up over the refrigerator door, checked with Bilba, snorted, and disappeared behind the door again. He came out a few seconds later, cupping one of my apples. "Let's go."

Bilba moved into the hallway. Away from the front door and the single window in my kitchen, it was the only place in the apartment to open a rift, as long as that rift was small. Bilba didn't cast the large rifts, and this one fit neatly in the narrow hallway. It helped that I hadn't hung my personal effects yet, not that I had many to hang. Most of those were split between the Overworld and whatever my parents had stashed away. The Zeke of the Fifth Circle hadn't made it to the Sixth in more ways than one.

Bilba mumbled his way through the incantation. Soon the air sizzled a few feet ahead.

"You're going to need to learn to do something about those white line things. In all the rifts I've seen, I've never seen one that has them. Except yours. One day, someone else will notice too, and they'll draw the wrong kind of attention," I said.

"From who? Fortunately for you, we're the only demons who care to come visit this repugnant apartment. Have you ever thought of opening a window?" Ralrek said, stuffing the apple in between his perfectly straight teeth.

I smirked. "Have you smelled the Sixth? This entire place reeks. I'll have to take you guys out for drinks sometime so you can imbibe everything this Circle has to offer."

The rift opened fully, or at least as large as Bilba could make it in a confined space. On the other side of the filmy barrier was what looked to be gray cement.

A bead of sweat clung to Bilba's hairline. "Since we've been to the Vigilante's headquarters, I figured we'd start there instead of taking a chance on the streets of Olympia."

"Genius." I patted him on the back and stepped through the rift.

The world tumbled and fell, rose and sank, and made a mess of my stomach. Just as quickly as normal became abnormal, and abnormal became normal, the world righted itself. I was standing in the middle of the hangar Virgo's Vigilantes used as their headquarters. Bilba and Ralrek came through.

"Can't hide well if we're popping into the middle of the hangar," I said when Bilba stepped through.

Ralrek grunted in agreement.

"Why do we need to hide?" he asked.

"We don't know who might be in here when we need to visit. We just might want to be more discreet, that's all."

"You want me to open rifts in the bathroom?"

"Right on top of one of the shitters," Ralrek snorted.

"A side office?" I said. "That would be safer."

Bilba tipped his head. "Sure. I'll talk to one of them or Virgo and see which is best."

Three Vigilantes watched a movie—I was believing they watched more movies than I did, which was true now that I didn't even have a television. They looked at us from the couches surrounding the TV. They weren't unfriendly looks, but I wouldn't say we were received like friends either. We were being watched the way demons watch unfamiliar, drooling devildogs. Based on a few expressions, I guessed we had a bit of a bite to our look. I'd blame that on Ralrek, but the fact was, we had to build trust with this group before they'd open their arms for us.

A long bench propped up one wall. It was covered in silver coils, springs, black grips and barrels, and just about any part of pistols and rifles imaginable. I only identified them because of my time in the mortal army. Not an aficionado by any stretch of the imagination, I enjoyed shoot-ing. These weren't props. The group was getting serious. Seeing the Vigilantes with a small armory was encouraging. They were formidable enough when they were a disorga-nized gang. Now that they'd fallen under the formal leader-ship of Virgo, they seemed capable of handling the hostilities that were sure to come.

By the sounds of Cassie's ominous and cryptic note, hostil-ities may already be rising. The group couldn't prepare soon enough.

A stocky woman in a bulky, green sweater, tan slacks, and combat boots rounded the bench. "What do you need?"

Friendly? Not so much. "We're looking for Virgo. Is he here?"

She bobbed her head toward the side of the hangar with the three doors where Virgo's Vigilantes was born.

"Thanks," I said, and we made our way to the meeting room. I knocked.

"Yo," Virgo's deep, rich voice said from the other side of the barrier.

We stepped in.

Virgo sat at the head of the table with Cassie in the first chair to his left. This time, Virgo's closest confidants didn't fill the room. Steve was here—I nodded, feeling the serious tone —as was another man. The unknown might have rivaled Ralrek's height. His skin was as dark as the mood. Whoever he was, he hadn't been in the previous meeting. He wore a long, white tunic and a bill-less matching cap that sucked to his skull. Long, black hair curled from underneath.

Cassie got to her feet, coming around the table and dishing out hugs. "Thank you for coming. I'm sorry about the cryptic messages. I hate sending those, but I don't know what else to do. "

"I totally understand," I said as we took our seats.

"Commandant, should we leave?" Steve asked.

I shot a look at Virgo. "Commandant?"

Virgo tipped his head into a shrug and the corner of his mouth twitched. Three smiles in two visits. Virgo was on record-pace here. "Not my idea. Everyone thought the leader needed a title. I disagreed. We took a vote. They won."

"I like it," Bilba piped in from two chairs away.

"Oh, if I knew you better, I'd give you such a hard time about this," I said.

"Don't worry. This lot does enough," Virgo jabbed a hand at Steve. "Though they tell me I'll get used to it. One day."

"Jawohl, Commandant," I said in German, receiving strange looks from Steve and the dark man at the end of the table. As a demon, I could understand every mortal language without translation. "To what pleasure do we owe this visit?"

The focus shifted to Cassie. "Just as I worried. Trouble is spreading."

"They're still harassing mortals?" Ralrek asked.

"Worse, unfortunately," Cassie said.

"They burned down my mosque," the dark man at the end of the table said with a burst of heat to go along with a sharp Middle-Eastern accent.

"This is Arham Assad, imam for the local mosque," Virgo said, with a dip of his head toward the stranger.

Ralrek loosed a low growl, so low I don't even think anyone but me heard. I kneed him. He squashed the noise about as well as he squashed his reaction to the man of Yahweh at the other end of the table.

Cassie flicked a scowl at Ralrek. Great, she'd heard. "It happened two days ago."

"Burned to the ground. My community has nowhere to go now," Arham said, his voice rising with pain and anguish. "What are we supposed to do? I was told you could help, God willing. We need help. Our people need help."

"Are your faithful being targeted?" I asked.

The imam shook his head. "Not personally. Not yet. God willing, not ever. But our spiritual home is nothing more than ashes. Might as well be a parking lot!" His fingers wrestled with each other and he snapped his arms back toward his chest. "My apologies. I shouldn't speak so harshly. I know you are here to help."

"It's okay," Cassie said, leaning toward him and tapping the table. "They are friends. They will help too." She sat straight again, looking at us. "That wasn't the only attack. A synagogue and a Baptist church were also burned on the same day, at the same time."

"A coordinated effort?" Bilba said with a gasp.

"For everyone. For one. For all."

I jumped at the sudden voice, intimately close. A voice that did not belong to either friend at my side.

Cassie tilted her head.

"Sorry. Knocked my shin on the table," I smiled apologetically, bending to rub my leg to really play off the lie.

Great, the disembodied voice was hanging in the Over-world with me. Awesome.

Cassie nodded, not thrown off by my interruption. "Definitely coordinated. These attacks required a number of... people to pull off."

We couldn't talk freely in front of the imam. That was a no–brainer. So I offered an out to the group. "If we could speak privately, I have thoughts on the matter."

"But you will help?" Arham said.

I gave him a slow nod. "Once we chat, I'll have a better

idea of what we can do. I'll make sure I let Virgo know my thoughts, and he can pass them on to you. Will that be okay?"

The imam looked at Steve, his fingers tap dancing on his chest. "Yes. Yes, thank you. Thank you all so very much," he said as he stood to leave.

I watched Cassie watch the imam leave. Her eyes were absolutely stunning—I'm sure I've mentioned that before. I didn't do it to be a creep. I just didn't want to be rude and watch the struggling imam walk out of a room of 'people' who were actually immortal creatures from the Underworld who were there to help. For a dark, snarky second, I wondered what would happen inside his brain if he knew he was consorting with demons. Mortals can be finicky about that.

When the door clicked closed, I asked, "Okay, what's really going on? You didn't ask us here because you thought we could help with a mosque. That's a matter for firefighters and police, not the spawn of Satan."

"I believe these attacks are growing because they're all coordinated," Cassie said.

"That's obvious," Ralrek interjected.

Cassie shot him a dark look—well, as dark is that smooth, perfect expression could. "What I mean," she said slowly, "is that these attacks hit the three major Abrahamic faiths purposely. One after another. Making it look like each was retaliatory. This was a deliberate attempt to raise tensions amongst them."

"Don't they do a good enough job of that on their own?" I asked, realizing too late that it sounded antagonistic. Cassie was an angel after all, and unless something changed recently, the three faiths weren't exactly on speaking terms with Hell's head honcho. An angel would see people of those faiths as one of their tribe. I raised my hand in apology. "I mean, the three have so much history between them this makes sense."

Cassie nodded. "Exactly. Why not leverage historical

animosity to your advantage? It's a great way to spark a conflict."

"But Olympia? Why now? I don't get it," Bilba said. "There are dozens of locations where this would have been more effective, especially if their aim was to elevate tensions. Olympia is hardly a religious hot-spot."

I turned to Virgo. "Did any of you get involved?"

He shook his head. "We didn't know about it until it was in the news. We didn't think about a supernatural influence, not until it was too late. But we've heard things."

"Like what?" Ralrek asked.

"After the arsons, we sent out members to see what they could find," Virgo said, his jaw clenching. "Because of the circles we've run in for years, we're connected around the city. Easier to get information from authorities and others. Mostly from the homeless. They trust us more than the fire investigators or the police. After talking to a bunch of them, finding other witnesses that were mentioned in the news or who we saw in interviews, we started piecing everything together. We don't have much, but we have enough to corroborate Cassie's information."

"What information?" I asked the angel.

"These weren't mortals," she said. "Magic was involved."

"Your operatives sensed the signatures of the spells?" I said, drawing my own conclusion.

Cassie shook her head. "Our sensors. The spells were demonic."

"Sonofabitch," I said, shaking my head. "So, the Council used and abused us and threw us away like yesterday's garbage, only to hire other agents and torch houses of worship? Great."

"No," Cassie said.

"But... you said the magic was demonic?" Bilba asked pensively.

"I did. But it wasn't agents or operatives of the Underworld who cast the most powerful spells. Not according to what we picked up on our sensors or to eyewitness testimony," Cassie said.

"Tell him," Virgo said.

Cassie's gaze fell on me. Somewhere deep, I quivered. Then she looked at Bilba and Ralrek in turn, spending the longest time on Ralrek. Good thing I'm not the jealous type.

"It wasn't an agent or operative who set the fires. It was Be —Beelzebub."

I groaned. Bilba shot back in his chair. Ralrek growled.

"That's why I wrote," Cassie continued, almost apologetically. "This isn't just a tactic by the Underworld, or even the Upperworld, to influence the Balance. This was an act of war. Be—b—Beelzebub is trying to play the sides off each other to create chaos. Chaos that is going to unravel the tense peace we have between our realms. He has to be stopped."

My mind spun. The Prince of Demons, likely without the approval or knowledge of the Council—no way Azazel was cool with burning down houses of worship—was committing terrorist acts in the mortal world. My gut said he wasn't acting alone. I'd bet the coin the rebel cell gave me that he had a half–tattooed-faced moron cooperating.

My jaw clenched. "I'm in."

"Me too." Ralrek snarled.

Bilba delayed before saying, "Oh, sorry. Of course I'll help."

Cassie sat back, her chest rising and falling in relief.

"I'll talk to the Vigilantes and ensure safe passage for the four of you and whoever you need to help. But," Virgo said, popping the table with a finger, his forearm's muscle rippling, "keep your numbers small. I don't want any of you bringing a horde of demons or angels here. We won't stand by and ignore it. I'll be blessed before the Vigilantes turn a blind eye to one side asserting too much power or influence."

"That won't be a problem," I said. "No one even knows

we're here. I can't exactly walk around the Underworld telling everyone I'm in open rebellion against one of Lucifer's own."

"I understand as well, and wouldn't think to abuse your trust," Cassie acknowledged. "I have permission to use the resources I need, but I only have a few of my kind in mind. Nothing more, I promise."

"Good," Virgo said, his hands closing in a fist. "So how do we ruin Beelzebub's day?"

12

UNDERWORLD, SIXTH CIRCLE

"You know, with all the drama going on in the Underworld, I think it'd be nice to chill in the Overworld for a bit. Maybe I should get myself Abandoned," Ralrek said, crumbling his napkin and throwing it on my plate.

"Joking about my personal trauma now, are we?" I said with a grimace, not at his comment, but at his soiled napkin, which I plucked from the middle of my unfinished pile of rice.

Ralrek stretched, pulling his shirt tight over his thin, fit chest. If I looked closely, I could see the ripples of a stomach with not a bit of fat on it. The chest of someone who looks like their second home was a gym, but who had never been to one. Ralrek had almost everything a demon needed.

"I don't know. Sometimes I'm half–serious. Not about what happened to you. That was wrong. But I get so tired of this stuff. Nothing ever changes. Can you imagine another sixty or seventy thousand years of this crap?" He said, a well–formed argument.

"Hard to admit, but I can't fight you on that," I said. "Except that if you were Abandoned, you wouldn't get to see me or Bilba. You'd start decaying. Lucifer knows how long that would take. Oh, and the constant longing, somewhere deep inside you, like an itch on the bottom of your foot when you're wearing shoes. A longing for back home. It never goes away. Just hangs over you like a cloud. Is that how you'd want to spend the last years of your life?"

Bilba returned to the table, his plate piled with rice and broccoli—I told you, Hell's food is bland. My mind drifted away to chicken wings. Maybe Ralrek's argument was stronger than I first gave it credit.

"Look at it this way, guys. Things are changing. We're part of that change," Bilba said.

Ralrek scoffed. "I doubt we'll live long enough to see the other side of any change."

Another point for Ralrek. This was turning into a rout.

"Well, maybe you're not looking at it the right way. For example, look at how we can move around the Underworld freely, to any Circle we want," Bilba said.

"We can only do that because you figured out how to open gateways and rifts," Ralrek said. "And the only reason we get away with it is because they're undetectable. The second that changes is the second your neck is in the same noose Gemini's was almost in."

"Wow, dark, buddy. Really dark," I said.

"My ability is just the beginning," Bilba said, his forkful of rice paused halfway to his mouth. "We have Virgo's Vigilantes up there. We can travel, and I think others will travel in the future too. We have someone close to the Council who is helping. We have the rebels."

Now it was my turn to chuckle, a hint of venom in it. "Yeah, all ten of them." Hey, I'm for idealism, but it has to be grounded in something viable for me to go full-in for it.

Bilba's fork dropped to the plate with a loud clink. Five kernels of rice tumbled onto the table. He ignored them. "You two are so frustrating. You only see what's right in front of you. You don't see what is possible. Maybe you think you do, but you get so focused on why things can't be done instead of how they can be. If I thought like that, I would have never tried to open that first gateway. A rift? Without trying something simpler first? Never. But I took a chance at being discovered by local authorities, or even the Council." He extended a finger, jamming it down on the table with each word. "Because it was worth it."

"You're right," I admitted after a moment. "Things are changing. If we want change for the better, we have to act instead of sitting around talking. If we don't do it, no one does. I want to see a little more excitement from my fellow demons. I mean, less than twenty rebels since all this crap started? How long ago did they spring up? Right after Aries. We've dealt with Taurus, Gemini and Cassie, and went to war, and still... Less. Than. Twenty."

"Give them time, and they will," Bilba said in a fatherly tone.

Sometimes my best friend was so annoying with his rational arguments.

"Speaking of demons who are excited to see things change, what would it take to get you to open a rift to Baghdad so I can check on Cancer? Leo hinted she's still alive. I want to check on her as soon as you think you can pull that off. We don't have to wait for someone to figure out how to cure any curses she might or might not have. I want to see her."

In my periphery, Ralrek's head lifted as he eyed me. Bilba met my gaze. I knew what he was silently saying.

We didn't know if Cancer was alive. Leo had passed on Azazel's message that her reported death was still unconfirmed. I hadn't seen Azazel since the trial by combat. I hadn't even heard a word from him or any secret messenger representing him. Completely in the dark. Again. With Bilba's ability to open undetectable rifts, I could pop into Baghdad and get answers.

"Do you know where she is?" Bilba asked.

I shrugged. "In Baghdad."

"Do you know how big of a city that is?" Ralrek asked. "She could be anywhere."

"If you remember, I was there along with you on those patrols."

"And that was only one section of a vastly larger city. One which, by the way," Ralrek said, holding a finger in the air, "is at the center of the world war."

"A world war where Cancer is helping mortals and in constant danger of her safety," I countered.

"Zeke, I would do it for you in a heartbeat if you knew where she was," Bilba said. "Have you reached out to her through a notebook?"

I had. A hundred times. And I got nothing. Instead of entering that dark thought tunnel, I said, "I haven't heard back."

"She's surrounded by war," Bilba said kindly, probably sensing the strain of my worry.

He had met Cancer, had been there through the struggles of her curse. So had Ralrek. But I had grown closest to her because of our mutual Abandonment to Seattle. We moved to Olympia together, not because we shared the experience of being rejected demons, but because we had built a powerful bond. We had started that end of our lives as a circle of two. My connection to the succubus was far deeper than either of these incubi imagined.

Yet, the back of my rational brain forced me to recognize both Bilba and Ralrek were only trying to help.

"You're right," I finally said, trying to focus on something that didn't bring about a bout of despair for my friend. "I'll keep reaching out. But the minute I hear from her, you're taking me there."

Bilba brightened. "Deal."

As if sensing the conversation needed a shift, Ralrek drew

a deep breath. "Imagine, the Underworld of the future, where demons travel wherever they want thanks to Bilba's gateways."

"Do you know how unrealistic that is?" Bilba asked. "It takes a lot to open a gateway and keep it open. Even small ones for the three of us. Gateways that move dozens of demons? Gateways that permanently stay open?" He shook his head. "I know I'm a badass, but I can't imagine the power that requires."

"The Council has them," I said. "Look at the mass transit ones outside their headquarters. Look at how they moved us for boot camp. If they can do it, you will one day."

"They have teams of older casters. Powerful demons," he countered.

"You'll get there. Give it time."

"And practice," Ralrek chimed in.

"Why not teach others, so it's not always you who has to open one?" I asked. "Since yours are undetectable, show others how to do it. At least those you trust, I mean. Before you know it, demons will move about under the noses of the Council. If enough learn, there's no way the Council can control it. They're too distracted by screwing with the Over-world, and they don't have the resources to police hundreds, maybe thousands of demons opening gateways. How awesome would that be?" I added for humor's sake. "How funny would that be?" Call me passive-aggressive, but after being screwed by the Council as much is I had, I figured I earned it.

"I—I wouldn't be sure where or how to teach," Bilba admitted.

"Why don't you start with Ralrek? Teach him."

The pair looked at each other like a couple at a dinner party in the middle of an argument they didn't want anyone else to know about. I almost laughed. To be fair, Bilba and Ralrek make it easy.

"I don't know if he's teachable," Bilba said.

"I don't know if you're smart enough to be a teacher," Ralrek retorted.

I waved my fork at them. "I'm serious. Why not? Plus, having two of you who can do it would be helpful if something... happened. Is it that hard?"

"Do you see anyone else casting gateways and rifts besides the Council and the lucky few they allow to do it?" Bilba asked.

"Well... no, but if you figured it out, you had the skill to do it with no curse of Lucifer or formal training, so why wouldn't that be the same for others?" My fork rotated toward Ralrek. "He can cast powerful spells. He couldn't hit the side of a blazeball stadium if his life depended on it, but that doesn't make him incapable. I say he's worth it. Give it a go. Ralrek, would you do it?"

The tall demon shrugged. "Sure. Why not? If he could teach me, I'd go for it."

"Then let's try it," I said matter-of-factly. "Should we use the hallway?"

Bilba shook his head. "See? The problem with that is I've been working on mine for a long time, and it takes practice to maintain control of the spell. You just can't cast it recklessly or it could get out of hand. We need open space, more than you have in this apartment. When I was learning, I went deep into Eve's Sanctuary. Just in case Ralrek lost control, I wouldn't want you to explain to your landlord how your walls were torn open. So, unless you have a secret hideout I don't know about, we can't try it."

I snapped my fingers. "We could go to the park."

"The park? Sounds fun," Ralrek said.

"Don't be a douche," I said with a mischievous snort. A quick look out the kitchen window revealed darkness had gripped the Sixth Circle. "At this time of night, it should be empty, and it's only a few minutes away. Plus, I've only ever seen younger families with implings using it. We can check if it's deserted. If it is, would that work?"

Ralrek's lips pressed together. "I guess if there are any imps hanging out, thinking they're cool and trying to cause trouble, we can scare them away and give this a shot. I'm up for it."

I fist pumped. Unfortunately, it was with the hand holding my fork half-full of rice. Kernels flew into the air, landing on the table and, more hilariously, in Ralrek's hair. "Let's finish up and go then."

As he tried to pick them out, Ralrek said, "Opening gateways would be cool. We could double our efforts at finding the Horn. You said Azazel gave you coordinates where it might be, right?"

I dipped my head over my plate since my mouth was full. Cracking open the corner of my mouth, I said, "Yeah. He's not sure that's where it is, but it might be a hint to where it could be."

"That would make searching for it a lot easier," Bilba said. "If we knew where it was, and both of us could open gateways to the area, we might be able to snatch it without anyone noticing."

I pointed at the other room with my fork, this time not spilling any rice. "The problem is, I have no clue where to start or where to begin. I'm hardly an expert at reading coordinates, and I know neither of you are."

"There aren't any other clues?" Bilba said.

I shook my head. "Just coordinates. And I'm not the outdoorsy type. With everything else we've got going on, I don't know if this is easy to take on. It might be better to stick with one thing at a time, no matter how important the Horn is."

"The Horn is very important, Zeke," Bilba said in an ominous tone that belonged in a cheesy mortal horror movie. "I told you what I read. If the Horn is lost, we can't be sure angels aren't involved. If they hold the Horn and the Halo..."

"I know an incubus. Outdoorsy type. Real rugged. So, unlike you, Zeke," Ralrek said with a wink as he cut Bilba off with his sudden epiphany. "He might be able to help."

"Is he trustworthy?" I asked.

"Well, he's not the two of you, but—"

I didn't let Ralrek finish. "Oh my Lucifer, that is the sweetest thing you've ever said."

"Shut up, asshat," Ralrek said.

"There he is. Good old Ralrek," I said.

"Anyway, he is a good incubus," Ralrek said. "Plus, I don't think we need to tell him what we're looking for, just that we need his help finding these coordinates. He'd be down, if I can find him."

Bilba groaned. "Don't tell me he's lost too?"

"No, he's just the adventurous type," Ralrek said. "I know him from a bar. He's there whenever he's around. The problem is, he's not always because he's off on some adventure more times than not."

"From a bar you go to, huh? Is he another one of your toys?" I teased.

Bilba's fork clattered to his plate. "I thought you'd given up on dating for a while?"

Ralrek's tone flattened. "Trust me, I am. I've got no interest in seeing anyone. Torlan ruined incubi for me,"

This wasn't a topic he wanted to explore, so I denied myself the opportunity to take a good-natured jab at him and kept our discussion focused. "So you think he could help find it?"

"We don't have a ton of options, and if one incubus can help, it would be him," Ralrek said. "We just have to be patient because I never know when he's off on some excursion. But, I'll keep my eyes out. In the meantime, why don't we try to see if you can teach me how to open one of these things?"

I stood, swiping my plate from the table, and scraping it into the trash can. "No better time than the present, I say. Let's get going. No one is paying attention to the park."

We made the short trip. Just as I'd hoped, the park was empty, even of troubled imps looking to drink and smoke and fling their lives down the wrong path. We moved into the deepest reaches, where the street lamps burning blue with Hellfire faded into distant points of light.

"Be careful. We're going to snap an ankle. I can't see a blessed thing," Ralrek said.

"We're opening gateways, not doing wind sprints," Bilba said.

"Like you would know what a wind sprint was." Low blow, even for Ralrek.

"We did those in boot camp, remember?" Bilba was completely genuine.

"I tried to forget the army," I said, pointing off to the left. "What about over there?"

Honey locust trees lined the area. Mature enough to stand over forty feet tall, they were full, providing coverage from the side of the park. In my short time in the Sixth Circle, this spot was rarely used. Those few times were restricted to imps and their romantic adventures. No one would traipse across us when most demons were putting their little ones to bed, drinking away the stress of the day, or binge watching television.

"Looks perfect." Bilba squinted. "It gives us enough space for what we need. Let's try it."

"So how do we do this? Teach me, oh, sensei," Ralrek said, stuffing his hands in his pockets as if chilled against the air.

Bilba moved in front of the arc of honey locust. He held his hands up in the air, elbows bent at ninety-degree angles, palms facing forward. He looked like he'd just run face–first into an invisible wall.

"Opening a gateway or a rift is basically the same thing, but it requires a lot of focus. This park will come in handy." Bilba looked around. "I was reading up on the topic in a book from Melchiot's personal library. It described the way the ancients used to teach others to open gateways and rifts. Back then, travel was open to everyone, so they taught capable demons. From what I read, schools and community centers used to host group classes on how to do it. Crazy, right? Anyway, the key is clearing your mind of all distractions."

Ralrek groaned. "Don't tell me this is that weird woo-woo stuff?"

"No," Bilba snapped. "But you can't expect to do something this monumental if you don't have a clear mind. Ralrek, copy my stance."

"Seriously?"

Bilba glared at Ralrek. He plainly took casting gateways and rifts, and now training others how to do it, very seriously. "Yes," he replied, waiting.

With a huff, Ralrek stole my best friend's pose.

"Good. Now, clear your mind of any distractions. Push them all away," Bilba said, closing his eyes for a moment, before opening them to a slit to ensure Ralrek was following directions. When he was satisfied, he continued. "Stop thinking about everything. No stresses. Nothing exciting or enjoyable. Focus on your breathing. Your mind has to be quiet."

"So they won't help in the middle of a fight?" I risked asking.

Bilba remained focused on Ralrek as he answered. "Practice, Zeke. With a practiced mind, we could. After years. This stuff takes high levels of skill and decades, centuries, of practice before someone can get to that level. Now, let's go."

I heard a low rumble from Ralrek, almost like his stomach grumbling. If Bilba heard, he ignored it.

"Just listen to my voice, and keep your mind clear," Bilba continued, his eyes closed now, without checking on Ralrek. "All demons... sorry, Zeke. Almost all," he said, "have magic. It is an innate trait of our kind. Think of it like consciousness. It's just there. All magic."

"All?" I asked, interrupting the proceedings.

"All," Bilba repeated, a hint for me to stop. "As I was saying, we all have magic. We're born with it. It is in us. Now, what happens is, as we mature, especially as we enter puberty, one Ability comes forward. Think of it like a preference, like how someone uses one arm over the other. They become dominant in the one they give preferential treatment to. It's the same thing with our Abilities. Most of it happens in our subconscious. We don't even realize we're doing it. We focus on one Ability, and with each incident, it becomes more dominant.

"So the key is to understand that from the beginning," he continued, straightening his stance. "Ralrek, you are not just a Fire user, a mage, if you will. You have numerous Abilities. They're just dormant. But I want you to imagine a string of Abilities in your mind, like vines in the jungle, hanging side-by-side, forming a curtain. Imagine any you'd like, it doesn't matter which. Fire is just one of those vines. Together, those vines form a wall shielding you from what is on the other side, but they're still individual vines. You can move all of them, a few, or just one of them. Push them aside or pluck them out of your way if you want to."

"So now we're plucking vines, are we?" Ralrek said with a soft snort.

"Focus, like I told you." Bilba's eyes scrunched tighter. "If it helps, think of them as strings on a musical instrument. I don't care. I just prefer the vines metaphor because of Eve's

Sanctuary. You do what works for you. Vines or strings on an instrument. Just imagine it, and that only."

Ralrek exhaled. "Fine. Vines it is. I don't play an instrument, so that'll be easier."

"Good." Bilba bounced on his toes. "Now, stop talking and focus on the vines in your mind. Each is like an Ability. One is bigger, thicker, than the rest. That is the one you have spent your life focusing on."

"My Fire Ability," Ralrek said, this time not sounding like a smartass.

Bilba nodded. "Your Fire Ability. But just because it's thicker than the others, its existence doesn't negate the existence of the other vines. They're still there, hanging alongside your Fire Ability. Vibrating alongside the thicker Fire vine. They're all humming, but if you don't listen you'll only notice your Fire, because it has been dominant most of your life. Now, we need to focus on the others. If you listen, you can hear them humming." Bilba pried his eyes open again. "Sort of like when you go to an orchestral concert and the musicians are warming up."

"Oh, great, another metaphor," Ralrek said.

"I told you I wasn't a good teacher. Focus." Bilba clicked his teeth. "Think of an orchestra. You hear the instruments as the musicians warm up, but there is always that low hum accompanying them. In the background. Lower than the rest. Full of bass. It hums and hums as everyone warms-up. It is the last sound to fade out right before the concert starts. That's what you're listening for now. Listen with your mind open and you'll hear them. Always humming."

I scooted backward, away from the pair, to give them space while watching with growing fixation on the lesson. Bilba was hypnotic, and I wasn't even the one being trained. Yet, I could see the vines in my mind's eye as well. This made absolute sense. Part of me listened for my orchestra while I watched. To his credit, Ralrek was following instructions.

"Keep listening," Bilba said, this time his tone much lower. "Forty, fifty different instruments, all playing at once. Listen for the low hum and start pushing the others away." He paused. Distant sounds of life around the outside of the park filled the night. Screeches of hundreds of bats. A howl from a very large dog, by the depth of the mournful cry. The *thump-thump* of a solitary chimera moving along a side street. Faint. "Focus on the hum."

After a silent moment, Ralrek made a sound that might have been a gasp.

Bilba encouraged but kept his voice level. "Keep focused on the hum. Find it. Separate it. It is the only sound you hear." He paused, cracking his eyes open.

Ralrek now seemed immersed. Heavens, I was hearing the hum too.

"Hold on to the hum. It's right there. A solitary sound. The other instruments have faded away. Only the hum. Now, slowly turn your wrist so your hands push out toward your sides, away from you. Keeping your elbows where they are."

I couldn't stop myself from watching Ralrek if I wanted. This was fascinating. Whether or not it worked, Ralrek was fully bought in. He was doing everything Bilba instructed and doing it with focus. No smartassery. His hands moved as instructed, as he isolated the sound Bilba wanted him to focus on.

I turned to my best friend, who was smiling. He was watching Ralrek, no longer focusing on his own posture and gestures. Bilba gave me a quick head nod.

"Find that hum, hold on to it, and push away," Bilba droned. "As you push, I want you to think about the Fifth Circle. Think about your apartment. Picture it. Now, focus on your kitchen." He paused, his eyes scrunching as if he was trying to picture Ralrek's apartment too. " Only that room. Focus on the small table you have in there. Keep moving your hands outward. Slowly. Very slowly. Push the vines away from the one that is humming. Think about your table. See the two chairs? See the cactus in the small pot you insist on killing? Can you see it?"

The question hung in the air. All the sounds in the park, the hooting of an owl, chirps of a billion crickets, the very faint *click–clack* of chimera hooves on brimstone, the rustle of leaves; faded as I waited for Ralrek's answer.

Finally, he answered in a hoarse voice, "Yes."

"Stay focused on the hum," Bilba said, his eyes wider than I'd ever seen them before. "The vine hanging in front of you is the only thing separating you from sitting at your table. Push it to the side, out of your way. Keep moving your hands apart. Push the vine."

And Ralrek was. His elbows still raised to shoulder–level, bent at a ninety-degree angle, he pushed his hands outward, away from each other. As he did, twenty feet across the hidden area we were using for this illegal activity, a pinprick of light hung in the air.

I was on my feet before I realized I wasn't sitting in the grass.

Ralrek pushed, and the light grew. At first, it was oval–shaped, but within seconds it elongated. Two spires of light shot up, away from that small center circle. The spires grew, reaching twice Ralrek's height. I shot Bilba a nervous glance. We were in the middle of the park, and it was late enough that no one would interrupt this session, but Ralrek's gateway was growing in size and brightness.

Bilba didn't look at me, however. Fascinated by what our friend was doing, he made a wide circle around Ralrek. His calm, even words pitched with what might have been excitement. "Listen for that single hum. Move the vine. Reach out to your chair. You want to pull it out from under the table and sit down. The vine blocks your path. Push it away."

Ralrek did. The spires on his gateway shot to twice their

height, reaching well over twenty feet. The small circle of light in the middle of those two vertical points shot sideways.

Bilba yelped, jumping back. Thank Lucifer I was already on my feet, because I also jumped at the sudden expansion of Ralrek's gateway.

Bilba's jaw dropped open as the gateway stretched, wide enough to fit the three of us side-by-side. Then it kept growing sideways. Ten feet. Fifteen feet. Twenty feet.

"Is it supposed to be that big?" I asked Bilba.

My best friend's mouth moved, but nothing useful came out. Still, Ralrek's gateway grew, brightening the small grove. So much for hiding.

Thirty feet. Forty feet.

"Bilba," I said in a warning tone, glancing around and hoping I saw nothing that resembled intelligent life.

"I—I..." Bilba struggled.

All the while, Ralrek's gateway ballooned.

Fifty feet wide now. This was becoming a problem.

"Stop him," I urged.

Bilba blinked. "Ralrek. Let go of the vine. Drop it!" Bilba said, panicked enough to snag Ralrek's attention.

The tall incubus twitched, his arms straightened horizontally from their previous position, as if someone had slung sandbags around his fists.

"Let go of the vine!" Bilba shouted.

The park was still empty, the night still quiet. We still had a chance to get away with this.

"Let go!" Bilba was now shouting.

Ralrek's gateway flickered.

Well, I pondered for a hopeless moment, if Ralrek's infant gateway didn't draw attention, my best friend's hysterics would.

With one last fierce jerk, Ralrek's arms dropped to his side. He wobbled, teetering. I raced to him, catching him by the shoulders.

"Are you okay, buddy?" I asked, trying to hold him steady. Demons as tall as Ralrek were difficult to keep upright, especially when you were half a foot shy of six feet tall yourself.

Ralrek cranked his neck in my direction, blinking as if he just woken from a deep sleep. "Zeke... whoa," he said as he stumbled.

I looked at Bilba, whose mouth hung open, and said, "Well, that was fun."

13

UNDERWORLD, FIFTH CIRCLE

"WELL, look at it this way. You didn't kill anyone this time," I teased.

"I didn't kill anyone last time either," Ralrek said.

"Only because we made you open the gateway in the sanctuary," Bilba said.

We had traveled to the Fifth Circle through one of Ralrek's gateways. Since Bilba's frightening training session with the incubus, he made Ralrek practice often, at least once a day. Over that time, they'd trained in smaller and smaller confines until Bilba was convinced Ralrek could contain his spell. He reported Ralrek was getting stronger and more accurate with them.

I wasn't so sure. This gateway was three times larger than required, but Ralrek at least had enough control now that he could open them in the hallway in my apartment. The first few times he tried that, he nearly burned holes in my walls, and that was after hours of practice. Now, he was adept enough to open them sideways so they ran down the length of the hall, and held ample control so it didn't rotate and bring the entire apartment down on our heads.

We'd even traveled through the gate and into Eve's Sanctuary without launching cataclysmic events around Hell.

Being back was surreal. I hadn't seen this garden in a long time. Too long. So much in my life had changed since the last time I stood in this tranquil realm. Now, I couldn't help but soak in everything around me. It felt right being here. Who knew if I would ever get another chance to enjoy it. The Council had left me alone, as Lucifer's laws dictated, since winning my freedom, but I trusted them as much as I trusted Beelzebub to babysit any of my future offspring.

Eve's Sanctuary. Home. My real home, at least to me.

The way the air smelled. The rustling of reeds in the pond. The familiar warmth of the Hellfire. The way a cloud of harpies flitted in the canopy overhead, chirping insults as they flew in the gloriously azure sky. All of it, so familiar, so comfortable. This was my home, but it was also a place where I wondered if I was still welcomed.

We'd find out soon enough.

"Let's get going," Ralrek said, clapping his hands together to close his gateway.

He was getting cocky, too adept at managing the gateways already. Before long he'd have another reason to brag. Lucky us.

"No time like the present," I said. We strolled out of the garden, taking time for me to breathe in as much of Eve's Sanctuary as possible. Then it was through the packed streets that led back to my childhood home.

Everything along the journey to my old stomping grounds looked the same. The Fifth was as loud as ever. Incubi and succubi filled the streets, dragging pouting implings. Chimera carriages, the few that dotted this part of the Circle, rumbled past without regard for anyone. Vendors shouted the benefits of their wares. Imps raced up and down the narrow pathways playing tag, bumping into older demons, oblivious to the nasty looks shot after them.

"Are you ready to see what they've done with the place?" Ralrek asked, showing a rare moment of compassion.

Bilba and Ralrek had warned me about my parent's improved lot in life. For long before I was a twinkle in Kanthor Sunstone's eyes, my parents lived in a massive angel oak that was degrading by the year. Far from dilapidated, the home had needed major TLC since I could remember. My father's Construction Ability was weak—the Sunstone's aren't a very magical family in more ways than one—so he couldn't rely on them for anything more than the most minor repairs. Angel oak trees had been converted to more modern homes, resembling mortal abodes, all around the neighborhood. The last of the conversion projects happened so long ago I barely had a memory of it. Conversions were a sign of status. For one's home to no longer hold its natural appearance was to signal to your neighbors that you'd "made it." My parents were the last one in the neighborhood still living inside a tree.

Well, until recently.

Somehow, someway, they found themselves the proud owners of a massive conversion process, where a new home was sprouting up from the ground near the tree that birthed it. My friends were kind enough to paint the picture for me to save me the shock.

"It's going to be strange, I can't lie," I said. And it was.

When we rounded the corner to the block they lived on, my eyes fell on the house my parents now called home. Scaffolding surrounded it. The new version of their home was a quaint, two–story dwelling painted a brash yellow. Who paints anything they appreciate that color of yellow?

My steps stuttered. "Wow. I thought I was ready. But that…"

"Welcome to trying to keep up with the Fireborns," Ralrek said with a tight chuckle. Even for immortals, status matters.

"Look at it this way, at least you get to see them again," Bilba said in his ever–cheerful tone.

"Right," I said, wondering if this was still a good idea, doubting it was, but feeling the tug of a mother's love for her son. A love that I returned in equal measure. Sometimes, you have to let your heart lead you. My mother deserved to see her son more than any mother in the history of Hell.

A thigh–high picket fence edged the patch of yard around the house. A latched gate guarded the entrance. I opened it and stepped onto my parent's property for the first time since I spent the Samhain feast with them, my aunt, uncle, and niece before leaving to fight for the mortal army.

When I knocked on their front door, it was like thunder rolling through the entirety of Hell.

Suddenly nervous, I swallowed. My heart skipped as footsteps approached from the other side.

Lilith Sunstone opened the door, her face going from confusion to elation in the batting of a faerie's wings. "Ezekial!" She fell into my arms.

"Hello, Mother," I said as I hugged her.

She squeezed. And squeezed. And squeezed. "What... How? Oh, my Lucifer, I'm so happy to see you!" It was only then that she blinked in recognition that I wasn't alone. Craning her neck to look around me, she said, "Oh, Bilba. Ralrek. How are you two?"

I interrupted, not wanting to have this conversation out in the open. "Can we come in? I was hoping I caught you cooking. I'm starving and miss your meals." I didn't, but since when did a white lie hurt anyone?

She shuffled back in short strides like an impling excited for Samhain presents. Her square jaw framed glowing cheeks. Mother was happy. That made me happy. "Come in. Come in. Your father isn't home yet, but he should be soon. He ran to the store. Come in. Sit down. I'll throw something together."

We kicked off our shoes once inside, and I took in the new place. As my friends went into the dining area along with my mother, I stood in the entryway and soaked in these strange surroundings. The succubus who greeted us was my mother. The home she resided in was definitely not our home. Not mine, at least. Everything here was square and nondescript, so unlike the inside of the angel oak with its curved walls and persistent damp wood smell. In that home, my parents creatively decorated around the curved rooms and piles of Mother's pyramid scheme—I'm not allowed to call it that to her face—boxes of product. In this new construct, everything was square and bland. The rooms. The ceiling. The door frame itself.

I walked into the dining area. The small table had a knitted runner down the center. Four chairs, two on either side, lined it. Hardly the setting for feasts. This could have fallen straight out of any department store catalog. The table in the old home sat twice as many.

My mother was busy in the kitchen, calling out when I paused too long at the unfamiliar set up. "Ezekial, we're in here."

"Coming," I called back, my eyes lingering on a parents' home that felt like a stranger's.

The kitchen was enormous, too large for my mother's questionable culinary skills. A marble counter wrapped around three of the four walls, separated only by a door. Jade was expensive. The only time I'd ever seen counters like these was during our mission to the Eighth Circle to rob Taurus of the Horn he illegally acquired. Demons at income levels shared by my parents didn't have jade—except that they did.

I whistled. "You and Father are pulling out all the stops."

Mother blew a stray hair out of her face. "Oh, that's your father's doing. He said I deserve the best since I waited so long for this conversion. Very romantic incubus, that one."

Bilba glanced at me in the silence that followed then filled it. "Well, I think it looks great, Mrs. Sunstone. It's a stunning place. Mr. Sunstone was right; you do deserve it. I'm so happy for you two. I know you've waited a long time for this."

"We have," Mother said, her back still to us. "I was sad that we lost our tenant. He was a quiet renter, and the income was nice. But with this smaller home, and what we sold the excess wood from the angel oak for, it made sense. We don't have to worry about upkeep anymore. We're enjoying it."

"Well, I'm happy," I said to her back just as the front door clicked open. Boots stomped in the entryway. The drums of war. Father had come home.

Shit.

We planned the visit for a time when he was supposed to be at work for hours still. The plan was to have a few-hour buffer so I could avoid coming across him, for a multitude of reasons. This was going to be a big problem.

Kanthor Sunstone had been halfway through greeting my mother when he walked into the kitchen. Upon seeing the three of us, he cut it off.

Father is a tall demon, enough so that I'd received thousands of trite insults throughout my life that I couldn't possibly be his son—short demon jokes are always in favor in Hell. Even at forty-thousand years old, he was fit, mostly due to his job at the Grand Chamber, where he worked on the maintenance crew tending to the contraption that sustains the Hellfire. His long jaw rocked to the side when he saw me in his kitchen. His stern expression didn't evaporate.

"What are you doing here?" he said. It wasn't a question.

"Hello, Father," I said, instead of sharing the greeting that was on my mind.

Bilba and Ralrek greeted him uneasily, while my mother said "Hello," with her back still turned. He crossed the room and stood in front, over, me. An untold score of messages and meanings were shared in that moment between the father and the son—too bad the holy ghost wasn't around or it would have been a real party—with a history of tension between them.

"How are you here?" he asked.

"A gateway," I said.

Mother's clinking cooking utensils ceased. "The Council opened a gateway for you to visit?"

"Not really," I said.

"How did you get here?" Kanthor's questions, now and throughout my life, were like a sledgehammer.

I didn't want to tell him how I was traveling nowadays. I didn't have to, even if he demanded it. As consistent as the Hellfire signaled the start and end of every day, Bilba blurted. "Ralrek opened one."

There was a clang in the sink.

My father spun on Ralrek, who shrugged. "How in Lucifer's Underworld can you open gateways?"

"I've had some training," Ralrek said.

In my most encouraging dreams, I would have hoped the fact their son was standing in their home would be the focus of the conversation. The mechanics weren't as important as the presence. Not to me. That seemed lost on Kanthor.

"I was missing you guys, and missing home," I said, hoping to draw the attention back to me. "That's why I asked Ralrek to open one. For me."

"You knew he could do this?" my father asked, staying on the topic that didn't need attention.

"Does it matter?" I asked. "I'm here for a visit. If I'm intruding, I'm sorry. But don't worry, I can't stay very long."

"Why not?" The question came out of Kanthor right on the heels of my statement, and over top a small sniff from my mother.

"I have things to do," I said with a shrug. "If this is a bad time, maybe I can come back later. Another day."

My father's gaze bore into me. I wasn't selling him on any of this. "I'm very happy that you were successful in your trial, Ezekial, but I don't remember the Council waiving travel restrictions for you. Unless you're telling me you're a special case. Is that what this is?"

I stared at my mother's back. The last time she had seen me, I was walking off the floor of the fighting pit, having taken a good incubus's life to save my own. The fact I was still alive should have overridden the illegal mode of transportation. I had to remind myself, Kanthor's world was one of black-and-white.

"Trust me, the Council still considers me a special case," I said with a fair bit of snark, I'll admit.

The tension in the room grew thick. My mother hadn't resumed her work at the sink.

Ralrek burst in. "I did it. I talked Zeke into coming here. I thought he'd want to see you guys, and you'd want to see him." I nodded at his well-placed, very-pointed jab. To think, once upon a time, he was Hell's asshole. "Plus, I needed to practice my gateways. This was the best way to do that. If we intruded or upset you, I apologize. It's my fault, not Zeke's."

There's something about fathers with powerful presences. Kanthor Sunstone definitely possessed that. He was so blunt in how he dealt with others, he dominated rooms with his fierceness alone at times. His history was littered with examples of awkward confrontations that ruined social events. Forget Construction magic, alienating demons with his stubborn insistence was his true Ability.

The way he turned his head at an achingly slow speed was a tried-and-true tactic. Kanthor wanted us to fixate on him, to show us how he could hold our attention with a simple turn of his blocky head. Unknown to him, it did nothing for me.

"You boys shouldn't be playing around with illegal things. This could get you in a lot of trouble," Kanthor said. "I expected more of the three of you. I'm greatly disappointed. I'm sure your father would be too, Bilba."

Oh no, he wasn't going to make targets of them. "And here I thought you'd be happy to see me," I said, looking more at my mother's back than my father's narrowed eyes. "Guess I was wrong. Again. We need to go anyway. I just wanted to let you know I'm all settled at the new apartment and doing well for myself. I hope that makes you both a little happier. Guys." I aimed the statement at my friends. "Are you ready?"

Bilba looked to Ralrek and then back at me, unnerved. "Sure, Zeke... no problem."

I gave my father a nod and walked behind my mother, hugging her. "Love you."

A slender hand slipped up to touch my arm. She squeezed, then released. "I love you too, son. Please be careful," she whispered.

I kissed her on the cheek and walked straight out of the kitchen without even acknowledging my father one last time.

As I clicked the gate closed, Bilba exhaled. "Whew, that was awkward."

"You can say that again," Ralrek said.

"Yeah, I don't know what I was thinking, coming to see them," I said, a not-so-direct apology. "Sorry for putting you guys through that."

"Don't apologize," Ralrek said, dismissing the house with a swat of his hand. "It's not your fault they twitch every time the Council says boo. That's just how demons are. That's why nothing gets done. Not to sound disrespectful, they're your parents, but they're also a microcosm of every blessed demon. No one is courageous."

"Welllll," Bilba said, "it didn't help that we dropped in on them unannounced. I'm sure it was a shock."

"Yeah, a shock," I said, only partially agreeing.

We had arrived without warning or permission, that much was true. But after everything we had been through as a family, a five minute visit should have been the best five minutes of their day, if not their month. That was far from the truth, though. Had the Council frightened everyone as much as it appeared? I knew demons were as individualistic as lemmings, but to capitulate on everything life offered, at every turn and fortunate opportunity, confounded me. Something had changed. Something I didn't understand, and didn't know if I wanted to root out.

I just don't understand demons.

Mood soured, I needed something to elevate my spirits. "What do you say we make one more stop before you take me home?" I asked.

"I'm not casting a gateway here. We're in the middle of the Circle," Ralrek said.

"We aren't going to use a gateway. We can use these," I said, pointing at my shoes. "I want to go see Dialphio. I need to walk through Old Towne again before we head back. There isn't any place in the Sixth like it, and I miss it."

So we did. The walk to the oldest section in the Fifth was a long one, but with each step I felt peace wash over me after the confrontation with my father. This was a familiar journey, one I could complete with my eyes closed. And it felt good. Really good. The old water bottle stand where I was first asked for an autograph. The cliff walls were tagged with twice as much graffiti now. The narrow streets of Old Towne which seemed to trap the sounds and smells of its restaurants.

The buildings here were older and narrower, reaching high above the street in this condensed space. Pillars blocked off the cobblestone so only pedestrians used the street. Armed guards, too. They also dotted the crowd who filled the path along the main thoroughfare. The restaurants had put tables out since the Public Works Division had given us a sunny day. Vendors with small booths and carts sold trinkets and conveniences along the middle of the pedestrian path. This zone of commerce allowed fantastic businesses like Chilly Willy's to exist. Thank Lucifer for bikini baristas.

We stopped by the stand, but Gigi wasn't working. Instead, an incubus was. Wearing nothing more than small, red bikini briefs and the layers of muscle Lucifer cursed him with, he asked if he could take our order. Ralrek was the only one to buy coffee.

While we waited for Ralrek, a trio of succubi passed. Their heads turned as if an invisible line connected them to us. One was so distracted, she ran into a lamp pole. I'll admit, I laughed. Sorry, but it's funny.

Throughout the walk, I noticed a few sideways glances. Neither of the guys said anything. It wasn't abnormal for demons to steal looks my way. Ever since the first mission to Seattle, demons had no problem examining the curiosity that was me. From the Fifth all the way to the Sixth, as my neighbors became more familiar with me, I was checked out more and more often. But unlike my early experiences in my home Circle, whatever motivated those snappy glances from Fivers, it was no longer hostility or repulsion. Strange, for a place that spent the last six thousand years treating me like chimera dung.

As we made our way to The Book Abyss, a few conversations at Old Towne cafés and restaurants stopped when we passed. Inside one clothing shop, a succubus moved to the store window to watch us.

Thankfully, any time we passed a guard adorned in traditional black armor, they were too far away, looking too bored to care about anything to bother with us. Count your curses where you can, am I right?

The familiar chime of the bell I'd hung over the bookstore door years ago resonated in my soul as we stepped inside Dialphio's realm.

I sighed. Dialphio's obsession with books was overtaking the store again, like weeds in an untended garden.

"What's wrong?" Bilba asked.

I shook my head. I couldn't risk telling him and hurting my ex-boss's feelings.

Chaos expanded in a slow creep over the shelves and promotional stands, disorganization being the natural status of life under Dialphio's reign. Apparently, the post-Zeke era had different priorities and capabilities. She had fiction titles involving demons falling in love with werewolves mixed with nonfiction titles about magic systems. Dialphio needed an intervention.

"Welcome to The Book Abyss. If you need help finding anything, let me know," an incubus said in greeting. He had spots of black stubble on his cheeks, the only sign that he'd hit puberty. His face was too smooth, too free of stress. This dude needed some heavier responsibilities.

"Is Dialphio here?" I asked.

"Yes, let me get her," he said, and went behind the towering stacks of books forming a wall that hid her make-shift office.

A mumbling moment later, she rounded the corner, pulling her glasses off when she noticed us. Her wary gaze shot to her side. "Loci, please give me a few moments with these wayward boys."

Loci nodded and went into the back.

Dialphio stomped forward. "What in the Underworld are you doing here?"

"I'm happy to see you too," I said. "We were in the Fifth and I thought we might stop by. Is this a bad time?"

Dialphio was rubbing the arm of her glasses between her thumb and her forefinger. "I didn't hear a gateway."

"We walked," I said, before Bilba could spill the beans on our activities.

"Walked here from where? Through Old Towne?" Her voice gained a pitch that hinted we might be in trouble.

"Zeke wanted to see his mom and dad, so we took him." Even as Ralrek and I groaned, Bilba continued, "Plus, Ralrek needs practice with gateways, so I figured we would kill two harpies with one stone."

I wish I could say it was comical to watch the way Dialphio blinked, rotating her head between the three of us as she processed this. It wasn't.

She lifted a hand, a single finger extended, and touched it with a finger from the opposite hand holding her glasses. We were in for it. "First, you can open gateways?" she asked Ralrek, not waiting for him to answer. "Second, you visited your parents?" She touched the second finger. That was for me. "And you didn't stop him when he took a tour of the Fifth, out in the open?" That last finger was aimed at Bilba. All three of us were facing a Dialphio–shaped burning by Hellfire.

"Well... I thought—" Bilba started, which was always a bad idea.

Dialphio slapped her side. "It doesn't matter what you think. You three are ridiculous. What do I have to do? Do I have to strap you to chairs so you don't do anything this foolish ever again? Do you realize what you've put at risk today? Even before today? You're training him on gateways? Where are you doing it? How are you ensuring your safety?"

Bilba's mouth fell open and snapped closed as he tried to answer, unable to.

"And you, going to see your parents after everything they've been through. After everything they've seen. Do you not remember your father's opportunities to denounce the actions of the Council, only for him to fail to do that? Is that a risk worth taking? Why would you put your mother in that position?" Her voice rising, she cocked her shoulders at Ralrek. "And you. Aren't you the skeptical one? You're supposed to keep these two dreamers in line, keep them grounded. Did you go comatose after opening your gateway?"

As she turned, spinning in a slow circle, her hands raising to the air in frustration, I said, "I'm sorry, Dialphio. I wanted to see you. I had a lousy visit with my parents and thought I'd feel better after a short visit with you before I headed home."

She spun. "Of course, you had an unpleasant visit. Your mother has been traumatized by everything that has happened. For years, they've been putting her through heartache. You are her baby boy, her little impling, no matter how old you are or how you want to look at it. That poor succubus is shouldering a lot of weight because of what the Council has done to you. And your father is in full-allegiance with them. He has had ample opportunities to stand against them, stand up for you, for what they've done to his son. And what has he done?" She made a little fist, slamming it into her palm with each of the next words she forced out. "What. Has. He. Done?"

"He's remained true to them," I said to the floor.

When she spoke, her voice was softer. "He is true to them, Ezekial." She was closer now. "The three of you have got to be more careful. You are no longer normal citizens. Not of the Fifth. Not of the Sixth. Not of any Circle. You were the Segregate. You are the Great Prince." She was in front of me now, rubbing both my shoulders. Her head swiveled to either side, including Bilba and Ralrek. "And you two are the most trusted demons in the Underworld. Demons everywhere depend on you to protect Ezekial from himself as well as from others. The three of you cannot take chances like this anymore. Did you not see the Council guards? They're all over the place."

"We saw a few on our way through Old Towne," I said.

Her hands dropped away. "And those are just the ones you saw on a single walk. If you were here more often, which I do not want you to be unless we've coordinated first, you would understand how prevalent they are. More each day."

"Why? What's going on?" Ralrek asked, looking perturbed.

Dialphio's head dropped. "We don't know. That's the problem. An uninformed citizenry and a growing law enforcement presence are never a sign of a stable and healthy society. You have to be more careful, okay?"

"Yes ma'am," came Bilba's prompt answer.

"Okay," Ralrek said.

"I will, Dialphio. I'm sorry," I said last.

Her shoulders rose and fell as if releasing a world of tension. "This brings up a good point. Something is afoot, something I can't quite put my finger on yet. Our mutual friend hasn't been able to help. Not more than a series of cryptic messages. I fear it's time for the three of you to take the next step."

I waited. The last thing I was going to do was set myself up for another—deserved, I admit—ass-chewing from my beloved bookstore owner.

"It's time to spy on the Council," she said flatly, as if she were putting in an order at her favorite restaurant.

"How in the heaven can we do that?" I asked, meaning every stunned word of my question.

"Our friend has mentioned interesting discussions taking place amongst Lucifer's Third. Interesting discussions that could become problematic. Since at least two of you can now open gateways, it would be possible to travel to a secure location where one might become privy to these discussions."

"What kind of secure location?" Ralrek asked.

Dialphio's emerald eyes flashed with playful deviousness. "In the Third Council's headquarters, of course."

14

UNDERWORLD/OLYMPIA

I LOOKED outside the front window of The Book Abyss, struck by the excited and entertained gestures and expressions of Old Towne's dining and bar patrons, its shoppers, its demons who just wanted to get out for a walk. The bright azure rays of the Hellfire brightened the day. Bless it, I love Old Towne. The second I stepped through the gateway, I was going to miss it.

"Look," a voice said from somewhere close, even though I swore only Bilba and Ralrek stood near me.

I spun, now paranoid even though we were upstairs in Dialphio's secret cell room.

Settled in the Sixth, no longer under the stress of facing my death, and I was still hearing things? From the Underworld to the Overworld and back. Great.

"Hey guys," Bilba said, interrupting my contemplation.

"What's up?" I asked.

He was looking at the notebook opened in his hands. He looked up. "We—" he stopped, swallowing, "—we have to go."

"Where?" Ralrek asked in his typical loquacious manner.

He pointed toward the ceiling. Dialphio's bookstore didn't have a third floor. This could only mean one thing.

"Cassie?" I asked in a rush.

He nodded.

"Let's go," I said, regretting that I hadn't carried my demonic notebook. "How long ago did she write?"

"No idea," Bilba said.

"Let me see the note," I said.

"Here." Bilba handed over the notebook and went to work opening the rift as soon as it was in my hands.

CASSIE: *Zeke, please come. Radicals harassing. Attacking —women's clinic. Need help.*

Horrible syntax. This was serious.

"Shit," I said, snapping the notebook closed.

The rift was almost open. The shimmering gray expanse of the Vigilante's headquarters peeked through. The hangar floor.

"Sorry, Zeke," Bilba said, already anticipating my complaint about jumping into the middle of a hangar floor. "But we're in a hurry and I can't concentrate in a rush."

"Don't worry, bud. Come on." As soon as I had enough space, I jumped into the opening between worlds.

After tumbling for a brief second, I was on solid concrete. The hangar buzzed with activity.

A lot of activity. Bodies darting everywhere, and even those who at first glance appeared static at stations around the hangar, hustled to prepare.

The weapons table was the busiest. A line of Vigilantes waited. Three of the group stood on the opposite side, handing out small firearms and running through safety and firing procedures. At the far end of the hangar, three vans had been backed inside, the rear doors stood open and Vigilantes scurried in a line like ants to load the vehicles.

"There's more of them than I thought," Bilba said.

I had to agree. In our previous visits to their headquarters, we'd seen maybe two dozen at the most. Now, that many were loading into each of the vans. Whatever Virgo was doing to build this organization, he was doing it well. Hell's rebels could learn a thing or two.

"Come on. Let's go find Virgo and Cassie," I said, and we crossed the hangar toward the meeting door.

This time I didn't knock.

"—when he gets here," Virgo was in the middle of saying as we stepped into the room.

Vigilantes filled the room. Bodies occupied every chair, and half a handful of humans, demons, and angels stood along the walls. They turned toward us.

Cassie got to her feet. "Thank Yahweh you're here."

Virgo nodded.

"What's going on? It looks like you are preparing for war," Ralrek said.

"Pretty near it," Steve said, sitting at the table, both elbows planted firmly on the wood. "The bastards just keep pushing."

"What's happening?" I asked, trying to find a starting point.

"They're back again," Cassie said. "This time they're getting physical, trying to intimidate innocent people outside and inside a women's clinic. It's a few blocks away. If we hurry, we can be there in a few minutes."

"We are hurrying. Making our last preparations. We had to wait for them," Virgo said, pointing at us.

"Why?" Bilba asked.

Virgo sat back in his chair, taking in the room. "Would you give us a few minutes?"

Chairs screeched as everyone pushed back. Papers collected, water bottles and soda cans were snagged into fists.

The room cleared with military efficiency. A quiet exodus. We were alone with Cassie and Virgo.

When the door closed, he said, "I wasn't going to act until you got here. We've been ready. Just waiting."

"You knew mortals were being attacked, and you did nothing?" I asked, disturbed.

Virgo seemed nonplussed. His fiery hazel eyes never flinched. "I'm not getting myself or the Vigilantes involved in this struggle without both of you present. I thought I was clear about that. If we do this." Virgo lifted a hand, his finger pointed at the table, making a circular motion as if he were drawing a circle. "We are going to do it on terms I'm comfortable with, or the Vigilantes will not get involved. The Upper and Underworlds can figure out how to proceed on their own if that's what you want."

"You know that's not what we want," Cassie said.

"But even with people getting hurt?" Bilba said.

Virgo's jaw clenched. "Even with people getting hurt." He paused, holding our attention. "Look, I know it may be difficult to understand, but what's to say there wouldn't be other repercussions of us getting involved with one side without the other present? If we had gone to support this harassment, some might see it as us supporting angels. What does that say to mortals on the team? What does that tell the angels who will find out about this? Or, the demons?"

"That makes sense," Bilba said.

I leaned closer and whispered from the corner of my mouth, "You're not helping."

"Sorry, but if the Vigilantes support either of us at a given time, it might create a dangerous perception. Just perception, alone, can be problematic. Once it exists, it's out of everyone's hands. It takes on a life of its own." He faced Virgo. "I appreciate why you did what you did. But we're here now. How can we help?"

"The group is posing as believers," Cassie said.

"Christians?" Ralrek asked.

Cassie's head rocked side to side in short, jerky movements, as her eyes crept closed, remaining like that for a brief second. "Yes. Yes, Christians. But they're not."

"And you know this how?" I asked.

She sat up straighter. "Because when I got the report, it was from an agent who is working undercover for us—"

"A spy," Ralrek said, his voice devoid of neutrality.

"Yes," Cassie said, elongating the word, "a spy. He's one who dropped the initial report of what was happening and who was committing the act. That's how I know they're agents of the Underworld."

"And that's why the Vigilantes weren't getting involved," Virgo said. "I'm sure the three of you can appreciate why I wouldn't want to be seen supporting an angel in a direct attack against demons, undercover or not. There's not enough trust between us for that."

A curious statement. "You don't trust us?"

Virgo, his forearms resting on the table, spread his hands. "I hardly know you. I know you're a good demon, and if you say those two are, I believe you. But to build trust, at least with me, it takes more. To be brutally honest, some of you have built far less than others."

Cassie shifted in her chair. It was subtle, but one I picked up. Was I the only one who noticed? "What's wrong?" I asked her.

She jerked. "Wh—what do you mean?"

I tipped my head toward Virgo. "His comment bothered you. Why? What else is happening?" I faced the leader of the Vigilantes. "You talk about the need to build trust. Well, that goes both ways, and right now, my gut tells me the two of you are holding something back."

"I'm not," Virgo said, staring straight ahead, addressing neither me nor my friends, nor the angel who sat to his left.

Noise drifted in from the hangar, and even that died a quick death in the confines of this stand-off.

Finally, Cassie spoke. Her voice was soft, restrictive. "Now is not the time. We have mortals who are being harassed. Abused. Some, probably hurt. We need to go."

"This is about trust. About me managing the Vigilantes to help both sides, or neither side. Something I'm responsible for when the four of you are back in your realms, and I'm left dealing with the fallout of what we decide right now," Virgo said, his voice cool, but firm. "It takes seconds for you to help establish that trust because this... event has massive implications."

An attack by agents of the immortal realm, be it from Hell or the Upperworld, was significant. It was a tactic that could influence the Balance and throw the Overworld into a spin it wouldn't come out of without completely wiping every smiling face from its surface. I understood that. Targeting mortals to gain power, and toy with the Balance at all to gain more influence, more power, was atrocious. If this event didn't have massive implications, it could be handled by an armed group of Abandoned and a smattering of invested humans. *If.*

My core temperature increased along with my growing frustration. The silent tug-of-war between Virgo and Cassie was annoying. Yes, Cassie was smoking hot, but if something was going on between the two of them, if they believed it was going to affect our operations, that could be dealt with at another time. It would suck, sure, but I'm not that shallow.

"I know how to build trust, at least between the Vigilantes and the Underworld," Bilba said, his high–pitched voice splitting the tension.

Virgo barked, "How?"

Bilba cleared his throat. "With our ability to open undetectable rifts between the Underworld and Overworld, we can do something no one has ever done before, at least no one I'm aware of."

I circled my finger, telling my friend to speed it up.

Blooming pink at the tips of Bilba's ears spread to his cheeks. "What I mean is, we could reach an agreement to take Vigilantes back to the Underworld. We could start bringing demons home."

"For what?" Virgo asked, his eyes narrowed.

"F—fo—for nothing," Bilba stuttered. "Well, I mean, so they can return home and live normal lives. Since we can travel without detection, we could get them home the same way. It would stop their decay. Being back there would restore their immortality." He turned to include Cassie in the conversation. "I'm sure angels could do the same thing. I couldn't do that for them, but someone on your side could. If we started this, then your Vigilantes could help both sides without the other being present, because we would already be building trust by returning demons and angels to their rightful homes."

"Sneaking demons back into the Underworld?" Ralrek mumbled, as though mulling over the proposition.

Bilba was a genius. What happened to demons once they were back in the Underworld, how they went about re-engaging in everyday life, was a more difficult question that could be ironed out later. Right now, Bilba had offered a feasible solution to a problem that was slowing everything.

"Sort of like how the mortals had the Underground Railroad?" Cassie said.

Bilba nodded. "Exactly. I mean, it wouldn't be that big. We could only sneak one or two back at a time until we're sure. But the concept is the same."

"What would you call it?" Ralrek asked. "You can't use the same name as the mortal's effort. That's offensive."

Bilba's cheeks wobbled as he shook his head. "I—I don't know. I haven't thought that far into it. It's something I've been thinking about since we met the Vigilantes. We could… call it the Highway to Hell, or something."

Ralrek smashed his lips together, jutting his jaw to the side, scratching it. "That's a mouthful."

"What about The Path?" I propose, wanting to move this along.

"Not very imaginative," Ralrek said.

"No, but it's simple, and ambiguous," I said. "We could use it and so could the angels, and no one who wasn't already in-the-know would have any idea what we're talking about. Plus, it has all the spiritual connotations worshipers need. It's perfect. We can always change it later. It's the idea that matters." Now I turned to Virgo. "Sound good? Does it do enough to earn your trust so we can help these mortals? Like now?"

His bottom jaw extended, showing teeth. "It does. It helps a lot." He pressed on the table, pushing himself up. His eyes bore into Cassie. "Trust is vital if the five of us are going to work together. We can't have secrets."

Cassie's head dropped.

"Are you telling him, or am I?" Virgo asked, not moving from the spot where he stood, but crossing his arms.

Cassie pressed her hands to the notched wood, pushing herself up. "We have more important things to do. We can deal with it later."

The way she enforced each word told me it was very much a big deal.

"Fine," Virgo snapped, "I'll put it out in the open and the rest of you can work it out after we're done dealing with this mess. But I'm not walking into this without everything being on the up–and–up. Guys," Virgo said, turning away from Cassie, whose eyes flared, "Cassie has been nominated for a position on the Upperworld's Council. Yahweh's Council."

By the time I turned my stunned face to Cassie, she was already watching me, her head hung low.

Cassie, serving on Yahweh's Council as one of the decision-makers of the Upperworld? One of its most powerful angels?

And she had never said a word.

Maybe Virgo was right about this whole trust issue.

"I AM SORRY," Cassie said, rounding the table and moving closer. Her fresh smell soured by hidden truths.

Virgo cast us a wary look before stepping out of the meeting room. Bilba and Ralrek followed closely behind, saying they would help. That left me alone with the angel who had lost some of her flair in the past few seconds.

"I just don't get it. Were you ever going to tell me?" I asked, trying to not sound like a pouting imp. "After everything we've been through, I thought you could trust me enough to share that."

She shook her head, a few strands of her cocoa hair falling loose. She tucked them behind her ear.

I swallowed. I think.

"Regardless of what V—Virgo says, it's not about trust. I didn't tell you because it never came up," Cassie said. "I don't want this to come between us. It's no big deal."

I did one of those cough–laughs that you do when you're ticked off and exasperated by someone. "No big deal? You're up for a position on Yahweh's blessed Council, Cassie!"

She flinched. "Please don't swear. You're better than that. And, I'm well aware of what I'm up for. There's been talk for a long time. Why do you think I keep getting these types of missions? They've been grooming me, going back way before the mission with Gemini."

"How in the world am I supposed to know how the Upperworld works? I just thought you were good at your job," I said. Yep, I sounded like a pouting imp.

"Z—Zeke, please don't. I swear, if everything were calmer, and I wasn't thwarting demonic activity, I might have had time to visit with you. We could have talked," she said. We hadn't had time. "All of this is stupid, really. I'm good at my job, but a nomination to the Council? It's not going to happen. I'm not going to actually be selected."

"Why not?"

Cassie opened her mouth and then snapped it shut, like she nearly said the last thing she wanted to say. Her shoulders rose with a dramatic sigh. "To be honest, I'm seen in a good light in the Upperworld. My work has been noticed by the right angels. Right place, right time. That's why. Plus, I'm not worried about it because it won't happen. I'm far too young."

Good decorum demands that you don't ask a lady her age. But since when was I anything but awkward around the female persuasion. "How young are you?"

One corner of Cassie's mouth curled up. "I'm eight-thousand and some change, since you're asking. You also want to know my weight?"

"Don't be a jerk," I said, feeling the initial heat of an embarrassed blush.

"I wanted to tell you, Z—Zeke, but the opportunity never came up, and I didn't want to sound like a braggart either," she said.

"Oh, don't worry about that. If your Council is anything like ours, a position on it is nothing to brag about," I said. "Still, I would have enjoyed celebrating that accomplishment with you."

"Are you asking me out on a date?" Cassie asked.

"We've already gone for drinks and look where that led us," I said. "Plus, I'm a beer drinker and you drink fancy stuff. You're not a cheap date."

That drew an ugly laugh–snort from the angel. Her smile dropped, her tone turning serious. "I would have told you... someday. It would have been a risk because of the attention on you. Please believe me when I say it wasn't easy to not tell you. Plus, the timing never seemed right. My attention was on other places, and it's not like we were close enough to talk about this during the events in Germany. Then we both went our separate ways for... what? Nearly two years? Even if I had the chance, I still might not have said anything until I knew it was actually going to happen. Not that I didn't trust you. Not that I *don't* trust you. But you've been in a bad spot for a while. Even if things were different, I still have no chance."

"Are you saying that if I'd come out directly and asked you, you would have misled me because you wanted to protect me?" I asked, my disbelief turning my mood sour.

"Probably," she said. "It would have caused too many... issues. For both of us. I'd always wanted to tell you. Our friendship means a lot to me. It's just... it's not that simple."

Before I had time to ask her what that meant, Bilba barged into the room. "Guys, come on. Something's happening." He dashed back out before we made a move.

Cassie shot toward the door, but I grabbed her wrist before she was out of reach. She turned, her crystal eyes wide.

"We're not done talking about this," I said, not without compassion.

She looked at my hand on her wrist. I let go, but she clutched my hand. I tingled. "I like that deal. And maybe I'll let you buy me that expensive drink. Now, let's go."

The angel spun and left the meeting room. I drew a calming breath before I followed.

Thirty feet away, Virgo oversaw the activity while in deep conversation with a short, hard–looking man. Enough space was between the pair for me to sense if he was Abandoned, immortal, or other. I extended my senses, not feeling any emissions. A mortal. Each time he spoke, Virgo leaned down so the man could whisper in his ear. With a sharp nod, Virgo dismissed him.

Virgo raised his arm, finger extended, making a circular motion. "Load up!"

Vigilantes piled into the backs of the vans.

Virgo jutted his chin in our direction. "Split up among the three vans. Don't ride together. We don't want to risk losing all of you with a single attack."

What did Virgo think we were riding into? During our army stint, Bilba, Ralrek, and I had deployed to Iraq. We were well-versed on the discipline of convoys. We under-stood how this worked. This was reminiscent of that time, just with less chest beating and with a lot less "hurrahing."

Virgo jumped in the passenger seat of the van on the left, so I went to the one on the right. Ralrek rode with Virgo. Bilba jumped in the middle one. Cassie joined me—sheer luck and all that.

Virgo's van shot out of the hangar, the side mirrors an inch away from scraping steel. The other two vehicles fell in behind. From my seat in the back, I couldn't see much through the front window. Within minutes, we were leaving the harbor area dominated by a log yard, racing up Franklin Street, and into the denser downtown area before turning east.

A new condo complex had grown up out of the parking lot since the last time I was in this part of Olympia, a three-story structure that made hiding and unloading the vans easy. The obstruction blocked the line of sight for any demons at the women's clinic.

"Everyone, check your weapons. We do this correctly," Virgo barked the order even as the vans were still unloading.

I looked behind me. The pub on the other side of the parking lot, which should have been open, was shuttered. At least we didn't have to worry about witnesses or casualties there. When we made our way to the street, both directions revealed that anyone who had been outside had scurried to safety. All signs of life in Olympia had been washed away for blocks east of the clinic.

"We do this quietly," Virgo ordered, waving his small army of Vigilantes forward. We sprinted down the sidewalk, crossing the road at the intersection.

I fell in behind the leader, even though I was one of the last to leave the parking lot. My adrenaline surged with the oncoming confrontation, blocking my brain from any thought but staying close to Virgo.

The clinic was shielded from the rest of the neighborhood by a tall, corrugated metal fence painted forest green, perhaps to match the spirit of the Olympic forests that surrounded the city. The gate had been closed from the inside, secured with a thick chain and lock. Virgo slammed against it, but that only resulted in the fence rocking open and swinging back closed.

"Get back," I said, pulling Creed from the loop and activating it. The steel blades clanged to life. As I brought Creed up over my head, I rotated it so that the moon-shaped ax head bit through the chain—hot knife meet butter.

One man growled. "Nice!"

Virgo shouldered the gate, and it flew open this time. The Vigilantes and us immortal supplements raced into the parking lot.

"Close that. See if you can bar it too," Virgo ordered the Vigilante at the end of the line. "I don't want any surprises coming up our backsides."

A woman in worn combat fatigues slid to a halt, spun, and reached for the gate with both hands. With a heave, she flung the gate and braced it closed with her knee until she secured the latch.

"On your guard," Virgo ordered.

The Vigilantes moved through the crowd of cars at a slow walk, each hunching over.

I stayed toward the rear, watching my friends spread out. Bilba took the far west corner. Ralrek slid along the fence to the east side of the parking lot. Cassie moved up the middle between the rows of cars, hugging one line for shelter. From the back, I extended my senses toward the three-story building.

There are things, whether Over or Underworld, that are eerie and unnerving. A forest at night comes to mind. Eve's Sanctuary can get like that too when no demons are around and the only sounds come from creatures hiding in its over-grown vegetation, especially the sprites, the spying little creeps. Empty streets at night are another. A silent parent sitting on the other side of the dinner table after you've done something you knew would disappoint them. And this parking lot.

It was too quiet.

"Liberate," a voice said near me, though I was standing alone.

I didn't have time to lose my mind.

My frustration grew at the lack of sound. We'd wasted too much valuable time at the Vigilantes headquarters fighting over how important trust was. Now, we might pay for that delay.

I extended my senses toward the clinic, unsure if I could pick anything up through the brick, steel, insulation, and whatever else was packed into that construction. As the wave pushed out, I picked up the signatures of the immortals and Abandoned. Easy enough now that every caster was conjuring.

Ralrek's Fire magic scratched my right side, the stickiness

of Bilba's Deception on my left. From the center of the parking lot came the joyful experience of a subtle migraine building at the base of my skull from my immortal-enemy-turned-friend, Cassie. Whatever she was about to do promised pain, and not just for her target. Sometimes, I can't believe how cursed I am—that's sarcasm, by the way.

Underneath it, from the direction of the building parallel to the lot, I felt... something. It was difficult to discern, partially because of the stimulus of the magic, but also because the clinic hid an untold number of immortals who may already be privy to our presence. If they were, they'd be preparing their response. The difference was, the demons on the other side of the brick wall were unseen and protected, their magic muted by the physical barriers.

Creed thumped. A window on the top floor shot open, and the muted sense I had of Abilities from within clarified.

"Get down!" I shouted a moment too late.

A thin stream of fire roared from the building. The flame caught two of the Vigilantes sneaking across the parking lot. They burst into flame, which roared five feet above their heads in a thin inferno. From toe to tip, they were engulfed, wildly swinging their arms in panicked pain. Their screams made me want to vomit.

Virgo shouted new orders as another window on the top story opened. With my body reacting to the diverse sources of magic, it was difficult to focus on what was coming from that second window. I had to warn everyone, but warn them about what? It didn't matter. Bad stuff was swelling in hiding.

"Be on your guard," I said.

Bilba held both arms diagonally away from his body at waist-level and then swooped them toward the building. I'd never seen him do that move, but I loved the result. Seconds after his gesture, a swarm of bats arced out of the sky and into the fight. Before they reached the building, a new sensation hit me from the second window. Inside my skull, a tickling. Bless it. Discernment magic.

Lucifer, I hate Discernment spells. Ever since my frightening experience with Taurus in the Eighth Circle, I haven't been at peace with the fact that some demons—too many—possess the Ability. Discernment magic screws with your head. Literally.

As Bilba's bats swarmed toward the building, I watched in helpless horror as a Vigilante turned toward Virgo's small army, aimed his pistol, and began firing. Three Vigilantes dropped to the blacktop before the rest took cover. A bright, white arrow of energy shot from Cassie's hand taking the poor bastard under the Discernment attack out. He was engulfed in a white orb that flashed to nothingness along with the victim. As if he never existed.

"There!" Virgo pointed toward the two open windows, and the Vigilantes focused their efforts on them.

Our gunfire was going to draw authorities. This had to end. Now. The problem was, we couldn't do that from the parking lot.

I sprinted across the expanse of blacktop, reaching the front door and trying to pull it open. It was locked, but made of glass. I stepped back, raising Creed with both arms, and thrust it forward from its high-guard position. Glass shattered, spraying the floor inside the clinic.

Ducking under the crossbar, I entered the building, bringing Creed up to mid-guard. A stairwell was directly ahead. I took it to the next floor, listening for any hint where I might find the agents of Hell. With the battle raging outside, I couldn't hear a thing.

From office to office I moved, searching each with wary steps. Toward the end of the hall, I found another stairwell which wrapped upward to the last floor.

Reaching the landing, I extended my senses, feeling Abilities in the room two doors to my right. I crept forward. As I reached for the handle, Creed nearly shocked me as its blades burst to life with Hellfire blue.

Immense power. My chest swelled. I felt indestructible.

Stepping back, I lowered my shoulder and rammed. The door flew inward. I stumbled into the room, shocking its occupants as much as I shocked myself. My accomplishment was the stuff of movies and Jason Momoa, not this little magicless demon—I guessed being the Great Prince had its advantages.

"Back off, Sunstone," an incubus, as tall as Ralrek, but half as wide, said. He reminded me of one of those waving blow-up stick figures at local car dealerships. "Or they die."

In the room's corner, three mortals cowered, all women, each young enough to not remember the greatest mortal musical era—the eighties heavy metal revolution, of course.

I snarled at the incubus. "Let them go." I lowered the double-axes at him to reinforce my message.

"Yeah, I'll get right on that. Letting go of the only leverage I have," he scoffed like my demand was only a suggestion. "Better yet, you take one more step, and I will light them all up."

He wasn't joking, of course. I had already sensed him holding his Ability active. The power of Fire magic radiated off him. But with the fight roaring outside and inside, it was difficult to separate his Ability from the others flaring from the parking lot and the other rooms of the building, even at this proximity. But he had given me a clue to his nature. He was a Fire caster, most likely the demon who had sent the first stream that killed the first two Vigilantes.

I inched forward. "They don't have a say in this. They've done nothing wrong. Let them go."

My order hung in the air, accompanied only by the crackle of Hellfire coming off Creed's blades. The halberd pulsed, low and dangerous. I felt... hungry.

The floor shook, and I stumbled, catching myself on the

wall. An explosion roared toward us. The women in the corner screamed. I screamed. The incubus who served as my adversary squealed.

"Get to the rift! Get to the rift!" someone shouted in the hall.

The incubus flicked his eyes toward the voice and then to me. I was the only thing stopping him from getting back to the Underworld.

I grinned.

"Don't do it," I warned, feeling the rising scratchiness of an oncoming spell.

As his hands glowed, I moved in a line between him and the women, spinning Creed to create a shield. As he loosed his stream of fire, Creed surged. The shield grew, increasing its radiance.

The women screamed again, but I focused on holding the shield and moving toward the incubus to push him back to the window. The last thing that was going to happen, besides the women escaping, was this twat scurrying back to some hole like the cherub he was. He had a decision to make soon. Did he want to remain alive and answer some awkward questions, or was he looking to be Abolished?

My skin raked like a million fingernails were trying to claw inside me. Glancing over my shoulder, I shouted to the women, "Run! Go, now!"

The incubus loosed a stream of fire even as they scrambled to safety. I lowered my head and pushed Creed's shield outward. My steps were slow. I took another step forward, straining against the strong stream. On the other side of Creed's shield, the incubus growled with exertion. His fire pushed me back, forcing me to plant my feet to stop the slide as he put more power into his spell.

Leaning into Creed, I panted, "Come on, buddy. Work with me on this."

Creed's shield colored a blue hue, brightening. With the

additional Hellfire added to the barrier between me and the incubus, the weight of force lessened. I pushed my foe toward the window to keep him away from the door. Even if I only delayed his escape, I had to keep him away from the rift.

Staring into his eyes, I grinned as I pushed him against the glass. A large part of me wanted to keep pushing, to squeeze him between the Hellfire–engorged shield and the window. But I never got the chance.

As he slammed against the glass, a burst of white light penetrated the incubus's chest from outside the building. It pierced him and slammed against Creed's shield, which shook but did not fail. I was going to have a talk with a particular angel at the end of this fight.

The incubus was swallowed in an orb of white, just as Cassie's spell had done to the Vigilante outside. Nothing remained of the demon. Not even a pile of ash.

I pointed at the clean floor, dipping Creed's ax heads. "See? That's how you take care of someone. Clean up after yourself from now on, okay?"

The threat removed, I ran out of the room. The rift had to be nearby. Listening for its sizzle, I passed office after office of frightened mortals. As I neared the end of the hall, the Hellfire fizzled and fell from Creed's blades, now nothing more than dull steel.

The parking lot was quiet. Voices drifted from the first-floor stairwell. The Vigilantes were coming.

Bracing myself against the wall, I peered around the corner into the office, noting lingering remnants of the rift that had been closed a moment too soon. The squad of demonic agents had escaped. That was going to be a problem.

"Zeke?" Ralrek's voice called from the stairwell landing.

"Coming!" I called back. As I raced along the hallway, I shouted to the mortals in hiding. "It's okay. You can come out. Call the police and ambulances."

Ralrek was halfway down the stairwell, looking up at me. "We've got to go."

"I know," I said, taking the stairs two at a time. Thank Lucifer for healthy, youthful knees.

We raced into the parking lot. The gate was cracked open. Virgo waited, waving to us. "Let's go. Let's go!" Then his head disappeared from the other side of the fence.

I kept my pace slow enough that Ralrek could keep up— I'm not bragging, I'm just showing how nice of a demon I am.

We reached the vans and sped away, back to the headquarters before the approaching sirens delivered the authorities.

The van was quiet during the short ride back. As we unloaded, I collapsed in a chair in Virgo's meeting room. Cassie sat across the table from me, her head thrown back. More of Virgo's leadership team filed in, along with my two friends.

"Thank you, everyone," Cassie said in a strained tone once the full team arrived and the door was closed. "I know what you just did wasn't easy, and I know you have suffered losses, but please know what you did today was important."

Cassie's gratitude gained grumbling acceptance. Virgo nodded.

"They were good people," Steve said solemnly, to which he received more quiet acknowledgement.

"Today won't be forgotten," Cassie said, taking in each Vigilante before turning to Virgo. "I swear to you, I will help, just as they are helping with this Path, or Highway to Hell, or whatever it'll be called. I'll work on it from my end so Abandoned angels can return home, if they choose."

"You would do that?" Virgo asked.

"I'll do whatever I can to right past wrongs," Cassie said, her eyes locking on me.

UNDERWORLD, SIXTH CIRCLE

DECOMPRESSING after a traumatic event is always a good idea. Even immortals do it.

Days after the events in Olympia, I'd gone into recluse–mode. I couldn't deal with All-Things-Zeke at the moment. Not that I blamed myself for what happened up there and the deaths of seven Vigilantes. I didn't. But I felt horrible every time I thought about the seven who weren't enjoying another day because some scumbag in Hell screwed with the Overworld.

The battle hadn't resulted in civilian casualties, though there were a few injuries. After hearing the status report from Cassie through the notebook, I tried to purge my mind. In the past, I dwelled on these things, and always found myself burrowing deeper. If my aim was to shake up the Council, I had to persevere and take better care of myself.

The old Zeke would have pouted about Cassie's secret keeping and the constant infringement on mortals by the Council—since I was convinced they were behind the attack on the women's clinic. But I was different now. I had been different. It was a slow change, but when you live as long as we do, you've got time to be thorough in making changes.

Instead of soaking in my frustration, I was out and about in the Sixth Circle on a mission.

The last time I talked to either Bilba or Ralrek was upon returning home after the demonic attack. I hadn't heard from them since because, honestly, incubi don't do that. We don't enjoy talking even when we're together, nevermind over long distances. Maybe it's just an incubi thing? Whatever the case, Ralrek may or may not be searching for his friend to help find the coordinates to the Horn. I wasn't going to wait around to hear word back. I was bored. I needed to get the heaven out of my apartment and learn about my neighborhood. I needed to take my mind off Olympia and the angel up there.

Walking the streets of the Sixth was my solution.

I headed out, armed with the coordinates on a new piece of paper since the old one had taken a beating, and my halberd, who hadn't shown a spark of life since Olympia. I think he was still recovering. Lazy stick. Creed can be temperamental at the best of times, and now I had to question his work ethic. I was taking him for a walk, whether or not he wanted to go. Of course, he'd come along whether or not I wanted him to. We were codependent like that.

The day was bright and blue, another beautiful, stinking day in the Circle. Like every day, the eternal flames burning from rooftops, sidewalks, city parks, and just about any orifice in the blessed Circle, greeted me. No, I still hadn't gotten used to that lingering stink. If a demon wasn't born in the Sixth, how did they get used to this stench? I mean, seriously, how could my nose not be offended? Noses, even immortal ones, weren't designed to inhale the smell of bad meat day in and day out. Well, unless the Circle was where you were born and raised. Regardless of how far or which direction I walked, the smells were worse here than in the blazebull stables I worked in through college. "Slinging mud," we called it, but trust me, it wasn't mud. And it stunk. Almost as bad as the Sixth.

I'd never take clean air for granted ever again.

Today wasn't the first time I'd gotten out and wandered around my new home Circle. Typically, I went for walks while looking for a job. The job search at least got me out of the apartment and forced me to familiarize myself with my neighborhood and pick up on the subtle differences in the way demons decorated their windows, some added potted plants to door stoops, and the small businesses that denoted one identical block from another.

One thing the Sixth offered was friendly demons. I realized within days of arriving just how kind everyone was. Each time I went out, my early experiences were reinforced. These were good demons. Maybe it was because of the environment they lived in. Maybe it was because their nature demanded kindness. I didn't know, but I embraced it. My native Fivers weren't rude, but with the Fifth Circle bustling with activity, it is a place where demons rarely paused to appreciate life. They filled each minute with something, be it work or pleasure. Whereas, everyone here embraced a slower lifestyle, which made it a heaven of a lot easier to unwind and relax.

Which I needed, thus the long, meandering walk around as much of the Circle as I could manage in search of a hint to the Horn's location. The... uh, open air was recuperative for my occupied mind.

In Olympia, I regretted not getting to the rift early enough to catch who had opened it. Not that its originator would be standing in the office of the women's clinic. But they might have been. Now, I'd never know. Without finding out, I couldn't know who was behind the attack. Of course, if the same demon who opened the rift also happened to serve on Lucifer's Third Council, they wouldn't have had to stand in the Overworld to keep it open. Another clue. They could have opened the blessed portal and walked away to catch a quick lunch while their hired thugs terrorized the poor mortals.

Finding the Horn would go a long way to unsettling what-ever nefarious plan were in the works. One of the most powerful artifacts in the Underworld, Azazel urged me to find it for a reason. According to Bilba, who reads everything printed about every dorky topic possible, the Horn dates to the beginning of our time and possesses immense powers that elevate the individual capabilities of the demon possessing it. By possessing it, someone could move undetected by Lucifer's Council. If they could do that, the entirety of the Under and Overworlds was theirs to enjoy. How that impacted the Overworld and the Balance was a problem too big for my brain. At some point, I'd have to sit down with Bilba and listen as he dumped his library of knowledge about the artifact. The Horn itself is one of a pair, with a matching Halo artifact possessed by the Upperworld. Bilba talked about a conspiracy called "the Horn and Halo Effect." Bilba loves conspiracies. I rarely listen when he talks about them. Maybe I should have. We never made it a priority. That, and it sounded absolutely nuts. He had said something or other about the two powerful artifacts coming together as a single piece, initiating the destruction of everything, including the universe.

Like I said, crazy talk.

Regardless of what the Horn could or could not do, it was important enough to steal from under the noses of Hell's most powerful demons.

The last time I saw the Horn, Seraph was carrying it through a gateway back to Council headquarters, leaving Bilba, Ralrek, and I in the Eighth Circle to wrap up our business.

Finding the Horn would cause a headache for the Council —an enjoyable thought. We just needed to find it as soon as possible. According to Azazel, that needed to happen yesterday.

The problem was, I had no idea how to use these coordinates. Until Ralrek came through on finding his friend, I was on a blind search.

Which led me to bumping into something. Or better yet, someone.

Holding my hands up, I apologized by wagging the paper with the coordinates on it at the succubus. "I'm so sorry. I was reading. Not looking where I was going."

The succubus, strands of wrinkles webbing out from the corners of her eyes, waved as she bounced on the balls of her feet. "No worries. May the Hellfire shine on you."

She was off before I could respond in-kind, the customary response.

Back on my way, I rounded the corner and found this street was short. Less than a half a block. Bordered by identical buildings hugging the street, rooftops smoked. The street opened to a rounded circle of open cobblestone. A large fountain sat in the center of the circle, which was filled with pedestrians. Instead of water, the fountain spewed a red sludge that could have been lava. Gray smoke billowed from the molten material as it oozed out of the decorative top and into the waiting pool below. A smattering of demons sat on the curved lip of the fountain's edge reading or eating lunch. A pair of succubi, their knees angled together, leaned towards each other, chitchatting. Behind the fountain, an elderly incubus in a wooden folding chair, a musical stand placed in front of him, played cheerful tunes on his trumpet. A thin line of demons stood in a half-circle, listening and clapping along to the ditty.

A row of food vendors lined the far wall of this festive circle. I grabbed a hot dog, piled high with mushrooms, relish, and a few peppers. In the Overworld, the peppers would give the dog the right kick, but here, it was all about different texture. As far as taste, this dog and garnish was going to be as tasty as hydrated Overworld noodles. Armed with this morsel, I explored the festivities.

The spirit was so light and joyful. Festive. I didn't want to leave. I no longer wanted to search for the Horn—at least for the moment. I didn't want to think about Lucifer's Council or the fact they might have operatives attacking mortals in the Overworld. I didn't want to think about Beelzebub working on his subversive power grab. I didn't want to think about Cassie, up for nomination to Yahweh's Council. I definitely didn't want to think about what that meant for my chances to see her if they selected her.

I wanted to enjoy this tasteless, if smoky, hot dog, listen to an elderly incubus trumpet fun tunes, and watch my neighbors enjoying themselves.

Sideways glances, elbow nudges, and finger points in my direction caught my attention. Maybe it was because I was a stranger, and this community was so tight knit they knew any outsider.

Maybe it was because the legend of Zeke was growing. The Council worked very hard in ensuring their propaganda was the only propaganda. They had the resources and the influence to ensure news programs and tabloids reported events in their favor. Even my trial by combat against Leo did nothing to paint me in a positive light with Hell's outlets. For a week, debates on talk shows centered on my actions, and I rarely came out in a positive light. Of course, you had to expect that when the outlets were nothing more than mouthpieces for the powerful.

Even though I was garnering attention, none of it seemed hostile. More curious, if truth be told. Okay, some appeared fascinated, especially the knee–touching succubi. I didn't have a problem with that. But hostility? None.

Smoky, bad-meat air aside, the Sixth was starting to grow on me.

Finished with the hot dog, I threw the wrapper away, and hung out to listen to the elderly musician until he apologized, saying he needed to take a break and rehydrate. Those who had been listening moved forward and dropped coins in an upturned hat in front of his music stand.

I dug into my pocket and pulled out a silver, dropping it in.

The elderly incubus followed it all the way into the hat, then looked up at me. "Very kind of you, Ezekial. Thank you for that gesture."

I straightened. "Do I... know you?"

Three demons were waiting behind me to donate.

The old incubus laughed like two tin soda cans knocked together. "Everyone knows who you are. Ezekial Sunstone, the Segregate. I might be an old musician, but that doesn't mean I'm not educated. I watch the news every night. I've seen you and your adventures. Quite the young incubus, you are. Now, you're holding up the line, and I've got coin to make. That's my dinner you're interfering with," he said with a smile, standing and delivering a grand bow. "Have a wonderful evening."

"May the Hellfire shine on you," I said, dipping my head in an awkward return bow. I probably looked ridiculous.

I walked away, still stunned, and left the festive cobble-stone circle.

Rounding the corner, I was back in the relative peace of the Sixth. Without wagons or carriages navigating the street, hearing footsteps was easy. The pace at which my follower approached set me on alert. My hand slid to Creed as I turned to face my pursuer.

The incubus pulled up short. My height—poor bastard. He had large eyes and ears that poked out from underneath his salt and peppered brown hair—a distinguished look. I could pick him out of the lineup of a hundred demons. He blinked rapidly and with such force that it scrunched his face each time.

"Hi... Hi... Are you... Are you Ezekial Sunstone?" he asked.

My hand was still on Creed when I answered. "I am. How can I help you?"

The incubus threw his head to the side with a broad smile. "Oh, man, this is so cool. To get to meet you. What a day. What a day."

"Well... thank you?" I said. "Not sure what I did to deserve that, but I appreciate your energy."

The incubus turned in the direction of the festivities. He pointed as if it were behind him. "I was in the circle and I heard the musician talking to you. Of course, I heard the whispers when you first showed up too, but I thought they were all crazy. Ezekial Sunstone, I said. Can't be. He doesn't live in the Sixth. But then I thought about it and thought I remembered hearing something about you moving here after your trial."

I rocked my head. "'Moved' is a relative term." Realizing how rude I sounded, I corrected myself. "Not that I have a problem with the Sixth. I'm enjoying myself here."

The incubus pressed his bottom lip into his top, pushing the corners of his mouth down. "Good to hear. Good to hear. Well, I don't want to take much of your time. I just... man, I can't believe you're really here."

I had to laugh. This wasn't hilarious, but his debilitating joy was infectious. "I'm not all that. Really. I promise."

He blinked rapidly, slamming those eyelids together over and over. "You don't know. You've done so much for demonkind. So many good things. And... I don't know." He craned his neck to look back toward the corner that tucked the informal street festival away before turning back, leaning to the side, and looking past me. He lowered his voice. "Maybe it's just my opinion, but what has happened to you is bullshit. Anyone with half a brain can see that. Now, don't get me wrong, plenty of stupid demons believe everything they're told. But isn't that the way of demons? Some, too gullible for their own good. But not me. I don't believe half of what I hear in the news."

"A good way to approach life," I mumbled.

"Definitely. Definitely. Just too much crap that doesn't make sense, you know?" He stopped, bringing his hands in front of his body and slapping his palms together. "Of course, you would. Of anyone, you'd understand. Just a blessed shame. Blessed shame. Well, I just wanted you to know that you're appreciated. The things you've done, that stuff travels. Demons know. Just a shame those in power don't listen."

"Oh, they listen. The problem is, they're only listening to those who tell them what they want to hear," I said.

Another hard blink before his shoulders rocked with a laugh. "Truth. Truth. I'll tell you, the Underworld would be a heaven of a lot better if someone like you were Lucifer. Let me tell you. You get it. Your heart is in the right place." He took a half step closer. I stayed where I was. Leaning in, he said, "My uncle is well–to–do. He has more coin than he'll ever use in his life, greedy bastard. Anyway, the reason I tell you is because he got a ticket to your trial. In the fighting pit. Remember?" He smacked his hands, forcing me to check around us to make sure he wasn't drawing attention. "Of course you remember! He told us about the fight, what really happened. Said it looked like you tried hard not to fight the other guy. Like you knew it was wrong. Until that day, he wasn't sure about you. Uneasy with what the Council was doing because so much of it didn't make sense, but still he wasn't on-board with what some have been saying about you. But boy oh boy, you convinced him at the trial."

My thoughts slipped to Leo, the dark harbinger of regret evident in my tone. "I killed an incubus. An innocent incubus. A friend."

This incubus's tone matched my own. "We get it. We do. A lot of us, too. There wasn't a straightforward way out of that situation, for sure. But it wasn't your fault. That's what a lot of demons are saying. All around the Sixth. Now, don't get me wrong. We don't go talking about it openly, but you have demons on your side. Trust me when I say that." He held up one hand in front of his face, crossed his middle and pointer finger. "Here's to wishing you get some breaks. Would love to see you take up a local Council position in the Circle. Heavens, maybe even Lucifer's Council one day." The incubus chuckled as he blinked. "Well, I've bugged you long enough. Just had to share my thoughts. Never thought I'd ever get to meet you, so had to take the opportunity when it presented itself, you know? Ha! Of course you do. Anyway, have a great one."

The incubus stretched out his hand. I took it and we shook. He gave me a long wink and then he was gone, back around the corner.

I turned toward home, shaking my head at the strange afternoon. I'd left the house to spend the day looking for the Horn and to forget everything else. As luck had it, I stumbled into a set of reminders that I could never escape my circumstances.

At least I'd found a new place to hang whenever I needed to get out. Who knew, maybe I'd even find someone looking to hire, or for a drinking buddy. Or a drinking buddy who was looking to hire.

I took a deep breath, inhaling the smoky air of the Sixth— a friendly place. My new home.

17

UNDERWORLD, FIFTH CIRCLE

THE BITTER AROMA of coffee filled the room, something I appreciated. Without it, I would have had to tolerate the cloud of body odor it covered.

The rebel cell had been in the room all day, Dialphio said, copying *The Histories of the Balance*. Without being sure how much of the task they'd accomplished, at least they succeeded in scenting the air with their efforts.

Thank Lucifer for coffee.

"The number of terrible events is increasing. Accelerating as well. And we're copying a book," Ret said, slapping the open page in front of him. By the relative thinness of the open fold, the incubus had done little copying.

"You're barely doing that," Dialphio said, tapping his copy as she walked by.

I smiled at my former boss. From customers with attitudes, to bullies, to my father in front of the rest of the family, and even the Council before they Abandoned me, no one intimidated this succubus. Dialphio wasn't going to go easy on a pouting rebel.

"We achieve what we can achieve, and we prepare for what will come," Dialphio said, now directing her comments to everyone. "We can't stop what they're doing, but we can make preparations for our response."

"Just be careful to not spend eternity preparing," Ralrek said. He hovered over the rear table covered with plates of junk food.

"Were we equipped to engage, we would," Dialphio said. "Unfortunately, that is not our reality. Not yet." She spread her arms out, turning. "There are less than twenty of us. Until our influence grows, we have to exercise extreme caution. Until we grow, we cannot act without it, unless we wish to unravel everything we've been doing for years. That is why we are doing this," she said, tapping the copy of a new *Histories* in front of Illis. The old succubus traded her garish purple blouse for an equally offensive mustard yellow one.

Nostris tapped his quill to his open book. "I understand why distributing copies is important."

Dialphio's turned, looking at his work. We waited. Nothing followed. She shifted her shoulders and sniffed. "Thank you for that, Nostris. Getting more copies of *The Histories* out is imperative. It may seem like an insignificant tactic now, but I cannot understate how important it is for long-term change. After all, isn't that what we want? Change. A different future where the atrocities being reported in the Overworld are a thing of a distant, dark past?"

"Because things are accelerating, Ret. You are correct," Dialphio said. "From what we are hearing about the Overworld, the number of hostilities grows each day. Hate groups are multiplying. They're becoming more brazen. Of course, what happens then?"

"There's a reaction, sometimes equal, sometimes superior," Bilba said. He sat at the table, next to a middle–aged, black incubus with a cleft chin and yellow eyes named Viztor. Bilba's writing companion only nodded his head at my best friend's answer.

"Exactly," Dialphio said. "One side acts, the other

responds. In return, that response draws another reaction from the side that instigated the situation. Then these things compound, becoming more egregious with each iteration. Keep this in mind. These actions perpetuate future actions, but this is happening under the cover of a growing world war. As horrible as it is, it can also be good."

"How in the Underworld is a world war a good thing?" Illis asked, her wrinkled hand pressed to her horrendous blouse. "It's terrible. Just terrible. All those tragedies. Those lost lives."

Dialphio rested her hand over Illis's and patted it. "The loss of life is tragic, that is true. Each one is as precious as the other." She stepped back, addressing the entire group. "But we cannot forget that it also provides us an opportunity to operate and grow. Without the world war, the Council and their spies wouldn't be as stretched as they are. Think back to what it was like before. How easy was it to move about without fear of being watched, being listened to? How often did you catch your comments before they tumbled out of your heads if they weren't complementary to Lucifer and the Council? And now?" Dialphio stopped pacing, giving time to everyone to ponder her comments before resuming. "Now, we can gather as a collective. We can work on propagating information to educate others so they understand this place in history, our history. Without the war, we couldn't do this without great risk."

"Before the war, they would have strung us up for what we're doing," Justis, the round-faced, blazeball cap–wearing incubus contributed. "Now, they're too busy."

Dialphio nodded. "That's right. We finally have a chance to be aggressive. Unfortunate that we have to, but each of us understands the consequences of not acting now. Without action, nothing changes.

Ralrek snorted. Not a humored sound. I elbowed him.

"Is it true that angels have been getting involved?" Zenas asked.

Dialphio prompted me with a look.

"Yes," I said, stepping away from the food. "It is true. That's what happens when demons screw with the Balance. Angels are going to react. Just like the mortals react to each other, so will our kind."

"Angels," Nostris said, his head hung over his book, shaking it.

"This isn't a bad thing. For example, if it weren't for angels, we wouldn't have known about the attack on the clinic in Olympia," Dialphio said, countering Nostris's disapproving single–word comment. "We will have to accept that."

"But… they're angels," Ret said. He had stopped writing again.

"Yes." Dialphio stretched the word out. "And some of them have helped us."

"Some of them have saved our lives," I said.

All quill action ceased. Every rebel eye fell on me. I had made a point they couldn't argue against. I was the icon. The Segregate. The Great Prince. A fistful of stupid titles rolled into one. But I was their hope, according to them. They had to understand how important Cassie was and could be to our cause.

"And they've taken lives. Let's not forget that," Viztor said, the cleft in his chin deepening at the memory of the attack on the First Circle.

"Never forget," Illis moaned.

"Never forget," Nostris echoed, as did a few other rebels.

I let loose a frustrated sigh. "Yes, the angels attacked us in the First Circle. Everyone knows that. And we also understand why they did. Is it horrible that innocent demons died? Yes, obviously. If the Council hadn't instigated that, if they hadn't made such a spectacle of Gemini's punishment, if they had worked with their counterparts in the Upperworld, those innocent demons would still be with us. But the Council focused on their vulgar display of power. They drew a line in the brimstone and expected everyone to accept their hard stance. They didn't suffer for it. In fact, I argue, most demons still think positively of the Council. And why not? The easiest way to control a populace is to make them afraid. And that is what the Council has masterfully done."

"Because we've let them," Ralrek growled behind me.

Now was not the time to confront his frustrations with the rebel cell's lack of progress. Maybe more than anyone in the room, I understood, because I, like him, suffered from the Council's continued power plays. But ostracizing allies and friends wasn't helpful.

"But... but, you're talking about working with angels," Zenas said, her large eyes widening.

"We can work toward mutual goals," Dialphio said.

Grumbling discontent followed. I turned to Ralrek and shook my head, bonding over our common emotion.

Behind me, the succubus who could pass for a librarian, Arin, nudged her horned rimmed glasses. "First, we should address the issues here, in the Underworld. We need to focus on class disparity and stemming the growing influence of the Council. Then we decide to consort with angels or not."

Justis adjusted his cap with his hands, pushing it forward and pulling it back tighter. He always wore the stupid thing backwards, so I still didn't know which blazeball team he supported. Better be the Sixth Zone Centaurs, my team. "Can't be working with angels. Could cause trouble."

"It could lead to demons mistrusting us. That will kill our movement before anything the Council does," Viztor interjected.

"How many of you have actually spoken to an angel?" Dialphio said.

No one raised their hand or spoke.

My ex–boss tapped her chest. "I haven't either. In fact, I

know of only four who have and all formed amicable relationships. One is my contact, and the other three are in this room. Before we waste too much time talking about why we shouldn't at least have cooperative conversations with angels, maybe we should listen to them. They might have information we don't. Ezekial, would you mind checking in with Cassie when you can and see what her thoughts are? I'll bet she has an interesting perspective on what's happening in the Overworld. She might also have interesting insight on our Council's wheelings and dealings."

I nodded. "Sure thing." My acceptance of the task was received with shock, if the expressions on the faces before me were any indication. "Look, everyone. This stuff is spinning out of control faster than our ability to stop it. If we are going to stop these demons causing actual harm to mortals, this is something we have to do."

"Thank you." Dialphio heaved with a big, calming breath. "This will require a lot of changes, even on our behalf. It's what has to be done. We believe Beelzebub is actively engaged in influencing the Balance." She thrust a finger in the air. "He isn't acting alone. He and Apopis are two harpies in a cocoon. If Beelzebub is active in the Overworld Apopis is as well."

"Two Founders who are nothing but trouble." Justis yanked his ball cap again.

"And so, we need to do something. Now," Arin the librarian said, her voice powerful and so contrary to her slight frame.

"By ourselves? That won't happen. We've been down that road. We tried it, and we failed," Ralrek snapped.

Bilba watched him warily. "There's a lot we can do, but I agree with Ralrek. Until the influence of this cell grows, our options are limited. We've lost our direct access to the Council. We're not trusted. I don't expect we ever will be. If they find out what we're doing…"

That had more to do with his actions than the rebel cell, and I agreed. Best to let that sentiment fade away, for now.

"I've said it before. The solution is to install Ezekial as the rightful holder of the title of Lucifer," Viztor said. "I'm not sure how many times we need to say that. We all agree it is the way forward."

"Yes, we do. Regardless of whether or not that's the solution, we need to figure out how we get him into that position." Arin gave her horn–rimmed glasses another nudge with a knuckle.

I almost asked the group to table the conversation when Ralrek slapped the counter. "This is why I'd rather be up there with Virgo, fighting the bastards until there isn't another one standing than being here, drinking coffee and talking in circles. Unlike what we're doing, at least the Abandoned and the mortals are acting."

"Believe," someone whispered.

I cranked my head, trying to find the commenter among the small cell. No luck. No one but Ralrek had spoken. Voices in my head again?

"We're doing things." Ret sulked.

"Are you dying?" Ralrek said. "That's what's happening up there. Abandoned and mortals are dying fighting operatives of our Council while we sit around copying a book and arguing for and against the best way to put Zeke on Lucifer's throne."

I slid to him and rested my arm on his shoulder. Ralrek flinched and held in a sharp, scant breath. He knew what my silent gesture meant. Beating up this group wasn't going to lead us to our goals. They were doing the best they could with what they had, which was very little. That's what the Council had been working on for generations, stripping demons of their ability to stand up for themselves. This was the outcome, and it wasn't the fault of the demons sharing this secret room.

A dark mood dropped over the meeting and Dialphio wrapped up the conversation, saying it would be better if everyone got back to work. She had scheduled another drop, her slang for distributing copies of the book around the Fifth like she was some drug kingpin.

We headed downstairs after a few stunted goodbyes. Halfway down, Creed warmed against my side. After a quick scan of the floor, I relaxed at Creed's possible warning. Maybe only a reaction this time? The street in front of the store was as busy as any other business day. Everything, so absolutely normal outside, while inside, a handful of demons scrambled to preserve our kind. Above us, someone scurried across the second-floor landing.

Dialphio moved with a grace I didn't know she possessed, stopping us before Bilba could open the gateway home.

"Please don't let yourself get frustrated with them. They're doing the best they can," she said.

"I know. I'm just running out of patience." Ralrek ran a hand through his hair.

"Please try?"

Ralrek inhaled through his nose, a drawn-out, nasally gesture.

"Thank you," she said. "I know this isn't easy for the three of you after everything they've put you through. Just remember, the Council is the true enemy here. We'll move forward and I will continue to nudge those demons in that room, but they are going to need something to hope for. Something tangible. I think you can do that for them."

"How so?" I asked.

"It's time to act," Dialphio said. She reached into her pocket, pulling out a folded piece of paper and handing it to Bilba.

He took it hesitantly. "What's this?"

"The coordinates to Azazel's chambers," Dialphio said. "The Council called an emergency meeting. For tomorrow.

That paper has the time you need to be in his chambers. Stay inside his room and listen. It's imperative you three are there."

Well, at least now I understood why Creed had decided to wake up.

"What do you know, Dialphio?" I asked.

She shook her head. "Just as he couldn't give you those coordinates himself, he didn't tell me why. He has to mitigate risk. He is already taking enough, so I didn't push." She reached out, tapping the fold of paper in Bilba's hands. "He stressed you must do this. He understands the risk, but says the future, our work, depends on it. I trust him. Be sure the three of you are there on time, and for the love of Lucifer, stay hidden. We can't lose you."

18

UNDERWORLD, UNDISCLOSED

"Do it," I said, swallowing hard, "before I lose my nerve."

Bilba's throat looked like it swallowed a dry cake, full.

Ralrek crowded into the hallway with us. We looked at each other and then at Bilba.

"Are you good?" Ralrek asked our pink-eared friend.

Bilba gulped. "As good as I'll ever be."

"One thing I've been thinking about? If you can open the gateway into Azazel's chambers just by having the coordinates, why can't you take me to wherever the Horn is located?" I asked.

The tips of Bilba's ears turned pink. "Because I don't know where those coordinates are or what Circle they're in. I don't know how to break this down into Circle, stratum, zone or sector. This is just... gobblygook. Heavens, we don't even know if it's in a Circle. That could be some celestial, inter-dimensional place I can't reach. It could be in the middle of the Acheron Ocean, for all we know. Not like I've got tons of experience at this. It may feel like it to you guys, but I don't. As many times as we've been in the Council chambers, I'm confident I can do this. Blindly trying to find obscure coordinates? It's just too dangerous, guys. It's better if we wait for Ralrek to find this mysterious lover of—"

"Friend," Ralrek corrected.

Bilba held his hands up. "For Ralrek to find this friend of his and see what he knows. Maybe then, I'll be confident about trying to open a gateway to it. Plus, we're sort of busy with other things." After a short pause, he said, "I can't believe we're doing this."

"I can't believe we have to do this," Ralrek said.

"If not us, then who, buddy?" I said, pulling Creed out of the loop.

"Not what I meant," Ralrek replied, sounding more of the Ralrek of old.

Bilba glanced at the halberd. "Do you think we're walking into a trap?"

I stepped back, tapping the collapsed weapon against my open palm. The halberd extended to its full length, three blades of destiny popping to life, filling the hallway with metallic resonance. "Do I think Azazel fooled Dialphio? No. Do I think Azazel is setting us up? Was he found out? Do I think we need to be ready for anything? Absolutely. I'm ready. You guys should be too."

"But—but I'm opening the gateway," Bilba said, gesturing to the spot in the hallway where he was going to carve a slice into thin air. "I can't open one and hold another spell. Not if we want me to be accurate where this thing opens, Zeke."

Ralrek patted him on the back hard enough to make him stumble. "We've got you."

Ralrek's spell scratched my arm long before his hands began to glow.

"Okay." Bilba blew out a slow breath. "Let's do this then."

Buzzing filled my hallway as the air peeled open, exposing the interior of Azazel's personal chambers—or what I hoped were his chambers, since I'd never been inside them before. Either way, the murky vision on the opposite side of the gateway exposed the interior of a room occupied by an exquisite desk.

I stepped through, lowering Creed and trying to keep it level as I tumbled through the emptiness between my home and the chamber of one of the oldest Council members.

I stepped out, ready for a fight against an empty room. Ralrek followed right behind, Bilba coming through last. Voices came from outside the chamber, far enough away to convince me that if this was a trap, we'd have a second to fight for our lives or dive back through the gateway.

"Best to leave that open," I whispered, nodding toward the gateway.

"Trust me, I wasn't closing it," Bilba whispered in return.

Ralrek tapped me on the shoulder, holding a finger to his lips and pointing at the door. Azazel's door was cracked open.

A third of the chamber was taken up by the desk. A rack where his black formal robe hung stood in one corner. The only other piece of furniture in the entire office was a chair, covered with black leather that was stretched and cracked with age. The arms of the chair were exposed wood, its hand grips carved with an exquisite demonic design of the seal of Lucifer. Not many obstacles to navigate around.

I held up my arm, blocking their path, before making a downward motion like I was patting the head of an impling, telling them to give me space and time. No sense in risking all of us. Extending my senses, I felt for any presence outside the door by feeling for emissions. Nothing. Azazel had removed his guards.

Stepping into the lead, I moved toward the door, taking the position closest to the slim opening. Ralrek stepped to the middle, pressing his ear close, and Bilba took the far side.

"This wouldn't be happening if you weren't doing what you were doing," Seraph was saying from somewhere in the main chamber.

"We are doing what needs to be done. What we should have done long ago," Beelzebub's deep voice shot back.

"You are doing it without approval. Without coordinating with the rest of us," the frail, shaky voice of Azazel said.

"The concern isn't yours," Apopis hissed.

"The fact remains, you took unilateral action," Michael said. "An action that was not yours to take. Look at the position you've put us in now."

"The position we are in is the position we deserve to be in," Beelzebub barked. "If the rest of you hadn't been so cowardly from the beginning, this wouldn't have been an issue. Your cowardice created this. Not my actions or those of Apopis."

"You launched multiple attacks on mortals in fourteen different countries," Seraph shouted. Something was thumped, like a fist smacking wood. "Do you expect us to sit by and not confront you? Are you insane? I've worked far too hard to achieve what we need for you to ruin everything. For the life of me, I cannot imagine what you're thinking."

"Maybe that's because it's not for you to know," Apopis said.

"We must maintain a unified stance. This infighting will be the death of us," Azazel interjected. It was a meek comment in comparison.

"I don't plan on dying anytime soon," Beelzebub said. "And we would be unified if you all had listened ages ago. Now look at what we have. We've got a world war involving angels we can't manage. Their influence is growing all over the Overworld, putting their grimy hands deeper and deeper into this mess. We've got a gnat of the incubus running around, interfering. A gnat with that halberd. If you think this is being managed with even an ounce of effectiveness, you've got a horrendous understanding of what that means. I, for one, am not willing to sit around and wait for you to gain that understanding."

Something slammed on the other side of the door. The three of us jumped. I shifted, ready to strike. Nothing happened. No fisticuffs in the main chamber. Nothing thrown. Instead, a tense silence, inside and outside.

"The reason we face these problems is because of your actions, Beelzebub," Seraph shouted. "Well, along with your scrawny sidekick. The pair of you managed to undo eons of careful work. Now magic is running amok. So many demons and angels casting we can't even tell who's doing what. The same could be said for the Underworld. Are you not bothering to read the reports? Every day, more hot spots of illegal use of magic pop up. Those reports mention travel. Dozens of reports a week. Do you think that's effective? Not even you can be that foolish."

"How dare you speak to him like that," Apopis said.

"And how dare he and you do this," Seraph's response was immediate.

"Focus on settling this so we can move forward," Michael said.

I pulled back from the door to look at my friends, who were listening intently with wide eyes. I'm all for juicy gossip about the implosion of this group of horrible demons, but for what purpose?

"Angels in the Overworld, influencing events," Azazel said. "That should be our priority."

"Don't let that distract you from the fact these two imbeciles have the Abandoned working together now. All over the Overworld, their network is expanding," Seraph spat.

"Sunstone is still a problem," Michael finally spoke up, his smooth voice calm despite the debate.

Bilba and Ralrek peeled their eyes away from the chamber to look at me.

"He must be dealt with," Apopis agreed.

"That's what I'm talking about," Beelzebub said. "If we hadn't been sitting on our hands for so long, we wouldn't be as stretched as we are. We could have taken care of the problems long ago. Now we're restricted to damage control. If we continue to sit back, we lose more control. Seraph, I know how much you hate that."

"Don't start with me," she said, her voice sounding like she was jabbing at the large demon. "This is all on you. Michael, we need to set this right."

"You think I don't know that?" Michael asked. "This… unfortunate decision by Beelzebub and Apopis, coupled with the continued challenge of finding the Horn, puts us in a difficult predicament."

"The Horn is still missing," Azazel said, sounding patient.

"Forget about the Horn right now," Seraph shouted over top of him. "If we don't manage these two, we won't have to worry about that artifact because the idiots will have kicked off Armageddon."

Even from this far away, Beelzebub's growl was clear.

"We can only be effective if we address one thing at a time," Michael said. "We need to determine our priority."

"I'm not budging," Beelzebub said.

"We have the superior position," Apopis said.

"Does anyone have a clue where the Horn is?" Azazel chimed in.

"Enough about the Horn already," Seraph spat. "We need these two to cease. Immediately."

"It will not happen," Apopis said. "We have the advantage."

There was a pause before Michael spoke, "So then we take the easy target first?"

"Sunstone." Apopis carried a threat in a single word—a word that also was my last name.

"Agreed," Beelzebub bellowed.

"It seems we have more pressing matters than a wayward incubus," Azazel said.

Seraph grated. "If getting rid of Sunstone will get these

two morons to agree to withdraw from their aggressive actions, I'm for it."

"Then how do we do it?" Michael asked.

Wow, kudos to the Council for not taking long to agree on my elimination.

"Ravenous is up for the Passage. We've already moved his test date forward twice. I say we take more drastic steps," Apopis said.

"How drastic?" Azazel asked.

"Why not immediately?" Beelzebub said. "Makes sense, doesn't it? A fine recommendation. We get Sunstone out of our hair if he's busy worrying about his little buddy. Let's move now, I say."

I looked to Bilba. His ears had gone far beyond pink now, burning red at the tips.

"Ravenous taking the test alone won't make much of a difference regarding Sunstone. A slight delay at best," Seraph said.

"You know, we could send the boys to the Isle of Dread? That would take care of this issue without moving around Ravenous's Passage," Azazel said.

Michael hummed.

"Don't even consider it, Michael," Seraph said. "Those three always find ways to get out of everything. They've managed it time and time again. How many more chances are we going to give them? No. Let's stick Ravenous in the Passage, but let's do it immediately. Giving him time only benefits him."

Beelzebub chortled. "According to his mentor, that's an accurate statement. He is struggling. Still struggles, in fact."

"Then let's move and get to other matters," Seraph said. "My operatives have reported concerning consequences of—"

"If we insist on this course of action, then let's allow the three of them into the Passage together," Azazel said.

Bilba, Ralrek and I shrank from the door in an instinctive reaction.

"Together?" Beelzebub's voice boomed. "Are you trying to give them every conceivable advantage? It's like you want them to succeed."

"It has been done before," Michael said like he was entertaining the proposal. "This could be advantageous."

"Exactly," Azazel said. Someone snapped their fingers. "This wouldn't be the first time an applicant was accompanied on their Passage. We know Ravenous isn't ready."

"And if he's not ready and fails... then none of them would come back out," Seraph said with a hint of bliss.

"Yes, true," Apopis said carefully. "But those times included the applicant's mentor, and we had... reasons. Melchiot Zeistane is Ravenous's mentor, and there is no way I will vote to support her attending him."

"Nor I," Beelzebub added. "She's too strong."

"I won't either," Seraph said.

"That is fine, I will agree to those terms if everyone agrees that Bilba being accompanied by Sunstone and Burning should take care of our challenge," Azazel said.

"The proposal does interest me," Michael said, pausing for a long time.

In the silence, I shifted. So did Bilba, as his future hung in the balance.

"This could be a perfect solution and allow us to focus our energies elsewhere. I'll vote in favor of it if the rest of you agree," Michael concluded.

"I second the motion then," Azazel said.

"Then let's put up for a vote," Michael said.

Beelzebub groaned. "Let's keep this simple. Is anyone opposed?"

I listened to the utter silence across the Council chamber.

"Then it is settled with a unanimous vote," Michael said. "We'll move Ravenous's test forward, and Sunstone and

Burning will accompany him. Seraph, would you mind handling the details?"

I didn't think Seraph would.

"Of course," Seraph said.

"Thank you," Michael said. "This should free us and get us back on course."

"Like making these two cease their actions in the Over-world?" Seraph asked, though it didn't sound like a question at all.

"Give it up, Seraph," Beelzebub said.

"That, and finding the Horn," Michael said, as if the constant bickering didn't perturb him. "I, for one, am dying to discover where it is, and who took it."

The Council moved on to other business, as if our fate was handily forgotten. We waited and listened, but Hell's leaders continued with unrelated topics. With Bilba's future determined, waiting for juicy trinkets from the Council wouldn't help us deal with what was barreling down. My friend needed as much help as he could get now.

I nudged Ralrek and motioned for him to do the same to Bilba. When I had their attention, I tipped my thumb toward the gateway.

Bilba nodded.

I don't think we breathed until we were back in my apartment.

"I've got to get home. They might have already sent a messenger," Bilba said, his words spilling out in a rush.

I didn't disagree. Getting him back to his father's house was imperative. I wouldn't put it past the Council to send a message for him tonight, and if his whereabouts were in question, their agents might go snooping.

I didn't want to mention any of that, so instead I said, "Yeah, you need to get some rest and talk to Melchiot as soon as you can. See what she says."

Ralrek tipped his head, but didn't say anything.

"Yeah," Bilba said, drawing a deep breath, closing his gateway from Azazel's chamber room and opening a new one. Behind the murky filter, Bilba's bedroom came into view. "I'll let you know through the notebook as soon as I hear something."

I watched my friends disappear without another word. My apartment was very quiet. Very lonely.

"Thanks a lot for the heads-up," I said to my halberd before tossing it on my ripped couch cushion and going to the kitchen to make a peanut butter and jelly sandwich. Ah, the lifestyles of the not-so-rich and infamous.

The Council still had the upper hand, but they didn't have the advantage they thought they had. Still, information in itself isn't much. We had to do something with the opportunity the elderly incubus handed us.

19

UNDERWORLD, FIFTH CIRCLE

BEING AWAKENED in the middle of the night is no fun. Being awakened in the middle of the night by a panicked best friend via a demonic notebook is an entirely different experience. Not one I would wish on anyone who wasn't a Founder. But that was my own fault. I'd been writing Cassie while laying in bed last night and fell asleep. The notebook had fallen to my pillow, propped against my head. I was basically face-to-Lucifer's seal with it when it strobed with the new message from Bilba.

I read my best friend's message and understood.

Bilba's Passage was in two days.

Two.

We had a lot of work ahead of us and no time to complete it, even though we were going to try our best, starting shortly.

He wasn't ready. There was no way he could get ready.

I wasn't ready to support him. We had yet to discuss that with Melchiot. Pushing him to anger in a test was one thing. Stepping into the Passage, where we could die, in a supporting role to help Bilba get us out the other side, was something I was completely unprepared to do. I would. I just wouldn't do it well.

Worse, the three of us were being thrown into the super-supernatural world with barely a clue of what to expect. The one who had training on the matter was spooked—I could tell by his middle-of-the-night letter—and most likely overwhelmed. Whatever I could do to help, I would. The problem was, I wasn't confident I could help.

We had Azazel to thank for this.

In a way, I couldn't be mad. The Founder's suggestion to force me and Ralrek to accompany Bilba pissed me off. But then, I stopped, calmed down—a little, okay? Let's not be dramatic—and saw what he was trying to do. If the Council had approved Melchiot, then we would have been four-strong going into the Passage. Having a Hex user may or may not have helped but having an experienced succubus who trained others on how to pass the life-and-death test, and had several students who had, would have given us our best shot at walking out alive. Which is why the Council crushed that idea, along with any hopes of us coming out unscathed. Or at all.

I did what I could for Bilba, which wasn't much. He was twisted sideways. Misspellings. Shoddy grammar. It was all so ugly to watch. No, seriously, Bilba is meticulous with that stuff, so I knew he was in an awful place. In the middle of the night, in a different Circle, there was no way I could help. He had to ride the long night out by himself on the other end of this magical communication.

For one of the few times in my life, I was up with the morning's Caller.

Funny thing about those animated walking spells; no matter which Circle of the Underworld they traverse, they always look the same, as if it is one entity that covers the entire demonic realm.

I peeked out my window with the morning's third cup of coffee in my hands and saw her purple-scaled body drifting along the sidewalk almost as soon as I heard her call. The eerie sound, the official start of the day, rose into the air, clear as if she were standing in my kitchen with me. Her long appendages swayed gracefully as she floated. Her long, purple strands of hair amalgamated into a single, thick braid, floating behind her as she drifted by.

"Well, time to get ready," I said to no one, jumping in the shower. Before I knew it, I would be whisked away to the Fifth Circle, this time with Council approval, where I was supposed to meet with the two incubi who'd face death with me.

Of course, that was something I didn't bring up to Bilba. He had enough to focus on, and casually, or not–so–casually, reminding him we could die would be a distraction.

As a location outside the Underworld, in some celestial neutral ground, the Passage was mysterious. What mattered most was that any of the three of us, or all three of us, could die inside it. The Passage, according to Melchiot's training, would test Bilba to his limits. Success came when he exited the dangerous illusion. The thing was, the test would deter-mine the how, when, and where of that exit. A fluid goal, for sure. Bilba could expect his worst fears to be used against him. Unlike our practice test, Bilba couldn't lose his cool. He had to maintain his rationality, staying unemotional and focused the entire test. But the thing was, he was already starting off on the wrong foot if his messages were a clue to his state-of-mind. Azazel might have thought he was helping by making us privy to the Council's planning session, but I wasn't sure. Bilba didn't seem to be preparing; he was panicking.

A buzzing told me a gateway was opening to whisk me away to meet up with Bilba, Ralrek, and Melchiot. Time to check in on my best bud.

I turned off the lights and made sure the windows and doors were locked. For all I knew, I might not come back. I was in no hurry to be Abolished, but I had to be a big boy. My job, besides protecting my best friend's wide ass, was ensuring none of us gained that new, undesirable status of being a memory.

Apartment secured, I stood before the murky image of Bilba's tiny front yard, drew a deep breath of stinking air, maybe my last in the Sixth, and stepped through.

I stumbled, exiting the gateway into the small patch of brown grass of Akimon Ravenous's yard. The Ravenous family budget was tight, always had been. I doubted Akimon had spare coin lying around for superior lawn care. The grass was as dry and cracked as a couple of the books Dialphio kept in her "special" case in The Book Abyss.

Ralrek answered the door when I knocked. I gave him a confused look. "Where's Bilba?"

Ralrek cocked his head backwards. "In the other room. Things are pretty tense. His father is stressed."

"And that's making him more stressed?"

"Yep."

"Well, this is the family's worst day since his mother left," I said as I stepped inside.

The house was quiet. If I hadn't known better, I would swear it was vacant except for me and the handsome demon behind me closing the door.

"Melchiot is back there with them, running through what to expect," Ralrek said.

"Is that why you're up here, answering the door? You almost opened it before I knocked."

He nodded. "It's too depressing. Everyone is on edge. I can't do anything, so I was in the kitchen making a snack when I saw you step out of the gateway."

"I'm going to check in," I said, walking into the room and greeting everyone.

Bilba looked like he hadn't slept, a nervous wreck who was trying to keep himself from turning to heated jelly. Melchiot sat on the couch opposite him, straddling the cushion's edge, her hands thrust before her as she gesticulated like she was trying to reconstruct something from molded clay. Akimon sat in the chair next to his son, watching Melchiot. He turned my way and did a double-take before struggling to push himself out of the chair.

Akimon Ravenous is one of the most invisible incubi I'd ever known. I don't mean literally, but the older Ravenous was always so non-intrusive. I swear, being hyperbolic for effect, there were probably days in his life where he didn't interact with matter. A large incubus with a mouth too small for his long face, his graying goatee hid a thick neck. If he wasn't so reserved, the older incubus could have been intimidating. Unlike my father, Bilba's didn't seem to care to be a demonic puppet. Never brusque, never rude, he was the personification of a wallflower. Even now, with his only child soon facing a life and death struggle, he was as reserved as reserved got.

"Thank you for coming, Ezekial. How are your parents?" he asked, shaking my hand.

Now was not the time or the place to talk about my parents. This was Bilba's time, so I lied in order to keep things as light and focused on my best friend as possible. "They're great. They say hi."

Clueless to the reality of my life, Akimon smiled. "Make sure you say hello for me."

"I will." I turned my attention to Bilba and his mentor. "Is there anything I can do to help?"

Melchiot glanced at me. Then her eyes darted to the floor, to the lamp, to a picture of Bilba and his father on the wall at a Samhain festival by the looks of the background. "We're making final preparations, and then we will talk our way through a simulation."

I said, "Talk? Aren't we going to your school so we can practice with another illusion?"

Melchiot shook her head in abrupt movements, as if invisible hands had gripped her ears and were yanking them.

Bilba looked at me. "The Council closed her school."

"We don't know that for sure," Melchiot said.

Bilba's chest rose and fell in a frustrated sigh. "Well, the Fire Marshal came by and forced her to close. He said the building wasn't up to code and that she couldn't reopen until it was."

I blinked, probably stupidly. "Wait. When did this happen? Was it not up to code?"

"My school has always met code. I am just as surprised as anyone," Bilba's mentor said. Her large nose flared, but her voice remained cool. "But that is a matter for another time. Right now, our focus needs to be on the exam and what the three of you will face."

"Ralrek!" Bilba called out, looking toward the kitchen.

"Yeah, coming," Ralrek said from the other room.

So, the Council was up to their dirty tricks. Not only had they cut Bilba's preparations short, but they closed Melchiot's school to make it harder to prepare. Maybe even as a punishment for helping Bilba. If only they put as much effort into equality for Hell's residents as they did ensuring Bilba failed.

"This might be a dumb question, but do you not have another space? An alternate location? Can we not go into Eve's Sanctuary and create the illusion there?" I asked, trying to brainstorm as many solutions as possible. Generating ideas helped me shut down the rising panic.

Melchiot answered, "I'm afraid not. My school was equipped with a mechanism to create the illusion."

"Oh," I said with a start, "I thought that was your spell?"

Melchiot's eyes darted left to right. "I'm a Hex user. I couldn't have created that illusion. It would take a hundred demons, working together to create something that robust. No, there's no possibility of re-creating it."

Looking at my best friend, I saw the fear. The trepidation.

I saw it eating away at him as he sat on a chair in his father's small, crowded living room. Ralrek slid in behind me, leaning on the door frame, eating a salad, as if the world weren't changing in two days.

Even if we came home, life would change. Bilba would be a Major demon, he'd have elevated status and privileges throughout the Underworld. Akimon's proudest moment. Government positions. Access to exclusive clubs. Security for his father so Akimon no longer needed to pinch every copper. All around the neighborhood and throughout the Fifth, neighbors and strangers would position to become friends with my friend, many in gross attempts to curry favor.

But there was a darker side, too. That Akimon was lonely, and had been for thousands of years, ever since Bilba's mother left. He worked long hours and was rarely home. Being socially awkward didn't help either. One of the nicest incubi in the world, someone I would gladly have as a father, Akimon had little time or skill for friends. Anything that happened to Bilba, good or bad, rippled across their joint lives. In my heart I knew, if Bilba were to fall in the Passage, it would be the end of Akimon as well.

It had to be weighing on my best friend. He was confident —if this was a happier occasion I'd call him cocky—he could successfully pass the Passage. Bilba believed in himself. I believed in him. He was a badass magic user. But the Council was doing everything they could to interfere so that he wasn't successful. The four Council members were licking their chops at what was to come.

If we were to die in the Passage, then Hell's rulers would be freed of more than us. The test takes place outside of the Underworld. If I died inside of it, Creed would also be left inside the outer realm. Unsure of where the test exists in reality, what would become of the halberd? Would Creed be trapped inside until someone opened it again? What if it was never open again? Would the halberd remain locked away in some super–supernatural prison for the rest of eternity? Had the Council already considered that aspect?

I glanced at Creed hanging listlessly in the loop at my belt. The dumb stick had no insight to offer except to warm slightly against my leg.

"Trust," a voice said, somewhere behind me.

I turned, shooting Ralrek a quizzical look.

As he chewed salad, his cheek puffed out. The fork raised to his mouth again, ready to shovel more in as soon as there was room, he scrunched his face, and grumbled, "What?"

"Trust what?" I asked.

"What about trusting what?" he said.

This was ridiculous. Either Ralrek was playing around when playing around wasn't appropriate, or I truly was losing my mind. Wasn't that wonderful?

Melchiot ran through a litany of possibilities Bilba might face. From previous conversations over beer and junk food, Bilba had let me know what the Passage might be like. But that was when he was excited, long before the Council was trying to wedge him into a life-and-death situation before he was ready. Now, it wasn't so exhilarating.

To think he could face dastardly creatures from the familiar to the fantastical was too open-ended for me. Creatures as small as nymphs, or even smaller, like fairies with attitudes, all the way to mountain giants. He could face natural and supernatural, living and dead. It was possible, Melchiot warned, Bilba might even have to come face-to-face with a squad of angels. The Passage could take place in the familiar streets of a replicated Fifth Circle, or it could be in the blackness of a universe beyond our universe. With those answers, she couldn't help, she said. No one knew, not even the Council, what Bilba was going to face because the Passage would know how he needed to be tested.

The uncertainty was doing little for my friend. Red blotches polluted his cheeks and his neck. By the time

Melchiot finished warning him what he might face, the entirety of his head had turned a shade or two darker.

Bilba was too deep inside his own head, becoming his worst enemy by psyching himself out. The old Bilba lacked confidence from millennia of being picked on over his appearance. That old Bilba was creeping through.

"You're going to be fine," I said when I saw him going into the dazed state he entered whenever he was overwhelmed. "You'll have the two of us along for the ride to remind you how awesome you are. Let's just focus on that. No matter what the Passage throws at us, we will be ready for it. You already are. Believe in yourself, bud. You're pretty kickass."

Bilba said, "Thanks, Zeke."

"You're a good friend," Akimon said from his spot deep in the chair.

Creed heated against my hip, feeling like I had dipped it in fire and made the wonderful decision to slap against my bare skin. I jumped sideways. Bilba squinted. I didn't have time to explain.

Buzzing from the other room drew my attention. The torturous sound of a slowly unzipped bag. My hand was on Creed's knob as I turned to investigate. Ralrek set down his salad bowl. Bilba got to his feet.

In the entryway, a gateway had opened. Creed pulsed. Throbbed. I gripped the knob, preparing to slip it from the loop.

Black feet, black legs. Armored. Black breastplates. Black helmets. The Council guard were here.

Four guards stepped out, forming a two–demon cordon on either side of the gateway. Once in position, they faced to close the cordon. Each held a spear, the small, triangular spear tip blazed blue with Hellfire.

"What are you doing in my home?" Akimon said, squeezing between me and Ralrek. His cheeks wobbled.

The guards didn't answer.

"I'll ask you one more time, what—" Akimon repeated, this time more firmly as he stepped toward the guards.

The Council guards didn't flinch at his approach. In the middle of Akimon demanding answers to know why his home was being invaded, another demon stepped from the gateway. The slender leg and soft steps gave away who it was before their not-so-grand appearance.

Apopis looked around the crowded room wearing a cocky sneer. On a worse day, I would have wanted to knock that sneer off his dumb half–tattooed face. Even on good days I have wanted to, being honest. Who am I kidding? All days. Antagonizing the Founder wouldn't do any favors for my best friend. Apopis would live to sneer another day.

Akimon took a stumbling step backwards. Ralrek caught him with a single arm, his eyes locked on the Founder. Melchiot mumbled something so quiet as to be indiscernible.

As Bilba stepped forward, I watched the guards for any sign of threat. Without taking my hand off Creed's knob, I extended my senses, not only feeling the natural magic in the room but also ensuring no one was tapping into their Abilities. We were safe, for now. Still, my hand didn't leave the halberd.

"Apopis?" Bilba asked. "Why are you here?"

Apopis lifted his arm, his fingers pointing toward the ceiling, and wiggling as he brought his arm back down toward his hip. As he did, a slimy sensation coated my arms, face, and neck—a Listening ward. I was the only one who could detect it beyond the visual clue the Council member gave. "I came to see how your preparations are coming. Do you feel as if you are ready to take the Passage?"

Had a Founder traveled to Ravenous home just to taunt a young incubus when he should be preparing for the most important day in his life? Just when I thought the Council couldn't be more pathetic, they proved me wrong and far exceeded expectations for depravity.

Bilba moved to the front of our group. On his own, facing down the Founder, one-on-one. "I believe so, yes."

Apopis didn't care whether or not Bilba was ready. He'd asked to antagonize my friend. "Believe so? You believe so? The Passage is a special privilege, given to those who have proven their superior Ability. Only those who have shown the fortitude are considered. It is not doled out to the undeserving. You have come so far in displaying your prowess, and the reports we've received from your mentor legitimize this opportunity."

I risked a glance away from the Founder to Melchiot. Her eyes, as always, flickered all over the place. She gave no indication one way or another about Apopis's statement.

Apopis continued. "In my time on the Council, I cannot tell you how many applicants we've rejected. Far too many to hazard a guess. Yet, here you are, at such an early point in your life, with this wonderful opportunity. And when I ask you, as a Founder, whether or not you're ready, you tell me you believe you are."

Apopis turned, gliding toward the gateway. He shook his head, as if Bilba were a wayward son who disappointed him. In front of the buzzing gateway, Apopis stopped, speaking as he slowly rotated to face us again. "Anyone who goes into the Passage less than completely confident in their Ability rarely comes back out again. A shame, but such is the honor of being a Major demon. The Underworld cannot afford to give such a title, and all the privileges that come with it, to just anyone. Though I'm sure their loss is tragic for their families, it is to the benefit of demons that those types never rejoin society. In the time you have left, I encourage you to think about that. Dwell on your lack of confidence, and how that could hinder your performance and your ability to stay alive. Of course, you'll need to hurry."

I felt it coming. Creed throbbed as if begging me to pull it free and birth life into it so it could chop the head off this snake. My jaw ached. I hadn't even realized I was clenching it. For a moment, I wondered how realistic it was to fight off four Council guards in the small room if it meant destroying one of Lucifer's trusted advisors. I wouldn't, of course, but the thought was tempting.

"I will think about it long into the night. I promise," Bilba said, bringing a smile to Apopis's slimy face.

"Oh, you don't have that kind of time," the Founder said.

Son of a cherub.

Beside me, Ralrek growled.

"Sir, may I speak?" Melchiot asked.

Apopis flicked his hand in an answer.

Bilba's mentor stepped forward to stand alongside my friend. "We would ask for a delay. I have mentored numerous—"

"I'm aware of how many you've mentored," Apopis said in a tone that communicated that he was not willing to be cut off again. "And I'm not interested."

"The delay," Melchiot said, her head cocked toward Bilba as if she was confused. "A delay would be beneficial to Bilba, giving him time to—"

"There will be no delay. Unfortunate circumstances have changed the schedule once again, which is why I am here. I've come to escort you to the Passage, Mr. Ravenous."

"Now?" Bilba squeaked.

A slow smile crept across Apopis's face.

Son of a salamander.

"But—but we were given another day," Melchiot said.

"You were given as long as you were given," Apopis snarled. "The Council has decided Ravenous will take the Passage now." He shifted to Bilba, a stupid smirk on his stupider face. "Collect what you need. We're escorting you, Burning, and… Sunstone without delay. Such are things."

Melchiot stepped forward, now standing in front of Bilba. "It is my responsibility as his mentor to attend to him in the

Passage," she said, her voice sounding stronger than I'd ever heard it.

"That won't happen," Apopis said. "You can spend this last minute providing any advice you have, but you will not be walking through this gateway. Ravenous takes his trial without you."

"But that puts him at serious risk. The tradition is—" Melchiot said, taking another step forward. She was parallel to the first guards of the cordon.

"Tradition doesn't matter. I will not hear another word." Apopis looked past Bilba's mentor to him. "Forget collecting anything, Ravenous. We leave now."

Apopis was turning toward the gateway when Melchiot shrieked. I was so shocked by her tone toward the Founder, by her intensity, I didn't recognize what was happening until after the fact. "It is my right!"

Apopis spun. "Enough!"

At his shout, the guard to Melchiot's right raised his arm and swung, catching her cheek and sending her sprawling to the floor. I tried to catch her but was too late.

She cried out when she fell, holding her face. Blood trickled from her nose. Under the hand covering her cheek were angry, red slashes from the guard's gauntlet.

I yearned to pull Creed free. To birth life into the magical halberd and free Hell from one of its oppressors and his protectors. I couldn't. I could not pull it out and rain devastation in this room. The confines were too small. The risk, too high. Bigger picture, I couldn't attack a Founder. That would be the end of the demons I loved. Even if I could take Apopis out, three other Council members remained. I'd never win.

Akimon stepped forward. "I will go with my son."

Bilba whirled toward his father. "Dad, no."

But Akimon tilted his head. "I will go. I am requesting to attend him. He's my boy. Please do this for me, sir. I have so little in this world. The one thing I have is him. If he is to take the Passage today, I want to be with him."

Bilba never talked about Akimon's Abilities. Strong or weak, it didn't matter. Though I appreciated the display of love, his presence would be a distraction to my friend, introducing even more risk.

Apopis's head bobbed with a silent laugh. "You would chance going into the Passage to be with him?"

Akimon's size seemed to grow by dimensions. "For my boy, I would do anything."

"Dad, I don't want you to go. It's going to be hard enough to do this without worrying about you," Bilba said, grabbing his father's hand.

Akimon faced his son, wrapping his free hand around the back of Bilba's head, and pulling it closer. They touched foreheads. "I want to do this. I want to be there with you during this trial. I know you can do it, son. I'm not worried about that. Give me this. Okay?" He ruffled Bilba's hair before turning to face Apopis and directing the same question at him. "Okay?"

"This is very touching, but I'm not here to entertain personal requests," Apopis said with a scowl. "We have delayed long enough."

"Why won't you let me go with my boy?" Akimon said, taking on a new personality, a fierce one.

Apopis strode forward. The guards shifted. Inch–by–inch, I pulled Creed out of the loop. It pulsed in my grip.

Apopis was face-to-face with Bilba's father. "Don't you dare presume you may question me or make demands of me. I will do what I deem appropriate. You want to go with your son? To watch as it pushes him beyond his limits? To see him attacked and tested, mentally, emotionally, and physically? You want to see what your boy is made of? See his demise? That's on you," Apopis said, tapping Akimon's chest with a narrow finger.

Ralrek made a hostile rumble from deep in his chest.

Creed was in my hand.

The Founder knew Akimon wouldn't lash out. Like a true coward, Apopis was only brave when he knew he had the superior position.

Spinning toward the gateway, Apopis snapped at the guard commander, "Bring them. Leave the succubus." He stepped through. Out of reach.

"I'm sorry, Bilba. I tried," Melchiot said, now getting to her feet, still holding her bleeding cheek.

"I know. I know you did," he said. "Thank you for everything. Thank you for preparing me. If—if I don't come out... we... we can settle what I owe you, somehow. My mother... she's in the Ei—"

Melchiot shook her head, her eyes no longer darting around the room. "Focus on this. Remember your emotions. The Passage is an illusion. You can master it. Don't forget your lessons."

"I will," he said, turning to the three of us. "Dad. Guys. Ready?"

I doubted we were, but we stepped into the gateway anyway.

20

BILBA'S PASSAGE

EXPECTATIONS CAN BE DANGEROUS. I figured as much of a big deal as the Passage was, entering it would be an awe–inspiring event. For the record, it's anything but.

First of all, the area around the gateway leading into the Passage was barren, devoid of hope. In fact, it wasn't even impressive on an esthetic level.

We stepped out of the gateway into a small room I figured was somewhere in the Council chamber. We squeezed in, trying not to bump into the rift a few feet away. Once we were through, Apopis closed the gateway to the Fifth and stepped into the rift without a word.

After tumbling for a fraction of a second of existence, we stepped out of the rift onto a sandy patch of the eternal plane. Dunes of brown sand rose up on all sides, cutting off any view of what lay beyond. A cliff face fifteen feet ahead held a shimmering black archway, dead center on the wall of rock.

Apopis went toward it.

The arch rippled, the blackness shimmering with silver slivers that added dimension to the impenetrable darkness beyond. Whatever it was, rift, gateway, or something else, the archway was silent.

Apopis stopped beside it. The guards pushed us forward. Closer.

From the surrounding desert landscape to the blackened archway, that blackness absorbed life.

"I can't see anything," Bilba said, more to himself than to the Founder.

"That's by design," Apopis said.

"What do we do? Just step in?" Bilba asked.

"No time like the present," Apopis hissed, thinking himself funny. He wasn't. "Of course, if you succeed, I will be here to receive you. The Passage will beckon me. Don't worry about that. For all we know, this will be the last time you see what lives outside the Passage. Your fate awaits. Step inside. I would wish you luck, but…"

Bilba ignored Apopis's attempt to antagonize and distract. "I'm ready, guys. Dad, please stay out here."

Akimon was about to respond when Apopis cut him off. "Oh no, he asked for this. He will get this. Your father enters with you."

"But—but," Bilba stuttered.

Ralrek stepped forward, his lips pulled back in a vicious grin.

Akimon put his arm on his son, in turn, blocking Ralrek. "I meant it when I said I wanted to be there with you, son. Let's not argue. Let's just begin. You're about to be a Major demon. I'm so proud of you."

"Thanks, Dad," Bilba said, drawing a deep breath. He faced the archway and the shimmering black. "I'm ready."

My best friend, the only incubus in the world who has stood beside me throughout my life, throughout every challenge and every time someone rejected me. The true friend who never wavered. Who saw the error of his ways when he took part in Aries's death. The stocky incubus who was a powerful magic user and a blabbermouth. The guy who tried his hardest at everything, and for everyone. The ball of joy with a good heart. The one who acted like an impling at Samhain carnivals even though he had attended them for thousands of years, treating each iteration as if it were his first. That is who Bilba was.

Maybe admitting for the first time in my life as I watched him approach that dark void, I loved him. His spirit brightened my world.

And he was about to enter the Passage, where he would suffer attacks designed to push him beyond breaking. My job was to protect him. Hell needed more demons like him, and I was going to make sure the special one they already had was going to return home tonight.

With a brief pause at the face of the magical hole in the cliff side, Bilba stepped through. As he disappeared into the archway, the black wrapped around him as if he were submerged in a vat of oil.

Akimon followed on his son's heels without delay.

"Looks like it's going to be a good time," I commented to Ralrek. He grunted and stepped forward, disappearing into the archway.

I stepped up, feeling Apopis's eyes on me. I faced him, never wavering. "He's not weak, you know? You might think you put us in the spot we can't get out of, but that incubus," I said with a tip of my head toward the shimmering blackness, "is one talented, stubborn guy. If you think you won't see us again, you're going to be disappointed."

I stepped into the murkiness, which rolled over me, pressing against my skin, against every orifice. The blackness pressed against my lips, yet I could taste nothing. Pushed on my eyelids. Filled my ears like a tiny yet persistent finger. It covered my hands, my arms. It pressed against my chest, pushing back as I entered. It coated my neck. Every inch of my skin, invaded. I didn't dare draw breath or open my eyes. I pushed forward.

And then I was stumbling onto smooth marble. Ralrek caught me.

Bilba laughed. "It did the same thing to all of us, don't worry. Dad almost face-planted."

"I wasn't ready for that," Akimon said.

"Don't worry, Zeke. You didn't look any dumber than usual." Ralrek smiled.

The narrow tunnel, twenty feet tall, stretched into the darkness. Far down its length, a single torch hung in a sconce on the right side, casting orange light to the floor and not much further.

"I guess we go in that direction?" I asked.

"I assume so since it's the only direction to go," Bilba said, characteristically cheery as though all his doubt was sucked up in the blackness.

"Lead the way then, future Major demon," Ralrek said.

My skin itched with the first sensations of a Fire spell. I eyed the tall incubus as he mumbled his incantation. Soon, his hand glowed, and a small flame appeared in his upturned palm. "So we can see where we're going, dummies," he said with a chuckle.

"Oh, that helps a lot. Thank you," Bilba said and skipped along the tunnel.

"Don't you think we should exercise a little caution?" I called after him.

Having just come through the Passage's barrier, I could have done without sticky sensations. Unfortunately for me, Bilba was drawing on his Ability now.

"What are you expecting?" Ralrek asked, his voice echoing down the tunnel, the only sound except for the crackling torchlight.

I think Bilba shrugged. It was hard to tell in the gloom. "I'm not sure. Running sucks, so I wouldn't be surprised if we get chased by something. Muscle-heads too. Definitely don't like muscle-heads. But a lot has changed since last time I fought one of those."

I laughed at the memory of Bilba trying to out-muscle the Seattle muscle-head body guard of Aries.

"Guys, I think I'm ready," Bilba said. "After all of our sparring sessions, and the two of you helping with training, I don't imagine they'll throw anything at me I can't handle. Not that I'm saying this will be easy."

"Just don't get too cocky," Ralrek said.

Ah, sweet irony.

"Just don't get emotional. You know what happened the last time," I said, reminding him of our recent training session. "Melchiot let us walk out of that place. The Passage won't."

"I'll make sure he stays level-headed," his father said.

Bilba stopped next to the crackling torch. "Do you think we should carry this with us?"

Ralrek lifted his hand, the one burning with flame. "What you think I have this for?"

"And what if you need to cast against a target?" Bilba said.

"I cast a spell. Either way, I'm going to need both of my hands," Ralrek said. "Carrying the torch is just one more thing that I have to drop. And for all we know, this place could be full of tinder. I'm not about to take that chance. Plus, it doesn't take much to hold the spell."

"Okay, that's settled. Can we move?" I said, encouraging us forward. "The sooner we get out of here, the better."

Leaving the flaming torch behind, we approached the mouth of the tunnel.

"What do you think is out there?" Ralrek asked.

Bilba crept forward. "Who knows? But I'm ready."

I pushed my senses outward and stumbled into Akimon, nearly knocking the older incubus over.

"Whoa, Zeke. Are you okay?" Ralrek said, catching me.

My head swam, but otherwise I was fine. "Yeah, I don't

know what in the heaven just happened, but there's a lot of magic in this place. I don't think it likes me poking around."

Far beyond the torch light, a deep, rich, smooth, yet light and almost feminine voice said, "Hold true to what you know."

I spun, seeing nothing except the mostly-dark, mostly-empty tunnel. I didn't dare project my senses again. Doing it could bring a blackout. "Did you guys hear something?"

They stopped, casting sideways glances at each other, and then toward the mouth of the tunnel.

"The only thing I hear is the torch," Bilba said.

"I did not," Akimon said.

Ralrek shrugged. "Me neither." He watched me for a second, concern passing over his face. "Why? Did you?"

I couldn't tell my friends I had been hearing voices since being pulled out of Abandonment. It was easy to push out of my mind when I wasn't sure I'd heard an animal or the wind. But I couldn't make that claim this time. Someone had spoken an entire sentence from the mouth of that tunnel as clear as morning Hellfire rays.

"Are you feeling okay, son?" Akimon asked, moving to me.

"Ignore me," I said, waving away their concern. "Just got a lousy night of sleep. Think it's screwing with my head."

"Well, focus. Bilba needs you," Ralrek said, holding me until he was sure I wouldn't topple over.

Ralrek was right. Bilba needed us. He needed the best of us. Which meant I wouldn't send my senses out again. Whatever magic was at work here, it was far superior to my Creed–enhanced abilities. It hadn't liked me prying into its mysteries, prying I would no longer do.

"I'm better, guys. Let's go," I said, shooing with my hand.

Bilba, in the lead, craned his head up and arcing from left to right as if we were back in the Overworld watching the sun transit the sky in seconds instead of hours. "Whoa. This place is immense."

We filed out of the tunnel and into a gigantic chamber. Gray slate stretched into the darkness. Smoky shadows fell over it, the walls hidden behind them. Every twenty-five feet, a torch burned in a sconce, casting weak, orange light that didn't even reach the floor, never mind penetrate the cloud of darkness hovering over this room.

I looked up, craned my neck and got lost in the dizzying heights of the towering chamber. If there was a roof, I couldn't see it. The sections of the walls I could see were identical to the floor's slate. Nondescript, free of designs or lines. The chamber looked as if giant engineers molded it from wet clay, every discrepancy smoothed over.

"What do we do?" Akimon asked from the rear of the group.

"I—I am not sure," Bilba said. "Melchiot said she couldn't tell me what we'd find because it's different for everyone. The Passage reflects the testee's worst fears."

Ralrek snorted, craning his head to take in the intimidating chamber. "Your worst fear is a boring room desperately in need of an interior decorator?"

"Ha. Funny. No, I have a lot of fears, just like everyone. But this isn't one of them." Bilba scanned from side to side. "Maybe we need to move. Inspect the chamber. See if we come across anything. Maybe this is a transitory place, and there's a doorway or something on the other side that will take us where we're supposed to go. Come on, let's see what we find."

We moved along the right wall, our steps hesitant. The petrified cherry of Creed was warm, putting me on high alert. The height of the chamber absorbed all sound. Except for our footsteps, the only thing I could hear was the crackling torches we passed. Those ahead and behind were soon muffled as if they didn't exist at all.

"Allegiance," a voice whispered close to my ear. My heart stopped—I swear, it did—at the voice. We were in a line, Bilba in the lead, with me behind him, Akimon behind me, and Ralrek bringing up the rear. No one could have whispered in my ear. To do so required stealth none of these incubi possessed. Why would the Passage torture me? This was Bilba's thing. The three incubi were looking into the shadows and the hazy center of the room as if they hadn't heard anything.

I was losing my mind. Absolutely losing my mind. And at such a young age.

I pushed the troubling thought away, trying to focus without accidentally sending out my senses and getting us— me—into further trouble. Creed thudded at my hip, and my hand dropped to it. Part of me wished the halberd would give me a heads-up the next time my broken brain decided to play tricks on me. Creed had no problem warning me whenever the Council was about to cause trouble, but if I was causing it for myself, the stupid stick seemed content to watch me fumble my way into a mess.

This thumping wasn't that type of warning, though. This time, Creed thumped insistently. The needy halberd wanted my attention.

"Be on your toes, guys," I whispered, pulling Creed free but not extending it. Not yet. I focused to my left, with the wall to our right. If anything lurked, it was doing so in the dark, smoky shadow of the great chamber's center. If we were being watched, I wasn't going to be the first one to move and give away our location. Pulling Creed out was fine. Activating the halberd was a different matter, one that might antagonize any magical adversaries waiting to test Bilba.

Heavy, padded steps and growling reverberated from the shadows. Something was approaching and coming fast. I didn't hesitate. Giving the halberd a shake, it extended, blades popping free. Creed didn't feel like bringing the magic of the

Hellfire to this party. One of these days, I needed to find the ON switch for that ability, because I was tired of the halberd deciding when and where it would be kick–ass.

The combined sensations of the three incubi's magic raked over my skin. Ralrek's Fire dominated the other two. Akimon's Water was the weakest, barely registering as a faint cold surface pressed against my arm.

Panting neared. Growls grew louder. Heavy steps thundered. Something—nails?—clicked on the slate. I had heard this combination once before. If what was coming out of that darkness was like that time, we might be in trouble.

"Get ready. I think we're about to face—" I tried to warn, but the hellhounds burst from the darkness, cutting me off.

Ralrek snarled, his spell coming to life in an instant. He hurled a ball of flame at one of the hellhounds, catching it in the breast and flinging it backward.

I stepped in front of Bilba, and lowered Creed, wavy dagger held before me. If this hellhound thought to charge right over my friend, it was about to get an invasive surgical procedure.

As the first hellhound charged back into the fight, slightly charred now, the one I faced dodged to the side, aiming for Akimon. As I adjusted, a leather lasso ensnared the beast's rear legs. The hellhound toppled, rolling over. The lasso cinched. As it fought and kicked to get free, the dog Ralrek scorched changed its direction and headed toward Bilba.

A stream of water sprayed the beast but did not slow it. Akimon was already sweating from his first spell.

Before the hellhound reached Bilba, I sprang into the air, rotating Creed to gain momentum and moving into Frigid Bite, bringing the half–moon-shaped blade down on the back of the beast's neck. Creed bit deep, crunching bone. The hellhound fell and slid to Bilba's feet, it's horrendously large mouth gaped, revealing teeth the length of my fingers. Even in death the stupid thing couldn't not display a snarl.

The surviving hellhound, its rear leg still bound by Bilba's lasso, kicked to free itself and failed. Instead, it used its powerful front legs to inch in our direction, its wide mouth and jagged teeth snapping open and closed. The powerful jaws could break any of us in half if it got ahold of us.

"I'm gonna put it out of its misery," I said, walking to it. The hellhound watched me with blazing orange eyes as if I were a tasty morsel delivered to its doorstep. I rotated Creed so that my asymmetrical blade hovered over the beast of Lucifer. It snapped, still full of fight. "Sorry, buddy. But you're only a spell." Creed sliced the air, through the hellhound's fur, through its neck. Creed's blade vibrated when it bit into the floor.

We were quiet as the beast leaked its life onto the gray slate.

"Well, that wasn't so bad," Akimon said with a chuckle full of adrenaline.

"Probably just the beginning," Bilba said. "Did those hell-hounds remind you of anything?"

I nodded. "They did. Just like the ones at—"

A series of fireballs lit the foggy darkness in the center of the chamber, arcing through the sky.

"Move!" Ralrek shouted.

We scattered as a volley of fireballs rained down, striking where we had been standing and splattering against the slate floor, spraying out in smaller orbs. The splintered remnants left thin, scorched trails. The impact points were now black-ened ovals. Another volley was sent skyward. The problem was, we couldn't see our attackers, but they could see us enough to target us. Additionally, we were now split up, unable to support one another. That might not be a problem for the magic users in the group but was for me.

This next round was aimed at Bilba. He was conjuring, unaware of the threat. Ralrek indiscriminately fired small fire-balls into the chamber's smoky shadow. Good thinking.

Putting our adversaries on the defensive would slow them. Bilba's father shot small streams of water at each of the approaching fireballs, sometimes hitting them. The fireballs he intercepted fizzled out while still in mid-air. But he missed more often than he struck.

Bilba was on the move, scrambling. The sticky sensations created by his Deception magic slipped each time he had to dodge. At this rate, he would never get a spell off.

I was left out. I could either move toward Bilba and try to support him the best I could by creating a barrier with Creed, or I could go on the attack and stop the fireball volleys at their source. The problem was, that required me walking into the shadow.

At the thought, Creed thumped in my hand, feeling like a small fist knocking against my palm.

"Are you sure, buddy?" I asked the halberd.

This time it thumped harder, as if it thought me ignorant. Me, a doofus to a petrified piece of wood.

I lowered the double–ax heads and slunk forward. "You know, if you would bring some magic to this fight, that would be great," I said in a whisper. The halberd didn't feel like responding this time. Convenient.

The attacks on Bilba continued as I moved into the unsettling smoky shadow. Soon, I lost sight of him and the rest of the party. They say no demon is an island, mostly because we only have a handful of those land masses in the Underworld's entirety and the most feared one, the Isle of Dread, is something no one wants to think about anyway. But right now, as the shadow of the chamber wrapped around me, cutting off my friends, I felt like one.

On a good note, forms took definition. Three incubi in a neat line tossed fire spells into the air. They wore black slacks with matching black dress shoes, white button up tops with black ties, and black blazers. The only thing this crew lacked were the cool sunglasses to complete the ensemble conspiracy theorists demand. As it was, I recognized these incubi in their matching outfits. The last time I'd seen them, along with massive hellhounds, was at the Hammerwolf estate in the Eighth Circle.

Behind the three Fire casters, another pair of identically dressed incubi held two hellhounds on thick chains. The metal chains thudded more than they clinked. The large beasts sat as if waiting for a treat, even though they could tear themselves free of their handlers with a flex of their thick legs. I was grateful for their training, because I was too far away, too lost in the shadow, to intercept them if they took the task of finding Bilba.

"Can you help an incubus out?" I whispered to my halberd and waited. And waited. Nothing. "Stupid stick."

I crept forward, figuring out how I was going to take out three Fire casters, four hellhounds, and two incubi whose magic Abilities I hadn't figured out yet. The nine-on-one proposition was not attractive.

As luck had it, I didn't have to worry for long. Keeping my eyes on my targets, I stepped onto something slick and my feet nearly went out from under me. Not only fast, I'm graceful when I need to be, as long as it doesn't involve talking to a gorgeous succubus—okay, or dancing.

My slip-and-slide routine may have kept me on my feet, but it also drew the hellhounds' attention. A few seconds of snapping, growling, and barking preceded them being released.

"Shit!"

I was on a long, smooth sheet of ice, revealing the magical Abilities of at least one of the hellhound handlers. The ice extended around my targets, shielding them from a sneak attack. That tactic obliterated, I now had to scramble off the ice and back onto slate, where I had traction and a chance to break away.

The problem was, I was still slipping as I moved toward

the slate, barely keeping my balance as the hellhounds charged.

As I jammed Creed's dagger into the ice to gain traction, cracking it, fireballs rained around me. One smashed so close its heat warmed my skin when it exploded. But the attack had its benefits. The ice sheet under me was melting at an exponential rate after the first attack against me. As more fireballs came, the ice splintered enough for me to get traction and back onto the slate.

The only problem was, the hellhounds were almost on me.

I lowered Creed to mid-guard and grinned. "Here, puppy, puppy. Let's see you get to me now, dummies."

It's not a good idea to antagonize hostile canines. In fact, I doubt Hell's history has even a few success stories. Unfortunately, I only learn life's lessons the hard way. Like now, after taunting overstuffed, drooling dogs.

They slunk backward, their humongous heads lowered, jaws almost touching the slate. All four snarled, pools of saliva at their massive, three–towed paws, crouching as they readied themselves to attack.

The hellhounds sprang forward. I retreated in a straight line toward the chamber wall. Reaching it would allow me to orient myself.

The fireball attack followed, and so did the dogs of Hell. For the record, hellhounds are quicker than fireballs, at least when they have the scent of prey.

I'd given up hope of appearing calm and collected. This was about preservation of life and limb. The four pursuing me were going to shred those principles. I couldn't fault them if they started with my limbs.

I am fast, the fastest demon I know. Call it one of the few curses Lucifer bestowed upon me—well, not Him, now that I understood He was nothing more than the face of the name. But in the middle of a raging battle, pursued by four hellhounds, I didn't have time to reframe my thinking. Fact is, I'm fast. Problem was, I'm not hellhound-fast.

As I ran in what I hoped was toward the friendly demons who could get me out of this mess, massive paws slamming against slate neared, accompanied by panting and growling. The only hope I had was reaching my friends.

Ahead, a long line of fire spread out along the floor, burning three feet high. Through the murkiness, the fire looked smudged, like a giant eraser had tried to wipe it away.

I stretched my stride, encouraged by the reference point. No way would I circle back to Taurus's imaginary henchmen. That firewall belonged to a demon on my side.

"Help!" I yelled. The slamming paws, the clicking of long canine nails on slate drew nearer with each step. I couldn't waste more oxygen pleading for a saving spell from an ally. I had to keep running.

One hellhound growled as the others barked, smelling a Zeke-flavored meal. It was overtaking me. Time to go down fighting.

Skidding to a halt, I spun and lowered Creed. Just in time. The beast was leaping. A second later and I would have been trapped under it. The halberd's double-axes sliced through the beast's stomach, spraying me in warm blood. Though Creed had torn open the hellhound's belly, it couldn't stop the momentum created by the charging animal. The full weight of the conjured corpse slammed into me, nearly knocking the halberd out of my hands.

My lack of size is well known, but I can pack a punch. I can also take one. The blunt force knocked the wind out of me, making my head feel thick as I flew backward.

Dazed, I tried to regain my feet, only remotely aware there were still three other dogs of Hell to deal with. Unsure if they were intelligent enough to recognize what had just happened, the three slowed their pursuit, hunkering. Their thick limbs bent, ready to launch as they close the distance.

Shaking my head, I lowered Creed again, no longer spending energy worrying about the fireball attacks from Taurus's men. I kept my attention focused on these three crouching animals.

"Now is a good time for you to help," I told my halberd.

Cold steel answered. Stupid stick. The hellhound on the right pulled its lips back, the fur around its snout scrunching as it snarled. Those teeth could shred brimstone. I was only seconds away from proving myself right. Its hind end raised up as it lowered its head.

This move was too obvious, as if I was being set up to allow the other hellhounds to maneuver for a better strike. But they only crept forward.

They had me backed to the wall. I would have to fight them off while cornered.

The threatening hound did as expected. It launched itself. As it bounded through the air, the other two charged. My final chapter.

21

BILBA'S PASSAGE

I WOULD LIKE to tell you I didn't cower and scream like a little impling, but what happened wasn't clear enough to make such a claim.

I know I saw the three hellhounds close in, two from the ground, and one from the air. A blur of action unraveled their attack, casting me into reaction mode. No time to think, just act.

The fastest ground-bound hellhound reached me first. It reared up to rip my head from my shoulders, and I didn't wait, rolling under and behind the beast. Spinning in a circle, lowering Creed to mid-guard, I swung in a horizontal strike and sliced through its hind legs.

Its partner, which had charged, was trying to turn to address my tuck and roll. Losing its grip on the slate, the dog toppled on its side.

The third beast, the air-born one, was still in flight when massive black wings cut through the sky, a shadow passing over the shadow of the chamber itself. Like a bat out of hell, this flying harbinger of the order of Chiroptera tore the hell-hound from midair. The bat clicked as it snared the hellhound in its over-sized claws, carrying the dog up and away. The beast howled, but its cries faded into the heights within seconds.

Down to a single hellhound, I stalked it as much as it stalked me. Side-to-side we moved, one trying to outflank the other, waiting for the other to make the first, fatal mistake.

I shifted Creed from hand-to-hand, trying to antagonize the beast. I lunged, and it snapped at air. Each second I wasted dancing with this stupid canine, the more time Taurus's men had to obliterate Bilba with their superior numbers. I moved to the right, putting myself near the wall, and the hellhound moved to the left. If this beast was as stupid as its cousins, this would be my decisive move. If it was the more intelligent of its line, I had just signed my death warrant.

The beast was a dunce. It charged once I made it believe it had me pinned. I raced to the wall, knowing its prey drive would encourage it to chase. Before reaching the wall, I leapt, pushing off the surface, tumbling heels-over-head, and landing behind the hellhound.

The beast never saw it coming. I thrust down with the wavy dagger, puncturing three feet into the animal's hide. It howled, swinging around to snap at me. I kept my grip on Creed, just barely, as the dog of Hell bumped me hard with its hind end. It whipped the other way, whipping me along with its ass. If the imaginary beast didn't die soon, I was going to sue the Council for a severe case of whiplash.

Whipping back the other way, the hellhound snapped, but this time with less force. One more twist of its body, and the animal wobbled.

I braced myself against its back and pulled Creed free before jumping to the ground, and taking a moment to put an end to the animal's suffering. Imagined or not, it didn't deserve to live any more moments in excruciating pain.

Panting, I raced to the firewall, jumping over it, landing and rolling into a standing position.

"Nice moves, Ezekial," Akimon said. "Are you okay? You're covered in blood."

"You got your ass kicked," Ralrek said with a chuckle that wobbled slightly.

I ignored Ralrek and looked at my best friend. "Nice bat. I was expecting snakes."

"I thought you might like that twist," Bilba said, his smile holding enough cheer to hint that he was proud of his accomplishment. "I've been working on that for a long time."

"It came in handy," I said. "Thank you, buddy."

"If you two are finished with this love fest, we have a battle that could use your efforts," Ralrek said, lines of strained effort carving the impeccable skin under his eyes.

I dipped Creed toward the firewall. "Isn't this one of those set–and–forget spells?" My skin still itched with the scratching of his Fire Ability.

"Holding it," he said. "At least until we know what we're facing."

I briefed them on what I saw.

"Taurus's men? Really?" Bilba said, surprised.

"Five of them and four of us," I said. "We fought them before and came out alive."

"We had Seraph then, and she saved our asses," Ralrek said.

I nodded. "True, but three of them are Fire casters, and we have Akimon. If we get him close enough, he could harass them while we defeat them. The other two appear to be Water users, so Ralrek, you won't be much use. But I'm sure you're used to that," I said, focusing on Bilba. "It will come down to you and me, if Ralrek and your dad can do their parts."

"Got it," Bilba said with a confident head nod. "Let's go."

I led them back to Taurus's men. The smoky shadow was too dense to see now that they weren't casting a continuous volley of fireballs.

I pointed where I thought I remembered them. "I think they're in that area. Roughly."

"Roughly?" Ralrek asked. "Not helpful. Could put us in danger if you're not sure."

"I have an idea," Bilba said, and the sliminess of a new spell crawled on me.

An army of small snakes, none longer than a foot but as thick as corn cobs, stood sentry in a long line. I stopped counting at thirty. It was as creepy as a demon's first time shaking hands with an angel, but I couldn't stop myself from smiling. Not that long ago, Bilba struggled to cast two simultaneous snakes. My, how times were changing.

I tried to laugh off my unease at the reptilian presence. "Was wondering how long it would be before you cracked them out."

"You won't complain if they help," Bilba whispered back, flicking his finger.

At the insignificant gesture, the grotesque snake line shot forward in an undulating approach. They'd overrun anything, even the supernatural hellhounds I'd just survived.

Within seconds, screams rose into the air.

"There they are!" Bilba shouted. "Let's go."

We sped into the shadow, me holding back on my sprint so we could stay together. To his credit, Bilba's father hung with us.

We found Taurus's men thanks to Bilba's snakes, who were keeping the five incubi more than distracted.

My skin prickled with a multitude of sensations between the three different Abilities. Ralrek shot a large fireball at one incubus, while Akimon provided a water shield from the spells of the other two. Bilba manipulated his snake army, having them slither around the four remaining guards before setting them to attack. The rest of the fight was almost unfair as we took down Taurus's men with relative ease.

I relaxed when Bilba cut off his spell and his snake army evaporated.

"How is everyone doing?" my friend asked.

"A little tired, but boy, am I having fun!" Akimon smiled.

"Doing fine," Ralrek said.

Bilba looked at me. I shrugged. "I'm sure once the adrenaline wears off, the exhaustion will hit me. Right now, I'm having the time of my life. Wouldn't want to be anywhere else."

"Good, because we're not done." Bilba looked around. "Though I'm not sure what we're supposed to do next."

"I hope you didn't spend too much coin on Melchiot," Ralrek said. "You'd think she would have given you a little more insight."

Bilba flipped his hand in the air. "There's no way she could have. It's different for everyone. Do you know how many variations of the Passage there could be?" Bilba went quiet. For a second, I was convinced he was running the calculations. "No two applicants have the same experience, so she couldn't hope to give me specifics. I'd worry if anyone claimed otherwise."

Bilba and his father shared a look. It was a deep connection, one between father and son who had already sacrificed so much for each other and would continue to do so. When I was Abandoned, Bilba had shared details of what his Passage preparation had cost this family. Not only was Bilba going to be in debt for a century, but Akimon had also taken on most of the loan, putting his house up as collateral. Such was the belief of this father in his son. I couldn't help but be envious. Deep down, I'm sure Ralrek felt the same.

"Well, how about we explore and see what comes?" I proposed. "I imagine the Passage knows best, so it will provide it when it needs to."

Bilba nodded, and we walked deeper into the shadow. It stretched on, seemingly without end. In an illusion designed to push Bilba in the direction required, wandering was still frustrating.

"Let's retrace our steps back to the wall and then move along it. At least then we'll have a point of reference," Bilba said.

We did. Moving along it, we walked for far longer than we should have had to in a single chamber, no matter how large.

"Stop," Bilba warned in a harsh whisper.

I listened, hearing nothing in the chamber.

"What is it?" I asked.

"A hole," Bilba said, stepping away from the wall, revealing a cube-shaped hole at the foot of the wall, three feet high and just as wide. "This is where we need to go."

Someone gulped.

"Let me." I stepped up.

Bilba put a hand on my chest. "No. It's my Passage."

I placed my hand on his, removing it gently. "Yes, but I have Creed. You'd have a heaven of a time trying to cast while crawling through that if something is waiting on the other side. Let me go through and make sure it's safe."

"Let him," Ralrek said.

Bilba sighed, dropping his hand back to his side. "Okay. But be careful."

"I always am," I lied and got on my hands and knees.

A slight but consistent breeze was blowing through the tunnel, hitting my face. It was cool, not cold.

"Here goes," I said, trying to sound happy.

The tunnel's floor was wet, slimy, and just about as gross as you'd imagine it would be, but I made it through untouched by anything that wasn't a silky spider web. The breeze became a stiffer cross-wind when I reached the end of the tunnel. I felt out in front of me and found solid floor. At least I wasn't about to tumble off a cliff into the utter blackness that greeted me in this new chamber.

"Zeke? You good?" Ralrek called down the tunnel.

"Think so," I called back. "Come through but use your light. I can't see a blessed thing. Bilba, you come through before your father. This is still your Passage, and I didn't crawl through…" I almost told him how nasty the tunnel was, but decided I didn't like being separated from him any longer than necessary. "Just, come on."

The rest of the party joined me in the chamber, Ralrek's handball of fire illuminating only a few feet around us.

"What is this place?" Bilba asked.

I tapped Creed's dagger against the floor at my feet. "Floor is solid, at least for a few feet. Can you send out one of those walls of fire again so we can see where we are?"

"I can, but I'd rather save my energy, if possible," Ralrek answered.

Turns out, he didn't need to. The room burst in a golden light from high above. I mean high, like at least a hundred feet. Blinding me against detail, I stared up for a source, not finding one, and allowed my eyes to drift down the sheer walls that formed this narrow room.

"Not much room for a fight," Akimon said.

"Maybe we won't need to," Bilba said.

A chorus of angels greeted his comment.

Literally.

Four angels hovered in the air of the narrow chamber. Complete in stereotypical white robes, they didn't so much as bob or drift. Golden hair hung to their hips. Their robes were cinched with golden sashes. Their hands were drawn together just underneath round breasts. The four were identical.

The angels hummed a melodic chant. Almost hypnotic. A beautiful melody.

"Angels? Really? You're afraid of angels?" Ralrek said, sneering up at the four.

"Don't judge me," Bilba said, less than humored.

I looked up in time to see the four angelic faces twist into open hostility. The smooth visions of stereotypical beauty morphed into what we demons think we know their kind to be—ugly, hideous mounds of flesh and bone, ligament and sinew.

The angels' melodic chants stopped, and they loosed piercing screams in a single voice, four complementing the greater. Jagged lines carved by an invisible hand split through their faces, peeling away their smooth skin and revealing their true nature—well, the stereotypical one in which xenophobic demons regard angels. Their hair faded to a blinding white, becoming a raging inferno of Angelfire atop their scarred skulls. Pale, putrid creatures of angelic lore. Bent and twisted things with enormous eyes and two holes against the flat of their face where their arched noses used to be. Their gaping mouths could have swallowed their heads if they tried. Fangs dripped with the blood of demon children.

I held Creed in front of me, spinning it to create a shield big enough for the four of us. "You need to work on your prejudices," I told my friend as the halberd picked up momentum.

"I promise, I will. But let's finish this first." Bilba chuckled nervously.

The smooth sensation of Akimon's water spell was a surprise, and large balls of ice formed over the heads of the angels. The balls dropped, knocking the illusionary angels to the floor.

I dashed forward, the shield of Creed extended. The angels screeched, shooting Angelfire from eight hands. Eight streams of the ray of destruction hit Creed's shield, stopping me in mid-stride and nearly knocking me down. If I hadn't been prepared for such a strike by spreading my stance, they would have succeeded. But the combined strikes still pushed me backward.

"A little help here!" I yelled.

Ralrek took the lead. From behind the safety of Creed's shield, he launched fireball after fireball, sending them raining down on the hunched figures causing an interruption in the angel's assault.

Angelfire is a powerful spell. I'd seen it in action too many times in the last few years alone. The disadvantage of Angelfire, I was now learning as I was on the receiving end, is its inflexibility. Whereas Ralrek could arc fireballs over my shield, and Akimon could create ice in the mid-air, the angels had to be direct. If it weren't for Creed's shield, the Angelfire would have taken us out in the blink of an eye. Because I had it, the attack of Yahweh's kind was inept as long as I had strength to keep the halberd spinning.

The four screeched when one of Ralrek's fireballs caught an angel's arm, setting fire to her robe. She waved wildly as if she could brush off the fire. The other three mimicked her panic. He sent ball after ball into the air. In the tight confines, the angels had nowhere to go. They tried to dodge, but space was limited.

Bilba was casting a Deception spell. This time, the master of creep outdid himself. From the floor of the tiny chamber, thick arms writhed upward. At first, I thought they were misshapen snakes popping from the stone itself. Then I realized they were anchored to the stone.

Hands protruded from the tops of the writhing arms. All around the angels, arms sprang from the floor, waving around and snatching at them. They no longer attacked as they struggled to avoid the combined demonic spells.

Their sultry siren's calls were hysterical screeches now, all different pitches, but in the same key. Their panic was horrendously beautiful.

One after another, Bilba's forest of swaying arms snagged the angels. One had her arm, and as she lurched to pull it free, another hand reached out and snagged her leg. The two arms held her laterally in the air as a third grabbed her remaining free arm. The three other angels were also ensnared by Bilba's arm forest. Whenever an angel used her

Angelfire to obliterate one arm, another grew a few inches away.

Bilba was panting now, but dominating the four on his own.

Ralrek got in on the fun, shooting a fireball that struck an angel distracted with fending off Bilba's arms. The fireball hit her in the middle of the back, catching and spreading. Her screeches were matched by her sister's.

The last free angel hurled herself toward Creed's shield. When she struck, she was thrown against the wall. Ralrek hit her with a fireball before she dropped to the floor.

And then there was one. But she didn't last long.

The last angel's four appendages were snared by Bilba's floor–arms. At once, I saw the sinews in the animated fore-arms flexed. The angel's scream was agonizing to hear as the arms pulled in opposite directions, ripping her arms and legs from her torso. The ripping and cracking of muscle and bone nearly made me vomit. Her torso splattered when it hit the slate.

At her death, the chamber went black again. An entire fight with angels and no migraine. I hadn't suffered any of the physical discomfort of the previous test's casters using Fire. The Passage was either blocking me from sensing the magic before spells were cast or, because this was all imaginary, there was actually nothing to feel. I could get used to not having migraines ever again, but I wasn't sure if being ignorant to spells was a good thing or not.

"Two for two," Bilba said in the darkness. He was a little too confident for my comfort.

"Be strong. It comes," a voice said, uncomfortably close. It didn't belong to any of my three partners. I knew that now. Still, I jumped at the intimate words in my head. It was the same voice that had been terrorizing me for weeks. The sound of a madness.

The voice, and whoever possessed it, left me with just the

four of us catching our breath after disposing of the angels. Someone gulped.

"Do we go back through to the other chamber?" Akimon broke the silence.

"I'm not sure," Bilba said. His clicking mouth when he spoke convinced me he was dehydrated.

I gasped—and I wasn't alone—when something clunked in the distance, like a heavy switch being thrown. Light shone from an unseen point above a figure so distant as to be unremarkable. We hadn't moved from the angel chamber, but this light, and the figure it illuminated, was hundreds of yards away.

"Well, I guess this is the next test." Bilba sounded tired.

"We've got this, buddy," I said, trying to be encouraging.

"I can't see much," he said.

"We take it slow," Ralrek said.

Bilba led. We neared with caution. The closer we drew, the brighter our surroundings until a sudden flash of white brilliance blinded me. I shielded my eyes against the stabbing pain, only dropping my arm when the white faded to red, and then to a pale pink.

I was speechless when I opened my eyes.

A vast field of wildflowers, whites and yellows, stretched into the distance, fading against a sky so bright at the horizon I could comfortably call it white. A steady wind blew across the rolling prairie. The figure was naked. The straight lines, and the sloping shoulders, the lack of voluptuousness hinted it was male. His back turned, flowing alabaster hair fell to his waist, and the way his skin wrinkled told me he was old, even elderly.

"Be strong," the annoying voice whispered.

I startled just the same. Everyone was fixated on the floating figure and didn't notice me.

The male rotated to face us. I drew back—a mixture of pain, horror, and shock overwhelmed me.

I looked into eyes the color of ice. Aries, the First of his Name.

I choked on a cry.

Ralrek groaned and Bilba moaned.

"Who—who is he?" Akimon asked, picking up on our distress.

"Aries," his son croaked.

Aries extended his illusory hand, curling his finger, beckoning.

We looked at each other, Bilba's eyes wide.

"It's an illusion," I said forcefully, not to be rude, but to make myself say the words that were so difficult to voice. Simultaneously, I wanted to deny and embrace that truth.

Bilba gulped and turned to face Aries, stepping forward.

As soon as he did, I felt an instant shielding. There was a definite separation between me and my best friend, an intangible barrier with very tangible sensations. I leaned forward and was stopped by something unseen. I reached out, feeling nothing but still unable to move in Bilba's direction. Akimon leaned toward Bilba, shouting something, but his voice was as silent as death. I reached to touch him, to reassure him his son would be okay, and my hand was blocked. Three feet separated us, and it might as well have been miles. Not only sealed off from Bilba, but sealed off from one another. The Passage only provided comfort in the sounds and feel of the warm breeze blowing across the prairie, somehow still able to touch us.

Creed was cool against my hip, almost comforting.

I lowered myself into the tall grass, plucking at it as I watched my best friend in the world approach the ghost of the incubus who'd liberated me.

Aries was just as I remembered, except naked. He had a fierce robustness to him. His icy eyes held a confident tranquility. His facial expression was serene. Even within the illusion that was the Passage, knowing Aries was nothing more than an amalgamation of the Passage's interpretation of Bilba's fears, I wanted nothing more in that moment than to call to the ancient who had gifted Creed to me and set me on this course. What would I say to the one who'd changed my life if given a few moments with him?

But this was Bilba's to face, alone. Not mine. I'd never get another moment with Aries. Or Leo.

As Bilba neared, Aries straightened. Spreading his arms and pinning his ankles together, Aries took on the form of a floating crucifixion. This was the cruelest of setups, the cruelest of exams. The Passage, if it was sentient, could kiss my ass for doing this to my best friend.

Bilba's stride hitched.

I looked past Akimon to Ralrek. Lines carved under his eyes. He clenched his jaw. Ralrek was being tormented, maybe even as much as our friend who faced a challenge of mind over will.

Aries's eyes locked on Bilba. He said nothing as he hung, splayed out in a replication of the way he left life.

Bilba's shoulders shook.

"No," I said to myself, recognizing the first signs of my friend beginning to cry. "No, buddy. Hold it together."

Bilba bent at the waist, placing his hands on his knees, shoulders still shaking. He bent like that for a moment longer, just long enough for me to worry that he'd cave to his emotions, fail his Passage, and trap all four of us for eternity.

The entire time, Aries simply watched.

I slammed my hand against the barrier, not even receiving the satisfying sensation of a smashed fist against a pane of glass. My frustration, an obnoxious gesture of nothingness, of helplessness. Unable to console my friend or to encourage him to keep his shit together and finish the task, I was useless. With a voice, I could remind him this was just an illusion. I could remind him he wasn't killing Aries again. With a voice, I could tell him he had been a pawn in a much larger game. I could scream in his face that it wasn't his fault. Beelzebub murdered Aries.

But I could do none of that. My role was to watch as Bilba stifled a cry and Aries stared.

Torturous minutes passed. Bilba never broke down. Maybe he came close, but he never did, that stubborn, clumsy, lovable oaf. Instead, he gathered himself and stood. He wiped away the tears with the back of his forearm, never turning to face us. His back straightened as he drew a breath. His hands moved as he conjured. Inside this barrier, I couldn't feel the slimy sensation of his Deception magic.

Before he released the spell, Bilba dropped his head, his chin falling to his chest. He shook it before snapping it up and thrusting his hands forward. Just as in Seattle, metallic bracelets zipped across the open air between Bilba and the Founder. Though he wasn't braced to a wall, the clamps slapped around Aries's wrists and ankles, pinning him just as he had been pinned in his very real murder.

The Passage was cruel to Bilba by making him relive this moment, but I thought that by clamping Aries, reenacting the role he had played, Bilba had satisfied the requirement. Bilba waited. Time passed. Ralrek and I shot each other questioning looks. Akimon's head swiveled between us as if we could help him understand what he was watching. Even if we could communicate, there was nothing to say. Bilba's test with the ghost of Aries wasn't complete. I didn't understand why and doubted Ralrek did either.

Bilba gesticulated again, creating the series of spells that had killed Aries. He conjured the beams Beelzebub had. He mimicked Ralrek's fireballs. He summoned the flock of bats Beelzebub had pulled from the Underworld into Aries's Seattle home. He slammed Aries's body against the invisible wall, just as Beelzebub had. Bilba reenacted every instance that led to Aries's demise.

After he did, the Founder's eyes drooped closed just

before his head lolled forward. Then the ghost of Aries hung limp.

I ached for my memory of the Founder who had changed the course of my entire life. I ached for Akimon having to witness this. But most of all, I ached for Bilba, who had only wanted to become a Major demon for the benefit of those he loved and the greater good of the Underworld, only to be pushed to relive his most shameful moment.

With Aries's second death, I felt the sense of freedom again. Bilba collapsed to his knees, leaning forward, his shoulders beginning to shake again. No longer restricted by the invisible boundary, I raced to Bilba and wrapped my best friend in my arms.

"I'm so sorry, Zeke. So... so sorry," Bilba said, choking back his cries.

I squeezed. "It's the Passage, Bilba. The Passage did this to you."

Akimon and Ralrek joined us, both trying to help Bilba keep his emotions in check.

"I killed him. I... killed him," Bilba said, his voice quivering.

"It made you, son," Akimon said.

Ralrek kneeled in front of Bilba, his hands on Bilba's elbows. "It was an illusion. Don't let it take your focus. You're already on the verge of being emotional. If that had been an antagonistic spell, it would have attacked, and killed you. Get your focus back. Now."

Bilba needed to hear this firm message. Nothing had changed. We were still standing in the middle of a prairie of white and yellow wildflowers with a warm breeze caressing our skin. The Passage had not finished. Something worse was coming, and Bilba needed to be ready.

Bilba sniffled but did not crack, and gave Ralrek a few jittery head nods. Standing, he said, "Okay. I'm ready."

He might have been ready, but he was not the incubus he

had been only moments before. Facing these fears was wearing on him. That was the Passage's intent, wasn't it? To break him before the final push.

I'd be blessed before that happened. "Come on," I said, wrapping my arm around his waist and turning him to walk back in the direction where we had entered the prairie.

My intent was to walk him back toward the first chamber. If the Passage wanted to push him, I was going to push the Passage back. We could let it lead us as it already had, forcing us to follow its script, or we could try to find the entrance and force it to respond for a change.

We made it ten feet when the prairie evaporated, replaced by a vast cavern, with deep sockets of black grottoes dotting the horizon. We stopped, looking around. Somewhere, rushing water crashed against rocks echoing into the open cavern. This place was immense enough to have its own atmosphere, I swore—but don't take my word for it, because I suck at science.

"Be ready," the disembodied voice whispered in my ear.

"Shut up!" I snapped, not meaning to.

Three heads turned toward me.

"What—what did I say?" Bilba asked, wide-eyed.

I shook my head. "Don't pay attention to me. I'm just busy losing my shit." I poked my chin toward the center of the cavern. On the opposite side, there was a pinprick of azure light, as if the Hellfire was calling us home. "Let's head that direction."

We crossed the cavern, the waterfall becoming clearer when we rounded a wall of stone pillars. Far off to the side, barely visible, a broad river tumbled hundreds of feet toward a massive lake of crystal blue.

The roar of the waterfall accompanied us as we traversed the cavern. Step after slippery step, we moved through the distant waterfall's spray. We navigated the slick, rocky floor. A painstaking journey. The last thing any of us needed was to slip, catch a foot in a crevice, and break an ankle. Our minds and bodies, exhausted. None of us were in the mood to carry anyone who got themselves injured.

We crossed halfway, the horizon a good distance away and the pinprick of Hellfire calling us home, still nothing bigger than a dust ball.

I shouted to be heard over the roaring water. "Maybe this is the Passage's way of making up for being a dick? Giving you a peaceful retreat before you're back in Hell accepting your new title?"

"We can hope!" Bilba shouted.

A boulder carried over the edge of the waterfall cast a sudden loud crash that echoed up and around. The spraying mists coated us, already soaking through my shirt. My jeans were heavy. The wetter I was, the colder the cavern felt. But hey, we were still alive.

Bilba shouted, "Can we please move? I'm drenched."

"Let's aim for that," I shouted back, pointing at the slit in the wall promising Hellfire.

"Sounds good," Akimon shouted, his voice hoarse.

We picked our way through the field of boulders as another loud thud came from the waterfall as it carried more of this realm's wreckage into the cavern's great lake. We paused when we came to a stream dividing one side of the cavern from the other. It was too deep and swift as it surged through the channel, to wade across.

"What do we do now?" I shouted.

"Move out of the way," Ralrek yelled back, barely audible over the roaring water.

The three of us moved to the side. He backed up. My chilled skin felt rough scratching, as if being rubbed raw by sandpaper only to have that turn into a power sander with the coarsest grit possible. This spell was going to be huge.

The stream of fire that leapt from his hands was impressive, I can't lie. Who knew he had that kind of power in him?

As impressive as the gateway that swallowed a good chunk of the Sixth's park was, this was a shock. The stream thickened as he spread his legs, taking a firmer stance. As it sped over the rocky floor, it grew taller and thicker, a cylinder of molten power. It struck the bank of rocks, sending dozens flying into the river. He didn't stop. Ralrek moved to his right at an angle that blasted more rock. As the pebbles, stones, and boulders were projected forward, they glowed, radiating the heat of his spell. They tumbled into the water, the collision of molten stone and the cool river casting billowing white clouds upward.

Before long, Ralrek had formed a land bridge across the river. His arms fell to his side, and he swayed. I caught him around the waist.

"You okay?" I asked.

He swallowed and nodded. "Exhausted," he said, waving lazily at the bridge he created. "We need to hurry. That might cause a flood, and I don't have the energy to swim right now."

"Akimon, can you cool it enough for us to walk on?" I asked.

The older incubus nodded at the prospect of helping. Seconds after I felt the first cold, smooth touch of his Water Ability, a modest jet of water covered the stone, shooting more steam into the cavern's sky.

"We should be safe now." He smiled, wiping his hands as if dust covered them. He started across.

Bilba followed.

"Let's get out of here," I shouted. Cinching Ralrek's thin waist, I helped him cross the uneven surface.

We were halfway across when the waterfall exploded again, this time multiple thuds that shook the ground under our feet. Whatever the river was tossing over its side, it was doing so with a vengeance, as if this illusory realm were mad at itself for not beating Bilba before he could escape.

We almost reached the far bank when Akimon stopped

and pointed back toward the lake. His eyes were wide and his extended finger shook. Bilba turned a fraction of a second before I did, flinching. I didn't see the rest of his reaction, because I was busy losing my mind.

Up out of the mammoth lake rose a beast of water. Not a water spirit or water spout, this thing was a giant, at least seventy feet tall. Its features were fluid, literally. Complete with a hairless head, two pools of darker water swirled where the eyes should be. Rivers formed lips that outlined its mouth, which swirled like a cesspool. The monster's legs were thicker than even the tallest trees in Hell, and its arms weren't twigs either. The water body rippled with the flow of currents, driven by forces unseen. Its fists were as large as a house. The magic holding that much water together was otherworldly. Lucifer and Yahweh could form a tag-team and never pull off something like that.

It lifted a leg, pulling it out of the lake in a sluggish movement. Its mouth, as wide as the chamber where we had fought the angels, yawned open as it moaned, a sound that might have found a home coming from the center of the earth.

Its watery foot landed, and the ground shook.

I'd been a fool. The thundering sounds from the waterfall weren't from the unseen river tossing boulders over the edge. Those perturbing noises had been the birth of this monstrosity.

Having emotionally weakened Bilba, the Passage was now going to crush him physically, and us along with him.

"Move," Ralrek barked.

Bilba snapped out of his trance, turning to his father and making a shooing motion. Akimon blinked, as if the goliath still stunned him, but turned and edged his way along the bridge, careful not to slip.

The colossus moaned again, the sound shaking the stalactites above our heads. It was sorrowful, as if each effort to raise its mammoth legs taxed the giant.

We were across the bridge before the next foot struck the cavern floor, this time on the rocky bank of the lake. In two strides, the giant had more than halved the distance.

"Move! Go! Go!" I shouted, trying to pull Ralrek along. He was taller and heavier than me, a combination that didn't work in our favor when navigating wet rock. This bank of the shore was just as rocky as the other, slowing our progress. I looked up at Ralrek, trying to keep the panic out of my eyes. "Can you run?"

His eyes closed, and for a second, I thought he might pass out. If I let go, he would collapse where he was.

"We need to slow that thing down!" I shouted my suggestion to Bilba.

"How?" came his response, full of dread.

Akimon stopped, spinning to face the water giant. Under my panic, I felt the smooth sensation of his spell. As I pushed forward, he released a stream of ice, spraying it along the rocks between us and this new threat in a wide arc. "Keep going. I'll catch up," he shouted.

I nodded in gratitude, adjusting my grip on Ralrek and pulling him along, slipping. Broken ankle, here I come… almost.

Bilba had stopped too, standing beside his father and raising his hands horizontally. Around him, small pebbles hovered in the air.

"We've got to… help… them," Ralrek said.

I agreed, but I didn't know what we could do. Akimon created a field of ice. Bilba was arming himself with hundreds of projectiles. Ralrek's last spell had taxed him. And I had a stick. What was I going to do against the colossus?

"Let me get you someplace safe," I said, pulling Ralrek forward. If I had more strength, I would have thrown him into a firefighter's carry and sped to one of the small grottoes the goliath couldn't invade.

"Just need... moment's rest... then... can fight," Ralrek gasped.

"Yep!" I said, choosing to conserve my energy with brief sentences, and to ignore Ralrek's delusion that he could contribute any more than he already had.

Taking the shortcut to the nearest safe place, I made it up the bank and into a small grotto. Unwrapping my arm, I got him into a seated position only for him to slide down and close his eyes. Behind me, the cavern shook with another footfall of the beast from the lake.

"... few... minutes," the oil-black-haired incubus said before he drifted to sleep.

I spun, using Creed like a walking stick as I crossed the field of boulders. The halberd vibrated, but I couldn't tell if it was from the giant's footsteps or the magical stick's temperament.

"Peacemaker," my crazy voice said inside my head.

"I wish you would give me peace," I shouted back to it, feeling relief and joy when Creed exploded with blue flame, engulfing the three blades. "Alright! Now we're ready to rock."

Akimon's field of ice was now fifty yards wide and still stretching toward the goliath. Bilba's rock display was still gaining mass. Spinning around itself, a thousand individual pieces become one as it picked up speed. Around and around it rotated, becoming a collective.

I ran toward them, raising the flaming Creed above my head, the dagger pointed at the rock bed. When I was as close to the giant as I dared, I slammed the blazing dagger blade into the ground.

Rock exploded with a thunderclap. Creed's strike propelled the prairie of pebbles, rocks, and boulders in a ripple toward the approaching water beast. The wave of rock picked up momentum and formed a small wall when it reached the banks.

Not high enough to slow the giant, never mind contain it. I had to do more.

I looked around, hoping to find a solution to my barrier building dilemma before the giant raised another incomprehensibly large leg. A single step and it would be over what I'd just built. My mind swirled, relieved only because Bilba's planetoid projectile was spinning so rapidly it obscured its individual pieces.

He pushed the formation forward, propelling it at the water goliath.

I watched in amazement as his ball of rock sped toward the beast. An escalating yell of excitement built inside me as it closed in.

But when the rock struck the goliath, there was no explosion, only a large spray of water as the mass punctured its body. The assault left behind a hole the exact size and shape of Bilba's rock. The strike didn't even slow the goliath. Its next step shattered Akimon's ice field, rendering it useless.

I lowered Creed, screaming and calling on the power of the halberd, the power of the Hellfire, the Flame of Annihilation. Creed roared in my hand, the double–ax heads gleaming blue. If I wasn't about to die, the halberd finally listening would have thrilled me.

The water giant acted first, swinging its massive fist into the barrier I had created, decimating it with no effort. Boulders shattered, chunks of sharp rock spraying outward.

I cut off my call to Creed, and the blades dulled, maintaining the power of the Hellfire they already held. A boulder, the size of a chimera, flew at me. I dove, barely avoiding being crushed to death. I hit the ground, yelling as the rock dug into my skin. Somewhere behind me, the bullet that had almost taken off my head smashed into the ground, projecting even more rock into the air. One, half the size of my torso, hit near me, spraying up more rock in this eternal ripple effect. I didn't get to my feet in time, and a small mound of loose pebbles and rock rolled over me, burying my entire lower torso and my strong arm. I screamed as the weight pressed. My legs and arm weren't crushed—I hoped—but pinned beyond the point of escape. Trapped, with a water giant on the prowl. Awesome.

With Ralrek passed out in the grotto and me trapped under a blanket of rock, Bilba and Akimon were on their own. Creed had fallen from my hand when the rock tossing contest buried me. I reached for it, but the best I could do was get in a good stretch. The halberd lay just out of reach. I craned my neck to see my best friend pull his father backward up the bank, away from the looming threat.

The water giant roared, a deep sound that shook the entire cavern. Stalactites fell from the roof, one dropping right behind Bilba and his fleeing father. Both incubi were shot forward.

"Creed!" I shouted.

The halberd responded, lifting off the ground on its dagger and flying to my open hand. I tried to block out the panic to focus. I needed to focus on drawing the Hellfire, calling on Creed's magic.

Now, if I could just figure out how I had done that.

Bilba was on his feet again, shouting to his father. Akimon lay in a heap too far away.

In a moment of clarity I questioned just what in the heaven was happening. None of this made sense. This was the Passage, not some incidental adventure where we stumbled upon the lair of a pissed off column of water with an attitude. This was supposed to be Bilba's test, to push him to his limits. But Bilba didn't fear water. Sure, giant things probably unnerved him. They unnerved everyone by them being so... giant. But after the Passage had forced him to relive his role in murdering Aries, this entire situation didn't feel like an escalation of his test. Something was wrong. Something was missing.

Movement caught my eye. Just to the side of the colossus, a tiny form dashed across the rock toward the fight. I squeezed my eyes to make out this potential new threat, swiveling Creed the best I could with my arm pinned.

Creed slipped in my grip. "No."

Powerful Deception magic was being cast. I felt it all over, even with my skin buried by a layer of rock. The succubus was drawing an immense amount of power, more than I had ever felt.

A rock wall formed between the water giant and its intended target, building around the back of the giant and imprisoning it.

Bilba's head jerked to the succubus. My watery eyes couldn't make out his expression, and that was a saving grace —for me, not him. I didn't want to see the effect this was going to have on my friend. Call me selfish, but I didn't want to witness how the Passage tortured Bilba in his last moments.

With blazing red hair and a red a-line dress, Fellia Ravenous raced to rescue her estranged son. Bilba's hands dropped. Fellia moved toward him more swiftly than I could take aim with Creed thanks to being pinned. Within seconds, she passed my line of aim. Creed was as useless against her as I was.

The rock wall around the water goliath exploded, spraying rocks to the outer reaches of the cavern. The colossus shook the world with its mournful call, raising its leg even as its prison walls rained down across the cavern. Boulders crashed against the rock bed, shooting smaller chunks, sharpened by fractures, in every direction. One grazed my cheek, slicing it open. I couldn't even put a hand to my face to stem the bleeding without setting Creed down.

By a saving grace, one struck near Bilba's mother, sending her flying backward, away from her son.

Bilba now stood in the middle of a rock field, facing the water goliath by himself. To one side lay his injured father. An equal distance in the opposite direction, his mother tried to roll.

Seventy feet of giant bent and picked up a boulder half the size of my parent's home. Lifting it into the sky, the beast readied to extinguish the life of one of the three Ravenouses.

Bilba swiveled his head to his father, then his mother. He was split from them. If the goliath flung the boulder at him, he would have to dodge over the uneven surface and hope to Lucifer he could avoid it and the collateral damage. Deciding which direction to evade the strike would only separate him further from one of his parents.

Slime covered my skin.

The water giant roared as it rotated its shoulder back to fling the boulder.

Bilba was screaming something I couldn't hear over the roar of the beast. I pushed against the rocks pinning me, hoping to rotate enough to get a shot on the towering monster. Not until I brought Creed across my body to aim at the giant did I notice that my distraction and pain had extinguished the Hellfire on Creed's blades. Once again, it was nothing more than a halberd.

Helpless, I mourned for my best friend as he ran to his left, along the bank, towards his father, casting glances back at his mother. Fellia Ravenous was conscious and trying to sit up, stretching her hand to him. Bilba was shouting, and I didn't need to hear him above the roar of the water goliath to know what he was saying. He was calling for his mother. Over and over. Even as he raced to his father, he called out to her while drawing on his Deception Ability.

As the water goliath's hand shot forward, a ring of blue flame burst around its feet, encircling them. The flames grew, building past its feet and reaching its ankles. Within a fraction of a second, the flames extended to its knees. Bilba ran to his father, almost by his side now, his hands weaving the air with his spell, rapidly working.

But not fast enough. The water goliath had momentum. Its arm shot forward—an unstoppable entity, powered by the magic of the Passage.

Bilba raged. The water giant flung the boulder.

As the flames licked beyond the goliath's knees to its thighs, the boulder descended on its target. My best friend screamed, his blue flame of Hellfire growing into a towering inferno around the water beast. Smoke rose, creating a white cloud above the monstrosity.

The flames grew to the beast's stomach, its elbows, and then to its shoulders. White steam billowed upward. The swirling vortex mouth disappeared. The dark-pooled eyes surrendered. The inferno swallowed the goliath's head as the boulder smashed to the ground, crushing Fellia Ravenous. Only by the grace of Lucifer was it large enough to prevent Bilba from witnessing what became of the illusion that was his mother.

My best friend howled and put more power into his spell. Mind cleared by the tragedy, fearing Bilba's mind was being broken, that he was allowing his emotions to overwhelm him, I used Creed to move stone after stone off of me. The halberd dug, one by one. I kept glancing over the pile, straining to see my friend before falling back and refocusing my efforts, unable to do both at once.

The column of Hellfire grew, reaching up, higher than the water goliath itself. The Flame of Annihilation heated, devoured. A white cumulonimbus cloud undulated over the column, spreading across the ceiling of the cavern.

Still I dug, knocking away rock, and panting with exertion. A blackout would have to take me before I stopped trying to free myself, if that's what was required to get to Bilba.

Before I succumbed though, I had moved enough rock to free my torso. I sat up, seeing Bilba on his knees, sobbing next to his father.

Digging back into the rock pile, I was moving rocks every second now that I had the use of both arms and my upper body. The weight holding my legs lightened.

Bilba's column of blue was dissipating, falling back to the lake's bank now. By the time I was free, it was less than twenty feet high but low enough to reveal the clever outcome. Supernatural heating of water dissipated a giant.

No way in heaven could he get me to admit to his absolute genius.

I scurried to Bilba's side, dropping to my knees and hugging him. He hugged me back. I looked over my friend's shoulder. Akimon's chest rose and fell. I squeezed Bilba. "He's alive, buddy. Your father is alive."

"I—I... know, Zeke." Bilba cried.

I pulled back, looking into his blotchy face. "She was an illusion. That wasn't her."

His head bobbed. "I know that too. But it felt so very real."

I hugged him. Nothing else needed to be said. Nothing I could say would counter the mess Fellia Ravenous had created, the mess the Passage had used against him in a last-ditch effort to break Bilba to see if he deserved the title.

Bilba Ravenous—Major demon.

22

UNDERWORLD, FIFTH CIRCLE

"I CAN'T BELIEVE you did it. I mean, I can, but... well, you know what I'm trying to say," I said, raising my beer. "To you."

Bilba raised his. Ralrek and Akimon raised theirs. Dialphio raised her wine glass. If you think that's bad, Melchiot held up a glass of water. We sat in the Ravenous's living room, celebrating the most monumental day of Bilba's life.

"A Major demon," I said, finishing the toast.

"Here, here," Ralrek said, taking a long swig of his.

"That's my boy!" Akimon said, downing his bottle before wincing and holding his side.

"Take it easy on the booze until you're healed, Dad," Bilba laughed, getting up from his chair and walking over to his father, leaning over and kissing his forehead. "Thank you for everything you've done for me."

Akimon blushed, tearing up before looking away and swatting at his son as if he was an annoying impling.

That only brought a round of laughter from everyone. I think even Melchiot joined.

"What now?" Dialphio asked.

"We relax for a century or two?" I offered.

Dialphio didn't bite. I didn't expect her to. I was only half serious. Now that Bilba was a Major demon, there was no throttling down. He had so many options he was going to spend weeks sorting through which path he wanted to take. I think the Passage distracted him so much that he hadn't planned for after he succeeded. I would nudge him the best I could, because I didn't think his new status would be one of peace, but I also didn't want to push him too hard. Not now.

We completed the Passage and were still sore and exhausted. Ralrek tried to cover it because he didn't want to lose cool points. He failed, but I kept that to myself. Akimon showed the most signs of the beating. Only Bilba was nonplussed.

The recognition festivities with the Council were reserved. The ceremony of Bilba joining the ranks of Major demons was nothing more than a publicity opportunity for the Council. The Master of Ceremonies spent more time praising the five Founders for their leadership in guiding yet another young demon to this elevated status than she did praising Bilba for his accomplishment.

That was for the best.

I didn't need the display to know that this issue between us and Hell's rulers wasn't over. The only way was slow, agonizing inch-by-inch progress. Now was not the time, though.

Melchiot had a successful student. Akimon had a son who was now a Major demon. Ralrek celebrated the occasion as if it were his own, he was so thrilled for our black-finger-nailed friend. For my part, I celebrated my friend as well, but I also recognized my excitement for the future. After his display of magic, I would never see Bilba the same way again. Now, I just had to figure out how to help keep him out of the clutches of Hell's rulers.

"This was great," Bilba said after we cleaned the dishes and sat for another drink.

Akimon had cooked an impressive spread to celebrate his son's accomplishments, and we ate heartily, as three young incubi are prone to do. Bilba's father was quite the chef, it turns out. The dinner filled the late afternoon and early evening. Afterward, Melchiot and Dialphio headed home, and Akimon excused himself to shower and rest, blaming the celebrations for wearing him down. I was tens of thousands of years younger, and I was ready to curl up into a ball in my bed.

We were sitting in the small garden the Ravenouses had constructed in their backyard. Bilba's father had not maintained it like he once had. Bilba said the garden was his mother's idea and that his father had tried to keep it for ages after she disappeared, only giving up after admitting she wasn't coming back and he got tired of hoping. By the way the garden grew wild and free, crowding the fence bordering the neighboring properties and cutting off the streetlights from the road, our presence was likely the first it had in decades. It was a pleasant retreat from the rest of the Fifth.

I lay back in the grass, trying to stare through the branches of the blue wisteria tree that was being invaded by the row of boxwood shrubs.

"I'm proud of you, buddy." I locked my hands behind my head and soaked in the moment.

"Thanks, guys. There's no way I could have done this without you," Bilba said.

"We know," Ralrek and I said simultaneously, drawing a chuckle from Bilba.

A peaceful quiet fell between us. I imagined all three of us drifting off to places in our own minds where we'd find solitude and reflection, untouched by the Council and their influence. A place where Lucifer Himself, only a title or not, couldn't even reach.

Things needed to change in Hell. The older and wiser me now understood I knew it much earlier but was too naïve to grasp its significance. I knew the other two incubi felt the same. They'd both been through enough Council–inspired crap.

We were three young incubi, sharing a tranquil moment in a backyard garden, ready to change the Underworld.

As I looked up into the night, enjoying my company, I knew this was going to be one of the last quiet nights we'd share for quite a while. I enjoyed every second.

23

UNDERWORLD/OVERWORLD

"YOU'RE LOOKING BETTER," Ralrek said as he backed out of my refrigerator, holding the half–sub sandwich I had saved for an evening snack. Not much of a snack, really, not unless you enjoyed subs with lettuce that tastes like paper and sandwich meat that held the flavor of smoke—and not the good kind.

The handsome jerk bit into it, nodding approvingly. Good sub or not, I was going to miss it.

"I was going to eat that," I said, then addressed his appearance after our trying experience in the Passage. "And you don't look like you were just run over by a carriage anymore."

Ralrek slid to the small kitchen table, sitting and eating my sub while we waited for Bilba to finish in my bathroom. The only one in my apartment. Sometimes I wondered why I missed having my friends around. "Yeah, it's strange. It took two days before I felt like myself again. I'd never thought to try a spell that large. Don't think I want to again."

"Did you do something different with it?" I asked. I had no idea Ralrek could cast such a strong Fire spell that could melt rock. Doubly impressive to turn stone to molten liquid within seconds. I'd be blessed before I told him how impressed I was.

"What are you guys talking about?" Bilba came into the kitchen, yanking open my refrigerator door and searching the contents.

"You better have washed your hands. By the way, don't either of you have food in your own homes?" I asked.

Ralrek held up the little that remained of my sub. "Food tastes better here. It's got a" —he waved his free hand in a circle as if he were a food critic —"certain smoky flavor."

"Oh, so funny." I smiled.

Bilba closed my refrigerator, empty-handed. "You don't have anything good."

"Sorry. I guess I'll shop before you guys come by again," I said.

"It's okay. I'll just get something in Olympia," Bilba said. "I'd rather eat Overworld food, anyway."

"Me too," I said, excited to go.

"Me three." Ralrek received disbelieving looks from both me and Bilba as he dusted his fingers free of crumbs.

We had been chatting through our notebooks the day before when we scheduled a meeting with Virgo and Cassie. There'd been enough dancing around without admitting that we were ready. I think each one of us found saying it out loud —in a notebook—was intimidating. If we committed the thought to words, we committed ourselves to action. I was ready; they were too, I'd bet, but without a firm plan, progress was stunted.

Today was going to be an important day for demons, angels, and the mortals who depended on them to not be asshats in the immortal realm.

"You finished? We're running late," I said, pointing at the corner of my mouth to tell Ralrek a crumb of my sub was caught on his.

He dabbed at his mouth with a finger. "Yep. Let's go. By the time this meeting is over, I'll be ready for lunch."

I shook my head at the tall incubus. Whoever got the title of Lucifer after Lucifer was no longer Lucifer, I was going to talk to that demon about re-balancing chance and dumb luck. If I ever took up the mantle the rebel cell wanted for me, I'd make sure no single demon got all the looks and curses Ralrek enjoyed. Too much for one demon just wasn't right.

Bilba opened the rift in my hallway and we entered the Vigilante's headquarters, which was quieter this time. Now that he was a Major demon, this was the last time I'd forgive him for opening a rift in the hangar. Before we left, he'd need to spend five minutes in a blessed side room memorizing it so we had a future of subtle entrances back into this realm. No one was watching TV. Two women played basketball at the far end of the hangar, the dribbling of the ball the only sound of life. The table where the group dispersed weapons was empty.

A door clicked open behind us. Steve walked out, smiling when he saw us. "Hey guys. Are you here for Virgo and Cassie?"

I nodded. "Are they around?"

He pointed at the conference room. "In there." He watched us for a second, and I could tell he was struggling whether to say something or not.

I laughed. "What's on your mind?"

He blinked. "I'm not sure. There's just something… different about you guys. Can't put my finger on it."

Bilba started, "Well, I—"

I had anticipated Bilba the Blabbermouth sharing too much information. Don't give me too much credit though; he always does. "We've had some things going on at home. That's all you're noticing. How have things been here?"

"I would like to say it's been quiet, but there have been minor incidents here and there." He crooked a corner of his mouth. "Hard to tell if it's the larger, organized group or just some idiots they've inspired who are acting on their own. But it doesn't help, either way."

"Sorry to hear that," I said.

"We change what we can and we don't stress about what we can't," Steve said. "There's a lot of division growing, to be honest. Depressing, because it seems to be gaining momentum, like no one wants to sit at the table and hash out differences anymore, come to some common ground. Instead, it's like everyone wants to pull the other away. But, that's why we're here, doing what we can."

Ralrek asked, "Where is everyone?"

I sensed the spirit behind his question. The desperation of violence drove the growth of the organization, bringing more Abandoned and mortals to our side. When the hangar was dormant, as it was now, I feared the dearth of activity might be a signal of the reversal. What if the mortals realized the impracticality of being a Vigilante, and the Abandoned had given up hope?

Great, one more task.

Steve made me feel better in an instant. "We've got teams out. Some are patrolling the city, but we have a few heading up to Tacoma and Seattle on recruiting missions. Virgo set us up with a few contacts in the area, and we touch base with them from time to time."

"Do you get people to join you that way?" Bilba asked.

Steve smiled. "Yes, people or immortals." He looked at me, shrugging as if he didn't just call me out on my hidden truth. "It's so hard to tell one from the other, isn't it? Anyway, I've got to run. Job calls. Being a Vigilante is fun, but it doesn't pay the bills. Catch you guys later."

Steve headed toward the hangar door and we headed to the conference room, finding Virgo and Cassie leaning over a map of the city.

Cassie looked up, her crystal eyes making my heart skip. "Hi guys," she said with her typical cheer.

"Hey," Virgo said in his typical flat eloquence.

"What are you guys doing?" Bilba asked.

Virgo pressed his finger to a spot on the map, the brown tip lightening almost to white. "We're scouting viable locations for the Underground, the Path, whatever we're going to call it. Still haven't decided."

Ralrek pulled out a chair and plopped into it. "Yeah, that's why we wanted to talk."

"Oh?" Cassie sounded surprised. "Is everything okay?"

Bilba gave them a not–so–quick rundown of events that led to him becoming a Major demon. I filled in the spots he missed, most importantly, about what spying on the Council had revealed.

"So, we have to lie low on this idea for the Path," I said, regretfully.

Virgo stood up straight, crossing his muscular arms. "So you're reneging on the deal?" He didn't sound pleased, but then again, Virgo never did.

"No, we're being smart about how we proceed," Ralrek said, matching Virgo's tone. "We can't take serious risks right now. With Bilba becoming a Major demon, it's only a matter of when, not if, the Council is going to do something to change that. If it wasn't for their in-fighting, they would have already tried to take out one of us."

"Probably all of us," I said.

Ralrek pursed his lips. "Yep. That's not a situation we want to antagonize, and it's not the right way to return demons home." He shifted to Cassie. "I'm sure you can understand. You wouldn't take risks with your Abandoned, would you?"

Cassie shook her head, a curl of cocoa hair falling forward. "No. Absolutely not. We have to stop this inhumane treatment of angels and demons. Letting them suffer like this in the mortal realm, decaying... it's wrong and needs to be stopped. Now that I have more influence, real influence, I plan on pushing forward on that. But, you're right. We have to be careful how we do this. If doing so puts you guys or this operation in jeopardy, then we figure something else out."

Here came the hard sell. I asked, "Would you be willing to hold off returning angels?"

Cassie studied me for a moment before answering. "Yes, it would only be right. Returning angels without you being able to take demons back to the Underworld would create an unfair perception, one that would be favorable to us and detrimental to your efforts. That would hurt everyone. That would lead to more and more incidents of swaying the Balance." She stopped until everyone was on edge, something I could almost touch and feel. "We all know what that means. None of us want that, of course. But I fear not everyone is so concerned. Yes, the angels can wait as well."

I gave her an appreciative nod.

Cassie sighed, taking a seat. "Plus, I might be able to change things if I have a little more time to think."

"Oh? Why is that?" Bilba asked.

Cassie opened her mouth. She paused. Blinked. Her shoulders dropped.

"They selected you, didn't they?" I guessed.

Her head dropped.

"Wow," Bilba said in a breathy tone. "Can you believe this, guys? We're at a table with one of Yahweh's Council members. Demons sitting with Yahweh's own."

Cassie gave an embarrassed smile, still looking down at the table. "Please don't make this a big deal. One of ours passed, naturally. They had to fill the vacancy. I was, undeservedly I think, chosen. Nothing changes between us."

The heaven it didn't. This changed everything. "How does it not? You're a Council member. You are now part of the body that makes decisions that not only affect the Upperworld and Overworlds, but you're going to be privy to things that affect us too."

"And I'm going to work toward the benefit of everyone, Z

—Zeke," Cassie said. "I mean... it's going to take me away from being able to help as much as I am now." She gestured at the map. "But in my new position, I'll be able to ensure the right angels are involved where I can't be."

"That could put you at risk," I said, trying to ignore the anxious thoughts bouncing around in my skull.

Cassie nodded. "It could."

In that moment I thought of a million things I could have said, ten million I wanted to say, and all would have made me look as ridiculous as a celebrity–struck imp. Cassie being selected to Yahweh's Council was nothing insignificant. It changed everything. Who she was. How she interacted with us. By its nature, it had to. Even if she remained friendly, she wouldn't be the same angel, because she couldn't afford to be. Proof of my opinion lay in the way Azazel had taken years to position himself to help in our cause. Even with the egregious violations to demon and Underworld, he still couldn't act boldly. Azazel was no coward. Yet he had to use different vehicles and agents to meet his goals. The same course was laid for Cassie now.

For all I knew, we could walk out of this meeting and I might not see her for decades. For centuries. The thought made my gut clench and my throat swell. Maybe I would never see her again.

I drew a deep breath, realizing how selfish my thought-train had become. More was at stake here than my enjoyment of being around Cassie. Lives were at stake. Cassie would find her replacement, and I would have to trust her choice. It was all about pushing toward a change in order to prevent the end of... well, everything—even if we hadn't figured out exactly what that change looked like. All that considered, I still didn't have to like it. Maybe I was being juvenile, but I couldn't see why it was so difficult to have an eternal realm where preserving interests wasn't divisive. Why was it so hard for the powerful to see the privilege of preserving the fulcrum, where everyone has a chance to live a fulfilling existence? What was it about being in a position of power that made someone want more and more, even more than their fair share? What was so unattractive about having 'just enough?' A pipe dream, I know, but without dreams, what point was there to existing?

"I'm happy for you," I said, the words forced out through my tight throat.

Cassie's lips curled up in a narrow smile.

"Will you be able to keep using our notebooks?" Bilba asked.

"Yes," Cassie said. "That won't be hard. It will be easier to stay in touch with you guys and not have to worry about being discovered. But don't worry about me. You three have enough going on. I wish I could help. Your situation is more precarious than mine. Just know," she said, glancing at me before sharing a look with everyone at the table, "you're not getting rid of me. I'll still be around, still worried about how you're going to stay safe."

Ralrek shrugged. "We can always go into hiding. There's plenty of places in the Underworld we could disappear to."

"You... you could find someplace safe?" Cassie asked. "What would your authorities say? Surely, they wouldn't leave you alone."

"They're so distracted with their problems and in-fighting they can't keep a finger on anything anymore," Bilba said cheerily. "They'd look, though. I'm pretty sure they won't stop until all of us and anyone who has helped us has been eradicated as a problem."

"The only problem is that it creates a lot more work for us," I said before this idea gained too much momentum. "Work that takes us away from important things like keeping the Balance balanced. That's what all of this is for. We have to stay safe. We'd need to restrict the knowledge of where we are to just a handful of demons. So, we'll have to level-up in the clear communication department and add layers between us and anyone acting to help. Just to keep everyone as safe as possible. That wouldn't be easy."

"No, it wouldn't be," Ralrek said. "But at least we would be alive. We can't guarantee that as long as the Council knows where we are. I'd rather act first than react when acted upon."

"Without our intervention, who knows what happens to the Balance," Bilba said.

"Where would you go?" Virgo asked.

Creed burned at my hip. I winced, inching the halberd away from my waist.

Ralrek leaned back in his chair, his head tilting side to side. "If I had my way, I would stay here. There's nothing like safety in numbers, and you guys have a tight operation. But, that would put the Vigilantes at serious risk. So, I don't know. We've been to the Eighth Circle, and that's probably the best bet. That place has been chaotic for so long, we could get lost."

The thought of living in the Eighth Circle offended me. It was a nasty place, full of nasty demons who ate treachery for breakfast. In a Circle that placed so little value on the lives and freedom of others, how could we find security enough to plot how we were going to change the course of Hell?

"There's always the Isle of Dread too," Bilba said matter-of-factly. I wasn't the only one who scoffed before he added, "What? We could. It would be safe. Well... safer."

Cassie leaned forward. "What's the Isle of Dread? That sounds like a horrendous place."

Bilba's head bobbed. "Oh, it is. Well, at least based on what I've read."

I agreed. We'd had this discussion, and a future on the Isle was as attractive as playing games of chance in the Eighth with a knife at your throat.

Ralrek tapped the table. "You tell her about that place," he said, standing. "I'm going to talk to the Vigilantes."

"Why?" Virgo said, his eyes narrowing.

"Because, I want to get information about them, as individuals. I want to learn about their stories, and where they want to go when we open the Path to sneak them back," Ralrek said, swiveling to the four of us seated at the table. "We're past the point of talking. We need to plan. That's what I'm going to do now. If we have to go into hiding, what we're doing won't be as easy as it is now. No time like the present to prepare. By knowing who these Abandoned demons are, and what they want for their future, I'll be preparing. I also want to know what resources they have back in the Underworld in case we need help. Could come in handy. Plus," Ralrek continued, looking only at Bilba and me, "if we have to hide in the Overworld, I want to make sure they trust us."

He left and an uneasy silence spread around the table.

Bilba cleared his throat. "Um, yeah, so, the Isle of Dread is a terrible place. It's basically an isolated part of the Underworld where our authorities discard demons, for lack of a better word."

Cassie scrunched her eyes. "I thought that's what Abandonment was about?"

Bilba said, "Well, in a way, it is. But for those demons they don't trust to let loose in the Overworld, they use the Isle. The demons sent there are restrained to the Underworld, so the Council can keep an easier eye on them, but they're not free to cause trouble either. There or here. The Balance goes untouched. It's a win–win for the Council."

"And a miserable existence for anyone sent to this Isle?" Cassie concluded.

"Exactly," Bilba said.

"How do you know?" Virgo asked, leaning forward, interlocking his fingers.

This was a question I could answer. "He reads. Everything. Literally."

"Don't knock it until you've tried it, Zeke. I know words are hard for you," Bilba, the Major demon, grinned.

"Ass."

"Well, let's hope you figure something else out," Cassie said. "I hate to think the three of you need to take such extreme measures to stay safe."

"Don't worry. We're going to stay ahead of the Council," Bilba said.

"You're going to continue to spy on them?" Virgo said.

"We have to," I said. "They thought we'd never come back from the Passage. As usual, they underestimated us, especially Bilba. But they won't stop. We can't either. It's a risk we have to take. Otherwise, we're constantly reacting."

Everyone at the table jumped when someone pounded on the door.

"Come in!" Virgo ordered.

One of the basketball-playing women, her face flushed, lunged into the room. Her hand remained on the door handle. "They did it again, Virgo. The women's clinic."

I spun in my chair. "What? The clinic? Why?"

"To make Yahweh's followers look bad," Cassie said with a deep scowl.

"What did they do?" Virgo growled.

"They bombed it." The woman's lip quivered. "Bombed the women's clinic. Casualties. And" –she stopped to swallow– "they're still there."

Virgo slammed a hand on the table. "Have James recall everyone. Tell them to bring whatever arms they have. Everyone goes directly to the clinic. Not here. We don't have time."

She nodded and disappeared back into the hangar.

Ralrek ran in even as she was leaving. "Let's go."

I was already on my feet

Virgo looked at each of us. "Can the Vigilantes count on you?"

As if the fierce expressions weren't enough of an answer, the head nods confirmed they could.

We ran into the hangar, towards the vans and the fight ahead. This time, no Mr. Nice Guy. If I had to do it alone, which I knew I wouldn't, today was the end for these terrorists.

24

OLYMPIA

DARKNESS SHROUDED the city of Olympia, the sun having set long before we left the compounds of the Vigilante headquarters. The block around the women's clinic was darker still. Power was out for blocks surrounding the building. The only light came from fires set at buildings around this section of the city. I'd seen a setting like this before, a setting I didn't want to ever experience again, but now was. This looked like a war zone.

I knew a Founder's fingerprint when I saw one. The fires had been set to distract and split authorities, keeping them busy so someone could execute the attack on the women's clinic with flawless cruelty. How else did you describe someone who would hurt women and children in need of services?

"Oh, my Lucifer," Bilba said, his eyes staring in widened horror at what remained of the clinic.

I found it hard to comprehend it as well.

A third of the building had collapsed, the rubble sloping into the road. Shattered glass sparkled orange. Wood beams still burned. Other building materials smoldered in piles.

Underneath one of those, a thin arm, covered in blood, poked out. Unmoving.

Creed throbbed at my hip the entire drive, as if it wanted to remind me I didn't listen to its first warning.

Sirens blared through the night. I imagined every available firefighter from any city that could get to Olympia was on their way. Black clouds billowed into the night, obscuring the moon and stars. The anguished cries of mortals punctuated the chorus of approaching sirens.

"I'm going to kill these bastards," Ralrek growled, his hands glowing with the spell he held.

Creed was in my hand, extended, the blades gray but threatening. "Not if I get to them first."

Virgo was dispatching the Vigilantes, choosing to not wait for those he'd recalled. They'd be too slow to respond anyway with the streets blocked off. Late arrivers would have to run for blocks once they got into Olympia. We couldn't wait. We had to act now.

I extended my senses, feeling muted demonic magic, just as I had the last time at the clinic. "There's at least twenty in the building," I said.

Cassie whipped her head around. "How do you know that?"

"You're not the only one working on your skills," I said. "I can sense demonic magic now, even a good distance away. The building is blocking a lot of the signatures, but I can feel the emissions. We need to be careful, or more will die."

We hunkered behind a broken section of outer wall that had collapsed into large piles of rubble where we could assess the situation.

From inside, a fireball raced across the night sky, striking a building further down the block. The rumble followed seconds later, the building already catching fire. More destruction. More death.

"I'm going in," I said, standing, Creed pulsing in my hand.

Ralrek grabbed my wrist. "Give me a chance. I'll blast them out of there. No sense putting yourself at risk, Zeke."

I knew what he meant, and I knew why he said it, but it didn't mean I was going to fall for it. Everyone in the blessed Fifth, in the entire Underworld, could call me whatever they wanted. Segregate or Great Prince, it didn't matter. You couldn't be a liberator, as *The Histories of the Balance* claimed the owner of Creed was, if you didn't actually liberate. And as long as that crew of demons boarded up in the standing section of the building was terrorizing the mortal realm, I was not a liberator.

Before I wrenched my hand free, a scream drew my attention.

The front door of the clinic burst open and a woman ran into the night. The leg of her slacks was ripped open, exposing bloody skin. Her blouse was torn at the sleeve. Her blood–stained face was marked with terror.

Behind her, the door hadn't even closed when another figure appeared, silhouetted against the light streaming from inside. I sent my senses and felt the emissions radiating from the silhouetted figure.

I jerked my hand away from Ralrek. He didn't grab me again. "Focus on the building. Suppress their attacks. I've got this," I shouted as I sprinted toward the woman.

In her terror, she wouldn't be able to distinguish friend from foe, and we couldn't have a sit-down to give me a chance to convince her I was one of the good guys while holding a six-foot long halberd. The figure in the door was conjuring. A cold, smooth stone sensation of water magic slid over my forearms.

The figure's hands raised toward the fleeing woman. I hefted Creed, the wavy dagger facing forward, and threw it like a javelin. Before the demonic figure released their spell, Creed brought an end to their magic and to them. The blade sank deep, propelling the figure backward, shattering the glass door. Creed's victim was an incubus. He shuddered for a second and then lay still.

"Creed!" I ran forward even as Creed stood on its end. Holding out my hand, I caught the halberd after it zipped across the open air.

Inside the foyer, I took a second to look at the young incubus. This incubus had to be a thousand years younger than me, maybe just out of school. Senseless.

Outside, the firearms popping told me the Vigilantes were engaging. Thudding of spells striking against and coming out of the building, hitting objects—and probably victims—told me that the fight was now on.

From my previous invasion of this clinic, albeit the collapsed portion, I was familiar enough with its layout to know where I could find the stairs. A military-esque strategy was at play here, dictating the demon's positioning. Wherever their forces were, they were attacking from the safety of the upper floors. That's where I headed as the battle escalated outside.

Reaching the second floor, glass shattered down the hall. Spreading my senses again, I felt the ebbing emissions from a dying immortal. One point for the good guys.

From my left was a strong signature. The demons had split their forces to both ends of the building. I crept forward, unable to spin Creed to create a shield in the narrowness of the hall.

"The Prince is here," a voice said, close enough to my ear to touch it with its lips.

I was alone.

Great, not only was I going crazy, but now I was going crazy with narcissism.

Creed jolted, and I almost dropped it—a warning I wouldn't ignore this time.

I reached the room where I felt the strong signature.

Backing against the wall, I raised my foot and kicked the door open. And froze.

Not one demon but three. And all were casting. As if that wasn't bad enough, I knew one of them.

From a mile away, I could have picked out the brooding incubus who wore a permanent scowl of hatred, even though I'd only met him once at a family picnic. The incubus I was supposed to take under my horns and mentor if we ever crossed paths again. The young incubus I would mentor in honor of Leo and Aries.

"Harvest," I moaned Leo's brother's name.

If the younger incubus recognized me, it never reached his face. Surprised hostility did.

Harvest Leto's small mouth pursed like an imp attempting his first kiss. My skin flushed with warmth, the sign of a Manipulative spell.

"Don't do it, Harvest," I snapped.

He blinked at my mention of his name, then resumed his spell.

The two other demons, one incubus and a succubus about my age, turned away from the window through which they were firing their spells at the Vigilantes below and focused on me. Three-on-one. Great odds.

Unlike the hall, this room had enough room for me to use Creed's shield. As they turned, about to spray their magic—and probably me—all over the office, I rotated the halberd. Creed didn't help matters by the way it thumped in my hands. I didn't have time for his attitude right now. We'd hash out our differences if I got through this.

On the other side of the wall, groaning overrode all sound. The roof caving in? Maybe I wouldn't die at the hands of these too-young, dumb, and full of themselves demons. Maybe my destiny lay under a pile of building materials molded by decades of Pacific Northwest rains.

The distraction hurt my foes more than me.

Their spells slipped as the building protested, straining against the call of gravity. I charged, Creed lowered. Done playing around with Hell's scum, I raised the halberd, catching both in the throat. Thank Lucifer—or whoever—they were about the same height, making my effort efficient and effective.

The petrified dark cherry haft connected with their throats, sending both head over heels—not for each other, but alongside each other. On the floor, they had similar reactions, grabbing their throats while raising hands toward me.

I glanced up, seeing Harvest sprint from the office, rounding the corner out of sight. The fine hairs on the back of my neck raised. One of these two floor-bound demons had Construction magic. The other had Water. I didn't want to see what the combination would create.

Not for the first time in my life, but something that was happening far too often, I raised Creed and thrust the wavy dagger blade into the incubus's chest. His cries shook me to my core. Creed pulsed with fury. I yanked the blade free, spun, and brought the double-ax head over in an arc. It bit deep into the succubus. She didn't cry out as her partner had.

Smoke drifted from the hallway. I crouched low, using an overstuffed chair to hide behind as I sent my senses outward. Abilities were being used everywhere, but one signature was far stronger than the others, even Cassie's.

Crawling toward the window, I forced it open, and a rush of chilly Pacific Northwest night air rushed in, pushing back on the increasingly smoky room. I leaned out, taking in the scene below and trying to draw a clean breath. Apparently, living in the Sixth wasn't effective conditioning for trapping yourself in a burning building. Who knew?

Bodies lay everywhere. Vigilante bodies spread across blacktop like an ant hill drowned by a cruel impling. Vehicles were crushed. Bodies and body parts marred others. Strewn across the blacktop, their twisted forms pronounced the cost of immortal greed. Creed throbbed, sending the jolt up to my shoulders.

Ralrek was below me, hiding behind a sports coupe while throwing fireballs toward an angled section of the building that formed an 'L'. The same direction from where this powerful signature came.

"Yes. There. He fights," the voice whispered. I felt a breath on my ear. Maybe it was the night's breeze?

Going crazy was a disadvantage at any point in someone's life, but in the middle of a heated battle, it's hardly the time to embrace the disintegration of mental faculties. The area where the strongest signature was coming from would require picking my way through these unfamiliar halls, fighting off Lucifer-knew-how many demons along the way. But, if taking care of the most powerful caster would discourage the rest of this terrorist band, then it was worth the effort.

As I leaned out the window, calculating a quicker, safer way to the strong signature, Creed decided for me. I had been holding it upright, bracing myself in a squat with the dagger cutting into the floor as a third leg. But as I considered my next move, the halberd lurched toward the door. When I say it lurched, I'm not talking about a slight tug. The halberd pulled me over onto my back as it flew at the office door. I almost let go, and I should have to save my shoulder. Plus, it would have been more graceful and less princely to let the stupid halberd do what it wanted. But I didn't loosen my grip, and it dragged me along until I ran into the table used to display magazines and information packets. It toppled over. I loosened my grip, but the halberd stopped pulling. By the time my hand was open, Creed fell and clattered against the table, resting at an angle.

I scrambled to my feet, snagging it. Defiant and stubborn, I wouldn't let the halberd's attitude lead me into a weaponless showdown should the wrong demon find me.

"What's your problem?" I said.

"Seek what you have sought," the voice said.

Great, not only was I losing my mind, but I was losing it even faster.

Sprinting out of the office, I crossed the hallway and shot out my senses. Very little magic was in this part of the building. Most of the muted signatures here were low, weaker still than the muted feel of the strong one coming through brick, glass, and wood. Wherever Harvest had fled, he wasn't close. Maybe that was him with the weak signal from the distant corner of this floor. I didn't care. I'd made a promise to Leo, and I planned on keeping it. Unless Harvest got in my way or put someone at direct threat, I was going to deal with him after handling the bigger problem.

Creed jerked in my hand, pulling me toward the stairwell.

"Bless it, I'm moving," I shouted, sprinting down the stairs, leaping to the landing with four steps remaining. Against the back wall, I checked around the corner, visually and with my senses. Safe, I took the stairs two at a time and raced past the incubus's corpse through the shattered front door, and into the parking lot, moving until I was alongside Ralrek.

"Good to see you," he said when I slammed against the car, my back to it.

"You're just as ugly as I remember," I said, spinning, but staying low and pointing at the angled building. "There's something over there."

"They're everywhere, Zeke," Ralrek replied.

To the side of the parking lot along the fence, Bilba kneeled behind a car, his hands moving in counter-clockwise directions. In perpetual motion, he looked like he was turning the tiller of a boat. Swarms of bats appeared above him, a black cloud against the black night. As he thrust his arms forward, the bats flew straight as an arrow toward a small group of foes on the opposite side, hunkering behind vehicles.

"No, someone in that part of the building is as powerful as ten of them. I've got to get to them. I just don't know how." I craned my neck. "I could pick my way along, but that will take a while."

"Can you tell where this strong one is?" he asked, flinging another fireball that exploded against the rear of the van, knocking the door open.

I shook my head. "Just the general vicinity. Right around there." I pointed to the third floor, to the right of the central doorway leading into the building.

"Get Cassie's attention, and then signal me," Ralrek said.

"What then?"

"If you can get her to use Angelfire on that section, I have something I've been saving up. If we combine our spells on that one spot, we might be able to shake out this leader."

"Sounds good. If she's on board, I'll raise Creed above my head like this." Laying Creed on the blacktop, I crouched lower and raised both hands over my head, probably looking like a poor imitation of a victorious boxer. "That will be my signal."

"Okay," Ralrek said, jumping when a large spray of water rocked the vehicle we were hiding behind. With a little more force, the demon who cast the spell could have rolled the vehicle over on top of us. "Just hurry."

Weaving in between vehicles, I crossed the parking lot to Cassie. Those crystal eyes that always made my heart flip were distant, focused on something that wasn't in the here and now. I explained the plan.

"Okay," was the only panting answer.

I raised my hands over my head, holding Creed horizontally. From his hiding spot, Ralrek nodded. Both of his hands glowed orange.

"Back up," Cassie warned as she weaved. Being this close while she drew on angelic Abilities was not a good idea. My stomach flipped. I gagged as pressure moved its way from my stomach up my esophagus. Bending over, throwing up on blacktop in the middle of a fight to the death was a glorious way to go out. Thankfully, I had little to vomit, only stomach acid. The discomfort of the growing migraine at the base of my skull didn't fade as quickly.

Moving alongside the car, I let her finish her spell. If I didn't, I would pass out against the fence hugging this side of the parking lot.

The further I moved from her, the less I felt nauseated as the pressure in my skull decreased. It was still there, very uncomfortable, and still distracting me. I increased my pace.

I neared a van and stumbled right into a succubus, dressed in black, and casting a Manipulative spell. My cheeks flushed with her magic.

She didn't see me until it was too late. I grabbed a fistful of hair and slammed her face against the van, dropping her to the ground, unconscious. Hey, at least she would still be alive to suffer through the headache that would come. But she wouldn't get a second chance if she made a subsequent poor life decision.

Keeping my eyes on the building, I moved away from the succubus as the night turned to day. Cassie's Angelfire, a beam half as thick as a vehicle, split the sky. It was followed closely by a swirling column of fire, two times as thick as her Angelfire. I stumbled, bracing myself against the trunk of a car. I squatted, amazed at the combined forces and anticipating the destruction that would follow.

Ralrek's Fire and Cassie's Angelfire spells hit the building at the third floor, shearing the roof off as they cut their way through. Their spells moved through this hardened building like a straw into water, continuing all the way through as it tore away the structure.

Immediately, the emissions cleared, flooding out from the building and overwhelming the signatures of the other demonic terrorists.

I wanted to scramble back and warn everyone, but I didn't have time. The owner of that power was coming, fast.

I moved closer, hoping I could get a read on the situation and maybe even outflank their leader. Now parallel to the building, I looked along its front exterior. Small piles of broken brick pocked the sidewalk. A car hood had been smashed by a fallen section from an earlier explosion. The gaping wound of the floor above was now out of sight. Along the sidewalk, every twenty feet or so, demons squatted, using their Abilities against the Vigilantes and my friends. Creed thumped in my hand. I could race along the sidewalk, shearing demons at the neck, and if I was quick enough, I could decimate this entire force with a single sprint.

"The Prince," the voice whispered urgently in my ear, breaking my focus.

Creed shook in my hands so forcefully I had to hold it with both hands. I edged along the building, pressing my back to it and holding Creed against my chest. "What in heaven is wrong with you?" I asked the halberd.

Peeking around the corner, there was no other way to get to the slinking terrorists. Just as my friends used vehicles to shield themselves, the terrorists were as well. I could have gone back into the parking lot and approached from their front, weaving in and out of the vehicles, but that would take too long and put me in the line of fire of both forces. The plan to sprint was going to have to work, because it was my only option.

Shooting out my senses one last time, I picked up the signatures in the parking lot. Overwhelmed by the rebounding sensation, one still stood out. I couldn't separate it enough to find its location now. It was close, and that's all I had.

I pulled Creed away, still having to hold it with two hands. "Now is a great time to call on some Hellfire, buddy."

The blades remained cold.

"Ass."

The halberd shuddered.

Drawing a deep breath, I turned the corner, ready to cut down every single terrorist along the sidewalk and bring this fight nearer to its conclusion. If I couldn't find their leader, I could take them out and allow my immortal friends and the Vigilantes to focus on the strongest.

Fire exploded. Water knocked over vehicles, turning to ice and imprisoning its victims. Someone with strong Manipulative magic mutated one of the parking lot light poles into a writhing column of metal, wiggling before it slammed down to squash its victims before rising back up again. The oblong light acted as its head, searching for fresh blood, before smashing again. Bilba's bats harassed terrorists, forcing most of them to defend themselves with their spells instead of launching them against the Vigilantes.

I bolted forward, my breaths and footsteps slamming on the concrete drawn into focus by adrenaline. I shifted Creed so the double–axes were to my left, ready to cleave.

Then the front doors exploded outward. A plume of fire roared from the building, shooting forward through the cars parked in its path, swallowing them. Fuel, ignited by heat, expanded. Cars exploded, shooting toward the Vigilantes. The inferno roared. Forty feet away, its heat licked my face, halting my sprint. I dove behind a sedan, only to realize too late that it was a stupid thing to do as parts of the closest vehicles were now raining down as the inferno swelled, swallowing two of the demon terrorists.

I stepped back. Creed jolted, making my teeth clatter.

Walking through the inferno, as if unaffected by its flames, strode the Prince of Demons.

Standing in the inferno that belched outward, expanding across the vehicles in an ever–widening swath, the large demon with blond sideburns flicked his forefinger with his thumb. In the air, a circle of fire engulfed Bilba's bats. In the millisecond it took to create the spell, the circle collapsed and extinguished against the black night. The cloud of bats was no more.

With a flick of his wrist, Beelzebub sent a ball of fire the size of a basketball arcing through the air. It struck a vehicle and exploded. Two Vigilantes, two mortals who sacrificed to keep the Balance, flew back, slamming against the other building and tumbling to the ground, limp.

Beelzebub had been a bully since the moment I was recruited to do the Council's dirty work. He had murdered Aries.

He was a part of every plot and wrongdoing I'd experienced since the blessed Council came into my life. A final spit of disgrace to Leo's memory, Beelzebub had somehow recruited Harvest into this terrorist cell. And now he was here, in the Overworld, a short distance away, and he was vulnerable.

Maintain the Balance.

Liberate.

Creed's double–ax and dagger blades burst blue with Hellfire.

As if sensing me, Beelzebub's head snapped in my direction.

I charged.

He spun, thrusting both hands forward conjuring a column of fire.

I lowered Creed, spinning it. The shield, instantly formed, alive and growing. Beelzebub's flames hit my juvenile barrier, pushing me back. I flew along the sidewalk, landing on my back, breath exploding from me. My head was cloudy, but I couldn't linger. A delay would cost my life.

I rolled to the side. The direction didn't matter, just as long as I moved. Beelzebub had to react to me, and that meant I still had a chance. In the grass now, I was shielded by a corner of the building. Getting back on my feet, I spun Creed again.

Once the barrier formed, I jumped around the corner. Beelzebub strode toward me. His confident walk hitched when I appeared and pushed forward.

He lowered his hands, and I charged. His flame struck my shield. I leaned into the strike, pushing against it. He was strong, incredibly strong—like frighteningly strong. My feet slipped. Lowering my head, I pushed harder, and the slide halted. Air hissed and a tire went flat on a late model sedan parked five feet away. At first, I thought he had melted the rubber, but the warm flush of Manipulative magic hit me. Taking another glance at the tire, it slid away from the car, exposing the steel rim. The black rubber amalgamated into a hand, its fingers curling in, making a fist.

The fist collided, sending me hurling through the air and crashing into the building. My head hit brick and stars filled my vision. Creed's shield dropped, but Hellfire continued to blaze on its blades. On my knees, I heard the deep, guttural laughter of the Prince of Demons.

He sauntered back into view as if a battle wasn't raging around him, except now he was holding a flaming sword. "Let's see if you're ready to dance, boy," Beelzebub boomed. "I'm going to make you regret ever meddling in my affairs."

"I always have," I said hoarsely.

Beelzebub raised the sword, and I brought Creed up just in time to block. From my fingertips to my shoulders, everything tingled with a single strike. I was on my knees, and he was standing. Beelzebub had a six-inch height advantage and a hundred pounds of muscle over me. But I had Creed and an attitude, and I wasn't going to pass up an opportunity to get a few blows in during this battle of princes.

Beelzebub brought his sword up again, and I rolled to my side, avoiding the strike that sliced through the air and into the dirt, scorching the grass as the blade sank into the wet Pacific Northwest muck.

Now I was on my feet facing him, rocking Creed, dipping its heads as I flipped the weapon from hand-to-hand.

"Pretty tricks don't impress me, Sunstone." Beelzebub snarled, facing me and edging forward.

He lunged, attempting a piercing thrust, which I knocked away. He stepped back with the speed and grace of a decent fencer and lunged again. I blocked that one too. Blow after blow, he pushed me backward with every strike, never allowing me an opportunity to land one of my own. Soon, he had me nearing the fence. I was running out of space.

I jumped to my right, and he shifted. Spinning Creed and using the momentum, I slashed sideways. Beelzebub used an upward blow to deflect my strike. But I was already spinning in the other direction, rotating Creed above my head and sending a single–arm reverse strike, a combination of *High Sun* and *Endless Dreams*, toward his legs. He blocked that too.

With each one of my strikes, I no longer looked into the face of a bully who loved nothing more than running roughshod over anyone he deemed inferior. Now, I was looking into the concerned face of the Prince of Demons who hadn't thought anyone would ever challenge him. I hadn't shattered his confidence, but he wasn't as cocky as a few minutes earlier.

I struck, he blocked. I thrust. He jumped back. I jumped to my side, much quicker than he could rotate. Beelzebub was on the defensive and being forced back toward the line of cars and his terrorists.

Behind him, a group of them stood together. They were combining their efforts, taking aim on anything that moved, but some of them were now glancing my way, not being passive observers to the fight.

The Manipulative magic user raised that rubber fist again, just behind Beelzebub's head. It flew at me. I raise Creed, slicing it out of the air. But the move had left me open for a counterattack, and that's exactly what Beelzebub did.

The Prince of Demons thrust.

The searing strike landed just above my hip. I screamed. Crackling flame filled my ears. Flame of Beelzebub's fiery sword. Flame of my halberd. The smell of burned flesh and the exquisite pain clouded my mind.

Holding Creed in my weaker hand, I pushed my other against my wound, feeling the wet warmth against my palm. The light coming off the double-ax heads was blinding me to anything beyond them, drawing my focus.

I grimaced and stood straighter. Beelzebub halted, his eyes widening as the blue orb of Hellfire expanded around Creed's ax blades.

I lowered the halberd and opened my mouth in a scream of fury. The orb grew, expanding as it pulsed, and a small beam appeared at the tip of the asymmetrical blade. Widening, the beam thrummed with life in rhythm with Creed's haft. I'd never felt so powerful. So indestructible.

Beelzebub was running, his hand gesticulating wildly.

A rift appeared a few feet in front of him just as Creed loosed the beam of Hellfire.

The beam closed in on the Prince of Demons, who didn't even chance to look over his shoulder. At the mouth of the rift, Beelzebub dove head-first just as my Hellfire spell struck.

The resulting explosion was beautiful. The Hellfire hit the Founder's rift, swallowing it in a white-bluish brilliance, roaring into the sky, sending a shock wave. It flung me backward. Cars were tossed in the air. Windows shattered, the sprinkling of glass tingling on blacktop alongside shredded metal. I struggled to sit up.

The new day pulsed, fading in and out.

Then I felt a presence. Not Lucifer calling me home, but Ralrek, kneeling over me. Bilba arrived seconds later. Standing a few feet behind them were Virgo and Cassie. Virgo's intense gaze swept the parking lot. Cassie had the most adorable line between her eyebrows.

"Zeke? Are you okay?" Bilba sounded like we were underwater.

I tried to nod. My neck, my head, my shoulders hurt. Every joint tightened, preventing much of a range of motion.

"Help me get him up." Ralrek tucked his arm underneath my head and shoulders and inched me into a sitting position.

Virgo grabbed my other side.

Cassie clutched her hands together. "You guys have to leave," she said, her voice edged with anxiety I hadn't heard since her role-playing escapades during Gemini's trial. "They've assembled a team in the Upperworld. They'll be here soon. You've got to go. Now."

"… have… to help," I said, using the last of my energy to form a partial sentence.

"There's nothing to help with. They're all dead," Virgo said. "You guys have to get back to the Underworld. I'll round up the Vigilantes. We're out of here."

Cassie glided forward, grabbing the sides of my aching head in her soft hands. She leaned in and kissed my cheek, still holding my head as she pulled back. "Thank you, Z— Zeke. Thank all of you for what you've done here. But you have to go. Now. Hurry. They're on their way."

Bilba mumbled something, but honestly, I was so distracted by Cassie's kiss that Lucifer and Yahweh themselves could have shown up and I wouldn't have noticed.

"Come on, Zeke," Ralrek said, not unkindly.

Bilba's rift sizzled open. Ralrek paused long enough at the tear between worlds to allow me to wave once more at Cassie and Virgo, before stepping through, back to Hell and the fate that awaited.

What did they do with demons who tried to kill a Founder?

25

UNDERWORLD, UNDISCLOSED

TURNS OUT, fate is a bitch.

I don't believe in it, of course, but I swear, I knew what was coming. Creed burning against my hip as Ralrek supported me through the rift was the first clue. Intuition got the assist.

Stepping back into the Underworld through Bilba's rift, it didn't shock me to see Council guards in my apartment.

"I don't imagine you guys are going to give me a chance to clean out this wound?" I asked the closest one.

He stared straight ahead.

"That won't be necessary, Sunstone," Apopis said, coming out of my kitchen, holding a small container of salad I had made for myself yesterday. What was it with everyone eating my food?

"Surprise," I said in a high-pitch, faked enthusiasm to accompany my feigned smile.

"The three of you have set down a new marker," Apopis said, casually looking at us, trapped in our narrow hallway with Council guards at each end, their spear blades lowered.

Creed burned, pulsed. throbbed. But I wasn't in fighting condition. My side hurt. My skin was seared. My wound gaped. For the bonus, breathing was not exactly a Samhain feast either. Somehow, I didn't think Apopis cared about any of that. I didn't care that he didn't care. But I did care about the inconvenient truth that I couldn't take on him and this squad of guards, even with my partners in crime there to help.

"How did you know we were coming back here?" Bilba asked.

Apopis's shoulders jutted forward in a quick shrug. "We didn't, not for sure. But we also had teams at Sunstone's parent's house, your house, and Ralrek's apartment. One way or another, we'd made sure you enjoyed a greeting party."

"So kind of you. Do I have time to change into a shirt that isn't ruined with blood? Being attacked by a Founder killing mortals in the Overworld isn't doing miracles for my appearance, I'm afraid," I said.

Without taking his eyes off of us, Apopis slid a hand backward into my open kitchen, moving it slightly. I couldn't hear it over the sizzle of Bilba's rift, still opened behind us, but I knew the Founder's gateway awaited.

"What's stopping us from jumping back into the Overworld?" I asked.

"I suppose you could, though I am unsure why you would want to." Apopis sneered. "We know where that rift opens to and have a team waiting there too. Or did I forget to mention that? Unfortunately for you, it's a tense situation, since there's also a squad of angels investigating the site. You'd be walking into a, what do mortals call it? Oh, yes, a hair-trigger situation. Might be difficult to survive if you decide to jump back through the rift. And you," he said, his beady eyes traveling up and down my injured body, "don't look like you're in the condition to fight anymore. But you're welcome to take your chances."

I snarled. The Founder had me. There was no way we could jump through the rift and expect to get away, even if

Cassie and the Vigilantes helped. Hell's contingent would still have to be dealt with, and unless the army of angels wanted to set off the Apocalypse, they'd likely defer to Hell's representatives and turn us over anyway. The Council would make meat pies out of me and my two friends.

Defeated, I said, "Where are we headed?"

"A short prison stay until we can establish the trial. But," Apopis paused, being melodramatic, "it won't be long. Tomorrow at the latest. There's a certain… sense of urgency to dispense justice for what the three of you have done. Come along."

The Founder returned to the kitchen, disappearing around the corner while Bilba and Ralrek helped me navigate the tight confines of the hallway, even tighter with the Council guard stacked alongside each other like over-sized knick-knacks. The guards fell in behind us.

Good to his word, we stepped through the gateway into a cell. The hum of the magical prison welcomed me back. So, the Council was making sure to strip Bilba and Ralrek of their Abilities and handicapping me.

"You remember this place, Sunstone." Apopis said. "Your magic is useless here, so don't even bother. Be a good guest and set your halberd in the brackets."

It was a pointless command. The Founder had no idea I could reach Creed anytime I wanted. It wasn't worth the fight. I needed to rest.

"He needs to get that cleaned and healed," Bilba snapped at the Founder.

Apopis's eyes slid to my wound. A grin spread across his half–tattooed face. "We're in the Underworld. Demons can't die here. He'll be fine."

Apopis slithered through the door as Ralrek barked, "He'll suffer."

The cell door clanged closed before Apopis said, "Well, isn't that unfortunate. I'm sure it won't take long to set up the trial. Sunstone can be healed after we sentence him, along with the two of you. That is, if we can't get Lucifer's approval to put you to death. He should suffer until then, to remind him of the suffering he has caused others."

With that, Apopis turned and glided out of sight. I panted at his departure until I was ready to pass out, which came on even as the armored footsteps of the Council guard faded.

I don't know how long I slept, but when I woke, my side ached, even if it no longer burned. I looked down. My shirt had been ripped open, exposing the wound which was closed and cleaned of blood, even though the skin was blackened.

"What did you do?" I asked Bilba.

He shook his head. "Nothing. You slept, and we watched over you just to make sure you were okay, but we didn't do anything. That" –his finger wiggled at my wound– "is all you. We cut your shirt, thinking we could help, but we didn't do more than that. You did. Amazing, especially since we can't touch our Abilities here."

We didn't get time to explore my miraculous healing abilities. From deeper in the prison, a door slammed and dozens of armored feet striking the brimstone floor echoed toward us.

"Ready for some fun?" I said, rolling to my side. "Help me up. I want to be standing before he gets here."

Because I have good friends, I was. Standing at the front of the cell, holding one of the bars in an attempt to look casual, I was disappointed to see the contingent of guards wasn't accompanied by a Founder. They escorted us straight to the Council chambers. When the tall doors were pulled open, I was hardly surprised to see fifty–odd demons, dressed in their elite-class finery, milling about.

"Looks like they want to make a spectacle of us," Ralrek growled.

"We're in for it this time, guys," Bilba whispered. I turned to see one of the escorts crosscheck my best friend from behind with his spear. Bilba stumbled. I caught him.

"Do that again and I'll disintegrate you where you stand," I snarled, not bothering to keep my voice low.

The guard, full of confidence and an attitude of entitlement, smiled.

They corralled us toward the center of the chamber to stand behind three sets of shackles bolted to the floor. This was new, but nothing the Council did any more surprised me, including their pathetic attempts to shame us.

Guards stepped forward and placed shackles on our wrists. Chained like uncontrollable hellhounds as the crowd of affluent demons moved in behind and around us. Many of them were eating, holding small, gold plates of an exquisite meal of fruits and cheeses. Others sipped wine from small goblets.

A guard strode toward the side doors, the personal chambers of the Council members. He rapped on each chamber door, once, before moving down the line, notifying each Founder that the room was ready to receive them.

The five Council members of Lucifer's Third Council marched out of their chambers in their formal black robes, the red embroidery lining the robes reminiscent of the inferno Beelzebub used to destroy half a city block.

Creed pounded at my hip so hard I was surprised it hadn't drawn everyone's attention.

The Council members moved to the riser, and behind their chairs. In a show of solidarity, they waited for the five to be in position before pulling them free and taking seats. Beelzebub grinned at me like I was a juicy piece of meat and he was a starving, oversized incubus on a protein binge.

Michael scanned the room, his head moved like a marionette on invisible strings. "We will begin now," he announced.

I found Azazel, trying to not make it obvious to the other

Council members. We needed help. We needed him to come through for us. But as usual, the elderly Founder busied himself with a small stack of papers, avoiding eye contact.

"This is but a moment," the voice of my broken mind whispered.

This time, however, I didn't ignore it or push it away. I let it be. This trial was going to be what it was going to be. I couldn't change the course of it. The Council would continue to push and punish. The key for me was to strip them of that allowance. How I was going to do that was still the mystery, but it wouldn't happen here.

Beside me, Bilba wheezed. I wanted to wrap an arm around him and tell him that no matter what was about to happen, he wouldn't suffer alone.

"We are faced with unfortunate times," Michael said. "These three incubi before you will defend their egregious actions to us and you, witnesses to Lucifer's justice. Prepare yourselves. The crimes they have committed are the most egregious and upsetting of our kind. What you will hear will unnerve you. Unsettle you. It will make you question that which you thought you knew. But we want you to take faith that we, Lucifer's Third Council, have taken great pains to ensure His justice. We never fail to protect the demons of the Underworld against such miscarriages. Today, you will witness our deeds. Carry word of what you witness to those who need to hear. A crime against one of Lucifer's Founders is a crime against us all. We must make an example."

Azazel grumbled something unintelligible. Beelzebub sat next to Michael, his massive chest puffed out, his thick hands clenched into fists. His smile said, "I just won." For their parts, both Apopis and Seraph were busy scribbling notes.

"Do we not get a say? Do we not get representation?" Bilba asked.

Michael cocked his head. Seraph's snapped up.

"There is no defense for what you've done." Apopis

hissed. "So, think carefully before you presume to speak again."

"It is customary to allow defendants to make remarks. We shouldn't be so timorous in our stance that we do not allow them that, should we?" Azazel asked from the far end.

Not only was he stationed at his customary spot as the last Council member, but Azazel sat even further away from Seraph than normal.

Creed heated, burning against my hip. Michael stared at me. When I focused, I noted a tickle in the back of my brain. He had tried to pry into my mind when I was distracted but was blocked once again by the magical halberd. Poor Founder. It must have been so frustrating to be denied that which he thought he was entitled.

I smiled.

"Customs no longer matter," Beelzebub barked, his voice booming around the large chamber.

A succubus somewhere behind me sucked in her breath.

Michael raised his hand. "We are not going to drag this out. We know what happened."

"Yet we have not discussed it," Azazel said. "We have not discussed the preceding incidents that led to the confrontation between young Ezekial and Beelzebub. Context matters."

Well, that answered my question about Azazel's courage. He wasn't backing down and had witnesses to prove it.

Beelzebub's chair creaked as he turned. "We're not here to discuss that."

"Far be it for me to be happy about agreeing with Azazel, but I do," Seraph said, slowly lowering the quill. "In this specific case, there are extenuating circumstances that contributed to this matter. However," she said, shifting her posture to talk down the table toward Michael, virtually blocking Azazel out of the conversation, "this is not the time or place for us to analyze the potential criminal acts of a Council member."

Someone in the room gasped. I was astonished Seraph didn't even bother to hint that one of Lucifer's Council members had committed a crime.

"Again, I will repeat this for the benefit of everyone gathered," Michael said, lifting his chin and looking toward the back of the room as if he saw someone standing along the far wall. "For the benefit of the Council, the witnesses, and the defendants. What is to be discussed here are not the decisions or actions of Beelzebub, but those of the defendants. Beelzebub is not on trial, these incubi are."

"Maybe he should be," Azazel said, drawing that line in the sand deeper with each comment.

Apopis hissed. Beelzebub growled, his chair creaking again.

"These three incubi," Michael said more forcefully, "are being charged. The charges are: illegal travel to the Over-world, using magic in the Overworld without permission." A gallery of gasps received the charges. "Illegal use of magic to open gateways and rifts." Murmurs this time. "And the attempted murder of a Founder."

He made the last statement with such ferocity the eruption of noise was hardly surprising. A large incubus, he looked like he'd come into riches after millennia of intimidating the brimstone out of anyone who denied him what he wanted growled. Another incubi threatened to rip our heads off himself if the Council guard didn't finish us first.

"Heresy!" an aged voice, smooth with wine, shouted.

"Lucifer, bless them for all eternity!" someone contributed.

When the initial blast of hatred died, I shouted, "I didn't want to kill him. I had to try, because that was the only way he was going to stop attacking innocent mortals!"

With the comment, I learned the nature of dead silence.

I hadn't planned on providing testimony because I knew how the Council operated. They would use anything I said against me. Regardless of having witnesses, anything I said would be repackaged in a way to make the Council appear to be the victims.

"So," Apopis said, dragging out that word, the sibilance so hard as to cut, "you admit you tried to kill a Founder?"

"I admit that at the time of his attack on mortals, I would have done whatever it took to stop Beelzebub from killing even more people. Yes." I locked my gaze on Apopis.

"Michael, cast the silencing spell on these three," Beelzebub said, his hand still fisted, raising and lowering it to the table in slow, light punches. "We shouldn't have to be subjected to their heretical comments. I shouldn't be subjected to their slander. Cast the spell."

This wasn't the first time I had found myself in the Council chambers, threatened with a silencing spell. But this was the first time the Council members agreed on the matter. With a quick vote, the measure unanimously passed. Even Azazel sided with Beelzebub, much to my surprise and disappointment. Just above the spot where my collarbones met, I felt a squeeze. A single focal point. An invisible finger of magic was pushed against my throat. I opened my mouth to protest but nothing worked. I couldn't even squeak. I turned to Bilba and Ralrek, and saw them straining to speak, their hands at their throats.

"Now, can we finish this? Time for sentencing? I have other things to accomplish today," Beelzebub said, grinning at his victory.

"The first action is obvious," Seraph said. "Even before he passed the Passage, Bilba Ravenous was opening gateways and rifts."

Astonished murmurs rippled across the gallery. Bilba's shackles clinked as he raised his hands, pleading, his mouth opening, but not making a sound.

"Don't bother objecting. We have a witness to corroborate this charge," Seraph announced, turning to the chamber guard stationed at the rear door. "Bring him in."

The guard snapped to attention and opened the door. A figure waited inside the room. This time, it wasn't Lucifer who made the dramatic entrance. It was someone much more surprising. Someone I never thought I would see in a formal capacity in the Council chamber. Someone, who by their very appearance, made me want to give up.

Kanthor Sunstone walked out of the rear room, escorted by the guard, and stood between us and the five Founders. My father never looked my way.

"Please state your name," Michael said.

"Kanthor Sunstone."

"What is your relation to the accused?" Seraph asked.

"I am Ezekial Sunstone's father. I know Bilba Ravenous through their friendship."

"In relation to the charge Bilba Ravenous faces, what is your testimony?" Seraph continued.

Somehow, I found the power to swallow.

"I've seen it before, but there was one day in particular where the boys—" my father started.

"By 'boys,' you mean the three defendants?" Apopis asked for clarification.

My father nodded. "My apologies. Yes, the defendants had traveled to our home in the Fifth. Bilba Ravenous admitted to opening an illegal gateway to the Sixth Circle to retrieve my son."

"And why were they coming to your house?" Seraph asked.

"For a visit," Kanthor answered. "They did it all the time. Every few days, Ezekial would come home. Bilba was the one who facilitated the travel."

Had I been able to speak, I would have been shocked into silence at my father's lie.

"Each time, it was Bilba Ravenous's gateways they used to bring Ezekial across the Circles?" Michael asked.

"That is correct," my father lied.

"Yet, even though it happened numerous times, you never reported these incidents to anyone?" Azazel asked.

"He isn't the one on trial," Beelzebub said before Kanthor spoke.

"And what about the rifts?" Michael put the proceedings back on track.

"The defendants used to mention opening rifts to the Overworld at dinner." Kanthor said. "We would tell them about the inappropriateness of their actions. I even demanded they stop, as did my lovely wife. But they weren't concerned. It was a joke to them. They took joy in the fact they could open gateways and rifts and use them to travel wherever they pleased. Whenever they pleased."

"Yet, you failed to report those as well?" Azazel pressed.

"Well... I..." my father stumbled. I couldn't remember the last time I had seen him so nervous. Of course, that's exactly what would happen when you were being questioned by your idols, I guessed.

"Again, he is not the one on trial." Apopis was the one to remind Azazel this time.

"You do not have to answer that," Michael advised. "In fact, I prefer that you didn't. Your actions are extraneous. The fact is, you have not only witnessed the use of gateways, but have also heard first–hand statements by the accused that they liberally used both gateways and rifts. Used both without permission. Is that correct?"

My heart broke as my father nodded. "It is."

"Thank you for your testimony. You are excused," Michael said.

Kanthor Sunstone walked from the Council chamber without a look at his son. Watching him go, my chest heaved with animosity born of rejection. My fists clenched.

"Well, I believe this matter is settled," Beelzebub said, bouncing a fist on the table. "We strip him."

"Yes," Apopis hissed.

"This is my session to run," Michael said, cocking his head but not so much that he faced Beelzebub. "But your recommendation is appropriate."

"Let's put it to a vote and proceed," Apopis said.

Michael fidgeted in his chair.

An incubus with a raspy voice said, "This is going to be good."

I never wanted to punch a stranger so badly in my entire life.

"Then we will take a vote," Michael said, his hand sliding to where he kept the gavel. "All in favor of stripping Bilba Ravenous of his title of Major demon, say 'aye'."

The approval to strip Bilba of his life's greatest accomplishment occurred before I processed what was happening. My friend's head fell at the loss of something he was so proud to have achieved. Shackled and silenced, I couldn't even comfort him.

"Let's move this along, Michael," Beelzebub said, whirling a broad finger as if he were flipping keys.

Michael's eyes closed, his nostrils flared as he drew a breath. He didn't speak until he opened his eyes again. "I'll remind you, Beelzebub, you are in no position to make demands. I am the leader of the Third Council. Until the time comes that you are, we move as I dictate."

Beelzebub looked at Michael as if the lanky, bearded incubus had lost his mind. His jaws bulged as he clamped them shut.

"Now to the matter of—" Michael had begun.

"Again, I must remind my fellow Council members, all actions by these incubi were in reaction to what Beelzebub did. Before we proceed, we must address that matter." The elderly Azazel wagged his quill at the muscle-headed demon at Michael's side.

"Silence," Apopis hissed, his narrow eyes sliding in Azazel's direction, but never directly addressing him.

Azazel blubbered at the verbal assault.

"Keep pushing this, and you'll regret saying anything," Beelzebub promised.

Creed thumped, bouncing in the loop.

"What—what is that supposed to mean? Are you going to attack me like you did those mortals? Without permission or even the knowledge of the Council?" Azazel charged.

The excited incubi and succubi from Hell's affluent groups, the political pawns the Council involved to witness this farce, spoke openly. Cries. Gasps. Shocked vulgarity. Most expressed astonishment at what they were hearing. Uncomfortable questions were mixed in, not out of earshot of the Council. Had they heard Azazel correctly? Was the Founder losing his mind? Was Beelzebub this much of a bully to his peers? If he was, how did he treat others? Was Michael not able to control his peers? Was the Council this farcical? Was something being covered up?

Watching Michael, I thought he might decompensate before my eyes. He blinked, his mouth opening and closing repeatedly. He was scrambling for a response to this unscripted twist in a very scripted process. Azazel had changed Michael's plans as the raven flew, and was forcing the leader of the Council to react while Hell's most influential residents watched. It was all so absolutely glorious.

Michael faced the crowd, tilting his chin up. "My apologies, everyone. It seems there are matters we have yet to clarify. The proceedings of this trial are of the utmost importance, but those matters will have to wait." He held up in an open palm. "I will ask for your forgiveness, but we must excuse you."

The chamber buzzed with disapproving grumbles. Some observers scowled at the incubus.

Michael nodded to a guard who snapped to attention and called the others forward. Five guards marched toward the congregation, who appeared more annoyed than unnerved by armed incubi closing in.

I moved my manacled hands to my hip, pinning Creed against my leg to stop it from jolting.

Within a matter of moments, the chamber was empty except for its guards, three unfortunate defendants, and the five bickering Council members.

"What in the world was that about, Michael?" Beelzebub asked. "You made us look like fools."

Michael slapped the jade table. Azazel startled. "All of you are doing a fine job of that yourselves. What in the Underworld do you think you're going to accomplish by exposing this situation to demons of their status?" Michael wrenched his head toward the crowd that had just departed. "Have you forgotten that we need their support? Do you know what happens now?"

"I imagine most of them will return to their homes and tell others what was said here. The situation is simply too interesting for them to not share, since so few ever get insight into how the Council operates. Or our secrets," Azazel said, a hint of pleasure in his voice.

Apopis snarled. "You did that on purpose. You intentionally planted seeds of doubt. What is your aim?"

"I have none," Azazel said, his aged cheeks wobbling. "I was ensuring we acted without impunity. If we seek justice, we must be just in our actions."

"I feel we have been as fair as possible," Michael said, his hand extending in my direction. "How many opportunities have we given these incubi? How many unfortunate circumstances have we had to deal with because of those opportunities?"

"And look where that has led us, Michael," Seraph said in a biting tone. "Are we better off now by putting energy into demons like Sunstone, or should we have been looking inside all along, at the actions of those who serve this Council?"

"Don't you start."

Creed twitched.

"And if I do?" Seraph shot back. "What are you going to do if I start? Are you going to threaten me too?" Beelzebub growled, but that didn't stop Seraph. "I don't give a hyena's ass about Sunstone. We have more important things to worry about than his feelings of fairness. What I am worried about is your lack of control over the actions of the members of this Council, Michael. We've had an opportunity to address this. Despite that, nothing was done. What will it take?"

"The matter can be… tackled, as you eloquently put it, after we deal with these three," Michael said, taking a position that said he would not be disobeyed.

"Or will it continue to be overlooked?" Azazel asked.

Beelzebub was on his feet. "What did I tell you? If you keep pushing this matter, we're going to have serious problems."

"And what would you do, Beelzebub?" Azazel said. The orange tip of his white goatee shook along with his jaw. "Are you going to put me to the flaming sword as well?"

Beelzebub spun, kicking away his chair, which toppled off the riser. By the sound of it hitting the floor, the chair splintered. "You will not talk to me like that anymore. Time has passed you by. Your ambition has waned, and that has blinded you. I'm not going to wait around until you figure out what needs to be done."

"So, you're going to act with impunity? Do what you feel needs to be done?" Azazel asked, still seated.

"If that's what it takes," Beelzebub spat, stepping closer to the elder Founder.

Seraph scooted her chair back and stood, moving out of the way.

"Enough!" Michael shouted. No one paid attention to him.

"So you will pursue whatever course of action you desire, without regard to our thoughts, the demons we serve, the

Underworld's needs, or even Lucifer's wishes?" Azazel prodded.

"I'll burn you to a crisp, you outdated waste of a vote," Beelzebub said, his lips curled back.

Apopis was on his feet now, moving to Beelzebub's side, the two approaching Azazel together.

"Ouch," I mouthed silently as Creed scorched through my jeans.

"See? See what you have led us to, Michael?" Seraph spat, gesturing with a hand that rotated between Beelzebub and Azazel. "We should have tackled this issue long ago, like I said. Are you going to do something, or are you incapable?"

"Don't act like you haven't been maneuvering yourself," Apopis said, spinning on Seraph. "Years ago, you were manipulating situations to your favor."

"I was not!" she shouted back. "I have been doing what was needed for the Underworld."

"Where is the Horn then?" Beelzebub boomed. "You were the last one to be seen with it. We've asked repeatedly for its return and you insist it's in safe keeping until we can be sure it won't disappear again. Could it be you're keeping it hidden from us for your own purposes?"

I had to check with my friends to make sure I was seeing what I thought I was seeing, hearing what I was actually hearing. Lucifer's Council was disintegrating right before us. So glorious.

"Let's focus on addressing these three," Michael said, moving between Beelzebub and Azazel, looking at both. "We will address everything else once this is settled."

"How can we worry about their supposed crimes when we have a Council member who has acted as Beelzebub has? He needs to be removed, Michael," Azazel said, his aged voice shaking. I doubted it was from fear. Azazel was showing more courage than the other four had ever displayed.

His comment stopped everyone where they stood, as if none of them believed they heard him correctly.

In a deathly quiet voice, Azazel repeated his comment. "He needs to be removed."

"We can have that discussion... later," Michael said, dipping his head.

"You would support it?" Azazel asked.

"I might," Michael said, holding up a finger. "We can investigate the circumstances of his actions. We have to give Beelzebub an opportunity to state his case. But later."

"I'm going to kill you," Beelzebub said, each word said with strained emphasis.

"He comes," my crazy internal voice said, not shut down by the silencing spell.

Who?

A sizzle from behind the jade table caught my attention. The Council members spun and separated, moving toward their chairs. How they'd fallen silent could only mean one thing.

Hard soles clicked behind the riser. Second-by-torturous-second, the Lord of the Underworld made His way atop the riser. He stood at the left of the table, the place of honor Michael usually held.

The Council members bowed.

Creed throbbed.

"Lord," Michael said from his supplicant position.

"We will stop. This is not the way. Not our way," Lucifer said in a voice so soft as to barely be more than a whisper.

"Yes, Lord," Seraph said, sounding every bit like an impling.

Lucifer faced us, and I'll admit, I sort of quivered. "We will deal with these three for now. Then we will discuss what becomes of the rest of you." His thick beard and mustache twitched. "Do any of you have a reasonable recommendation?"

Azazel shuffled forward, raising a finger. "If I may, Lord?"

Lucifer lowered himself into the chair, the guards assisting him. "Go ahead, Azazel. Just... please... make it reasonable."

"I think it will find favor with You, Lord," Azazel said, demurely. "In order to allow ourselves time to debate the issue of the crimes committed by the Prince of Demons, Beelzebub, I propose we—"

"Speak," Apopis hissed.

Azazel cleared his throat. "I propose we banish these three to the Isle of Dread."

Beelzebub's enormous chest jerked with a laugh. "That's your great proposal?"

"Let him speak, Beelzebub," Michael said.

"As I was saying," Azazel restarted, this time more slowly, "we could send them to the Isle. We have tried prisons and had unsatisfactory results. We attempted to Abandon Mr. Sunstone, with very poor results. Banishment to the Isle solves the issue of what to do with them, while also freeing us to discuss what we should do about the matter of Beelzebub affecting the Balance."

Beelzebub growled, but kept whatever comment he had to himself.

Lucifer mulled over the comment, the long hairs of His mustache and beard intertwining as they twitched. "That is an interesting proposition. Is anyone opposed?"

"I'm not opposed, Lord," Seraph said. "The Isle of Dread will weaken their Abilities. Burning won't be able to light a candle after a few months there."

"There is no need to be hostile, Seraph," Lucifer chided. "Anyone else?"

Beelzebub grunted. "A slow, natural death is more than they deserve, if the natives don't kill them first. I'm not opposed to it," Beelzebub grumbled.

"Liberate," my constant, crazy companion teased.

For the first time, Lucifer looked at me. My insides seized.

His eyes traveled to Bilba and Ralrek as well, but glided back to me. Creed seared. I felt the slight mental tug of the Lord of Hell trying to pry around in my head. Creed kept my thoughts unreadable even against Lucifer.

He tilted His head, staring up toward the ceiling, His mouth twitching as He blinked. After a brief pause, Lucifer said softly, "Yes. The Isle of Dread will suit them just fine."

26

ACHERON OCEAN

WHO KNEW serenity could be found at sea? Having grown up in the Fifth Circle, I rarely had the opportunity to be around water. Only during my short stint to the Second Circle, an island, was I near a body of water. I had more exposure to it during my time in Seattle and Olympia—I'm choosing to ignore the long flight across the Atlantic Ocean for my deployment. Being in the air over so much water, for so long, was not something I willingly want to recall. Now, here I was, okay to float on a large raft in the middle of a body of water that stretched to the bounds of the Underworld. I had to be okay with it, because it was happening anyway. Heavens, I guess I could not be okay with it and my fortunes weren't going to change.

To call the vessel we were on a raft is sort of unfair. It was large enough for me and my best friends, the newest exiles to the Isle of Dread, Azazel, the Founder who Lucifer tasked to accompany us on the journey, and his contingent of guards, each allied to him. Four large, wooden chests filled the center of the raft. Supernatural means propelled us across the Acheron Ocean, with no need for a crew.

That gave us an abundance of privacy, to talk through our

future with the Founder, who had risked his own safety for us. The tranquil journey across the open water cleared my head enough to think about what was to come as the vessel rocked over short waves toward a wall of fog hanging on the near horizon. The salt water smell in the air purged the toxicity of the recent interaction with Hell's other rulers.

"I thought this was going to be a much more... rugged ride," I said, laying on my stomach so I could reach over the edge into the warmth of the Acheron, lazily lapping the water.

"Most times it is bumpy," Azazel said from his seat at the rear of the raft. The wood chair looked uncomfortable without padding, and the elderly Founder's constant shifting confirmed that. "With me accompanying you to the Isle, we're given safe passage. Otherwise, you wouldn't have been able to traverse this body of water, even if we borrowed an ocean liner from the Overworld."

"Is that to prevent any of the inhabitants of the Isle from returning to the Underworld?" Bilba sat with crossed legs on the other side of the raft, peeling a banana.

"Well, we can't very well have the worst of the worst returning and stirring up trouble, now can we?" Azazel answered with a wink.

"Is that what we are? The worst of the worst?" Ralrek smirked, stretched out on his back, hands locked behind his head, soaking in the Hellfire's glory. He said he needed to work on his tan. That was crap. He could tan by just thinking about the azure beauty of the Hellfire.

"It is what everyone says about the inhabitants of the Isle," Bilba said.

"How do you know that?" Ralrek asked.

"He read it," I said, just as Bilba admitted he had read it, which was said over top of Ralrek mentioning that Bilba had probably read it in a book.

Our simultaneous answers drew a rough chuckle from

Azazel. "It is fortunate you are so well read, young Mr. Ravenous. Because I have unfortunate news. You'll find little in the way of reading materials on the Isle. What you do find will likely be in poor condition and lacking in educational or entertainment value. However, the lack of good reads may give you time for other pursuits."

I rolled over, looking back down the raft, away from the wall of fog that hid the horizon. "What kind of pursuits?"

Ralrek tilted his head back. "Yeah, I thought we were being sent here to die slow, miserable deaths?"

Azazel rocked his head. "You can, if that's what you choose. But, with what the three of you have accomplished, it would be an absolute shame were you to not take advantage of this opportunity. It's not every day demons find themselves in the fortunate position of not having to worry about the Council or any of our spies or security forces. Imagine an existence outside the influence of meddling Council members, but not yet in the Overworld where you have those genuine concerns of decay. With enough focus, imagine the wonderful things you might accomplish."

"But we'll be without magic," Ralrek said.

"Will you?" Azazel asked.

"Won't they?" I asked on behalf of my friends.

Azazel looked off to the horizon, the Hellfire-y side. "There's a lot you will learn in this journey. You won't know for sure until you try, am I correct?"

Bilba's shoulders rose and fell. "I guess so. I hadn't thought about it."

"Sure," Ralrek said, closing his eyes and adjusting to even out his tan.

I sighed. "Since I don't have to worry about testing my Abilities," I said, my hand sliding to my hip, holding Creed close, "I guess I can spend the rest of my natural life dwelling on the fact I won't be able to help everyone struggling in the Overworld. Or looking for the Horn."

Azazel harrumphed. The raft creaked as if agreeing. "The three of you seem to know quite a bit about what life is like on the Isle of Dread. I advise you to not draw too many conclusions. And don't worry about events in the Overworld. I will work with your angelic girlfriend—"

I shot up straight. "She's not my girlfriend. She's just an angel."

Azazel chuckled. "And I will continue to assist matters with the vigilante group and the cell Dialphio has formed. It's time for them to step up their game, anyway. I figure I will give them the necessary nudge."

Even though I knew Azazel was friendly to our cause, it was still remarkable to hear him talk so openly. He had done something similar when in Olympia, readying to bring me back to the Underworld. Back then, we had been alone with a few of his guards. Now, Bilba and Ralrek were privy to the conversation, and there wasn't a Listening ward.

"Won't that get you in trouble with the other Founders?" Bilba asked.

"Mayhaps," Azazel said, flicking his wrist. "But I expect we are going to be distracted with a number of issues." He stopped to chuckle, lifting his head, breathing in the cool ocean air blowing across his face. "Ah, I love the smell of the Acheron. Nothing like it in the entire Underworld. I don't get out here often enough. Maybe, after all this settles, I will take time for myself and do just that. We shall see. But, returning to the matters at hand, I want to highlight how advantageous it was for the three of you to witness that blow-up in the Council. At times, I feared you wouldn't see my secret intent."

Azazel had a playful look on his face, even with his eyes closed and his head tilted back. The Acheron's breeze blew his long goatee over his shoulder.

"You were poking the hellhound there, for a minute." I snickered. "I thought Beelzebub was going to torch you where you stood."

"I'm sure he would have liked nothing more than to do that," Azazel admitted. "But I knew if I pushed him hard enough, I could get him to focus on protecting himself more than the three of you. That put the pressure on him I wanted. Beelzebub enjoys being able to do what he wants, when he wants, and if he's allowed to focus only on his target, it does not bode well. However, if you get him riled up by putting the attention on his failings, he becomes putty in your hands."

"Did you know Lucifer would intervene?" Bilba asked, fascinated.

"I did not," Azazel said nonchalantly, as if Bilba had just asked him if he preferred to watch an action movie instead of a fantasy. "Only hoped."

Bilba whistled. Ralrek, his eyes closed, smirked, nodded his head.

"That's a heaven of a gamble," I said.

"A gamble worth taking to get you out of their clutches and somewhere safe, where you might be able to find an advantageous situation," Azazel said. "I encourage you to consider that. Test your Abilities, but also test yourselves, and remember that the Council will be too busy deciding what our future looks like to worry about the misfits on some isle we think can no longer interact with the Underworld. Even you, Rebel Mage."

Bilba blinked. I looked at him, and even Ralrek disturbed his tanning session to crane his head up.

"Rebel Mage?" Bilba asked.

"That's what I hear you're being called around the Circles," Azazel snickered. "From what I hear, some who are less than happy with the way we are administering the Underworld have taken to it. A popular name, it seems. You might attain cult hero status after all is said and done."

Ralrek groaned, but with a smile, and laid his head back.

"Wow," Bilba said. "You're not the only one with a nickname now, Zeke."

"Don't get cocky." I winked. "They come with extra responsibility."

We shared a laugh before Bilba asked, "What is going to happen to the Council?"

"Your guess will be as good as mine, " Azazel said. "I imagine we are going to struggle for quite some time, if we even manage to find a common ground to start. That will be a challenge in itself."

"What happens if you can't?" I asked.

Azazel pinched his lips. "That will be up to Lucifer's will. Do not be surprised if the Council as you know today does not exist when you return."

Bilba whistled. I agreed. That comment was whistle–worthy in more ways than one.

Azazel lowered his head, smiling. "You boys saw what Lucifer is. The secret behind the curtain has been revealed. He's been like that for almost as long as I've known him. Eon after eon, always the same. He was weak when He was younger, and back then He had the energy. As He's aged, He seems to have become less interested in managing the Under-world, much to the harm of its inhabitants. Such a shame. So, I don't expect much, definitely not miracles, when it comes to His intervention in the Council's deterioration."

"Will you be safe?" Bilba asked.

"I'm safe knowing the three of you will do great things if you set your minds to it. That is what matters," Azazel said. His eyes drifted away. "The Underworld is changing, and not for the better. We cannot settle, for if we settle, we accept that which is prescribed for us. I truly hope you boys take advan-tage of your time on the Isle. What it holds for each of you, we cannot guess. Test the boundaries. Now, more than ever in your lives, is the time. Accept no less from yourselves than you would from the Council who has harmed you. Try not to worry about those you've left behind. You have plenty of demonic notebooks, yes?"

"I have a few," Bilba admitted.

"Me too," Ralrek said.

"Yes," I said.

Azazel extended a crooked finger at the row of wooden chests bound by black iron bands at the middle of the raft. "In those chests I've ensured you have the supplies you need to start a very successful life on the Isle, including more demonic notebooks than you could use. They should make your continued coordination with friends and family around the Underworld and Overworld much easier. If you need anything else, of course, just write. I will make sure you have what you need."

"Th—thank you," I said.

"It's the least I can do," Azazel said. "I'm encouraged and excited to see what you will do. I imagine glorious news coming from the Isle in the very near future."

We casually floated along on the timid current, carrying us toward the wall of fog, each lost in our thoughts. I knew I was. Azazel definitely looked as if he was. Bilba picked at his banana peel. Though Ralrek may have been asleep.

After a while, Bilba said, "I can't believe we can still use our Abilities and the Council" —he paused, looking at Azazel — "well, those who oppose us, won't be able to interfere. We don't have to worry about our safety, and we can still stay in touch with everyone until we figure something out. This is going to be great."

"As long as the Hellfire rays are always like this, I'm going to love it," Ralrek said, tilting his chin to tan his underside. Can't have any imperfections now, could he?

Azazel laughed. "I hope you boys don't expect a vacation. Life on the Isle will not be an easy one. You'll have plenty of work to do just making friends."

I blinked. "I—I didn't think it would be a hostile place. Is it?"

Azazel rocked his head as if the entire raft was being

thrown side to side. "Lying to you does you no favors. For ages, the Council has approved Circle Administrator requests to send the worst of demonkind to the Isle. It's our way of shoving aside society's rejects so we don't have to deal with them. The Underworld's underground, if you will. That includes those we've Abandoned who proved a threat to the Balance or to the Council's interest." He smiled at me. "So, you could say the crowd is rough. You'll have to choose your friends carefully. The Isle's economy is one of relationships. Trust me, having played a part in most inhabitants, from the distant past to now, you will need friends."

"Sounds like fun," I said, still embracing the fact that I could soon be outside the reach of the Council. I could still talk to Cassie. I could still check in with Virgo and Dialphio. My mother could receive sanitized letters from me, if only to let her know I was okay. My father could kiss my ass. I'd deal with him when I was able. Bilba and Ralrek were with me, and if Azazel was half accurate, my friends could access their magic. The Council would continue its implosion while we organized our future, stretching from an isle in the furthest reaches of Hell to a Fifth Circle bookstore, and the Over and Upperworlds.

"Will you let me know what you learn about Cancer?" I asked.

Azazel's face softened. "Of course, young Ezekial. I'm sorry they did that to you. A ploy. To deceive and throw you off. We don't know anything for sure. The Overworld is impossible to search with any efficiency, and the world war doesn't help. Yes, of course, as soon as I have something solid, I will let you know."

"Either way?"

"Either way," the elderly Founder said.

"Thank you," I said, looking toward the looming wall of fog. The end of the Underworld.

It didn't scare me. A future on the Isle of Dread didn't sound so dreadful.

As the first tendrils of fog enveloped the raft, cutting off the rays of the Hellfire and gripping the air with chill, we hushed. The day darkened the deeper we floated into the fog's grasp. Even the waters of the Acheron Ocean lapping against the raft were quieted by this new world.

"The Isle of Dread is not the end of your journey, boys, but the beginning," Azazel's voice thundered in the shroud of fog.

"Listen," Crazy-Zeke whispered to me to as Creed vibrated against my hip.

THE END

WHAT'S NEXT?

Wasting away on the Isle of Dread cannot be the end of Zeke's story. Not if he has anything to say about it. And who in their right mind thinks Bilba or Ralrek will sit by, soaking up the beach Hellfire rays? On the horizon, an eternal storm brews. What mysteries and opportunities await?

Find out in the next chapter in Zeke's story. Book 7, "Libra's Liberation," coming in 2022.

REVIEWS HELP

If you enjoyed this book, I would appreciate your review.

Your time is valuable, but reviews not only help other readers find something they might like, but they help me as an author. They are important to me because they allow me to see what readers like you enjoyed about the book and what I could have done better.

Thank you to every one of you who takes the time to leave a review!

DON'T MISS OUT!

Get the latest news, special deals, exclusive stories, first looks at book covers, and more by signing up for Paul Sating's newsletter!

Sign up for Paul's newsletter to follow all the news and special deals for upcoming novels, and to catch up on the latest regarding his podcast at http://www.paulsating.com.

EXCLUSIVE STORIES AND CONTENT!

More stories! More exclusive Paul Sating fiction, including free audio books, in podcast form!

Get more stories each month by becoming a Patron! New exclusive fiction each month!

Become a Patron & enjoy more content!

ACKNOWLEDGMENTS

This book was written between February and April of 2021. The world was just started to reset itself after a long bout with a worldwide pandemic, and I, like you, was stuck inside, looking for ways to keep myself creative. Thankfully, I'm a "flow" writer. Once I find my momentum, I can usually fly through a project. *Virgo's Vigilantes* was no different, after a few days.

I was surprised, to be honest. You see, over the winter, I spent my time with an upcoming fantasy series called *Battleborn.* This series is very different from the world of Zeke. It's violent; it's dark; it's written in the third-person point of view, so you get to meet a lot of new characters; it's a mashup of Conan and The Witcher-types of fantasy. To go from something like that to jumping into Zeke's head took time. As an author, I "become" the characters you read on the pages—inside my head, trust me. I do not run around my neighborhood with a Creed-like halberd strapped to my back—though I'd love to, trust me. So to "be" so many dark, violent characters, and then try to become Zeke again takes time—I'm just not that delusional. But, wow, after a day or two of writing

Virgo's Vigilantes, I was rocking and rolling—often hitting ten thousand words a day. Seventeen days and over one hundred and twenty thousand words later, the book was done, and ready to sit around while I edited *The Pride of Leo*. Zeke was fully reborn, to the point I have a deep itch to jump into the next books in a series—Zeke is needy like that.

Over the spring and summer of 2021, however, Zeke is going to be put on the shelf so I can focus on the *Battleborn* books. The good news for fans of Zeke, though, is that I've found by jumping out of his world to work on other things really helps me think more deeply about Zeke's world, something I think you have seen over the past two books, which are much larger than any of the previous four were. Who knows what impact working on six *Battleborn* books will have on Zeke, but I can only imagine it will make me hungrier to continue to throw a ton of problems at him and see how he and the gang react. After all, I've left them on the mysterious Isle of Dread, separated from the rest of the Underworld. Stranded on an island, surrounded maybe by friend, maybe by foe—who knows? As long as fate allows me to explore the future of Hell's favorite chicken wing-loving demon, I'm going to see what lays in wait for everyone we adore (well, except for most of the Council).

Just like every single book, I needed some special people around me to pull it off.

My sun and stars, the moon of my life, my alpha reading, dancing-loving, 80s-wannabe wife, Maddie. She's the first one to tell me everything I've done wrong in a book, and I adore her for it. That's true love, right there!

My daughters, Nikki and Alex. Whenever I leave this rock flying through space, I'll know I'm leaving it better than I found it because of these two amazing, young women. I've screwed up a lot in my life, but my wonderful daughters prove to me each day that I wasn't a total screwup.

SciFi author Blaze Ward and I were sitting around, chatting about book stuff, as you do. This was back in the dreaded 2020, during a shut-down pause, and he said something that changed my writing life. When I asked him how he could put out so many books, so quickly, he responded with "trust your writer voice." Sometimes, it's the simple things. This was one of those seminal moments for me. Such an apparently innocuous piece of advice that helped me write my two longest Zodiac books in record time (and do so in a halfway-decent way that stops my editors from yelling at me). Onward and upward!

Kevin Rowlands is such a positive force in my world. He has been a long-time Patron, one who always listens to episodes right away, always leaves feedback so I know if I'm sucking or not, and he was even the first outside my family to encourage me to chase this dream. What human! Another soul-recharger is Stephanie Mikkelsen. Having met her through my old podcasts, she quickly became a superfan, which is weird, because the show that led her to my fiction was a crime drama—not exactly in Zeke's wheelhouse. Yet, I haven't scared her away, and she is consistently the first person to throw her hand up to read the new books and help get word out. That stuff is gold, people! Lori Peterson, Natalie Aked, Alli R., Erica Stensrud, and Matt Guerin—thank each and every one of you for being part of this project. Virgo would not have launched as it did if it weren't for all of you.

If you didn't notice, Zeke is looking much-enhanced since the earlier books, starting with *The Pride of Leo*. That's all down to the cover designer, Jake at J. Caleb Clark Designs. We had some conversations about updating the series covers, and Jake knocked it out of the park. Thank you for the long days and weekends you put in to make Zeke look as badass as he does, Jake.

As always, my Patrons are the most epic fans in the world!

Thank you for being part of this wild ride! You all (better know) you mean the world to me!

Lastly, to you, the reader. Without you, Zeke wouldn't bother getting out of bed in the morning.

ALSO BY PAUL SATING

Fiction

Fantasy

Horror

The Scales

12 Deaths of Christmas

The Plant (Free for newsletter subscribers)

Suspense

RIP

Chasing the Demon

Nonfiction

Novel Idea to Podcast: How to Sell More Books Through Podcasting

Podcasts

Audio Fiction with Paul Sating

(Free for Patreon supporters!)

Urban Fantasy Author Podcast

(Available on all major podcast apps)

ABOUT THE AUTHOR

Paul Sating is an author, podcaster, and self-professed coolest dad on the planet, hailing from the Pacific Northwest of the United States. At the end of his military career, he decided to reconnect with his first love (that wouldn't get him in trouble with his wife) and once again picked up the pen. Years on, he has published eight novels and he hasn't even screwed up his podcasts, which have garnered over a million downloads.

When he's not working on stories, you can find him talking to himself in his backyard working on failed landscaping projects or hiking around the gorgeous Olympic Peninsula. He is married to the patient and wonderful, Madeline, and has two daughters—thus the reason for his follicle challenges.

Find out more about his other books and free podcasts from his website: paulsating.com.

CONTACT PAUL

How to Contact Paul Sating

Published by Paul Sating Productions
    P.O. Box 15166
    Tumwater, WA 98511
    paul@paulsating.com

Follow Paul:
    Facebook: www.facebook.com/authorpaulsating
    Bookbub: bookbub.com/paul-sating
    Goodreads:
goodreads.com/author/show/16982359.Paul_Sating
    Instagram: @paulsating
    Pinterest: pinterest.com/paulsating
    Twitter: @paulsating